"*In Case of Emergency* begins with a phone call and unfolds into a sharply plotted, dark story packed with lies, betrayals, and so many secrets. Fast-moving and clever!" —Samantha Downing,
author of the #1 international bestseller *My Lovely Wife*

"With more twists and turns than a mountain road, *In Case of Emergency* will take you on one hell of a ride. Buckle in as E. G. Scott expertly spins a story that will have you guessing until the final pages, culminating with a blockbuster ending. A must-read!"
—Liz Fenton and Lisa Steinke, authors of *The Two Lila Bennetts*

"A smart whodunit that brims with human insight about the surprising ways in which we heal and the importance of coming face-to-face with our role in the trajectory of our lives. *In Case of Emergency* is a fast-paced volley of a story batted back and forth between a cast of entertaining characters, all while stylishly concealing more than a few tricks up its proverbial sleeve."
—Chandler Baker, author of *Whisper Network*

"When a brilliant but troubled doctor is listed as the emergency contact for a woman found dead—a woman who's a complete stranger—she finds herself the prime suspect in the murder. Razor-sharp narration and witty dialogue keep the pages turning in this fantastic follow-up to E. G. Scott's breakout sensation *The Woman Inside*." —Wendy Walker, author of *The Night Before*

"Twisty, sharp, and superbly plotted, *In Case of Emergency* kept me on tenterhooks until its explosive and wholly satisfying conclusion. A dark thriller with a brilliant, troubled female protagonist at its core, this is a summer read you won't want to miss."
—Cristina Alger, *New York Times* bestselling author of *Girls Like Us*

"[*In Case of Emergency*] builds its twisty way to a suspenseful climax."
—*Booklist*

"An utterly twisted standalone thriller." —*PopSugar*

"A true page-turner that will keep you guessing." —*Hasty Book List*

"*In Case of Emergency* is a fast-moving and sharp thriller that examines the roles that loneliness, trauma, and friendship play when deciding who to trust."
—*BuzzFeed*

ALSO BY E. G. SCOTT

The Woman Inside

IN CASE OF

EMERGENCY

A NOVEL

E. G. SCOTT

DUTTON

DUTTON

An imprint of Penguin Random House LLC
penguinrandomhouse.com

Previously published as a Dutton hardcover in August 2020
First Dutton trade paperback printing: August 2021

The Library of Congress has cataloged
the hardcover edition of this book as follows:
Title: In case of emergency: a novel / E.G. Scott.
Identifiers: LCCN 2019034183 | ISBN 9781524744557 (hardback) |
ISBN 9781524744571 (ebook)
Subjects: LCSH: Murder—Fiction. | Missing persons—Fiction. |
GSAFD: Suspense fiction.
Classification: LCC PS3619.C6623 I5 2020 | DDC 813/.6—dc23
LC record available at https://lccn.loc.gov/2019034183

Dutton trade paperback ISBN: 9781524744564

Printed in the United States of America

1st Printing

For our sisters and brothers;

Gordon, Susan, Madeline, and Thomas

IN CASE OF EMERGENCY

PROLOGUE

THIS IS GOING to end badly.

It's chaos in here. They're not listening to me. I've told them that we need to stop operating, but they're talking over me, drowning me out. I know what I'm doing. I'm an integral part of this team. Hell, I'm the smartest person in the room.

Her vitals are a mess. Her breathing is shallow and labored. Her color is all off.

"She's been under too long. We need to close her up."

"Almost there. Just hang in. Just a minute longer."

The beeping ramps up.

The ego in this room has pushed out the common sense. "We're going to lose her."

"This is *my* operating room!"

"She's coding!"

PART ONE

Date: October 2, 2019
From: CharlotteKnopfler@gmail.com
To: Braindoc67@gmail.com

H,

I know you told me not to reach out to you this way, but you aren't leaving me any other choice since you haven't returned any of my phone calls. We really need to talk.

I know you got the same message I did last night. This isn't going away. Your pride is blinding you from doing the right thing here. Coming clean is the best path ahead for everyone involved.

I want to be able to look in the mirror every day and know that I fixed the mistakes I made. I don't want to ruin any more lives. Please contact me.

Charlotte

ONE

WOLCOTT

I HEAR THE cracking sound and look up just in time to see the splintered wood flying toward us. I drag the shrieking woman hanging on my arm out of the way as the massive branch thuds onto the pavement.

"Lionel!" she screams.

When I look up again, my partner has managed to get his footing under him, narrowly avoiding the same fate as the chunk of tree. I put my arm around the frantic woman and take her hand with my free one. "It's going to be okay," I say in my most soothing late-night-radio deejay voice. "My partner has it under control, ma'am."

"But Lionel isn't supposed to be out of the house," she protests. "He's scared. And confused!"

"The big guy's going to be just fine, ma'am," yells Silvestri. "Detective Wolcott, can you get over near the trunk here? I'm going to lower him down to you."

"Oh, please be careful!" she insists.

"Ma'am," yells Silvestri, "your cat is in wonderful hands, I assure you. My partner here is as steady as they come."

I squeeze her shoulder reassuringly before I slip her grip and move toward the tree. As I do, I notice two teenage boys standing across the street, pointing their phones at us. It occurs to me that a couple of kids that age probably could have had Lionel down from the tree in about half the time it's taken us.

Silvestri cradles the cat with one arm as he lowers himself onto his stomach. He balances himself along the length of the branch and lowers Lionel down to me. The cat appears to be paralyzed with fear, limbs jutting out like a panicked crossing guard. I take him gently around the rib cage and lower him slowly into the crook of my elbow.

His owner nearly bowls me over as she retrieves him. "Oh, Detectives! Thank you so much. I'm so glad you were passing by. You saved Lionel's life!" She turns her attention to the cat, lavishing kisses on him as she chastens his behavior. "You're such a bad boy, aren't you? Yes, you are. Yes, you are."

Silvestri drops down from the tree and joins the lovefest, scratching Lionel behind the ears as the cat nuzzles him.

"Thank you so much, Detective!" The woman eyes my partner. "You're so brave." She begins whispering into the cat's ear, all the while keeping her gaze locked on Silvestri. "Say thank you to the handsome detective, Lionel. Yes, that's right. Say thank you."

"Think nothing of it, ma'am." He nods to the woman, then the cat. "Lionel. Now, you two get back inside and enjoy your day."

◆ ◆ ◆

"You really came through on that one, Silvestri." I'm pulling the unmarked back onto the street as Lionel's owner waves at us from the front porch of her house.

"Long Island's finest, at it again," he deadpans. He tugs his sleeves up to inspect his forearms, and I notice a smattering of tiny puncture wounds.

"Shit, man. You okay?"

"All good," he answers, waving back to the woman on the porch. "Glad I had on the thermal, though. That situation had the makings of a fucking acupuncture session gone wrong."

"Odd day today," I say.

"Dead-slow week is more like it."

"Well, you did good. And where'd *you* learn to climb a tree, city slicker?"

He chuckles. "It might surprise you to know that I wasn't always the model citizen you see before you today."

"That right?" I ask.

"I had some behavioral issues as a youth." He flashes air quotes around the diagnosis. "My folks sent me off to one of those Outward Bound camps for the summer. You think the tree climbing's impressive? You should see me tie a square knot. That'll *really* get you hot and bothered."

"A real outdoorsman," I say.

"Why do you think I'm so comfortable out here in the boondocks with you?" he asks.

"And a regular Cesar Millan with the animals these days," I add.

"The love of pets will do that to a man," he says.

"How *are* Molly and Duff?"

"Big, happy, and slobbering, the both of them," he responds, and turns to me. "Kinda like someone else I know."

"Enough with the ass-kissing, Silvestri. It's been a roller coaster of a morning. Let's hit Gus's for some sandwiches, eh?"

"Sounds good to me," he answers. "I've been dreaming about that Reuben, with the fresh—" He's interrupted by the sound of his cell vibrating inside the cup holder. He fishes it out and answers. "Detective Silvestri . . . Mmm-hmm . . . Yeah, we can be right over . . . You got it . . . Yeah, thank you." He hangs up and turns to me. "Wolcott, we're gonna have to put off lunch for a bit. Sorry, pal."

"What was that?" I ask.

"Looking like a day at the park."

"That puts a different spin on things," I say. "What's up?"

My partner shakes his head and shrugs. "Sounds like a body."

◈ ◈ ◈

We pull into the lot adjacent to the park. The sprawling lawn is empty, except for a flock of seagulls scavenging near a garbage can, and what appears to be a human form splayed out on the grass beyond the commotion.

"Any idea who called it in?" I ask, scanning the expanse.

"Whoever it was didn't bother to stick around, I guess."

Silvestri and I climb out and approach the lawn, which sends the birds packing. "Looks like she's left the building," I say as my partner and I pull pairs of nitrile gloves out of our pockets and stretch them over our fingers. I drop into a squat position and press two fingers gently against her carotid artery. After a moment, I look up and offer Silvestri a solemn shake of the head.

He drops down to get a better view of our victim. "Man, she looks young," he observes, a frown on his face. He shakes his head as he studies her. "What a shame."

He's not wrong. The woman appears to be in her midthirties. She's dressed in spandex pants, a thin hooded sweatshirt, and running shoes. Her hair is pulled back into a ponytail and secured with an elastic band. The position of her body is consistent with someone having suffered a sudden physical collapse. I examine her face. The color has drained, but I don't pick up on any overt signs of trauma. Her clothing appears to be undisturbed. I examine her hands. The unpolished nails are clipped short but evenly, with smooth edges. The wrists and forearms that extend from beneath the rolled-up sleeves of her sweatshirt are free of bruises and marks, save for a couple of light superficial scratches. I pull out my pen light and shine it into her eyes, and I catch a whiff of vomit on her breath as I lean in. I check the surrounding area but see no pools of sickness close by.

"How's she looking?" he asks.

"Pupils look dilated," I say. "Smells like she's thrown up recently. That's what's jumping out at me."

"You thinking natural? Some cardiac issue? Out for a jog, and then this?"

"Could be," I answer, shaking my head.

He studies the length of her body carefully, then moves his hand toward the front of her sweatshirt, where he's located the lone pocket on her outfit. He slips his hand inside and fishes out some loose cash and an inhaler.

"Damn," I say. "Asthma attack, maybe."

"Could be," he says with a forlorn expression. As he counts out twelve dollars in fives and singles, a card falls out from among the cash. "Coffee money?" he guesses as he sets down the bills and inspects the card.

"What do you got there?"

He looks at it, then flips it and hands it to me. "Just this."

TWO

CHARLOTTE

"Today is the day," I say loudly, using volume as much as enthusiasm in my attempt to conjure Peter. He said he would be back this week, and I am running out of days on the calendar and doubling down on positivity.

When I woke up this morning, my intuition was strong. For the first morning since he went away, I genuinely felt the hopeful excitement of finally seeing him outweighing the negative, nagging pull that he's gone away for good.

"He will come for me today." I am specific in my intention. I close my eyes and picture a strong white light entering my body and radiating through me while time is suspended in the red traffic light, and I relish a few composing breaths before I start my day of interactions. The only sound I can hear is the soothing metronomic turn signal, click, click, click, click.

It's a quieter-than-usual suburban weekday afternoon at the mouth of the parking lot, and I'm alone at the intersection. There is no one to look at me in judgment for talking to myself at full volume. Not a harried mom on her way to Pilates, or a car full of teenagers side-eyeing me, thinking, *Crazy*.

Then, as I enter the lot and near my corner of the complex, I practically jump out of the moving car when I see a man standing in front of my office, his back to me. He is tall with dark hair, too far away to positively identify, but it has to be him. I slow the car and squint, my heart blooming with hope, and I bounce in my seat like an excited toddler, but he's moved out of sight behind one of the storefront pillars.

"Wait!" I bellow, then whip into a lane of open spaces. He's already walked a good distance away by the time I pull into a parking spot mercifully close to my office door. I barely remember to shut off the engine and unfasten my seat belt before I'm out of the car.

"Peter!" I call after the steadily shrinking figure. He doesn't hesitate in his next step or turn around. My heart sinks.

"Peter?" I say a little louder in volume, but lower in hope. He's disappeared around a corner before the "er" leaves my lips. I check the time on my phone to see if I have a few extra minutes before my next patient to give chase, but I only have two minutes until the appointment is scheduled to begin. I chastise myself for getting out of the car; I could have driven alongside him and easily caught up.

Fuck. I want to follow him, but I'm out of time. He'll come back. Of course he will. I pull out my phone in the hope of a text from him, asking where I am. Nothing.

I shakily put the key in the door. Was it really him? My desperation may be distorting my ability to see people clearly. I'm doubting everything lately. I should be able to recognize him by now, even at a distance. I fight against the negative self-talk that is bubbling over.

"Honestly, Charlotte. You can barely recognize yourself anymore. Get your shit together," I mutter as the door glides open with an easy push.

"Excuse me? What did you just say to me?" The voice is so close, I feel the hair on the back of my head stand up.

I pivot sharply and we are face-to-face.

◖◗◖◗◖◗

My hand is steady and I am poised to strike. The sun through the window glints off the tip of the metal. Her blue eyes are wide with fear at the sharp point moving toward her chest. She swallows hard and looks away. In one quick move, I push the tip into her skin. She exhales sharply. I smile.

There are points on the outside of the human body where if you apply enough pressure, say, with a sharp object, you can change an entire internal energy flow. You can turn someone into wet spaghetti or bring them to unconsciousness with the know-how. I pride myself on having mastered these vital points, outside and in.

I've never lost the thrill of seeing how they respond the first time. It's a reminder of how powerful what I'm doing can be, and how powerless people are. How they confront the things that scare them tells a lot about their personality. In this case, she is openly afraid. I have only known her for inside an hour, but she already is an open book of insecurity and fear. It's a large part of what has brought her to me. And makes her an ideal candidate for what I do. I keep one hand on her arm to comfort her while I home in on the next entry point.

"How are you feeling, Lucy?" I say gently as I move around the table and push the point into the crook of her left arm.

"When are you putting the next one in?" she questions nervously.

"Already done. You didn't even notice. How does it feel so far?" I ask her.

"Strange. Tingly. Does that mean it's working?" she responds.

"Tingling can indicate that your qi—your energy flow—is being moved along, which is the goal. So you are doing great." I know based on her consult interview earlier that she is highly self-critical and suffering from majorly low self-esteem, two character traits that can manifest physiologically in a number of insidious ways.

"Oh good. My body doesn't always cooperate when I introduce it to new things. Mainly exercise or dieting." She releases a laugh that sounds more wounded than amused and self-consciously puts her right arm over her midsection. Body-image issues are very apparent in her. There is a lot to work on here; she is the kind of challenging patient I like.

"The wonderful thing about acupuncture is that you don't have to do much. Just lie back, breathe deeply, and let me do the hard part."

Once I explained my negative self-talk at the door when she was arriving at the same time as I was, we had an awkward laugh and she graciously let me properly introduce myself before we got started. It was not how I wanted to begin with a new client, and I'm lucky she has a sense of humor.

"How does it actually work? I tried to do some research online, but you know how unreliable the Internet can be." She groans. "I try to stay offline as much as possible, so I decided to hold off and ask the professional. I'm also hopeless with anything computer related."

"Smart thinking. Googling *anything* is often more frightening than educational. I can recommend some great books about acupuncture if you are interested."

"Sure. I love to read."

"Great. I'll write them down for you before you leave." I put a needle in her third eye, the space between her eyebrows, which is an incredibly calming point.

"Basically, we are made up of energy, and sometimes what is happening in our heads, coupled with our diet and lifestyle choices, can negatively affect our bodies' ability to connect all this powerful energy flow, and things get blocked. In Chinese medicine, organs correlate to particular emotions. Stored-up trauma from our lives can accumulate and manifest in a number of physical ailments. Everyday stresses and daily pollutants, from the air we breathe to the food we put in our bodies to the toxic people we encounter, can overload our systems. All of these factors add up and our organs can't do their jobs fully, so problems arise. The needles help open your pathways." I've moved to her large intestine meridian. "If our body is a racetrack of energy, the places where energy gets blocked are like little car accidents along the way. I use the needles to clear the road and keep everything moving smoothly."

She seems impressed with my explanation. Her breathing has deepened and her nervous system has calmed. I am happy that she is reacting so positively, and so quickly.

"How are the needles feeling so far? Anything bothering you? Any aching or sharp pains?"

"I'm great, actually. I can barely feel them going in, and once they are, I feel a nice body buzz. Like I'm in one of those massage chairs at the nail salon, but on a low setting."

"That is a great metaphor! I might have to use it."

She's pleased. "Of course. Use away."

I don't have my next needle completely out of its plastic casing when I hear the front door buzzer. Damn. Since Rachel isn't in, and we don't have the budget for a receptionist these days, I can either ignore it or interrupt my session, which I'd rather not do with a new patient. I decide to ignore it and pull the needle the rest of the way out. The buzzer sounds again and is followed by a pretty aggressive knock. Whoever it is clearly is not going away. My stomach flips. I don't have any other patients today, and according to the schedule, neither does Rachel. It has to be Peter. My heart does a triple axel.

"Lucy, I'm so sorry. Would you excuse me for a minute? I wasn't expecting anyone. I should go check and see who it is." I put the still-sheathed needle on the side table.

"No problem," she replies amicably.

I slip out the door and make my way past our shared "reception area," which is simply an IKEA desk topped with a box of Kleenex, my laptop, and a wood-and-stone Cairn fountain. When I open the door, my eyes are met with jade irises so striking that a small current of electricity travels from the top of my head to my feet. It's the man from earlier. And he clearly is not Peter from this angle. Disappointment envelops me.

"Hi. Can I help you?" I stay squarely in the doorway so he doesn't enter the office.

"Hi. I'm Jack." He reaches his hand out confidently. I peg him as a salesman, but I'm not sure what he's selling yet. I give him a small friendly wave instead.

"I'd shake your hand, but I'm treating someone right now."

He looks me up and down quickly and corrects himself by casting a laser focus on my face. "Charlotte?" he asks.

"Have we met?"

"Nope, just a lucky guess." From each of his hands, he waves our two business cards, which live in two slots next to our entrance door. He looks at each of our cards again and chuckles. "My odds were good."

"Are you looking for Rachel?" I shift to lean on the door frame to further my not inviting him inside, trying not to let the impatience in my body escape into my words.

"Maybe? Or maybe I'm looking for you?" He lets that sink in and is clearly pleased when I don't respond right away aside from looking away from him quickly.

Normally, I'd be more repelled by his brashness, but he's got sexual energy and appeal wafting off of him that I'm picking up on pretty strongly. I'm surprised by how much I'm reacting to this complete stranger standing a few feet away from me, in the midst of my disappointment.

I clear my throat. "Do you have an appointment with Rachel?" It's possible that he was a late add and she didn't put him into the system, or one of them got the day or time mixed up.

"No. But I was walking by—I've passed your office a number of times, actually—I like the China Panda lunch special—and finally decided to come in. I think you, or Rachel, might be exactly what I need to feel better." His smile is crooked, and on a less handsome man, it could look more like a case of dental neglect.

I'm struggling to parse innuendo from confidence. He could easily be a creep who only saw "massage" on the door, totally disregarded the other words, "reflexologist," "acupuncturist," and "Reiki healer," and slithered in thinking he would get a hand job after his dim sum. Sadly, it wouldn't be the first time.

"Well, I'm actually with a patient right now, but if you want to come back in half an hour, I could help you make an appointment. Were you looking for a sports massage?" I'm not getting an openness-to-Eastern-modalities vibe from him. His clothing and haircut paint more ex–lacrosse player turned broker type. Not my type in any realm of my life, yet he is annoyingly magnetic. I check myself. I am not available. I am deeply in love with my boyfriend.

"What do you do?" He's kept eye contact well enough and his body language is open and nonthreatening, but there's something about him that isn't sitting right with me.

"Acupuncture and Reiki."

His face draws into an expression of thoughtfulness, and he tugs at an invisible beard for effect. He reminds me of someone from my past, but I can't figure out who.

"Force of habit. I actually had a beard up until last week, but I gave myself a makeover. I feel naked without it."

I'd rather not think of this man naked, but of course that is where my mind goes. I quickly drop that image and think about Peter's beard. How much I've thought about kissing him in the last month. I hear Lucy cough and shift on the bed from behind the closed door. The office is smaller than ideal, but it is what I can afford right now.

"Sorry. I really need to get back to my patient."

"Patient? Or client?" His face hardens momentarily before he softens into a smile when he sees my posture go from neutral to rigid fast.

"Excuse me?"

"Oh, sorry. No disrespect. Wasn't sure how that worked with non-MDs." He grins.

Technically, I'm still an MD, but I won't correct him. His charm has jumped the shark and I'm ready to be free of him. I used to only spend my days with men like him. Working alongside, sleeping next to. Loving and fearing. I frown and I can see him register this change in me.

"I apologize. I offended you. I am trying to work on that."

I don't take the bait. I don't need to hear about whatever this man is working on in himself. I'm retired from worrying about the self-improvements of charming but flawed men.

"No problem. Why don't you check out our website and you can book an appointment that way." I make no attempt to line my tone to sound particularly inviting. He's fully under my skin and I'm not liking it.

"Maybe you can even fit me in this afternoon?" The cognitive dissonance between my distaste at his arrogance and the curiosity of what his body would feel like against mine is disorienting.

"I'll have to look at my schedule for this afternoon, but I don't believe I have any openings." The practical side of me is yelling that not only do I have openings, but I desperately need to fill my dwindling patient roster if I want to stay in business. All the other parts of me are preferring to ignore the conflicting attraction-and-aversion piece, as I'm really not in the mood to endure low-level harassment from this dude in the form of James Spader in *Pretty in Pink. That's it!* I'm relieved to land on who his behavior is reminding me of, and now that I have, I don't know if I can see him any other way.

"You can also book online," I reiterate.

"I prefer to live my life offline," he says without a trace of irony and runs a hand through his hair and moves to leave, having the last words. "See you later, then. Looking forward to it." He turns on his heels and makes his way in the direction of the China Panda. He's clearly a man who doesn't take no for an answer.

My least favorite kind.

"I'm so sorry about that, Lucy." She rolls her head toward me, a smile settled across her face. I wash my hands at the small sink to the right of the door before resuming my position next to her.

"No problem. I was just getting in some much-needed me time. Nice to just be in my head for a change."

I'm relieved that this new patient is seemingly very laid-back given her self-described anxiety. Usually self-critical and low self-esteemed people don't take to disruptions easily. But who knows what she's concealing in the interest of making a good first impression. "That's great. Glad you had some good alone time. Do you feel ready for some more needles?" She takes my face in for a long time, and I feel a blip of déjà vu. She nods and smiles and returns her gaze to the ceiling.

"I'm lucky to have stumbled onto your practice online. I'm so glad I didn't take those Yelp reviews to heart; otherwise, I really would have missed out."

Her comment seems well-intentioned, but it stings. I've likely lost a lot of potential new business because of the scathing online reviews, but I've long given up on trying to get them taken down. I gave up once I realized that for every screed I successfully got removed, two more would crop up in a futile and hateful game of Whac-A-Mole. All I can do is preserve the few loyal patients I have and cultivate the new ones, like Lucy, into hopefully becoming regulars.

"You have very steady hands! I guess that is important in your line of work."

I nearly mention my former life, when my steady hands were my biggest asset. I hold back, knowing that opening that topic of conversation is potentially riskier than satisfying my ego.

"Yes. Steady hands are very useful. But mostly, it's about having an open mind and a love for healing. I'm especially passionate about helping people who haven't been able to get relief from Western medicine."

"Amen." She closes her eyes in response.

"It sounds like that has been your experience." I know I'm leading the witness, but I want to know more about what has brought her here, and Lucy's been tentative with the details so far. I can sense that there is a lot more under the surface.

She nods thoughtfully as I begin placing needles along her lung channel. She described depression, lack of motivation, and body-image issues during her consult, which can all be a result of stagnant energy flow in the areas where grief and loneliness reside.

"Unfortunately, I haven't had a great track record with traditional doctors. I gave up on trying with them. It was very discouraging when I was at my sickest, but I've come to peace with it. For a bunch of know-it-alls, they struggle a lot with the basics, like how to treat patients as people, not just symptoms."

I think about how much this statement applies to me, but in a very different context. I remain silent, and happily, she continues emerging from her shell. Often needles are very effective in drawing introverted people out.

"No use in blaming others for not being able to make you feel better. That's what my mother always used to tell me, anyway." She sighs. I get the impression that this conclusion has not been easily won for Lucy.

"Very wise. Some people live their whole lives without learning that."

If I'm lucky enough that she returns, I'm sure I'll be learning a lot more about her. People tend to increasingly open up on the table the longer they come to me. My friend Annelise has told me that I'm more effective than her therapist with my "sharp points, soft words, and healing vibes."

"All you can really do is take matters into your own hands," Lucy says with more confidence than I've yet heard from her.

"Absolutely." I like her. She's got good, positive energy underneath the pain. Something I can relate to and that I've been trying to unearth hourly. But my sadness keeps creeping back into the lead. I lean over her and put a needle in her pericardium point and feel the channel open intensely.

"Whoa!" she cries out. "What was that?"

"Are you okay? Was it painful?" I take a step back to give her some space. The first major opening can be overwhelming for patients.

"No. It was just . . . wow. Like a jolt of energy through my whole body. All that from one little needle?" She is wide-eyed.

"It's a point that correlates to the protective casing around your heart called the pericardium, which, among other things, protects it from overwhelming emotions. It's a very powerful and moving point in acupuncture." I lean farther over her to insert another needle into one of her large intestine points, which opens significantly as well.

"Jesus! What was that one?"

"Your stomach channel—which can be related to anger, among other things."

"Hmm. Funny. I'm not an angry person," she says amicably.

I see her looking at the medallion Peter sent to me for my birthday a couple of months ago. It has come out of my shirt and is hovering above her heart area.

"Pretty! Is that an heirloom? It looks old . . . but in a good way!" We both laugh.

"Actually, it's from my boyfriend. I should ask him if it's an heirloom." I pause from needling and take the copper coin in my hand, looking at it for the hundredth time.

"What does it mean?" she asks. My fingers trace the raised metal. I have gotten into the habit of absently fiddling with it when I'm daydreaming so often that I sometimes wonder if I'm going to rub the Rod of Asclepius from the metal completely.

"It symbolizes health, healing, and peace." She smiles. Peter sent it at the height of my being angry at him, and once I unwrapped it, I couldn't stay mad. It was so thoughtful. He appreciates how much the aspects of my old life are still a crucial part of me, and how I want to heal myself as much as others. He gets me.

I place the necklace back in my shirt and take a pump of Purell between my palms before I resume with her needles.

"Well, it's lovely. And so great that you have a man in your life who gives you nice things. I never had one who really got the art of gift giving. I only got presents in the form of apologies." I don't share with her that the necklace was exactly that. I've moved on, so there is no need to dredge up the negative. She continues. "I've all but given up on men." She sighs into a laugh. I sense more resigned sadness than humor.

"I understand. I'd all but given up too when I met Peter. Funny how that happens."

"That is always the way, isn't it?" She flutters her eyes open. "Do you treat him?" She nods in the direction of the needle I've just inserted along her inner elbow and twisted slightly. "Needles-wise, I mean."

"I don't. As a general rule, I don't treat romantic partners or family members." I smile at the thought of having Peter on my table. I wonder if that will ever be a possibility. My mind shifts to an image of treating Mom, and I cringe. Luckily she's just as averse to my treating her as I am, one of the rare things we agree on.

"What about friends?" she asks.

"Depends on the friend, but yes, generally I'll treat friends," I respond lightly.

"Good to have boundaries and keep business and pleasure separate. I've seen the opposite situation end badly more than once," she says knowingly.

I reflexively think about my time with Henry and going from protégée to romantic partner. I'm batting a thousand with the negative thoughts today.

"Some people really struggle with that." She holds my eyes for an uncomfortable moment and I wonder if she can read my thoughts. I have been one of those people, for sure.

I swat away the memory of my Henry days and swap in Peter. I really try not to think about him too much when I'm working, but it's getting harder the longer he is gone. Handsome Peter. Dangerous Peter. Missing Peter. It has been three weeks and no word, not even in code. But he swore that this was the week he would return.

He made me promise that I wouldn't tell a soul if he disappeared and I've kept my word . . . for the most part. My heart aches thinking about him. I try not to let my mind wander to the worst. He'll resurface again; I can feel it.

I finish inserting the rest of the needles. "So now all you have to do is breathe deeply and meditate if you can."

"Meditate? I don't really know how," she admits.

"Try to focus on something simple that makes you happy, and keep coming back to your breath if your thoughts wander."

"Okay." She flutters her eyes closed and a smile spreads across her face. "Got it."

"How do you feel?" Her shoulders have lowered from her ears and her mouth has gone slack.

"Wonderful. Actually, kind of stoned. Did you dip those needles in something?" She giggles.

"Nope. That is all you. You are experiencing the wonderful natural high of your body's circuitry system flowing smoothly. Pretty incredible, isn't it?" I beam. It never fails to fill me with happiness when a new patient feels good.

"Remarkable. I feel like I'm healing already," she says dreamily.

"I'll be back for you in about twenty minutes." I switch the overhead lights off.

"You're going to leave me here in the dark, alone?" The smallness of her voice surprises me. But the needles can be very disarming. "What if something bad happens?"

"You'll be fine. I promise nothing bad will happen." My heart opens for her. "I'm right outside the door." I've gotten it nearly shut when she speaks again.

"Charlotte?"

"Yes, Lucy?"

"Thank you. I really hope someone does this for you. You deserve it."

❖❖❖

Back at my desk, I log in to Yelp, something I vowed to myself and to Rachel that I would stop doing. The practice became so habitually masochistic that I would often find myself checking in mindlessly multiple times an hour, even though it was repeatedly as painful as the mindless time before. But today, because of Lucy's comment, I feel a strong pull to check. Part of me hopes that Peter might use the online review page as a place to communicate with me. "In plain sight can be the best place to send messages," he'd told me when we started mapping out our secret codes.

The last time I logged on was four months ago, and Rachel, wonderful friend that she is, kindly offered to screen them for me and share any positive ones, and skip the negative ones so that I didn't have to read how awful people think I am. Or the one person who does, who goes by many names, apparently. The most recent review is from just after I stopped looking at them, written by "Truthhurts," with one star.

> I would give Acupuncturist Charlotte Knopfler a negative 5 stars review if this app gave the option, but what I can't communicate in stars, I'll hopefully succeed with in words. THIS WOMAN IS THE WORST!! She shouldn't be allowed to treat any other human beings for anything, let alone stick needles in them. She's a careless and dangerous CRIMINAL. Take my word for it; do not give this woman access to your body or to your wallet unless you want your life ruined. She should be in jail.

The sudden sensation of wanting to fall through the floor into some alternate reality is acute. I can't lose my shit while a client is in the office. No wonder Rachel offered to look at these; I should have known better. This one is the worst so far, or maybe it just feels that way because it's the newest. I'm about to scroll through to challenge my theory and upset myself further, but my phone vibrates in the top drawer, where I keep it during sessions. I'm relieved for the distraction from the cruelty.

"Hello?"

"Can I please speak to Charlotte Knopfler?" I don't recognize the overly official-sounding voice.

"Speaking." I respond quietly for the sake of my patient.

"Ma'am, my name is Treat Allen. I'm calling from the Suffolk County medical examiner's office."

The world around me starts to tilt. I'm speechless and the voice continues.

"You were listed as the emergency contact of an individual who has come into our custody, and we are going to need you to come to our facility to make an identification. Are you able to do that today?"

All the saliva in my mouth has evaporated and I feel the hallmarks of a panic attack coming on. I put my head between my legs. My braid rests on the floor in a heap.

"Who . . . ?" I am unable to contain the tears as they run down my forehead and into my hairline.

"Ma'am, unfortunately I cannot give out any further information. We'll require you in person before we can continue this conversation. Do you need our location?"

"Yes." I grab a pen and copy the information on the back of one of my business cards. "I'm on my way."

I shakily gather my cell phone, bag, and keys and proceed to drop everything on the threshold of my office. I nearly fall into a heap and start sobbing. Peter. I know it's him. My love. Dead. The worst possible thing that could happen, has.

Heart racing, I struggle with locking the door behind me. I spot my green Prius and hate myself for being happy this morning about something as meaningless as finding a nearby parking spot. Now this seeming stroke of lucky convenience will bring me that much closer and more quickly to my biggest fear.

A cold incoming winter wind bites the tips of my ears and I shiver through my tears. I've forgotten my coat in the rush, but I decide against going back for it. A couple of stoned teenagers walk by me and burst into laughter before entering the China Panda next door. I start the car, attempting to still my quaking hands, and prepare myself for the fifteen-minute drive from Smithtown to Stony Brook.

The afternoon sky is dark-to-light ombré. It feels much later than five thirty P.M. It takes me ten minutes of driving well over the speed limit and disregarding yellow lights before I realize that in my panicked state, I've left Lucy full of needles in my locked office.

Desperate, I forge on in the same direction and fumble for my phone to call Rachel, who doesn't pick up. I hear the desperation in my own voice as I cry my need for help through the voice-to-text and hope she's nearby. As soon as I get the last of my plea into the phone, the sky opens up and torrential rain engulfs my car, a sign from above that I should slow down or else. I feel reckless now, and panicked, and instead of decelerating, I glide through a very yellow light. A car coming from the opposite direction in the turn lane slams on its horn and brakes, the loud honking reverberating in my head at top volume. The sky has darkened considerably and the rain is hard on the roof of my car and the wipers can barely clear the view for long enough to see mere inches in front of me. With each swish I pray for him to be okay and for my view to become clearer, and the harder it becomes to see in front of me.

Catastrophe is surrounding me on all sides now.

THREE

RACHEL

"HAVE YOU TOLD ANYONE?" He sips the steaming coffee tentatively as he looks at me through dark glasses. We are indoors, so he looks like an incognito celebrity or, more fitting, a mobster.

"You are the only person who knows." I look down at my tea and pull on the string attached to the bag filled with hibiscus flowers.

"Rachel. We are only as sick as our secrets." His Rolex catches the sunlight as he takes another sip, the overflow liquid from the saucer dripping from the bottom of his cup onto the table between us.

"Yeah, well, in that case, I guess I'm terminal," I say flippantly as I swipe my unused napkin across the coffee puddle.

He frowns. "I don't think you should be making mortality jokes at a time like this, do you?"

"I don't really care what you think," I counter.

He catches my eyes. "This is serious." He clasps his hands in front of him. "Listen to me. This is happening."

I take a gulp of air to encourage my lungs to relax. "Don't you think I know that?" My voice cracks and my eyes fill.

He leans back, satisfied with my display of vulnerability. "What are you going to do about this?" His voice rises.

I look around at the surrounding diners who've paused their conversations to look at us. "Jesus. Keep your voice down."

"I'm upset," he says, lower.

"You and I have very different opinions on this, that much we know. I don't want to keep having this conversation. I should have just handled it on my own." I pause, realizing I may be pissing him off. "No offense."

He shrugs. "It takes a lot more than that to offend me. Another important thing about me that you should know is that I'm not in the habit of letting people off the hook."

"I've already told you. This isn't negotiable," I restate for the third time this hour.

"I don't want this on my conscience. Aside from the fact that I actually kind of like you, I value my reputation. If anyone found out that I had anything to do with letting you get away with this—"

"No one is going to find out. That's the whole point of this." I gesture to him and me. "What we've shared is nobody else's business. That's the agreement."

"What about Charlotte?" I don't like the way his voice changes when he says her name.

"What about her?" I reply defensively.

"Can't she help you? Surely she'd want to save your life?"

"You are being unnecessarily dramatic and mean right now." I shake my head sadly. "This is not her problem to fix."

"Well, the person whose problem it is, is doing jack shit." His eyes bore into me.

I tap my fingers on the table nervously. "She would not handle this well." He looks wearily at my fidgeting and I retract my hands into my lap.

"If she's really a friend, she's going to want to help," he responds.

"She'd be furious with me. She and I have very different outlooks on the right thing to do as far as this is concerned." I look out the window and watch the steady stream of traffic flow by.

"Rachel, now more than ever you want to be living truthfully, don't you?" he asks.

"Don't start that shit," I spew.

"All the work you've done on yourself?" He makes a tsk-tsk sound and it makes me want to drive my unused fork through his hand. "Secrecy is a slippery slope," he pushes.

"I'm about to get up and walk out of here," I warn.

"What about if I talked to Charlotte? Explained things to her in technical terms? I think she'll like me; I tend to have a soothing effect on the ladies," he says.

My mouth goes dry.

"Don't you dare." I grit my teeth and double down. "Besides, if you don't keep my secret, then what's to keep me from telling yours?"

"I have nothing to hide." He laughs. "I'm an open book."

"You have everything to hide!" I say seriously.

His face pales a few shades and he's about to reply when my phone vibrates in my bag for the third time in ten minutes. I've been ignoring it, but it's getting increasingly harder not to worry about who else is coming for me.

"Maybe you should get that?" he says, his irritation apparent.

I remain still. Better not to incite him.

"Go ahead, check it," he says. "It could be a matter of life and death," he adds glibly.

"You have a really fucked sense of humor, you know that?" I say as I flip over my iPhone, and he shrugs. I see that I have three missed calls and a text from Charlotte. My stomach climbs into my throat as I read the text and shoot back a quick response without asking his permission.

"Everything okay?" he asks.

"I need to go. I'm sorry. There's a problem at my office," I stammer.

"Charlotte?" he asks. I shoot him a dirty look.

"She needs my help." I reach for my purse to retrieve a twenty, but he waves it away when I extend my hand.

"I'll add it to your tab." He smiles wryly.

"Fine," I shoot back.

"This conversation is not over. I'm not going away." He means every word. My hand is on the door when he lobs one last grenade at my back.

"Rachel," he says gravely. "Save yourself, while you still can."

FOUR

SILVESTRI

"Ms. KNOPFLER?" I try my best to maintain a warm but reverent expression as the distressed woman approaches me in the hallway. This is about to be the worst part of my day.

"Yes, I'm Charlotte Knopfler." In spite of her obvious unease, she extends a firm handshake and offers up the kindest smile anyone in her position can be expected to muster.

"Miss Knopfler, my name is Detective Silvestri. Thank you for coming in." In a fun twist, the grief counselor who's usually on hand for these moments called out this morning with a death in the family. Wolcott is off chasing down a stolen pool-cleaning van, which leaves Mr. Sensitive to walk this poor woman through the bereavement process.

"Please, call me Charlotte." She wears her dirty blond hair tidily in a braid and bun arrangement. She's dressed in loose-fitting clothing and slip-on shoes, and I pick up the scent of candles and incense. I suspect she's a massage therapist or some sort of holistic practitioner.

"Okay, Charlotte. I'm going to walk you through the process. I'll be with you every step of the way." I give her my arm and lead her in the direction of the sitting room.

"Are you taking me to the body?" she asks.

"It's not quite the way you might expect from the cop shows."

We're met by the medical examiner, Fisk, who leads us into the sitting room and gets us situated. I'm relieved to have another woman in the mix, as I'm hoping this will help put Charlotte at ease. I calmly explain that she'll be handed a photograph attached facedown to a clip-board, that the photo will be of her loved one's face framed by a blue sheet, and that there are no markings or trauma to the face that she needs to prepare for. I tell her that she can take as much time as she needs before turning the photo over.

As I watch her absorb the information, I find myself taken with this woman's level of self-possession. Aside from being quite beautiful, she exudes positive energy. Even now, with her friend lying on the slab in the other room, she seems tuned in to Fisk and me in an almost deferential sense. Under normal circumstances, I can imagine what she brings to the situation. A real caregiver.

I watch her closely as she turns the photo over and forces herself to look at the image. I register surprise, then confusion, on her face before she faints in her chair.

❖ ❖ ❖

This has happened once before. During my NYPD days, I had to accompany a next of kin to identify a body. We spent several days tracking down the sister of a young woman who turned up dead in a hit-and-run, and then had to wait until she returned home from an out-of-state visit to a boyfriend. When the woman finally made it in, begrudgingly, I sat her down while the medical examiner and grief counselor ran her through the drill.

The woman seemed more put off than concerned and became increasingly impatient and belligerent until she was handed the clip-board. She huffed, snatched the photo, and looked at it before freezing in place, becoming ashen, and passing out where she sat. When we finally revived her, she looked at me with eyes the size of saucers, her lips quivering. There was a detached glaze in her stare, and she seemed to be looking just past me.

"Are you okay, miss?" I asked.

"Well, ain't that a motherfucker?" she answered absently.

"What's that, miss?"

"Felt like I was staring into a mirror just then." Her gaze continued to hover just beyond my head.

"I understand," I said, patting her hand reassuringly. "These circumstances can be unsettling. Can I ask you the last time you were in contact with your sister?"

She looked at me for the first time, genuine shock dripping off of her face. "In *contact*?" She frowned incredulously. "I didn't even know I *had* a sister 'til just now."

Charlotte is taking short sips of water from the paper-cone cup she holds with two hands, as if warming herself by a fire. She wears an expression of what I read as pleasant, relieved surprise coupled with mild shock. Her unfixed stare settles somewhere on the wall at the far end of the sitting room. I let her eyes settle back to mine before I pick up the conversation again.

"You seem relieved," I say finally.

"Of course," she answers, allowing herself a deep exhale. "I thought that was going to be someone I know in that picture. Or knew, I guess."

I do my best to temper my surprise. "Are you saying that you don't recognize the woman in that photograph?"

"I have no idea who she is," she responds. There's the slightest hint of hesitation in her expression.

"And you're sure about that?"

"I've never seen that woman before in my life." She betrays a smile, then catches herself. She looks at me sheepishly. "Sorry, I probably seem callous. I'm sure she has loved ones out there who are worried about her and looking for her."

"No, no. It's understandable." I pause to consider. "It just raises more questions than it answers."

She cocks her head slightly and furrows her brow as she looks at me. "And you're saying that I was this woman's emergency contact?"

"That's correct," I say. "Your name and number were written down on the card we located in the pocket of the deceased."

I don't register any of the usual hallmarks of deception as I study her face. She takes another deep breath and shakes her head. "Well, Detective, I have to say, I'm as baffled as you are." She looks to Fisk for a moment, then back to me. "Who was she, anyway?"

"Well," I say, "that's exactly what we're trying to figure out."

FIVE

CHARLOTTE

I'M GRATEFUL when Detective Silvestri walks me to my car. In spite of my reassurances that I'm stable enough to make it unescorted, the shakiness from the last couple of hours is still intense, and I feel like a foal on new legs when I step out into the evening. I immediately begin shivering like one without my coat, which I'm now wishing I hadn't left in my office in my earlier panic. I wrap my arms around myself while we near my Prius.

"Are you sure you're feeling well enough to drive? I'd be happy to give you a lift home and arrange for someone to bring you back to your car in the morning. It's been a jarring day for you." He seems overly formal for someone who's just spent what felt like hours in a small room with me. He holds eye contact a beat longer than expected, as though he's searching for something subconscious in my movements.

"I'm much better now that I've eaten, thanks to you." I smile and it occurs to me that I very possibly have bright orange remnants between my teeth from the peanut butter and cheese cracker sandwiches he scared up after my fainting spell. The snack paired well with a cranapple juice box. I wish I had a compact mirror handy to check my teeth. I can't believe that I'm thinking about how I look at a time like this.

"Ah yes, the fine dining of the Suffolk County medical examiner's office employees. They have the palates of kindergarteners. Apologies for not having something more sophisticated on hand." His smile is nice when it emerges. In the course of the afternoon there were mostly pensive looks. Something about leaving the sterile surroundings of our previous venue has loosened him up.

"Actually, peanut butter crackers and juice boxes is one of my favorite snacks." We both laugh. This is true. "I shouldn't admit that out loud, since I tell my clients to avoid sugary and processed foods, but the comfort of flavor nostalgia sometimes wins out over common sense. And that used to be my winning combination of sustenance when I was in school." He smiles and nods. I realize I'm standing somewhat awkwardly in front of my car and angle myself closer to the driver's-side door.

"Do you have someone at home to keep an eye on you this evening?" he asks protectively.

I was careful not to mention anything about Peter when Silvestri's earlier questioning veered to who I thought I was brought in to identify. It would be too complicated, and I'm not prepared to answer any questions, nor would Peter want me uttering a word about him to local law enforcement. Not that he's reachable to call to come and get me.

"My friend Rachel is coming by to keep me company," I say hopefully. I haven't been able to get through to her yet. "We're partners in our practice."

"Nice. Someone to do needles on you?"

"Actually, she's a reflexologist and massage therapist, among other things." I don't know why I say the last part. What "other things" am I even suggesting? I haven't been doing a good job today of being clear in my communication. That happens when I'm hiding things, and I hate that my situation is such that I have to be that person again. Especially to a detective.

"Reflexology, eh? I was never one for people touching my feet." He chuckles. "Glad to hear you have someone." *Someone.* A sour thought about my absent group of so-called friends pops into my head as I extract the car keys from my purse and unlock the door. Silvestri leans across me and grabs the handle before I do, opening the driver's side and guiding me in.

He's gentle for a cop. He doesn't have the usual aggressive energy wafting off of him that other men in his line of work do. He has the quiet calm of someone who's been around the block enough times to know that there is far more power in stillness and patience.

"I will go through all of my client records tomorrow and see if anyone's name jogs my memory, but I feel positive that I've never seen that poor woman before today." *Am* I positive? She did look familiar, but for all I know, she reminds me of another movie character from my youth. I worry the admission of familiarity might get his hopes up, and I don't want to disappoint. "I really want to help, though. Will you let me know what you find out?" I pull the seat belt across my chest.

"Absolutely. In fact, I'm sorry to say it, but you and I will probably be seeing a lot more of each other in the next few days. My partner and I need to determine what exactly befell Jane Doe, and why she had your contact info in her pocket."

"Yes, of course." I worry about potential regular interaction with law enforcement. Peter has a way of keeping tabs when he's not around. Any contact with the police taken out of context could be bad. And it may cause him to stay away longer.

Silvestri shuts the door and I watch him back away a few steps and realize that he's going to wait until I pull out and drive away before moving any farther. I wave at him and check my mirrors twice before making my way to the exit. In the rearview, he is watching and waiting, and for a moment I feel safe.

I drive home, where no one will be. I replied to Rachel's text from earlier confirming that she'd made it back to the office to free Lucy, but she hasn't replied to my text giving her the broad strokes of today's roller coaster and an invitation to her to come over this evening for moral support, something she is always eager to do. Her phone goes straight to voicemail when I try her now. I don't want to be alone, but I may not have a choice in the matter. Maybe I need to process everything that happened today by myself.

I feel a little drunk with all the conflicting emotions roiling in me. The relief of seeing Jane Doe's face, and not his, has wrung me out. I shudder at the thought of seeing Peter's face. I have escaped tragedy for one more day, so there is an enormous weight lifted. But he's still gone. And then, *her.*

Who *is* this stranger who made me her emergency contact? The confusion of never having seen the dead woman before today, mixed with the unsettling feeling of her being familiar, is unshakable. I hit the gas impatiently and pass a car in front of me. The driver makes an exasperated face and flicks his middle finger when I glide by, and I smile sweetly while telling him to fuck off in my head. The exchange brings me back into the moment. I look down at the speedometer and realize I'm racing toward sixty miles an hour. In a school zone, no less.

I pull over to the side of the dark road and place the car in park. I close my eyes and breathe deeply as I try to place her. When I open my eyes, I see her in the glass looking back at me for a split second and flinch. I pull out my phone and text the number I've been trying him on for weeks now.

I need to talk to you. Something bad has happened.

In the darkness of the trees outside my car I see the nearly autumn branches moving in the wind, and my loneliness is magnified. I stare at the screen, knowing in my heart there will be no response. I feel a breath on my neck and whip my head around to inspect the back seat. Empty. Spooked, I start the car and take in the warm air pushing out of the vents. I drive slowly and carefully home, feeling haunted and shaken by dread.

I pull into my driveway and look at my dark house.

I think about the first night I slept in it by myself, after moving out of my mother's house for the second time. I'd taken refuge there for an incredibly difficult year of recovering from my hospitalization, the end of my career and relationship, and the slow but sure new beginnings of my life now.

Rachel and I were sitting on the front stoop in the summer evening humidity, exhausted from moving my few belongings into the sweet little rental I'd found, soaking in the smell of the burning sage we'd just passed through the house.

"Can you stay over?" I'd asked her. This would be the first time I'd ever lived completely alone. I'd gone from my mother's straight into years of college and med school roommates to living with Henry.

"You are going to have to sleep here alone eventually. Why not have it be on your first night? It's very symbolic. Besides, I have to get home and feed the fur babies, or they'll claw my eyes out tomorrow." She'd hugged me tightly and left me to start my second attempt at an adult life.

I don't think I'd have made it out of my mom's or found my own place without Rachel's encouragement. She was the first friend I'd ever had who treated me like I was strong when I was feeling my weakest. "I can feel the fight in you." She'd said that the first time she worked on me. She saw strength and courage in me that I didn't know I had or how to tap into at that point. I'm having trouble accessing that courage right now.

I lift my phone in the hope that Rachel has responded, but I have no new messages. I text her again, letting her know I've just gotten home. It's our pact. For whenever we are apart or leave each other, we always have to let the other know we are okay. As I type, it dawns on me that Rachel is my "in case of emergency" person. My chest swells with love and gratitude that I have someone who cares about my whereabouts and safety. I finish typing and send.

Home safe.

SIX

WOLCOTT

"Mornin', sunshine." I catch Silvestri in the hallway and hand him his tea as we walk toward our desks.

"Thanks, partner." He tests the heat with a tentative sip. We round the corner, where he's greeted with a hero's welcome. His desk is papered in a couple dozen of those "Hang in There!" cat posters, there are several bags of feline treats tacked to a corkboard, and our colleagues are clapping and hooting. Even Captain Evans has gotten in on the fun.

Silvestri assesses the scene and suppresses a smile. "No wonder our budget's gone to shit around here. Get back to work, you derelicts."

A couple of the detectives make meowing sounds as they return to their desks. My partner and I remove our coats and settle in. "So," I say. "Heard you got to don your grief counselor hat. Can't tell you how much I would have paid to see that."

He looks suddenly perplexed. "Yeah, quite a curious fucking case with that one."

"How so?" I ask.

"Well, this woman, Charlotte, comes down to identify the body."

I notice he refers to her by first name only. "Usually how it works."

"Right, except she gets here, looks at the photo, and claims to have no idea who she's looking at."

I feel myself perk up. "Okay, *that's* unusual."

Silvestri takes a moment before he speaks again. "It's . . ." He shakes his head. "Odd."

"Do you think she's on the level?"

"That's just it," he says. "She seemed genuine. That's a hard thing to fake in the moment. I thought I caught a flash of hesitation, but she could have just been processing. There was a palpable sense of relief. It seemed as if she was expecting to see someone else on the slab."

"And we're sure she's not just an exceptional liar?"

"She's some sort of holistic practitioner. Really open, positive energy, warm. Does not strike me as the devious sort. Unless I'm completely misreading the situation."

"You tend to have a good gut with these things," I say.

"I'd like to think so."

"So, we've got a young woman found dead in a park, and we're no closer to answers than we were before."

"Thankfully, *you* cracked the case of the hot-tub bandits. Otherwise, the day would have been a total wash," he says.

I ponder the situation. "I'm just curious why in the hell someone would be an emergency contact if—"

I'm interrupted by the rattle of my partner's cell phone against his desk. "Detective Silvestri," he answers. "Oh, hey, Fisk . . . Yeah, we'll be right over . . . Thanks a bunch." Silvestri nods, and we get up and grab our coats.

◆ ◆ ◆

"How's our favorite croaker doing today?"

Our medical examiner looks at me with a arched eyebrow. "Hey, three-piece. Missed you yesterday." It would understatement to describe Fisk as an odd sort. Then again, I'd be le if I had to clock in to this place every day. And I do appreciate her nd of humor.

"Yeah, heard you had Nurse Ratched her st with the grief therapy," I say, nodding in Silvestri's direction.

"He was a real prince," she answers. I can't tell if she's being sincere.

"Enough with the sentiment," Silvestri quips. "What's doing, Fisk?"

"I got a weird one for you two," she answers.

"Thank fuck," says Silvestri. "I was getting restless."

"So," she continues. "The tox screen on your Jane Doe came back. She seems to have been poisoned."

"That right?" I ask.

Fisk continues. "You two ever heard of *Atropa belladonna*?"

"Sounds sexy," answers Silvestri.

"If you're into that sort of thing," she says. "*Atropa belladonna*, more commonly known as deadly nightshade, is a highly toxic plant, albeit one used for a variety of medicinal purposes."

"You'd think with the word 'deadly' right there in the name . . . ," begins Silvestri.

"That's where it gets interesting," says Fisk. "There are a handful of toxic plants that are used for medicinal purposes. Belladonna is very effective for treating anything from asthma to sciatica to Parkinson's."

"We found an inhaler on the body," I say. "You think they were using the stuff to treat her asthma?"

"Quite possibly. I can go ahead and test the inhaler. The key with these remedies is potency. If you dilute it enough, it's rendered safe. But it can be a tricky practice. There was a pharmaceutical company a couple years ago that recalled a line of children's earache medicine that contained belladonna."

"But you said it's safe . . . ," I begin.

"At the proper level of dilution. The dose makes the poison, as they say. Belladonna shows up mostly in homeopathic remedies. A lot of those pass under the FDA's radar, so these gray areas pop up."

My partner's eyes meet mine. "Homeopathic?" he asks.

"Yeah, it's not as regulated a market," she explains.

"So, you can just get your hands on this stuff without it being evaluated?" I ask.

"I mean, any responsible company will adhere to accepted standards of potency. But you could always get some yahoo who whips up his own batch without knowing any better."

"And are these plants widely available?" asks Silvestri.

"Sure," says Fisk. "Anyone can buy a bag of seeds and plant them in the garden. Little tricky to grow in this climate, but it can be done."

"So," I ask. "What's your guess with our Jane Doe?"

"Hard to say. This is so rare that it took me a few different rounds to figure out what was going on here. Obviously the asthma component could explain it, where she OD'd on something that was prescribed to her. Or could be that someone dosed her. In any case, she was swimming in the stuff."

We're standing in the hallway outside Fisk's office. Silvestri is looking off into the distance, perturbed. "Well," is all he can manage.

"I'm suddenly curious about your holistic healer," I say.

"You and me both," he answers, shaking his head.

SEVEN

CHARLOTTE

BY THE TIME my alarm goes off at eight A.M., I've been staring at the ceiling for an hour. I've repeatedly tried meditating, but seeing Jane Doe's face every time I shut my eyes has put a major damper on my hopeful calm.

I can't stop obsessing over the possibilities of who she could be, and who I was to her. After a restless night of trying to conjure a forgotten patient, classmate, or even passing acquaintance, my nerves are shot and my head is a kaleidoscope of people I haven't thought of for years. So far, I've come up with nothing. The only consolation is that her identity search has replaced my constant thoughts about Peter's whereabouts and my unsuccessful attempts to reach Rachel or Henry, so at least there is some variety from the last handful of sleepless nights and restless mornings spent ruminating.

I've never had a good short-term memory recall, especially for faces and names. It was a quality that Henry used to chide me about. "You really need to get better at that if you are going to be a surgeon."

I don't like thinking about Henry, but the message has made it un-avoidable. After my hospitalization, I promised myself that I'd never contact him again. Our relationship feels like it happened to someone else.

Things looked so different then; all my long-held dreams were coming true, or at least I thought they were my dreams at the time. I felt unstoppable. I was pioneering major things in my field, being given the runway to create and explore in directions few people in my position had been allowed to, all with the support of one of my heroes.

Dr. Henry Thornton was a rock star. I'd been following his career like a medical groupie since my undergrad days, when I saw him speak about the work he'd done with PTSD in the survivors and families of terrorist attacks. He was the resident surgeon of the best psychosurgical medical program in the country, which I'd been gunning to work in from the first day I saw him present to a room filled with hopeful pre-med students.

And I'd been one of the lucky few who landed my internship in his sphere. Not just lucky—I worked my ass off to be there.

He'd barely looked at me during my year one as an intern, but I later found out that he was well aware of me and amused himself by watching me grind through the grueling eighty-hour work weeks in the trenches, desperate to get into the OR.

In my second year, I was assigned to his team. I was shocked; I didn't think he knew my name, let alone would want me to work with him. I'd written a few bold papers in medical school on trauma-reversing neurosurgery that had crossed his desk, and I had a reputation for keeping my cool in very intense situations, so he'd sought me out before I'd even begun to try to endear myself to him.

I later found out that he requested me, and I didn't know whether to be grateful or disturbed, since he'd treated me so badly that year. He justified it as fair treatment. "I treat everyone badly, you know that. You aren't special." Henry had an impeccable talent for making me feel simultaneously like the most and least important person in the room. He never hid who he was, and I should have believed him when he told me. But I was starstruck and he knew it.

My professional success had the opposite effect for me socially. My fellow residents in years two and three were hateful because I'd leapfrogged right over them. People thought I'd slept my way into his operating room, something I found out when someone accidentally put me on a group text discussing my undeserving ascension as "screwing my way to the top, one gurney at a time," but the truth was that we never crossed the line until well into my junior residency in year three. It wasn't like a medical TV show where everyone was nailing one another in break rooms with abandon. It was discreet when it actually happened, after the rumor was old news. Part of me rationalized that if it was already assumed we were sleeping together, we might as well be. Henry didn't care either way what people said about him. I think he was more worried people wouldn't say anything. He reveled in being the front-page news in all situations, negative or otherwise.

Regardless of the truth about how I'd ascended so quickly, the collective belief, being what it was, left me extremely lonely, in my professional triumphs and in general. I leaned hard into becoming a certain way: detached, unbothered, and all business. I started to shut off the feeling parts of myself and only lived in the thinking spaces. A profound disconnection from my real self took hold.

Henry appreciated my confidence and drive, and my natural ability to compartmentalize. When more than one intern would leave an operating room to lose their lunch or put their head between their legs, I was always up front, eager to suction while the cranial saw cut through skull or hold the bone flap while the attending was uncapping the awaiting gray matter.

My boldness further alienated my peers, who thought I was arrogant in my ambition to do new things in the field. I didn't think I was. I believed I was confident and fearless. Now I realize how much of a character I'd created around my identity as a surgical intern and resident. It was like I'd stitched together all the collective qualities I'd observed in the most successful teachers I had along the way, mixed with TV and movie surgeons I'd idealized in my youth, and stepped into the persona as soon as my scrubs went on. I did it so effectively that I completely lost track of who I really was along the way.

Sometimes obsessing about my former life is a good thing in small doses. I can reflect on how unhappy I really was and appreciate how different my life looks now. How much happier and healthier I've become. But if I spend too much time looking back, the old stress level seeps in. I start to slide into the old feelings of being the victim. I refuse to be that woman ever again.

The morning light streaming into my window is persistent. "You are strong. You are resilient. You are present," I say to myself as I roll over onto my side. I bring my thoughts back to the present, where there is plenty to mull over. I need to stop being so self-centered in trying to figure out who I am and focus on who Jane Doe might be. And I need to keep as positive as possible. When I surrender to negative thinking, things get bad.

I can hear my phone vibrating on the bureau a few feet away The sound of the phone motivates me up and out of bed. Even the possibility of Henry being the caller helps, though the conversation we need to have makes me want to disappear. I spy the caller ID and see the call I've missed is from Rachel, and I'm happy to see she's resurfaced. Her missed call is followed up with a text: *I'm on my way.* I shoot her back a thumbs-up emoji.

I'm eager for a recap of her experience with Lucy once I abandoned her on the table. The fact that this occurred after I told her nothing bad was going to happen makes the whole situation particularly cringe-worthy.

It's generally our routine for Rachel and me to spend a few mornings together when Peter is out of town. She's an earlier riser than I am and usually calls me twice before I've even looked at my phone. She'll have already meditated for an hour, hit two consecutive morning yoga classes, and run errands by the time I'm rolling out of bed. Rachel is admittedly a woman of extremes, first realized with her voracious and nearly deadly heroin habit. She miraculously kicked it ten years ago but effectively substituted one lifestyle of unhealthy obsession with another of extreme health and wellness. The alternative being much better for her survival rate.

I've no sooner gotten our smoothies blended than I hear her familiar knock and then her key in the door. She enters with full hands: two chai lattes and something I surmise is from the vegan bakery down the street from her house. I am still not a vegan in spite of Rachel's proselytizing, but I humor her. I cannot and never will give up cheese.

"Morning!" she sings. She looks like she's stepped off the cover of *Yoga Journal* in her flowing gauze dress, adorned with multiple strands of mala prayer beads hanging from her neck and wrists. She is a dead ringer for a young Stevie Nicks. We've been mistaken for sisters more than once, which I always take as a compliment.

"Good morning." I lean into her for a hug and her incredible head of soft reddish blond curls engulfs my face. The smells of coconut and lavender are comfortingly familiar. She sits on the stool across from me and pushes the latte, which I accept gratefully, into my hand.

"I'm so sorry I was MIA last night. After I rescued your patient, I went to a yoga class and then fell asleep super early. I didn't see your missed call and texts until this morning," she explains. It seems odd that she would have gone to sleep without checking back in after getting my text about my having to identify a body yesterday, but I choose not to push it since she did me such a big favor.

"Thank you so much for going to the office to retrieve Lucy. You saved me."

"Of course! I was happy to help." She looks at me for a moment. "You look tired, Beautiful, but tired." If it was anyone else, I would take offense, but I know it is genuine love and concern, which I appreciate. She can, and often does, say whatever is on her mind without any filter. She is the most honest person I've ever met, and I strive for her integrity and truthfulness. I've been coming up short on that recently.

"I didn't sleep well at all. Yesterday was . . . stressful." I drink the warm, nutty liquid.

"Oh my God. We have so much to discuss!" She's as exuberant as I am mortified.

I pause, reconsidering if I should question her unavailability last night, but conclude that it isn't important.

"I've never left anyone on the table before." I put my hand over my face, cringing at the thought. "And she was a *new* patient."

Her enthusiasm ratchets down and I can tell she is calibrating the degree of her own energy based on my evident distress. She speaks gently. "Don't torture yourself. Seriously, let it go, right now. You had an emergency. It happens, honey."

This is one of the many reasons she is my best friend. She generously reminds me to be nicer to myself, often.

"You are a lifesaver," I gush.

"Of course." She replies. "You would have done the same for me."

"How mad was Lucy when you got there?"

"She'd fallen asleep, so that was good. She didn't know how much time had passed."

"How much time *had* passed?" Again, I have an impulse to ask her about where she was when she wasn't picking up my calls. The question is more rooted in my general unease with the fact that she's been sending me to voicemail lately.

"Only about an hour. I was able to get there pretty quickly." She takes a breath. "I was nearby." She doesn't elaborate.

My chagrin rises again. "I can't believe I forgot about her. I was in such a panic, everything just went blank and I flew to the medical examiner's office. By the time I got there, I couldn't even remember the drive over."

"Lucy was a sweetheart. Said she hoped everything was okay and that she'll make a follow-up appointment." This is a huge relief.

"I was expecting a scathing Yelp review from her, not a follow-up appointment." Rachel nods sympathetically. She's incredibly gracious about my awful online reputation, given her shared space with me. I know she's borne some of the brunt with a few of her clients—guilt by association—and I feel endlessly responsible about it.

"You haven't gone on Yelp, though, right?" My silence tells her every-thing. "Oh, sweetie. No wonder you are feeling so down. Try not to dial that stuff in. The online trolls are scared and judgmental. We should have empathy for them, but don't let them do this to you."

"It's really hard not to look. And I keep thinking that I can handle it."

"I know. I know." She turns her attention to the window. "It's so hard not to care."

"I tried calling Lucy last night to apologize, but I haven't heard back." I take another sip; the chai is sweet and spicy going down my throat.

"Don't fret, you'll hear from her. I told her I would give her a free massage, so she's definitely coming back."

"You are the best. I'll pay you back for the massage. Can I do your needles this week?"

"Don't think twice about it," she responds, waving me off. I'm not sure if she is referring to the offer to pay her back or the needles. She hasn't let me work on her for a few weeks, which is out of character.

"So, the Lucy crisis has been averted. It sounds like you've got plenty else to worry about. Do you want to talk about it? Or not yet?" This is our trusted routine with our catch-up sessions. We need to warm up before digging in. I appreciate that she is taking my temperature.

"Um. I don't know. I think so?" I take a long inhale. "It was all so sur-real." She comes around the island to give me a hug. I let some tears free on her shoulder but don't give in too much further.

"Let's get some fresh air," she offers.

We put on our coats and she threads her arm through mine and leads me to the back deck, where we get situated on the comfy chairs. The air is brisk but refreshing, with bright sun in the cloudless fall sky beating down. I turn my face upward and bask for a moment. Once we are com-fortable in our usual seats, legs in lotus position, facing each other, we both drink from our cups.

"Okay. I'm ready." I pull my knees up and close to my chest.

"Start at the beginning. I want to know everything," she says eagerly.

I begin with the phone call from the medical examiner's office, sparing no details. She sits patiently, uninterrupting, her face open and quietly reacting to each part of the story. When I finish she closes her eyes and exhales.

"You must have been terrified."

"I was."

"I'm sorry I wasn't with you and you had to go through that alone." Her eyes are wide. "Imagine seeing him like that? It would be so traumatic."

"I've imagined it about four hundred times since yesterday, and it's horrific every time."

"Charlotte. I had a premonition this month that major change was coming. I thought that feeling was about *my* life, but maybe it was about yours." She unfolds her legs and stands to pace in the space between us. This is her usual choreography; it's challenging for her to stay still for too long. "Now the question is, who is this woman and what does she represent in your life?"

"Or why did she have my information on her? It doesn't make any sense."

"It's definitely a mystery. Maybe she's trying to tell you something." She holds her hands up and out like she might take flight.

"I just don't understand why I have absolutely no recollection of her. That isn't like me. Even at my worst, I had enough awareness to remember someone I was close to."

"Is she from your Manhattan days?" Rachel is careful.

"Maybe. I just don't know." I feel defeated.

"Mistaken identity? A different Charlotte Knopfler?"

"She had *my* phone number." Rachel's asking all the same questions I did.

"Maybe this is a good thing. The most uncomfortable scenarios are the most transformative." She looks at me knowingly.

"I can't imagine any scenario where a dead woman is a good thing."

"I didn't mean that." She pauses. "But, whatever the reason, I'm sure all will be revealed, soon enough. What do you know about her?"

"Hardly anything at all. Nothing, actually. Just that she had my contact info on her, and not much else. It's eerie."

"Weird. She didn't have any identification? Was she robbed? Did they say the cause of death?" Her energy is a little too upbeat for the subject matter. She loves a good mystery.

"Whatever I know, I've told you. I have no idea about the other details, Sherlock," I tease.

"How are you otherwise?" She pushes her bracelets up and down her arm and they make a click-clack sound, a regular and endearing nervous habit of hers that I've grown so used to. Funny how certain little mannerisms of the people we love stick out. With Henry it was the way he would bounce on his heels when he was cooking up a brilliant idea. With Peter it's his way of humming into the phone when he is thinking.

I am desperate to spill how I really am but worried that if I do, she will say all the things out loud that I've been thinking. I'm not ready to face the truth, even if I don't yet know what it is.

She knows what I'm thinking without my opening my mouth. "So, have you heard anything from him?" It bothers me that she won't refer to him by name. I should tell her, but it seems like a small, stupid complaint in the grand scheme.

"Nothing yet. But I'm sure I'll hear from Peter soon." I need to temper my worry in front of Rachel. Even the minimal information I've told her about him has drawn too many questions that I can't answer.

As far as Peter knows, no one in my life knows he exists. When we started to get serious, Rachel was the only friend I told about him. Peter asked me to keep our blossoming relationship under wraps, but of course I had to confide in my best friend about a potential new boyfriend. In the rock-paper-scissors of new love interests versus best friends, friendship is always paper, and new boyfriends are rocks. I was a little put off he'd suggested otherwise, but I told him the white lie that

I was superstitious anyway and wouldn't talk about new connections until I felt confident things were going in the right direction.

Meanwhile, I was keeping Rachel apprised of the unfolding situation and decoding the subtexts of his texts with her. It was a little juvenile, sure, but I was so focused on my studies growing up, I hadn't had many relationships, serious or otherwise. I'm a late bloomer in that particular area. Rachel is much better at the psychology of people in romantic relationships and far more insightful about little things I wouldn't have picked up on or batted an eye about. We both agreed that Peter was fascinating, handsome (I shared a couple of photos of him with her), and very funny. He was also extremely elusive at times. But I had a feeling about him that I couldn't shake. A feeling that he was going to change my life completely.

In our first two months together, it wasn't until he dodged enough of my invitations that I realized the extent of his job and the privacy it required. It explained his caginess when talking about our relationship with other people and his mysteriousness. "It won't always be like this, honey," he'd promised. "The job I'm working right now requires me to be deep undercover. I'm risking a lot just by talking to you." I was so far gone by then, I really did keep our relationship under wraps beyond Rachel. And the more my relationship resembled a spy novel, the more details I'd leave out of my updates for her. Lying to my best friend by omission should have been my first red flag. Well, maybe not the first, but a brightly colored one that I chose to bypass.

I had a lot of questions for Peter but was patient with how much he could tell me about what it was he did. I knew the basics: that he was working for a sector of the government that required him to travel constantly. I guessed it was the FBI, but he made a comment once about the FBI being the "Coast Guard" of government agencies. He'd been a Navy SEAL and then had been tapped for an intelligence job. He was a self-described savant, self-taught in computer science and criminal psychology, and was recruited by the government out of high school but deferred to go into the military first. He "wanted to have some real-life experience." His bravery was undeniable, and endlessly attractive to me.

I knew he had to be on call pretty much twenty-four hours a day, and his living six hours away, near Quantico, didn't help matters. I offered to make the drive a few times, but he was embarrassed by his government-subsidized "pitiful bachelor's pad," and, more worrying, he thought it was a bad idea for his "enemies" to know I existed. We agreed it was safer for him to come to me when he could, but I was deeply disappointed.

Naturally, the more I fell for Peter, the more I wanted to know about him. But my curiosity seemed to be pushing him away, and I always feared coming off as needy. So I reserved my musings about who he was for Rachel, who was just as fascinated and excited about him as I was. She was so happy to see how happy I was, considering the depressed, adrift woman I was when she and I met, who swore she'd never be in a relationship again. It had taken a lot of healing, but I was ready.

After a few minor Peter disappointments—broken plans, unpredictable moodiness, and short disappearances—Rachel's fascination morphed into suspicion, which stoked my own. I continued monitoring how much I told her. I wanted to keep my feelings about him separate from hers. The more serious Peter and I got in between his assignments, the less I shared with Rachel. I was so enamored with him that I kind of glossed over the fact that I was placing an ever-growing wedge between Rachel and me by holding back. If pressed, I'd feed her curated information and details that weren't always completely truthful, or lean toward painting him in a positive light. Or I optimistically painted him as the man I knew he could be if he wasn't so stressed and overworked. But Rachel's no slouch, and she knew something was amiss. You can't mind meld with someone regularly like she and I do and not have them pick up on a shift in energy like the one that was happening with me.

Now that things felt so unsure with him, I wish I had been up-front all along. If I tell her everything now, I know she'll assume the worst and tell me as much.

"Are you going to have a real talk with him when he's back on the grid?" Rachel's tone is tentative. She's sensed my defensiveness about this particular topic the past few times she and I have mulled it over and has been careful about bringing it up.

"I need to find the right time to do it. But, yes."

"What will you say?" She's twisting and untwisting a length of curl between her fingers, examining the hairs for any split ends. There are none.

"I'm going to tell him that I need him to show up in this relationship. That the long-distance thing isn't working anymore."

"Good." She nods approvingly while I break for a sip of chai.

I hesitate. "I'll tell him that I want all of the normal relationship milestones."

"Great. Love it. What else?"

I feel my throat constricting slightly. "Um. That I want him to meet my friends, and I need to meet some of his, before we go any further." I know my growing defensiveness stems from my frustration with myself. For letting my relationship with him get as serious as it has without knowing very much about him, for allowing things to get as far as they have with the obvious red flags apparent.

"Are you going to ask him for some proof about his job?" She's edging into territory that I don't like. I'm started to feel strangled by all of the repressed feelings snaking up my esophagus.

I put my hand lightly on her upper arm, to reinforce my love for her, and mete out each word carefully. "I told you this. He texted me pictures of his work ID, and plane tickets and his passport, last month." And he had, after some uncomfortable exchanges between him and me and a few days of not hearing from him. But I was glad I'd pushed. Seeing these objects reassured me that he wasn't a figment of my imagination or a con artist. He'd gotten in the habit of sending me links to national news stories to give me vague hints of what was taking him away from me.

"Right. Right. You never showed them to me. I forgot he had." We both know that she hasn't forgotten anything, and I know she's angling to see the proof herself, but I'd decided I needed to keep some parts of him to myself. Now I'm getting frustrated, and kind of pissed. I wouldn't show her the images, even if I had saved them, on principle.

"Can we change the subject? I've got too much noise in my head from yesterday." I rub my temples with some of the essential oil remnants on my wrist.

"Of course." She squeezes my hand supportively and releases it to pull a carrot and pumpkin seed muffin from the wax paper bag. She tears it in two and hands me one of the halves. I accept.

She chews her muffin slowly, and I can tell that she isn't going to change the subject. "You know, I wonder if Peter came into your life to help you finally get over everything with Henry and what happened?"

"How do you mean?"

"Sometimes we meet people who hold a mirror up to us, right? They force us to see the things we don't want to about ourselves. Make us confront who we really are. And if you are frustrated with Peter—"

"I didn't say I was frustrated," I say, annoyed.

She effortlessly detaches from my tension and stays sunny. "What's Peter's sign again?"

"Gemini," I say through an aggressive bite of muffin.

"Hmm. Right. It's a tricky sign, especially with Sagittarius." She considers.

I've never fully embraced Rachel's tendency toward the esoteric. This skepticism has kept me feeling like something of an outsider in our world of alternative healers. It isn't that I'm close-minded or completely nonbelieving—switching from Western to Eastern medicine prompted a major adjustment in my attitude about the mystical, unseen side of life. But it's a lot to embrace, and my roots in science and analytic thinking often hold me back from viewing the world at the same cosmic level as Rachel. And this is one of the many reasons she has been so important in my healing. After everything happened, I wanted to believe in something bigger than myself. I wanted to see the mystical power of things outside conventional wisdom and thinking, to internalize the self-compassion and forgiveness so badly. But that is no easy feat coming out of twelve years of hardwired "God complex" training. Ironically, I think my relationship with Peter has helped me open my mind much more to the power of the unseen. Being with him has required a major leap of faith into the unknown, for sure.

"Rach, I want you to be happy for me. I'm really in love."

"I'm happy you are in love. I get it. Just because I haven't had a serious boyfriend since the Clinton administration doesn't mean I've forgotten the thrill of it. If you are happy, then I am. I just wish he'd walk through the door already. I know his absence has been tough on you."

Strangely, the image of Peter walking through the door plays out vividly in my mind as Jack walking through the office door yesterday. There's that excited tickle of a feeling again that I want to squash. I feel guilty and ashamed to be thinking about this other man.

"Oh, that reminds me, did a guy come into the office yesterday afternoon to make an appointment?" I see her look down at her pocket, where her phone is. She takes it out of her jacket and looks at it quickly before replacing it. "Rach?" I push gently.

"Nope." She's elsewhere. "No one came into the office when I was there. I walked out with Lucy and locked up, assuming you wouldn't be coming back. Were you expecting someone?"

"No. Well, I thought maybe Peter was going to surprise me yesterday. Anyway, this guy came in when I was in the middle of Lucy's session and he was kind of pushy and wanted to schedule an appointment. I asked him to schedule online, but he was insistent that he was going to come back in person."

"Huh. That's the first walk-in we've had in a while. Maybe your luck is changing." Appropriately, the wind has picked up and Rachel's curls are dancing around her face. She looks like a Greek goddess.

"Yeah. I mean I should be happy about any potential patients, but something about this one got under my skin." I'm not sure how much I want to reveal to her, but I find myself wanting to talk about him.

"Under your skin in a good or bad way?"

"A little bit of both, I guess." I'm honest.

"What in particular?" she cues.

"He was really confident, annoyingly so. But also really magnetic. And he was doing this thing—he kept stroking his chin like he had a beard—that I found kind of creepy until he said he'd just shaved his beard."

She stops nodding and looks alarmed momentarily.

"And he has these ridiculously bright green eyes. Piercing."

Rachel's expression changes, but I can't decipher into what.

"What?" I ask.

"Oh, nothing. My mind is wandering. Sorry. I'm a bit scattered today."

"Everything okay?" I ask, concerned and hopeful that she is going to fill me in on whatever she's been hiding from me.

"Oh, totally. I haven't been sleeping well. That's all." She shivers. "I'm getting chilly. How about you?"

I nod slowly, unsatisfied with her evasiveness. "Let's head back inside," I say, and she follows me back into the house.

"I've got to pee. Be back in a flash," she says.

I feel frustrated but attempt to shake it off and make my way to my laptop and open it to see what my schedule is shaping up like for the next few days, fully expecting that it will be more of the same. One client a day, if I'm lucky. I open the tab with an ad for my treatment-room space for rent and work on the wording. I need to try to get in a practitioner who actually has clients and make up the money I haven't been able to get together to pay rent.

Then I see that there is a new appointment notification. Tomorrow at nine thirty A.M., for Dr. Jack Doyle. He's a doctor. Of course he is.

EIGHT

SILVESTRI

"You a regular around these parts?" We're back in the park where our Jane Doe was found, and my partner's calling out to a young woman dressed in a pair of shorts and a Windbreaker as he flashes his badge.

"Sure am. I run the tennis program here," she answers as she approaches.

"You must be wrapping up the season pretty soon," I say, rubbing my hands together.

"Yes," she says. "We're at the tail end." She looks to Wolcott, then back to me. "Is everything okay, Detectives?"

I pull the phone out of my pocket and turn it toward her. "Does this woman look familiar?"

She considers it for a moment before her eyes widen. "Oh goodness," she laments.

"You recognize her?" I ask.

"I'm pretty sure, yes. I think she volunteered at the community garden down the way there." She points in the direction of the garden, shaking her head. "I would see her here on her lunch break now and again. What happened?"

Wolcott shakes his head. "That's the question."

❖❖❖

"Okay, folks. We're on root-vegetable duty today. Give a holler if you need anything."

As we near the garden, the director is setting her team up for the afternoon. She stands in front of a greenhouse abutting a planting bed. She sees us approaching and eyes our outfits.

"You're a little overdressed for digging around in the dirt, fellas." She gives Wolcott the old up and down. "Especially you, Dapper Don."

Wolcott responds by flashing his shield. "Afraid we're here on a different sort of chore."

She studies it, then smirks. "This place isn't exactly a hotbed of criminal activity." Then, looking around: "Forgive the pun."

"Not half bad," I say, before pulling up the shot of our Jane Doe. "I need to ask if this woman looks familiar."

She studies the image for a moment before her face drops. "Oh no." She sighs. Her chin falls to her chest as she lets out a deep exhale. "I had a bad feeling."

"Would you like to sit down?" asks Wolcott, indicating a wooden stool next to the greenhouse.

"I think I ought to," she says, as we help her to her seat.

"We understand that this woman—"

"Brooke," she interrupts, dazed. "Brooke Harmon is her name."

"I see," continues Wolcott as he slips out a notebook and jots down the information. "We understand that Miss Harmon was a volunteer here?"

"She certainly was. Big part of this organization. I mean, not just the garden, but the whole community of volunteers. She'd only been with us for about six months, but it felt like she was here from the start. She'd really turned a corner."

"How's that?"

"Well, Brooke originally came to us as part of her community service requirement, but quickly fell in love with gardening. It became a therapeutic practice for her. She'd recently finished her required hours but had decided to stay on with us."

"Community service?" I say. "Can you tell us what Miss Harmon was in for?"

"Aggravated harassment. I will say, when Brooke was first assigned here, she was quite angry. But I watched her really grow, in an emotional sense, over the course of her time here." Her shock appears to be morphing into anger. She looks me in the eye intently. "Detective, what happened?"

"We're working on piecing that together now, ma'am. Can you tell me the last time you saw Miss Harmon?"

"Day before yesterday," she answers. "Brooke left a little early, said she wasn't feeling so hot. Seemed agitated."

My partner looks at me, then to the garden director. "And what time would that have been?"

She thinks for a moment. "She normally gets off at five. I guess it would have been around four or so. I remember looking at my watch and thinking it was unusual. She never left early."

Wolcott writes in his notebook before addressing her again. "Had she been feeling unwell lately, or just that day?"

"She had some respiratory issues but was in good health otherwise, as far as I knew. Great energy, very active."

"I see," says Wolcott. "And do you know what Miss Harmon did for work, outside of here?"

"She had some sort of administrative assistant position," she says vaguely.

"And she lived here in town?"

"Just over in Port Jeff."

"Uh-huh," I say. "Now, when I showed you her photo a moment ago, you mentioned having had a bad feeling. Can you elaborate?"

She looks off into the distance, then back to us. "The last couple of days she seemed rattled and on edge, which I noticed because it was so unlike her. It reminded me of the Brooke who first came to us."

"Any idea if she was having trouble in her personal life?" my partner asks.

"I'm afraid I don't really keep tabs on that sort of thing with the volunteers." She shakes her head before her eyebrows perk up. "Although she and Julie were pretty close. I think they may have started socializing outside of their hours here. Excuse me for a moment. I'll grab you her contact info."

As she dips into the greenhouse, Wolcott leans toward me casually, speaking just above a whisper. "With the timeline she's giving us, sounds like our friend here could have been one of the last people to see our victim alive."

The garden director returns with a slip of paper. "I wrote down the address and phone number on file for Julie Merrill," she says, handing the paper to my partner. "She may be able to answer some of your questions better than I can. And I put my info down as well. Please don't hesitate to reach out if you have any more questions. I'm happy to help. Brooke was a real doll."

"Much appreciated." He nods. "And thank you for your time."

"Think nothing of it."

As she turns back toward the greenhouse, I stop her with a thought. "Just out of curiosity," I ask, "do you grow deadly nightshade here in the garden?"

She looks at me as if I've just stepped on a rake and smacked myself in the face with the handle. "No, we avoid that stuff. It can kill you, you know."

NINE

Woundedhealer: Hi, ladies.

MaxineKD: How are you?

Woundedhealer: Things are still feeling out of sorts. I'm trying not to spiral.

Makeupyourmindcontrol: Something is in the air. I keep thinking about that Disney movie from the eighties, "Something Wicked This Way Comes." They used to put it on at school assemblies when Flag Day was rained out.

Miserylovescompany: Well, that is completely weird and random.

Makeupyourmindcontrol: I never claimed to be anything other than.

Biggirlsdontcry54: Things are always weird by me. But, I'm a weirdo. And I was homeschooled, so I have no idea what "Flag Day" is.

MaxineKD: I preferred the book. Bradbury is everything.

Woundedhealer: I'll have to add it to my list. So, is Harmnoone82 ok? I haven't seen her on here in a few days.

Makeupyourmindcontrol: She was having a rough one the other night. But the proverbial wagons were circled and all is okay.

Woundedhealer: ????

Makeupyourmindcontrol: Well, I was half in the bag, so no help, but MaxineKD and Biggirlsdontcry54 came to her rescue.

MaxineKD: It was no big deal. We had an impromptu "ladies' night out."

Woundedhealer: Really? Wow. Sorry I missed it. Although, meeting up in person sounds kind of strange.

Miserylovescompany: Strange, huh? Thanks a lot!

Woundedhealer: No offense! It's just that we've all been confiding in each other for a while now without ever meeting, and you all know more about me than anyone else. The veil of the computer being lifted feels . . . intimidating . . . exposing?

Makeupyourmindcontrol: I know what you mean, Woundedhealer. And I don't want any of you to find out that I'm actually a creepy middle-aged man pretending to be a single mom with a taste for boxed merlot and Lifetime movies.

MaxineKD: Don't even joke about that!

Miserylovescompany: It's funny, once we were in person, it felt like we'd been meeting that way all along. It was all very familiar.

MaxineKD: And we recognized each other right away. We are undeniably bonded.

Miserylovescompany: Yeah. Trauma bonded.

Makeupyourmindcontrol: Is that a bad thing?

Miserylovescompany: Depends who you ask.

Woundedhealer: How was Harmnoone82? I felt like she was feeling pretty strong the last few chats?

MaxineKD: She was shaken up but we calmed her down. She just needed to talk.

Miserylovescompany: Everything is fine now.

MaxineKD: It was just a misunderstanding.

Woundedhealer: I should reach out. I've been so preoccupied.

Miserylovescompany: She said she might be taking a break from being online for a while. Get off social media.

Makeupyourmindcontrol: I'm too much of an addict to ever do that. Good for her!

Woundedhealer: I feel bad I've been so self-involved. She's always supportive of my stuff. I should have been there.

Miserylovescompany: No reason to feel bad. We all have life getting in the way of our best intentions. She understands.

Woundedhealer: Still. I'll message her just to let her know I'm thinking about her.

Biggirlsdontcry54: I'm sure she'd appreciate that. You are always so thoughtful, Woundedhealer.

MaxineKD: And we should do it again!

Biggirlsdontcry54: All of us together in the same room? I might actually leave my house for that.

Trauma Survivors Private Chat Room: 10/3/19
12:00 p.m.
Private Message from Woundedhealer to Harmnoone82 (offline)

Woundedhealer: I wanted to check in and see if you were doing okay? I thought I would reach out since you haven't been online for a while. I heard that you had a rough night and when I went back to check the chat history, I couldn't find anything. I've been thinking about you a lot and would love to chat one-on-one. Something happened this week and I can't bring myself to talk about it with the group yet. I was hoping I could talk it through with you first. Anyway, I hope you are okay. I'm here if you want to talk. Always.

TEN

CHARLOTTE

"EVERYTHING HE TOLD ME was a lie." She gratefully accepts the Kleenex from the box in my outstretched hand. She asked for an emergency session for nine A.M., and while I'm happy to have the appointment, it's hard as ever to see her discomfort.

At twenty-two, Cameron is my youngest patient, and her sessions typically start in tears. She is a highly sensitive person carrying a lot of trauma. The hardwired stress wreaked havoc on her nervous system, and after many fruitless attempts at Western medical intervention for her myriad immune disorders, she found her way to me, thank goodness. I feel more protective of her than most patients, because I see a lot of myself in her. After a year of our working together, her body is stronger than ever. Her self-esteem, on the other hand, could use some strengthening.

"You can't ever *really* know someone, can you? I thought I did with Kyle, but wow, I was *so* wrong." Her body and voice are shaking.

I put my hand on hers to keep her from upsetting the needles I've just placed along her wrist, and she continues spewing, unfazed. I feel bad, but my attention is not on her as completely as it should be. Rather, it's on the bouquet of flowers that was waiting for me on the stoop of my office this morning. My pulse hasn't taken a break from sprinting since I came in an hour ago.

"*God.* I am such an idiot. I thought I knew him." Her pulse is slippery, and I know she needs to unleash the energy spilling out of her before I can effectively calm her. I take a step back, with my next needle waiting.

"He told me that he was ready to be in a committed relationship. I thought it was safe to assume someone who says that is actually single at the time."

Cameron's neck-deep in dating quicksand, an unfamiliar place for me.

"You are *not* an idiot." I catch a break in her animation and work in a needle on the first spleen point, the organ of obsessive thinking and processing emotions. I mentally suggest giving myself a spleen tune-up after my appointments today. I am having a little trouble focusing as well, and the excitement/nervousness that I'm feeling about Dr. Jack Doyle's imminent arrival is distracting.

Cameron continues. "I don't even understand why he would lie about that. What is the point of emphasizing that you want to be with one person if that isn't what you actually want?"

I don't tell her what I'm thinking: that Peter would classify that particular tactic as sociopathic misdirection.

"Maybe he aspires to be the kind of person who wants to be in a monogamous relationship but can't quite get there yet. Sometimes people tell lies because they believe they are true, or want them to be." I place a needle in an especially calming point in her ear called "the heavenly gate."

"Charlotte, I love you, but you have to know how utterly naive that sounds." She's precocious as hell, and I laugh hard. "It's pretty scary if you think about it. Anyone can say *anything* they want about themselves and you just have to decide to believe them. But it's all bullshit." Tears are running down the sides of her face and into her ears. I'm reminded of an early conversation with Peter about the unbelievable ways people misrepresent themselves online. It's such a big part of his job to suss out the truth, I wish he was here to talk to Cameron and reassure her about how common what she's going through is. It wouldn't take away the heartbreak, but maybe she'd beat herself up less.

The needles are taking effect and she is becoming calmer with each spoken thought. I can see her breath deepening.

"I can't believe how wrong I was about him. I thought he loved me. Three whole months of my life just wasted." My heart breaks for her.

"It feels like you can't trust anyone right now, but I promise you that there are good, honest people in the world. This is a rough patch."

"My whole life feels like a rough patch. How do I keep making the same stupid choice about guys? Ugh! I'm so mad at myself."

"Trust yourself, don't blame. Your instincts are right; it may just take some time to fine-tune how to interpret them. Look, you knew something was off with him and you found out early; take solace in that. Your intuition is on point. Your gut is a powerful compass."

"Oh, I don't need my gut. I have his secret Instagram feed. Evidently, he is someone who likes to take a lot of pictures with skanky girls perpetually dressed for Coachella named EvieDD and Beckysweetlips. I can't compete with that!"

"You shouldn't feel like you need to compete with anyone, or compare yourself. It isn't real, even if it seems like it is. Remember that filters and staging make things look like people want them to, not how they actually are."

She nods and scrunches her face up. "My brain hears you, but my heart is stuck. I still love him. What do I do?" I hate to see her suffering.

"Stop making the story about him. Look at this pain as information. You were attracted to this person to see something about yourself. Instead of focusing on what he's done and is doing, how about looking at all of the ways this is going to make you smarter, stronger, and more centered in your life and in your next relationship." I hear the words coming out and realize that I'm channeling Rachel.

"That all sounds Oprah AF, Charlotte, but I'm trying to be a pragmatist. What would you do if you were me?" I'm honored that she asks my opinion. It makes me feel sisterly.

"Maybe don't look at his pictures? Can you be kind to yourself and focus on something else? Maybe get offline for a while? Or block him."

She side-eyes me as though I've proposed sticking needles directly into her pupils. I rub my hands together to create healing energy and place them on her stomach. "Okay. Deep breaths. I want you to repeat 'I forgive myself, I release him' twenty-eight times. Let go as much as you can. I'll be back in thirty-five minutes."

❖❖❖

After I shut the door, I wash my hands in the bathroom, which carries the faint odor of next door's burned cooking oil and soy sauce no matter how much essential oil we put in the diffuser.

The warm soapy water feels good on my skin and I leave my hands under the tap for an extra minute as I look at my reflection. My face is puffy from bad sleep and my eyes are dull. I turn the water temp in the other direction and splash cold water on my face to perk myself up. I dab some lip gloss on my lips and rub them together, then think better of it, wiping the gloss off with a Kleenex and flushing it.

I check my phone and see that the doctor is due in a matter of minutes and head back to my desk to unsheath the flowers. As I enter the waiting room, the door buzzes, ten minutes early. I open it for Dr. Jack, who is commanding even before he opens his mouth, his confidence coming off him in energetic waves.

"We meet again." He beams.

"Good morning. Have a seat and I'll be with you in just a few minutes." I'm jarred by the instantaneous nervousness his presence brings on and open a new window on my computer to appear like I'm doing something while I gain composure. He steps closer and peers over the monitor.

"Thank you for seeing me."

"Sure. No problem."

"Pretty flowers. From someone special?"

"They are pretty," I agree.

"So, what do I call you? Charlotte? Ms. Knopfler?"

"Charlotte, please."

"Charlotte, how long does an appointment with you usually last?"

"For your first appointment, depending on how much we need to cover, it's usually about seventy-five to ninety minutes."

"Good. Good. I have surgery at one P.M.," he states proudly.

Ah. He's a surgeon. I'm sure he relishes this part of the conversation, when people swoon over his career announcement. I always did.

"Not a problem. We'll get you in and out in plenty of time," I say mildly, not celebrating his proclamation, which seems to stump him.

"I was disappointed when you weren't here when I came back the other day. I hope I didn't scare you away." He ignores my attempts at looking busy and my suggestion that he take a seat.

"You don't scare me, Dr. Doyle." This comes out way more flirtatiously than I intended. My regret is overtaken by curiosity. "You came back in person yesterday?" I ask, this time careful of my tone. "What time?" Rachel said she walked out with Lucy; he must have come after they'd left.

He looks up at the ceiling. "Um. Not exactly sure. It was late afternoon. I guess you closed early for the day?"

"Sorry. I had something come up." I immediately regret apologizing. I have been trying to stop using "sorry" as my default when there is really no reason to apologize. I bet Dr. Jack Doyle doesn't apologize to anyone.

"I hope whatever it was wasn't anything serious," he says gently.

I pull my gaze from the monitor and make full eye contact with him. His face is open and he seems genuinely empathetic, not the typical bedside manner of a surgeon. His intense eyes and the scar running the length of his jawline contradict the warmth in his smile. I feel tempted to ask him what the scar is from, and if he wore a beard to cover it. But these aren't appropriate questions for a patient. These are personal questions. Date questions.

"It wasn't." I'm hardly going to introduce Jane Doe into the conversation, though oddly, I feel moved to tell this complete stranger about my experience and get his take on it. I open my drawer and pull out my new-patient packet, attach it to a clipboard, and hand it to him.

"Old school, huh? Most places are using iPads for new clients." He chuckles as he accepts it.

"I guess we are pretty vintage around here," I say lightly. If only we could afford an iPad. "If you wouldn't mind, could you fill in your basic info and your health insurance info here, and we can see if they'll cover your visit. More of the major providers are recognizing acupuncture and reimbursing patients. Once you've got that completed we can go through what brought you in today."

He takes the clipboard from my hand and glances down at the paper. "Actually, I'm going to pay in cash, if it's all the same to you. I'd like to keep insurance out of it. Too much of a headache."

I'm a little surprised by this, but it isn't unheard of. I haven't told him my fee yet, but if he's a surgeon, he won't likely be deterred by the cost. "Sure. The first visit is three hundred dollars, because it's a longer appointment with the consult, and two hundred thereafter."

"Fine. Fine," he replies, head down as he jots down his information in surprisingly legible handwriting, and quickly hands the personal info back to me.

"Great. Let's get started, then. We are going to be in here." I gesture toward Rachel's treatment room and he looks at my closed door, where Cameron is hopefully in la-la land. "Not in there?" He points. "Isn't that one yours?"

I'm taken off guard by the question and wonder how he knows which treatment room is mine, but I realize that the last time he saw me, I was coming out of it. "Not today. There's another patient in there right now," I respond. "We'll be using my colleague's treatment room."

"Oh. Right. Rachel." He has a good memory.

"Is there a problem?"

He hesitates. "No. Not at all. I guess I'd pictured this happening in the other room. Glad business is good."

I lead him into the room and invite him to sit in the chair across from me. I put my clipboard on my lap, poised with a pen, and give the info he's filled out a cursory once-over while he gets settled and looks around the room. He's forty-five, born in January, single, and a nonsmoker. He exercises six days a week and eats a very healthy diet—at least according to what he's written down. In person and on paper he seems to be in overall excellent health, given his lack of check marks next to preexisting conditions. We'll see what his body tells me when he's on the table.

"So, Jack, how are you feeling today?"

He smiles big. "I'm feeling very well. Thank you."

"Great." I write the word "great" on my blank page and feel immediately embarrassed when I see him watching me write it. "And what brings you to acupuncture?"

"This feels a little like therapy," he quips.

"It can seem like that a little bit. It can also help in some of the same ways, or be a nice complement to seeing a psychologist regularly. Are you currently seeing anyone?"

"No one exclusively." There's that grin again.

I muscle through the nervousness I'm feeling. "There is a big connection between your mind and body. Often your emotions appear in your body as physiological issues."

"Just don't make me talk about my childhood."

I wait for the inevitable Western attitude to reveal itself and gird myself against defensiveness. He's a cocky MD, yes, but also a patient sitting in my office. I realize how standoffish and resentful I'm feeling in his direction.

He clears his throat. "Actually, I'm here because I have been experiencing some preoperative anxiety, which is new for me. I've been operating for twenty years and have never had this problem," he says quietly.

"When did this start?"

He rubs his hands together. "About six months ago."

I make a note. "Was there one incident that sticks out as the beginning of the anxiety, or was it gradual?"

"Um. It was pretty gradual. I haven't had anything disastrous happen," he replies, unconvincingly.

I nod, sensing there is more for him to say. We sit for a few moments in silence.

"Well, my wife left me last year." His voice quality has altered. For the first time since he walked through my door, I see his soft underbelly. I feel for him. "It wasn't happening before then."

"I'm sorry. That's very difficult." And traumatic enough to make the most confident person anxious at work, especially someone whose job deals in life and death, even if he doesn't categorize it as "disastrous." I do wonder what made her leave.

His momentary vulnerability recedes quickly. "I haven't lost anyone on the table yet, at least not because of my error."

I feel exposed, as though he knows exactly what I've done. A trickle of sweat slides down my back.

"What symptoms are you having? Panic attacks? Vomiting? Experiencing tremors in your hands?"

"All of the above." I nod and note his symptoms. "It sounds like I'm not the first surgeon you've treated," he replies.

"Something like that," I mutter.

He frowns. "Hmm?"

"Yes. I've done a lot of work with doctors. I actually specialize in the physiological presentation of trauma and have a lot of hands-on experience with surgeons." All true, just not in the way that he probably assumes.

"Well, out of all of the acupuncture joints in all the world, I walk into yours. Play it again, Sam."

I offer a small smile. "I just hope I can help you." I know I can, if he'll let me.

"And how does sticking tiny needles all over my body help me get my mojo back, exactly?" He's playfully patronizing.

"Well, firstly, you need to have an open mind. This work is about energy, and skepticism can block that energy flow even further than it already is."

"I'm here, aren't I?" By the way he's clasping his hands, I can see that he is actually nervous, and I feel a little bad about taking a tone with him.

"Yes, you are. That is a great start." I put my clipboard down. "Why don't we start with some basic work."

"Sounds good to me." I see his smartwatch illuminate, and he looks at it. "What do you need me to do?"

"Let me take a look at your tongue."

Now it's his turn to try to conceal his grin. "You move fast, huh?"

I glance at him sideways. "It can tell me a lot about what is going on inside."

He sticks it out against his obvious skepticism. It's pale and coated.

"Have you been feeling cold easily? Lost your appetite? Been experiencing weakness?"

His eyes widen. "Yes, actually. You can tell that by looking at my tongue?"

I grab a hand mirror from my shelf and hand it to him. "It isn't magic; take a look." I lean into him while he extends his tongue in the reflection. He smells good. Like recently showered-and-shaved good.

"Tho thow than u thell wuh ith . . . ?" He tries to talk with his tongue still outside of his mouth and we both laugh.

"I can tell that you are yang deficient by the color and coating on your tongue. The most common symptoms that go along with that particular stasis are the ones I asked you about, and a few others. Panic, anxiety, worry." I'm don't mention impotence, but it's also another hallmark of male yang deficiency. I'll let him bring it up if he wants to.

"You can close your mouth now."

He retracts his tongue, closes his mouth. "Very cool trick," he says. "What now? Are you going to tell my future from the lines in my hand?" he teases.

"I'll treat you faceup today and get a sense of how your qi is flowing overall. We can talk more when you are on the table, and I'll be able to tell a lot more about what's going on in your body. I will step out and have you undress down to your underwear and give you a towel to drape across yourself."

He nods, winces, and quickly moves his hand up to his shoulder and rubs.

"What's going on with your shoulder?" I ask.

"I play tennis, and this shoulder's been giving me some trouble lately."

"Well, I can do some needles to get the energy flowing, and try some Reiki on that spot."

"Rakey who now?" He chuckles. His relentless condescension is getting old.

"Or my partner Rachel does massage, which you might be more comfortable with. She'll be here by the time our session is out if you'd like to speak with her."

Again, I pick up the same weird energy from earlier, when he was asking about her office. "Would you like to talk to her instead? I know you have surgery in a few hours, but she might be able to do something this morning to help with anything acute." I don't know this to be true, but I'm curious to see how he reacts.

"No, that's all right. I'll see my usual girl. Thanks." I roll my eyes when I turn away from his line of vision.

"Okay, then." I look back at him and stand. "Let's get you on the table. I'm going to step out now. I'll give you a few minutes to undress and then I'll knock before I come back in. I can put a bolster under your knees if you have any lower-back issues."

"And if I'm not wearing any underwear?" I can't tell if he's joking. I crack a small smile and hand him a small folded washcloth.

"That is what this is for."

He blinks a few times and I laugh before reaching for a normal-size towel. He laughs loudly and grabs it from me playfully.

I shut the door behind me tightly, feeling good that I've made him laugh—and immediately bad, because I feel giddy.

◈ ◈ ◈

I'm barely in my chair before the light mood drains out of me. I see an email slide into my inbox from Henry. Just the sight of his name conjures a fist-size knot in my solar plexus. I feel nauseous as I open the message.

From: Braindoc67@gmail.com
To: CharlotteKnopfler@gmail.com
Re: IMPORTANT

Charlotte,
I'm taking care of it.
    Consider this matter closed.
    Don't contact me again.
Henry

Before I have a chance to process, the door behind me opens and Jack walks through, fully clothed, pulling his jacket on.

"Everything okay?" I ask him as I swivel in the chair in his direction and stand.

"Something came up with my patient. I'll need to cut our appointment short and rain-check becoming a human pincushion."

"Okay," I reply.

"I'll pay you for the whole time, of course."

He fumbles in his back pocket and withdraws a fat wad of cash secured with a gold money clip and speedily peels off three hundreds.

"I hope everything is okay."

"I'll call when I can make it back in."

He is already out the door before I have a chance to say goodbye.

ELEVEN

WOLCOTT

"Give me a minute, Detectives."

Silvestri and I stand near the entryway of the Pilates studio where Julie Merrill has just finished teaching class. The last of the students have exited. She towels off her face and hair, then drops the towel next to a large tote bag and returns her attention to us.

"Sorry," she says. "Tough class today. So, how can I help you?"

"We understand you volunteer at the same community garden as Brooke Harmon?"

"I do, yes." Her smile drops as her eyes toggle between Silvestri and me. "What's this about?"

"Were you aware of anything unusual going on with Miss Harmon as of late?" I ask.

"What's . . . is she okay?"

Silvestri clears his throat. "I'm sorry to have to inform you that Miss Harmon was found dead."

Julie drops into a squat and rests her palms on her knees. She closes her eyes, breathes deeply, and returns her attention to my partner. "Oh God. I'm so sorry to hear that. I can't believe . . . Jesus. What happened?"

"We were hoping you could help us figure that out," he says. She starts to let out tears.

"We're very sorry, Miss Merrill," I say. "We understand that the two of you were close outside garden hours?"

"Yeah," she says, in disbelief. "We had gotten to be friends over the last couple of months. I felt like we were really getting to know each other."

Silvestri maintains eye contact with her as he drops into a squat. "We understand this must come as a shock. Would you be up for answering a few questions?"

She looks at a clock on the wall. "There's another instructor starting a class in a couple of minutes. Can we sit and talk somewhere else?"

╪ ╪ ╪

"Thanks, Detective."

I hand cardboard cups of tea to Julie and my partner as I join them at the table. The coffee shop we're sitting in is slow with the midafternoon lull. I sip my coffee as Silvestri leans forward. "You were saying . . . ," he continues.

"Well, things had been going really well with her lately. She'd made the decision to go back to school to study child psychology, and she'd begun applying to programs. She was excited. Then, over the last week or so, she just seemed short-tempered and on edge. I tried to ask about things, but she kind of deflected. I got the feeling that she was touchy about whatever was going on, so I didn't push things."

"Did you have a sense of Miss Harmon's personal life at all?"

"So, she and I had just gotten to the point where we were starting to open up about our love lives," she muses.

"And what did hers look like?" I ask.

"About the same as mine." She laughs. "Although I'm really amazed at how well adjusted she seemed about it. Especially considering the divorce."

"Miss Harmon was divorced? Was that recent?"

"A year or so ago, I think."

"And you didn't know her to be dating anyone, it sounds like?"

"No. But again, she seemed really happy alone. And she was doing a lot of work on herself, so that was cool. She had a tight circle of friends that she mentioned, outside of our crew from the garden, and I think they really helped her through a lot, with the divorce and everything."

"Had you met any of these friends?" asks Silvestri.

"Not yet, no. But we only recently started hanging out outside of work."

"You mentioned that," I say. "And you hadn't noticed anything out of the ordinary with her that you can think of?"

"Hmm." She looks into her tea. "Aside from her being kind of stressed last week, not really." Her eyes widen. "Gosh, I should have pushed her more about whatever it was. Maybe I could have helped." Her chin drops.

"Miss Merrill," he says. "There's no use wondering what if, believe me. We're sorry about your friend."

"Thank you," she says, doing her best to pull a smile.

I remove a card from my pocket and set it on the table in front of her. "Please let us know if anything comes to mind. And we may be in touch if we have any more questions."

"Of course," she says. "Thank you, Detectives."

As my partner and I rise from the table, I lay a hand gently on her shoulder. "Take care of yourself."

TWELVE

CHARLOTTE

With Jack's abrupt departure, I have a few minutes to absorb Henry's email before I need to rouse Cameron. I feel stung by his curt tone but hugely relieved that he's taking care of things. I know that I don't have it in me to go through anything else with the hospital lawyers, or my own lawyer. I don't want to think about going through any of that painful process again.

After I close the message, I shift my worry to the flowers. With a pounding in my head and chest and sweaty palms, I discard the outer cellophane casing in the wastebasket and scrutinize the arrangement. The bright orange and white splashes of tiger lilies surround a smattering of purple flowers and baby's breath. There is no personalized card included, and none needed. It is undeniably Peter. My heart sinks like a stone. The purple means he has to stay away longer. The orange means that he's been compromised, so communication will be extremely limited. The baby's breath means he's safe, which is a sliver of comfort amid the disappointment of his extended absence. Originally, I'd found the game of learning his floral codes fun and exciting, but his quizzing me on the code of flowers for a week straight became tedious and struck me as incredibly unecessary. He'd been very unhappy when I suggested it was bordering on paranoid, and I was given the silent treatment for ten days until I acknowledged how smart it was that he'd come up with the system.

My mind is a hundred worries all mixing together. Peter's flowers.

Jane Doe. Rachel's strange behavior. Henry's email response. Peter's whereabouts. Jack Doyle. I feel like I'm sliding into the calm crisis mode of my medical internship days in the ER, when there was too much input to focus on one particular emergency for too long. My mind moves to practical matters, a reflexive mode in times of emotional deluge. I get up and start straightening the office space, even though nothing is out of place. I stretch my arms up and side to side. I move to my computer and start a spree of deleting junk mail. I need to try to sit still and meditate. I move back to the couch and set my meditation timer for five minutes, the amount of time Cameron has left in her treatment, and shut my eyes tight.

I think about Cameron. Disappointment in love is one of the most common complaints on my table, and the brokenhearted store that hurt in so many places aside from the heart. So many of my patients talk about how they are preoccupied with what their partners are doing when they aren't together, and with more interest and energy than when they are. There's no time left to spend self-reflecting, so their complaints and worries are wrapped around other people's lives. It's a wonder that anyone can have a healthy relationship with all this access to one another.

The office is silent except for the white noise machine. Cameron is likely hovering in that lovely middle place between awake and asleep, hopefully calm. I feel lonely and jarred by the last couple of days, and the familiar obsessive longing for Peter. Before the flowers, his silence lasted four and a half weeks, the longest yet in our relationship. I know this is part of being with him, although coming to peace with it is one of the harder adjustments in my life.

Peter was between assignments when we met, so the first months of our courtship he was always around. It seemed like all I had to do was think about him and he'd light up my phone or be waiting in my inbox. We had an instant, uncanny connection. He knew what I was going to say and where I was going to be without my telling him. He predicted things happening before they did, and he made me feel completely safe with his seeming omniscience. Before I fully understood his job, I joked and maybe believed a little that he was psychic.

We were communicating constantly, to the point that I felt like I was losing myself, and breaking my own rules about boundaries in relationships. He told me he loved me on week four. He texted me every hour and got concerned if I didn't reply quickly. It was exciting at first, and then too much. It had been two months of nonstop communication and I told him I needed to come up for air. He said he understood and then he was gone without a trace. When I reached out to let him know how much I missed him and wanted to resume, there was only radio silence.

I didn't know if he'd completely misunderstood what I meant, or if something bad had happened to him. We were in a relationship gray area. We hadn't intertwined our worlds enough for me to know his routines or how to find out if he was hurt or missing. And we were definitely not prepared for major life events. I had a vague sense of where he lived, but driving across state lines and telling him "I was just in the neighborhood" seemed excessive and clingy. The original number I'd had for him was going straight to a generic voicemail, and my texts were unanswered. I'd already googled him when we first connected, so I knew there wouldn't be anything about him online. He'd explained to me that his employer made it so he would be absolutely untraceable online.

By the time he resurfaced three weeks later, the only communication I'd gotten from him was one answered text from a number I didn't recognize. He'd simply responded, *Alive,* weeks after I'd asked him if he was. I was crestfallen but resolved to move on as quickly as possible.

I mooned over him silently for a few days, finally admitting to Rachel what had happened. We analyzed and dissected and ultimately concluded that I'd dodged a bullet. But when he wrote me one of the most heartfelt apology emails I've ever gotten, along with images of travel documents, photos of some of the locations he'd been, and a forwarded email from one of the people whose life he had apparently saved, I was reeled in again. I felt reassured and proud of him. We communicated every single day after that.

Eventually, he became vague and evasive about his job again, and there were more than a handful of tense and frustrating exchanges between us. I began to lay down ultimatums about having more specifics about what it was he actually did, or I would end things between us. Once he explained what he did and I believed him, I understood that his omniscience wasn't precognition; it was professional.

Instead of the meditation app gong sounds bringing me out of my meditative state, the door buzzer jolts me back into the room. I jump up and make my way to the door, unlock it, and find two men standing on the sidewalk outside my office. One is Detective Silvestri, and the other is a man I've never seen before but I assume to be his partner. They both have neutral expressions, although Silvestri seems to be suppressing a smile.

"Good afternoon, Ms. Knopfler. This is my partner, Detective Wolcott."

Wolcott nods, but his gaze is on the flower arrangement. "Nice to meet you."

"Hello."

"Mind if I use your facilities?" Silvestri asks.

"Sure." I point him to the bathroom and he moves toward it, leaving Wolcott and me alone.

"Nice to meet you, Dectective." He accepts my outstretched hand, his attention still on the contents of the vase. Wolcott is taking in every inch of my office. His energy is even more grounded than his partner's, and I can tell that he is highly perceptive.

"Needles, huh? I've never had the pleasure." He smiles.

"I'd be happy to get you on my table if you have any complaints," I respond lightly.

"Just this one right here," he says, as Silvestri rejoins us. "Don't think you have enough needles for that, though."

Silvestri smirks. "Thanks for the hospitality. Too much tea. By the way, that's a beautiful tapestry hanging in the bathroom."

I laugh. "Thanks. It is more utilitarian than decorative. It's covering an unsightly door that leads to the China Panda. Unfortunately, it causes the bathroom to have a constant and apparently permanent odor of lo mein."

Both men chuckle. I turn to Silvestri as Wolcott continues to survey the space.

"I was wondering when I'd see you again. Have you learned anything about Jane Doe? I haven't been able to stop thinking about her." Out of habit, I put my hand on Silvestri's arm, which he registers with an unsure smile before quickly looking at Wolcott, who has also noticed the gesture. I have to remember not to touch everyone in the familiar way I do with my patients.

"That's why we're visiting. Would you be free to talk with us right now?" His cadence is different than it was during our first meeting. He seems more clipped.

"Sure. I have a patient on the table. Let me finish with her and then I'm all yours."

As I head for the room to remove Cameron's needles, Wolcott meets my eyes and chimes in, "Beautiful flowers. What's the occasion?"

I stumble to answer. "Nothing special. Just a grateful patient."

"Interesting arrangement, isn't it, Silvestri? You dabble a bit in flowers and plants and such, right? What do you call this purple flower here?"

I'm stunned a little at the question. It's as pointed as the petals on the flower he is asking about. Silvestri examines the arrangement somewhat reluctantly. Curiously, I see disappointment pass over his face.

"That looks like nightshade to me."

Wolcott looks either impressed or teasing about his partner's knowledge. "Hmm. Interesting choice. You don't see that one every day, do you?"

THIRTEEN

SILVESTRI

"DEADLY NIGHTSHADE?" I say. "That's a rarity, for sure."

Behind her desk, our healer's shelves are teeming with various plastic and glass jars and dropper bottles with handwritten labels indicating the names of corresponding supplements, extracts, and tinctures. As Wolcott takes in Charlotte's office, I look directly at the flower arrangement, all the while keeping my peripheral focus on our person of now great interest. She doesn't seem to blanch at the mention of the lethal flower, but instead studies the arrangement with renewed curiosity. I detect nervousness behind her facade.

"Hmm," she says, forcing a smile. "My friend has great taste in flowers. I guess her taste tends toward the exotic, too."

My partner jumps at the opportunity to pause his visual scan and lock eyes with her. "I'm sorry, it was a friend or a patient who sent these? I'm confused."

"Both," says Charlotte. "Some of the people I treat find their way into my life in more personal ways."

Wolcott pulls the notebook from his pocket. "And may I ask the name of this patient turned friend?"

I watch Charlotte's shoulders tense as she draws in a long breath. If we were at the poker table, this is the moment I'd go all in. "Rachel Sherman," she answers.

Wolcott jots the name on his pad and returns his attention to the shelves behind her desk.

"I'm sorry," I interject. "During our first conversation, I believe you mentioned sharing this space with someone named Rachel. Would that be the same woman?"

There's the slightest hesitation before she answers. "It is, actually. Yes."

"So, really, it's colleague-patient-friend, then," I say. "Quite the trifecta." I feel my stomach tighten. I'm letting her dishonesty get to me. I need to let up a touch.

She reaches for a glass of water and takes a sip, all the while maintaining eye contact with me. "We sometimes trade sessions. So when you asked about the flowers, I was thinking of her in more of a patient capacity, I guess."

Wolcott slips in and downshifts. "Ms. Knopfler," he says. "I see that you deal in a lot of herbal remedies. You mix your own, or no?"

"I don't. Those need to be mixed by a licensed herbalist. Certain roots, for instance, need to be cooked, so as to nullify the toxic effects. Do you have a particular interest in plants and herbs, Detective?"

Wolcott looks at her thoughtfully. "One that's increasing by the minute, thanks largely to my partner here. He's taught me all sorts of fun facts."

Charlotte looks at me as she answers him. "Nature provides us with so many of the remedies we need. It's really quite amazing."

"And occasionally lethal," he says.

The remark yanks her gaze back to his. "Detective, I realize there's a fair amount of skepticism around what I practice. But I assure you, there's a science to all of this, just as there would be with any course of treatment you'd receive from your general practitioner."

"I see," he counters. "But you're telling me that some of these remedies are derived from deadly plants, correct?"

I study her posture as she considers my partner's question. She holds her ground, not displaying the usual evasiveness of a guilty conscience. She appears defensive, however, her shoulders turned inward and her chin dropped. I'm having a hard time getting a clean read on her.

"Dosage is key, Detective Wolcott." Her answer is clipped, but my partner's employing a goading tone. "And I'm of the mind that natural remedies are far less dangerous than the synthetics that wreak havoc on our systems."

"I see," he answers. "Ms. Knopfler, would you—"

Just then, Wolcott is seized by a violent coughing fit. Charlotte's expression softens into one of concern as she retrieves a pitcher of water with floating slices of cucumber from the side table and pours a glass. My partner hunches over a wastepaper basket, steadying himself against the desk with one hand as he turns a lung inside out in the direction of the trash.

"Here you are," she says, setting the glass within inches of Wolcott's hand. She places a palm on his back and moves it in slow, deliberate circles. "Try to breathe."

After a moment, he straightens up, reaches for the water, and takes a sip. The coughing abates, and he considers the glass in his hand. His eyes tearing, he turns to her and chuckles. "Maybe this holistic care really *is* the ticket."

She breaks into a grin, then fakes a stern expression. "I haven't lost anyone yet, and you're certainly not going to be the first to go."

"Well," I say. "Now that my partner's made a spectacle of himself, I suppose we'll leave you to your practice."

"Detectives?" she asks, with a look of concern. "Have there been any developments with Jane Doe? That poor woman has been on my mind quite a bit."

Wolcott catches her eye. "We believe we have a positive ID. We're waiting to speak with the next of kin before we can release that information."

"*Any* idea how we might be connected?" she asks. "Sorry, I've just been racking my brain, to no avail."

He straightens up and tugs on the top button of his suit vest. "Well, we're narrowing down our theories. Hope to know something more definitive soon."

I study Charlotte carefully. She offers a steady glance. "I'll continue to send positive energy your way."

"Thank you for your time, Ms. Knopfler," I say. "We'll be in touch."

◆◆◆

A gust of wind swoops through the parking lot as we approach the car. I turn to Wolcott. "You okay, Smokey?" I ask.

"Just doing some recon," he answers with a grin.

"In the trash bin?" I laugh.

He pauses before he climbs into the driver's side. "Well, that's where the tag from the florist was hanging out."

"You're a wily one, partner." I shake my head as I sit, then pull the door closed. "Let's hit it."

He backs out of the parking space and cuts through the lot. "Do me a solid and look up the address for a June's Floral Shop."

"No problem," I say, pulling my phone from my pocket. "Oh, and that 'next of kin' bit was pretty slick. You liking her for this?"

"Have you noticed what I've noticed?" he asks, pulling into a stream of traffic.

"What's that?"

"Of the people we've spoken with, she's the only one who hasn't asked how Brooke Harmon died."

FOURTEEN

RACHEL

PETER IS A PROBLEM. But Charlotte has more than a few.

She has a genius IQ, at one time could perform brain surgery that only a very small number of people in the world could, and was on track to be one of the youngest, most celebrated female psychosurgeons in the world. Why she isn't any of those things any longer isn't even the problem. The issue is how shortsighted she continues to be about trust and the true intentions of people. I should try to respect how trusting she is after everything she's been through, but it's difficult when I see her getting hurt.

Charlotte and I are yin and yang in matters of reading people. Where she falls short in spotting the obvious deceptions and ulterior motives that most people carry, I am too acutely aware of these qualities. As the person closest to her and who cares about her the most, I want Charlotte to see people for who they really are. Peter in particular. Her mother. Her group of so-called friends. They are all imposters in some way. Yes, we all are. But they all want something from her, and give her little in return.

The problem with the desire for her to see people's true motives cuts both ways, of course. Because if she could truly see people for who they really are, I'd probably be weeded out pretty quickly. I live in fear of that. But my lies are by omission, not commission, and are for her own good. They are protective. I only have her best interests in mind. I would take a bullet for her, or pull the trigger to protect her.

Charlotte is amazing in how she's been able to transform her previously reserved and emotionally withheld bedside manner as a surgeon to the emoting, openhearted practitioner she is today. I didn't know her then, but based on a handful of unguarded moments when she's dug into that time in her life, I've been able to piece together quite a bit. I know she's been lonely, scared, and defeated. I only want to keep her from feeling any of those things ever again, if I can.

I am extremely protective of my friends. I have a hard time when people lie to me or keep secrets, and she is increasingly doing both. Yes, it makes me incredibly hypocritical to point fingers, I know.

Each day that this situation with Peter continues, the harder it becomes for me not to come clean. I want her to be happy, but this has gotten out of control.

╬ ╬ ╬

He's waiting right where I told him to be. He looks anxious.

"Hey, Rach," he says when I step out of the car. "How's it going?"

I don't do him any favors by downplaying my anger. "What the hell do you think you are doing?!"

"I'm trying to help you," he counters.

"By meddling in my life? That is not what I asked for. Charlotte was not a part of this."

He takes a gentler approach. "I like her."

This enrages me. "You have to leave her out of this."

"Rachel, I thought we trusted each other." His nice-guy routine has no effect on me any longer.

"You have crossed all kinds of boundaries, and it is not okay." I keep my voice firm.

"Rachel, I understand you are scared. But if you let me help you, you might have a fighting chance."

"You don't want to help me! You want to kill me." I gnash my teeth with each word.

"Think about what you are passing up here. You are making a decision that may be your only option to live to see forty," he says seriously.

"This is not your business or your problem." I'm struggling to keep grounded, and dig my heels into my shoes.

"You kind of made it my business," he counters.

"I don't have to listen to anything you tell me to do. Worry about your side of the street, bud."

He mulls this over. "You certainly don't have to listen to anything I say. But think about the position you've put me in. Doesn't that matter to you at all?"

"I want you to stay out of my life, and to stay away from Charlotte."

"That is going to be a problem for me. I can't just walk away." He crosses his arms.

"It isn't up to you to decide who lives and dies." I'm terrified of anything else he might say.

His voice is stern. "Actually, it kind of is. And unfortunately, you are running out of time." He moves toward me and I take a big step backward. "Rachel, you need to make the rational decision here."

"Or what? What are my options?" I assume a stance of confidence. "You'll poison me? Watch me die slowly? No, thank you."

"That's not fair. You have to work with me here. I'm trying, Rachel."

"Just leave me alone." I duck and weave, avoiding his grip, and slide into my car. He says something as I close the door and start the engine, but I don't catch it. He moves close to my window and says it louder.

"I'm going to have a tough conversation with Charlotte if you don't do the right thing. Protect her even if you don't want to protect yourself."

I gun the engine and peel away from him. I really don't want to do something drastic, but if he tries to interfere again I might not have a choice.

FIFTEEN

Woundedhealer: Can we talk about mothers?

Miserylovescompany: Depends on which mothers we are talking about.

MaxineKD: As long as we don't talk about mine.

Biggirlsdontcry54: Sure. I love my mother.

Makeupyourmindcontrol: Really? After everything she put you through?

Biggirlsdontcry54: Like I love getting the flu or gum surgery.

MaxineKD: HAAAA.

Biggirlsdontcry54: But she made me who I am today. Right?

Woundedhealer: You are much more evolved than I am.

Biggirlsdontcry54: Twenty-five years of therapy helped. Or as I like to refer to it, the "long con."

Woundedhealer: A con to get what out of you exactly? (LOL.)

Biggirlsdontcry54: To get me to say, "I love my mother."

Makeupyourmindcontrol: A very long and *expensive* con. I always wondered why shrinks would want to actually help their clients get better. Isn't that ultimately just creating a patient retention problem?

Miserylovescompany: Keep 'em crazy and you can get a pool with a Jacuzzi and a view.

Makeupyourmindcontrol: You've been in therapy for twenty-five years?

Biggirlsdontcry54: Yep. And it was an inside job. Mom paid for it.

MaxineKD: I think Woundedhealer should have the floor now on this subject, ladies.

Makeupyourmindcontrol: I'll keep my fingers off the keyboard for as long as it takes me to open this pinot grigio. Then, no promises.

Miserylovescompany: I'll see your box of wine and raise you frozen calories. Tonight I'm having a ménage à trois with Ben & Jerry.

Woundedhealer: You guys make me laugh.

MaxineKD: Tell us about your mom, Woundedhealer.

Woundedhealer: Well, I've been trying to be less hard on her. I mean, she does her best, I guess.

Biggirlsdontcry54: It's hard to imagine you being hard on anybody.

Makeupyourmindcontrol: Seriously, you are like the most patient person I've never met.

Woundedhealer: She brings out a side of me that is like all of my worst qualities amplified.

Makeupyourmindcontrol: I can relate to that. There are things that my mother says, especially after "the tragedy," that make me want to punch her. Like the fact that she refers to my brother's death as "the tragedy."

MaxineKD: I flat-out hate that word.

Biggirlsdontcry54: That word is a tragedy.

Woundedhealer: It's the anger that my mom brings out in me that worries me.

Makeupyourmindcontrol: Sometimes mothers just suck. And bring out the worst parts of us. Which is ironic considering we are probably the best things that were brought out of them.

Woundedhealer: I feel like I've painted a worse picture of my mom than she deserves, though.

MaxineKD: Or you could have Stockholm syndrome? You feel defensive of your abuser? That is a thing.

Biggirlsdontcry54: Someone's been dusting off their copy of *Trauma of the Gifted Child*!

MaxineKD: Middle finger emoji.

Biggirlsdontcry54: MaxineKD, did you just type the words "middle finger emoji," thinking it would actually be a middle finger?

MaxineKD: 🖕🖕🖕

Biggirlsdontcry54: Oh good. I was hoping you'd google how to do a middle finger emoji next.

Miserylovescompany: Ladies! Ladies! Woundedhealer, keep going. We are listening.

Woundedhealer: She was the person I was able to turn to when my life fell apart. When I had nowhere else to go, she took me back, let me sleep in my old bed and not get out if it for two weeks. No questions asked.

Miserylovescompany: So, she loves you. Wants to be there for you.

Makeupyourmindcontrol: That's something. My mother always loved my brother more than me. She couldn't wait to get me out of the house, even though he was really the problem.

Miserylovescompany: Focus Makeupyourmindcontrol! Woundedhealer has the conch shell.

Woundedhealer: Right, but by being vulnerable with her when everything went so sideways, I feel like she now uses it against me anytime I have a bad day or show any feelings.

MaxineKD: Aw. I'm familiar. She treats you like you are always on the verge?

Woundedhealer: Yes. Sort of. But at the same time, acts like nothing is ever really wrong. And like my feelings are wildly inappropriate. It's more about using what she knows about me against me.

MaxineKD: Woundedhealer, I think your mom and mine would get along.

Woundedhealer: You'd think so. But my mom isn't great at keeping friends.

Biggirlsdontcry54: The only thing my mom was great at keeping was an impressive cache of snide remarks about how I stole her youth and potential.

Makeupyourmindcontrol: Wow, we are a cheerful bunch, aren't we?

MaxineKD: Seriously. We should start our own line of Mother's Day cards.

Woundedhealer: Do you think if someone isn't close with their mother or doesn't feel loved by her, they are doomed to never really be well adjusted or happy?

Biggirlsdontcry54: Hmm. I don't know. Norman Bates was close with his, and look how that turned out.

SIXTEEN

CHARLOTTE

"You were a strange child." I can hear my mom exhaling. Whether it's tobacco or medical-grade sativa, I don't ask. The chance that it's a combination of the two is as high as she likely is.

"Well, thanks, Mom. But I actually just asked if you remembered any of my childhood friends who I was particularly close to." I'm desperate to figure out why Jane Doe is familiar but completely erased from my mind. Childhood seemed like a good potential lead. I've been on with her for six minutes and I'm already wishing I hadn't called.

"I assumed you were referring to Socket? You were friends for so long. I always thought she looked just like you."

She never misses an opportunity to remind me of the ways I'm different from everyone else.

"Mom, Socket was genderless. *And* an imaginary friend. No one knew what Socket looked like."

I haven't thought about my imaginary childhood best friend in a very long time. "I mean like *actual* friends. A best friend I forgot about? A pen pal? Or maybe a half sister you never told me about?" I mean it as a joke but consider the scenario and shudder at the possibility.

"Honey, trust me, you'd know if you had any other siblings. You know how terrible I am at hiding things." She is.

"Awful, Mom." I try to rid myself of the images of things seen while snooping in her room as a kid.

She snorts. "Oh, I was successful in hiding plenty. And for your own good too. I know you think I was a terrible mother, honey, but you could have done much worse."

This is our banter. She always maintains that she did the best she could as a single mom raising a "strange child." I think she could have done better.

"Mom, how did I end up parting ways with Socket?"

"Well, let me see if I remember. It's been a long time." The reason I called her was because of her memory. It's like a steel trap and she prides herself on it but likes to make me work for the information.

"The guidance counselor from the elementary school, Mrs. DeHirsch—she's dead now—called me in to talk about how we could get you to socialize better. You were spending a lot of time in the corner talking to yourself—or talking to Socket—and your teacher, Ms. Bordeaux, was getting concerned. When she asked you what you were talking about, you apparently said, 'We were talking about Socket's head surgery.' It was dark, honey, but no one can argue that you didn't know early on exactly what you wanted to be when you grew up."

"Shockingly, you never told me that, Mom." New anecdotes like these make me wonder how much revisionist history she's peppering in. There are numerous origin myths about my surgical predisposition. All told by her. Funnily enough, I recall none of the instances of wanting to become a doctor, only the feeling I had when I was told that it's what I'd always wanted: that she was describing someone other than me.

"Didn't I? Huh. Oh yeah. You were fascinated with medicine at a very young age. Thankfully you didn't take to operating on the neighborhood pets, like that one little psychopath who lived two doors down. What *was* his name? He's the president of some bank, which his mother will remind you of every time you run into her. Is it Douglas? Oh, it's going to bother me. Miraculously he lived to adulthood with that horror show of a father." I hear ice in a glass clinking as she pauses.

"Mom. Focus." I don't hide my exasperation; as usual she's undeterred.

"God, remember that teacher, Ms. Bordeaux? She was a piece of work. I'm pretty sure she's dead now too. She shame-walked right into class in last night's outfit more than twice. You could smell the Tanqueray and Parliaments on her a mile away. When I did parent days in the classroom—"

"Okay, off topic, Mom. But since you brought it up, why didn't anyone say anything about my kindergarten teacher being a degenerate alcoholic?"

"Charlotte, honey, it was a different time. People weren't so uptight about child rearing. I would have drunk too if I was spending my days with six-year-olds." She sighs dramatically. "The world was not as scary of a place as it is now. I used to let you walk to school by yourself all the time, and you only had a babysitter until you were able to unlock the door by yourself."

"And wasn't there a spate of kidnappings around that time, in our town?" If she won't drive us back to the topic on hand, I will.

"Anyway, Mrs. DeHirsch—newly married—she was so proud to be a guidance counselor, she had a sharp mind too, and she was really interested in you. She wanted to make sure you didn't leave kindergarten without some friends. Very sweet, such a tragedy."

"Mother. You are a walking obituary." I sigh. "What happened to her?" I don't even want to know. But she'll tell me regardless.

"Cancer," she stage-whispers.

"Terrible." It is, but it also may be completely untrue, given the source, so I choose to live in the world where Mrs. DeHirsch is still with us. "Can you tell me what happened at school?" I'm gentle but impatient.

"After the conversation at school, I took you to McDonald's and we talked about how it was time to start playing with other children and leave Socket at home. You got sad but were very mature about it. You asked if we could take flowers to Grandma's grave, and you had a talk with her while I waited in the car. When you got back into the car, you just said, 'Socket is with Grandma now.' It was a little spooky, honestly.

And I didn't notice the poison ivy until we got home. You'd picked flowers for Socket to put on Grandma's grave, and apparently grabbed a hand and faceful of poison ivy in the process. Poor kid. You had it everywhere. Even rubbed your eyes with it. You looked so bad, I thought they were going to call social services on me when I took you to school the next day. They sent you home immediately, called me at work, and that nurse, what's her name, gave me an earful." She laughs mightily.

"Hilarious," I deadpan.

"Charlotte, are you feeling okay? What is this all about? You sound off."

I backpedal quickly. "I'm fine, Mom. Just thinking about the past a lot this week, no reason in particular." I'm as terrible a liar as she is, but in place of convincing deception, we are extremely well versed in deflection.

"Thinking about the past too much never ends well."

We've got a strong repression game too.

She pivots. "How's your love life? Seeing anyone special?" It took her much longer to ask this time around than usual.

"Still looking for Mr. Goodbar."

"Ha!" Never fails to get a laugh out of her. "God forbid. What a movie that was. Tuesday Weld was incredible. You know it was her only—"

"Oscar nomination. I know, Mom." We have this conversation at least once a month. Because she's been told more than once that she looks like Tuesday Weld, Mom acts as though they are old friends.

"Char. Are you sure you are okay? Maybe I should come over. We haven't had a visit for a while."

"No, that's okay." I wish I'd given a pause before unleashing my emphatic no.

A tiny part of me considers changing my mind. I could let her in on everything that's going on. But where do I even begin? She doesn't know about Peter. I certainly won't tell her that I've been back in contact with Henry. And why worry her with the added plot twist of a mysterious dead woman who I can't place for the life of me? I just don't want to feel so alone in all of this.

"Probably for the best anyway. I've got big plans tonight." She doesn't elaborate, and I don't push.

"Mom, I'm going to hang up."

"Okay, sweetie. Talk to you soon. Call me in a few days."

"Will do. Thanks for the trip down memory lane."

She laughs. "You really were, honey." She exhales again into the phone.

"I really was what, Mom?"

"A strange child. But such a sweet one. Once you started to make friends, you couldn't stop. You loved everyone, even the bad apples. *Especially them.*"

SEVENTEEN

WOLCOTT

"THOSE. THE CRABAPPLE branches."

The pair of bells strung to the door chime as we enter June's Floral Shop, drawing the attention of a woman who uses a set of clippers to direct two young assistants between a refrigerated case and the large vases set up along a marble tabletop. She props her spectacles up to eye us, as if trying to determine whether we're more buttercup or daffodil guys.

"Good afternoon, gentlemen. Let me know if I can help you with anything, okay?" She offers a smile before turning her attention back to the bustling assistants.

I wait for a moment, to give my partner a chance to do the honors, but he's absorbed in the botanical paradise. I take the opportunity to address her. "May we speak with you for a moment?" I say, flashing my shield discreetly so as not to alarm the small handful of customers perusing the displays.

"Of course," she says, and crosses over to where we're standing. "What can I be of assistance with?"

Silvestri's tongue is practically mopping the floor of the shop. "This place"—he beams—"is gorgeous."

She chuckles slightly. "Why, thank you," she says, then pauses awkwardly.

He snaps out of his trance. "Where are my manners? I'm Detective Silvestri. This is my partner, Detective Wolcott."

"A pleasure, Detectives," she says, studying my partner curiously. "A real anthophile, huh?"

"It's just . . . you have some very exotic types on hand here." He catches himself and blushes. "As you know."

She smiles. "Certainly nice to have an admirer in the shop." Suddenly, the corners of her mouth drop. "Oh goodness. You're not here for a condolence arrangement, I hope."

"No, ma'am," says Silvestri. "Nothing that grim. We're just tracking down some information on an order that came through your shop within the last few days."

She exhales. "Thank goodness," she says, and nods in the direction of the cash register. We follow her to the counter, where she flips open a laptop and begins hitting keys. She pauses to look up at us. "Now, was this a pickup or a delivery?"

"We're not entirely sure," I respond. "Basically, we're trying to figure out who placed the order."

"I see," she says. She tips her spectacles down and eyes us over the top of the frames. "Cheater?"

"I'm sorry?" I respond.

"It's a philandering husband, isn't it?"

I stifle a laugh. "We're not at liberty—"

"Oh, come on!" she protests. "I could use a little intrigue around here."

"Are you kidding?" asks Silvestri, looking around the shop. "I'm spellbound."

"You're making my day, Detective. Okay, what was the name of the recipient of the arrangement?

"Charlotte Knopfler," I respond.

She clacks away on the keyboard for a few seconds before her eyes light up. "Oh right." She hits a few more keys. "One of my assistants took the order." She continues tapping the keys. "Okay, it was placed yesterday and delivered to Ms. Knopfler at her office same day."

"Can you tell us who placed the order?" I ask.

She finishes tapping, props her spectacles up, and studies the screen. "I sure can," she says, and looks at us. "The order was placed by a Brooke Harmon."

EIGHTEEN

RACHEL

I'm not afraid of dying. Being alive is much harder than the alternative.

I once flatlined in the back of an ambulance and was dead for an hour and twenty minutes. There was no bright light, but instead a feeling of being suspended in a warm, thick darkness filled with the sensation of complete emotional and mental weightlessness. I was awash in a euphoria stronger than my first hit of heroin. I didn't want to come back.

Alas, it wasn't my time, thanks to a paramedic who shot me full of Narcan and brought me back from the dead. When I opened my eyes and saw his looking down at me with tears brimming, he confided that there was no way that he was going to let me die that day because I bore a striking resemblance to his little sister.

Those eighty minutes of death saved the rest of my life. When I came back, I knew I didn't want to feel the way I'd been feeling pre–death experience any longer. I never used again, and I came back with a burning desire that I hadn't ever had previously: to live. I had little to start with, so building any kind of life for myself was progress.

What I *am* afraid of is being abandoned by people. This is the fear that one of my first counselors suggested was the primary reason I'd started using in the first place. Drugs were a means of self-medication to allay the pain of being afraid, something most people do, but generally with less lethal modes. Now I chase clarity with the same verve I did getting high.

I had a pretty uneventful, normal childhood until my dad went into a routine surgery when I was fourteen and never came out. My mom never really recovered and kind of faded into the background of both of our lives, a shadowy figure who moved quietly to and from her job and the couch. I was an only child, so I sought friends as siblings and spent a lot of time at sleepovers and going on other people's family vacations as a de facto foster kid.

I had a strong curiosity about friends' older brothers who made questionable life decisions, usually in the form of motorcycles, weed, beer, and Metallica, gateways for people with a certain brain chemistry and a deeply laced need for rapid reality removal.

It could have been anything that I chose to self-medicate with, but my choice in company greatly influenced my tools of self-destruction. The older brothers became men and the anesthetizing effects of beer and weed stopped cutting it for them. My unfortunate preference for love interests with death wishes and the absence of an off switch in my brain were a dangerous combination. My lack of fear or ability to moderate anything made me an attractive partner in crime, and there was no shortage of dangerous partners willing to gun it toward trouble at top speed with me.

When I met a beautiful man-boy named Bo, the king of parlous choices, like turning his headlights off at night when we were drunk and high so the police couldn't see us going ninety miles an hour, I clung tightly to him until I become so subsumed in shooting drugs that there ceased being room in my consciousness for anything or anyone else. I lasted three months on the black tar diet before I took my reviving ride in the back of that ambulance. By some miracle, Bo had the wherewithal to call 911. It was the last high–thrill ride the two of us took together.

He didn't survive the ride.

◈ ◈ ◈

When Charlotte and I met, we had a lot in common. For starters, our love for needles. Granted, her passion was using them to heal, and mine was a dormant desire to fill them with smack, but it was a starting place.

Thankfully I'd had more than seven years clean by that time, but there was always that twinge of desire hanging in the fringes of my brain if I let myself get too overwhelmed, tired, or out of sorts. I'd actually gotten acupuncture done in the first year of my recovery by my rehab roommate, who was an impressively powerful healer in between her drinking benders. The needles were extremely effective for cravings, so I became an acupuncture junkie. I dabbled in all of the healing methods available: Tibetan bowl sounds baths, qigong, Reiki, cupping, craniosacral massage, and reflexology. If it had the promise of healing my damage, I binged on it. Eventually, I decided to become a healer myself.

I was volunteering to be a test patient in a class Charlotte was in while I finished up my reflexology training at our school, and we were partnered up on the first day. She became my test subject as well. It was the beginning of the most important friendship either of us has ever had.

I'd learned a lot about myself getting sober and in general found other people to be more problematic and triggering than positive influences on me, so up until that point, I tended to roll through life alone. I sporadically went to NA meetings and felt secure in my sobriety most of the time, but I probably should have tried harder to build a support system in the rooms I was spending time in. Always being on guard prevented me from making any deep connections, and the rate at which people would cycle in and out was frightening. I never wanted to get too attached to any one person.

It wasn't until I met Charlotte that I came out of my shell and trusted more than I could have imagined. She was really the first solid friend I'd ever had, and it opened me up in a major way. I appreciated the path she was taking, especially after she confided in me what had brought her to that decision.

Being stuck with a bunch of energy-moving needles can really open the emotional dam of stored-up feelings. One of the first times I was on her student table, she did a series of needles that had me crying like a baby. She hadn't experienced how powerfully emotions came through in practice yet, only in theory.

"I'm so sorry!" she said when she witnessed my emotional flash flood.

"This is what is supposed to happen," I reassured her.

"I guess I knew that intellectually, but I wasn't really prepared for it. Are you sure you are okay?"

I managed to smile through the onslaught. It was always good to dump the hard feelings. Crying was cleansing as hell.

"I'm great. Every time I experience a purge like this, I feel better for days after. Just another onion layer being peeled back. There is always more and deeper, but it feels important to be getting there."

She'd lit up. "It's funny. In my previous work, I was working toward the same goal with my patients. But they were always unconscious, so it was one-sided. It's a surreal experience to go from that to this. Getting feedback in real time . . . it's amazing."

Our strong desire to release our guilt and move on was what really bonded us the most. The passion to heal people who were suffering was the second thing. We didn't share our darkest marks on our consciences that day, but we would soon enough.

◈ ◈ ◈

Trauma Survivors Private Chat Room: 10/4/19
6:15 p.m.

Harmnoone82: Hello, hello!

Miserylovescompany: There she is.

Harmnoone82: Sorry, ladies. I know I've been MIA.

Woundedhealer: So good to see your name! Are you okay?

Biggirlsdontcry54: I was worried you weren't going to come back after your late-night diner summit with MaxineKD and Miserylovescompany. I thought maybe they scared you off . . .

MaxineKD: Thanks a lot, Biggirlsdontcry54! I'll have you know that I'm just as charming in the flesh as I am on the keyboard.

Harmnoone82: Of course I came back! And the impromptu meet-up was just what the doctor ordered. The pie and good company fixed me right up. (That, and getting out of town and offline for a beat.)

MaxineKD: Harmnoone82, glad that our crying over key lime pie didn't put you off us.

Miserylovescompany: If ever there was a dessert choice to cry over . . . not a lick of chocolate. Have some respect, ladies.

Woundedhealer: So that's where you've been? You are feeling better?

Harmnoone82: Better than ever.

Woundedhealer: I was worried. Are you okay?

Biggirlsdontcry54: You got out of town? Color me jealous.

Makeupyourmindcontrol: Where to?

Harmnoone82: I went upstate. It was heaven. I sat around in nature and slept like the dead. I feel like a new woman.

Woundedhealer: So things are good, then?

Harmnoone82: Better than good!

Woundedhealer: Oh great. I was worried. Are you sure everything is okay?

Harmnoone82: Yes. I thought you'd be happy that I'm back, Woundedhealer.

Biggirlsdontcry54: For real, Woundedhealer.

Woundedhealer: Sorry. The last couple of chats, you mentioned that you were worried about things?

Harmnoone82: Honestly, Woundedhealer. I'm good. Jeez.

Woundedhealer: I'm sorry, I guess I'm projecting my shitty week.

Makeupyourmindcontrol: What's happening?

Woundedhealer: I had to identify someone who died.

Miserylovescompany: Oh dear.

Biggirlsdontcry54: Terrible. So sorry, honey.

Makeupyourmindcontrol: Sending you hugs and love.

Woundedhealer: I'm still trying to process it all.

MaxineKD: So sad.

Miserylovescompany: Were you close with this person, Woundedhealer?

Woundedhealer: I didn't even know her.

Makeupyourmindcontrol: That's difficult. Sometimes we don't realize how little we know about the people in our lives until they are gone.

Harmnoone82: *Is now offline.*

Miserylovescompany: Looks like we lost Harmnoone82 . . .

MaxineKD: So much for the long goodbye.

Biggirlsdontcry54: More like the "Irish exit."

Woundedhealer: It was probably my fault. I can't seem to say anything right this week.

MaxineKD: I hope she doesn't stay away for too long again.

Makeupyourmindcontrol: Try not to beat yourself up, Woundedhealer. (Even if it is something you excel at.) She'll be back.

Miserylovescompany: We always come back. No getting rid of us. We are like support group herpes.

Trauma Survivor Chat Room: 10/4/19
6:45 p.m.
Private message from Woundedhealer to Harmnoone82 (offline).

Woundedhealer: H, I'm sorry. I don't know what I was thinking. It has been a confusing week. I hope you can accept my apology. You've been so supportive and kind to me in this group, and even though we've never actually met, I sometimes feel closer to you than some of the friends I have in real life. (Not that this isn't "real," but you know what I mean.) Hope things are okay with us. X WH

NINETEEN

RACHEL

Before I can pull into a spot, he idles his Mustang alongside my car in the 7-Eleven parking lot. His cigarrette is burning down to the filter between his fingers, but he doesn't seem to notice. I have the briefest indelible nicotine craving, even after a decade of not smoking. There are a few things I'll never be completely free from, and the desire to smoke is one of them.

Our cars are facing in opposite directions, and to the casual observer, we might look like undercover police officers, or shadier characters brokering something only suited for a convenience store parking lot.

I'm surprised he was able to identify me so quickly, since we have never seen each other outside of our usual setting. But then I realize he knows my car. I lower my window and say, "Hey," and he looks to his left and right dramatically.

"Follow me, it isn't safe here," he whispers before he pulls out of the parking lot slowly. I pull a U-turn and follow his lead out of the exit and toward my house.

As he pulls into my driveway, I'm momentarily nervous. I've never had him over to my house; I've always gone to him. I don't tell many people where I live for good reason. But of course he knows my address for the same reason he knows my car.

He gets out of his car and zips his jacket before donning chrome Ray-Bans and a skullcap.

"Why the theatrics?" I jokingly accuse. He's left his car on and the bass of some indecipherable seventies rock ballad serves as our soundtrack.

The temperature has dropped significantly since this morning. I stand against the hood of my car and lean into the heat from the engine. I'm tempted to invite him inside, but I don't want this encounter to last longer than necessary, and Charlotte's expecting me for dinner.

"I could get fired for this," he says as he hands me a manila folder.

"I know. I'm sorry." I accept it, unsurprised that it's as scant as it is.

"Whatever. I fucking hate this job anyway. Gotta pay the bills, though."

"Thank you so much, Matty." I put a grateful hand on his shoulder and he blushes. I know he is hoping for something more than our casual acquaintance, but he's not even friend material, let alone anything more. He's a child, for starters, and his taste in music (while from the same era as I am) is as misguided as his willingness to steal from his job.

"I don't know how helpful this will be. I wasn't able to find *anything* on this dude."

"That is exactly the reason I asked you to do this." I flip the file open and take a quick look at the single sheet of paper inside. "A-plus, bud."

He beams. I don't think he's gotten many high marks in his life. He means well, but he's definitely short on some of the life basics.

"Can you send this info to me via email as well?" This is what I'd asked him originally, but he pushed for an in-person meet-up, probably in the hope of a quid pro quo arrangement. Plus, there isn't a lot of excitement around here in general, and I could sense his craving the need for intrigue. We all want to feel like our lives are more important and exciting than they actually are. Truth is, I don't think anyone at his job is paying enough attention to the on-the-clock goings on, let alone the extracurriculars of their disgruntled employees.

"Oh yeah. No problem." He pulls out his phone and touches the screen a few times. I feel my own phone vibrate in my coat pocket.

"Thanks again, Matty." I look toward his car and hope he gets the hint.

"Anytime. Hope you get the bad man, whoever he is." I nod seriously and he seems pleased. We stand for a minute until he finally catches the cue and leans in for an awkward hug, which I sidestep completely. Embarrassed, he gets into his car and revs the engine.

I wave lightly as he drives away, and once he is out of sight, I pull my phone from my pocket, remove my gloves, and click into my email to make sure it's come through. Matty's work email address is at the top of my messages, with the subject line PETER STANTON. I click on it to see what I already hold in my hands. It feels good to have the truth in all forms.

I just need to figure out how to break the news to Charlotte.

TWENTY

CHARLOTTE

RACHEL LOOKS ABSOLUTELY POSSESSED. Her eyes are as wild as her hair when she blows through the kitchen door with a large bunch of alstroemeria and an armload of Whole Foods bags. Her expression softens slightly when she meets my eyes, and she quickly twists her pensive look into a smile, as if I've caught her by surprise being in my own kitchen.

"Hi! Sorry I'm late. It feels like hurricane weather out there. Perfectly atmospheric for the coven meeting tonight." She laughs hard and drops the grocery load onto the table before going for a vase on the top of the fridge.

"Everything okay?" It isn't like her to be late—it's half an hour later than we planned. But no sooner do I have the thought than I realize that she has been late a lot recently, and cagey about why. I'm fighting the sick feeling in me that she's pulling away from me like everyone else in my life.

She hesitates just slightly before responding. "Yeah. Everything is fine. I just had an appointment go later than I expected."

"Oh, I didn't think you had anyone on the schedule today." I'd just looked at the shared calendar earlier in the day and she wasn't due for any clients this evening.

"It was a late addition. I didn't put them into the system." She is busying herself with the groceries and not looking at me. "I'm the first to arrive?"

"The only. I'm pretty sure you need at least four to constitute an actual coven, so that is out for this evening." I say this drily to mask the very real pain I'm feeling over the ongoing group rejection of my friend circle.

"No word from *anyone*?" She shakes her head. "Well, we don't need them. We'll conjure the four winds just the two of us, then."

We aren't actually witches. We are a monthly women's group that I'd been successfully hosting for more than two years, with a collection of smart, thoughtful women in the area who needed to get together with other women to decompress, laugh, and vent. Most of the women are friends from growing up who stayed in town or came back.

It especially is an escape for the mothers of the group, who are the majority. "The coven" is what Rachel's most recent ex, Eric, called our group. The label stuck longer than he did. The nickname was less affectionate than it actually was backhanded and, frankly, misogynistic. She broke it off with him shortly after he made the comment. Him stealing all of her jewelry contributed as well.

"Fine with me. Honestly, I wasn't in the mood for a big group tonight. Glad to just hang with you." She already seems lighter than when she walked in the door, and I have a nagging feeling of irritation that she isn't as frustrated by the group's unexplained silent treatment as I am.

She must sense this and she shoots me an empathetic smile. "Don't worry. Whatever the reason, they will come around. This can't be about anything you did—you haven't *done* anything. Don't take it on."

"Maybe. But I don't understand why they are cutting me off. I'd like to know. If I did do or say something wrong, I'd like the chance to apologize."

"Apologize for what exactly? People have things going on. You don't know what each of them is dealing with as far as kid stuff and work."

"Yeah, I don't know. I was taken off the endless text stream about kids and husbands."

"But that group text was annoying you," she reminds me. She's right, but now that I've been removed from the nonstop updates about childcare and marriage dramas, strep throat and diarrhea, I miss being included.

"It was, but I'd rather the constant updates and griping than the radio silence. This feels intentionally exclusive."

"If that is what is going on, then it's some high school mean-girl shit, and they are all being exclusive and petty. You don't need that in your life, honey."

There are moments when Rachel lets down her love-everyone earth-mother vibe and I catch glimpses of the anger and bitterness that lie beneath. There has always been a thin layer of tension between Rachel and the rest of the women's group. But I've never brought it up for fear that acknowledging it would make it worse.

"I guess," I concede. But the group rejections cut deeply and feel like another heavy sandbag of disappointment in the growing pile.

"My blood sugar is on the floor. I need to eat something. How's the hummus coming?" she asks.

I add more roasted garlic and sea salt to the pulverized chickpeas and give the Cuisinart another pulse of power until the consistency looks right. I unplug the processor and dredge a carrot stick through the mixture before handing it to her. She accepts it gratefully.

"Maybe a smidge more tahini?" Rachel licks her fingers and then arranges the flowers she's brought. When she's satisfied, she pulls her curls into a bun before starting to unload her bounty onto the countertop. I left Peter's arrangement at the office, knowing that the flowers would only garner excitement and unanswerable questions from the women who were supposed to attend tonight.

I survey the spread. "This is a lot of food for just the two of us. Maybe we should scale back on the menu?" It's hard to conceal the disappointment in my voice.

Rachel nods. "Let's just make the roasted veggies and the mushroom steaks. We can skip the guac and salad. I'm starving, so I'll make short work of the hummus. Oh, and I brought those raw chocolate truffles you love."

"I thought you were cutting out the all evil sugar?" I tease her.

"I've decided to give up giving up sugar. Life is too short to deprive myself," she declares.

I don't have the heart to tell her how sick of the raw chocolate truffles I am. And the regular appearances of sprouted bread, which isn't really bread, and the gritty cashew cheese. I'm sick of the "healthy" food that doesn't taste like food. What I really want is a cheeseburger and a Diet Coke. My medical school diet. "Great. Love those."

Rachel is unscrewing a bottle of bubbly water and pouring two glasses full. I uncork a bottle of organic pinot noir while she toggles Pandora to set a new station without asking. She puts on the Greg Scott station, which I always listen to, so I don't protest. Our shared favorite song starts and we both say "yay" and "turn it up" at the same time.

Rachel sings along as I spoon some of the chickpea mix into a bowl.

"A moment I will not forget / We met our match, the day we met;

"We shared a laugh, we shared a brain / You drove me nuts, you kept me sane.

"We leapt at the sky, howled at the moon / We whistled, we sang the same sweet tune;

"You might have known before I did / What it means to love, what it means to live."

While I watch her and realize how self-absorbed I've been and how little I've been checking in with her about what is going on in her life, I belt out the chorus with her and we laugh-sing at top volume together.

"My rock, my heart, my air, the part / Of me that sees the light, the ease / You set me free, aflight, abreeze / Can't tell you what you mean to me."

"Come sit down and talk," I say to her gently. "I feel like I don't know what is going on in your life."

She reaches for a carrot, and we both laugh as she dramatically begins singing into it while spinning around the kitchen. She serenades me while I abandon trying to talk during the song, and instead wash the portobellos. She has a great voice and I let her have the spotlight.

"The inside jokes, the smiles, the tears / You're the balm that calms my fears;

"You get to me, you let me be / You lend a smile, you let me grieve.

"You're a part of me that will never leave / In my bones you live, you breathe;

"Away from the crowd, you're never alone / You're on my mind when I get home."

I turn to face her and see that her eyes are filled. I reach for my phone to lower the volume as the chorus comes on again, but she grabs it from me and continues the performance. I watch, mouthing the lyrics along with her but letting her bring it home.

"Woke from a dream, was soaked in sweat / I'd never known you, we'd never met;

"I'd never known how sweet life gets / When you find the piece that fits.

"The one who sees you, knows your soul / Knows each part and loves you whole.

"I'd never said, to my regret / How much I love you, my best friend." She sweeps her arms upward in a dramatic finale before opening them for a hug, which I oblige. When I break away we laugh hard as she bites the top off her carrot microphone before collapsing into a chair.

"You definitely missed your calling." I slide into the chair next to her and we take a moment before recovering from our giggling fits. It feels so good to laugh.

"Okay, will you now tell me what you've been up to?" I look at her expectantly.

"Hmm." She looks down at her hands. "There's not much new with me."

Her laid-back response stings. "Oh. Okay. Are you sure?" Her phone chirps and she scoops it up quickly before I can see the screen. She reads something and I swear I see her recoil slightly before she puts it in her bag. "Sorry."

"Everything okay?"

"Oh yeah. Totally." She walks over to the unbagged produce and starts chopping cilantro as though she hasn't just been singing and dancing around the kitchen. "Any word from the detective?" she asks, clearly looking to take the focus off her. I concede.

"Actually, he and his partner, Detective Wolcott, came to the office today."

Rachel raises her eyebrow. "I missed them? Darn. What's the partner like? Is Wolcott a he or a she?" She pauses chopping to grab another carrot and holds it like a cigarette.

"He. And suspicious. Or maybe 'inquisitive' is a better word."

"Well, that is his main job requirement, no?"

"True. But, I felt like he was overly skeptical of me for some reason."

"He's probably freaked out by acupuncture. Men usually are, especially uniform-wearing men."

"Even so, I wasn't trying to put needles in him. I was trying to be helpful."

"So what is there to be suspicious of?"

"Well, my name is being attached to a dead woman that I have no recollection of, for starters. And I was jumpy before they even got there."

"You have nothing to hide." There is the slightest touch of doubt in her voice when she says this.

"I didn't make a good first impression with Wolcott, or second impression with Silvestri."

"That doesn't sound like you, Char."

"I was on edge, I guess. And there were the flowers. They had questions and I had to lie about who they were from. I said you sent them."

She instinctively looks at the bunch she's just lovingly positioned. "What flowers? I'm confused—"

"Peter sent flowers."

Rachel's face contorts. "Oh. Wow. That's news. Is he back?"

"He's not back; he just sent a bouquet."

The mood in the room has changed substantially, the lightheartedness being replaced by thick tension.

"Where is he? What did the message say?" She seems to have forgotten about the detectives altogether.

"His work assignment is taking more time than he originally thought."

"Of course it is," she says to the carrot.

"Rach, his job is important to him. It isn't his fault or choice that he is going to be away for longer than he expected." The defensiveness in my voice makes me question my own faith in the matter.

"Whatever his job actually is." Her words are razors.

Sometimes, I wish I'd never told Rachel about Peter.

She begins to arrange the portobello steaks on a cutting board and rains Himalayan salt and black pepper down on them. I busy myself with slicing veggies and retrieving the skewers from the utensil drawer. We work in silence for a few minutes and the sounds of a haunting piano melody build in the background.

"Let's talk about something else, okay?" The phrasing as a question is only to suggest that I'm being considerate of her opinion on the matter. I am not. We are absolutely going to change the subject.

She turns her gaze out the window, the last of the daylight fading quickly. "Fine. Back to the detectives . . . What's the latest on the dead woman?"

I shoot her a disapproving look. She's been oddly cavalier about this very grim situation, and it's irking me.

"They said they are getting close to figuring out what happened to her. They have some leads."

"Huh. They came all the way to your office just to tell you that?"

I feel the patience slip from me at the same time as the knife slides from my hand and clatters to the floor. "Oopsie!" Rachel exclaims and goes to retrieve it.

"*Leave it,*" I yell.

Rachel is startled and takes a step away from me. She raises her arms in a gesture of "What?" and then into a pose of defense.

"Char? What is it?" She's wide-eyed. I suddenly feel foolish.

"Sorry. I don't know what is wrong with me. I'm so frazzled. I miss Peter. This business with the dead woman is awful. I definitely don't love having detectives showing up at the office—even if they are well-meaning. I'm having a hard enough time getting new clients and keeping them. And . . ." My brain is spitting out words, but I am unsure if I want to really get into things with her.

"And?" Rachel has taken a seat at the table and has clasped her hands in her lap, waiting, like she knows what is coming. "Are you upset with me about something?" I sit across from her and mirror her body language.

"I feel like you are being more negative about Peter than usual. You've never even met him, Rach, but you act like you know him better than I do." She opens her mouth to counter this, but I hold up my hand to stop her. "Every time I bring him up, you become really judgmental."

I look down at my hands on the table instead of meeting her eyes. I immediately begin to doubt everything I've said before she can respond. She is quiet for a long time and then clears her throat.

She pulls her phone out of her back pocket and clicks around, and I feel a surge of annoyance that she's decided to start texting in the middle of this conversation. After a moment, she hands the phone to me.

Onscreen, there's an email from a name I don't recognize at the top—MathewHart@usdmv.com, subject line PETER STANTON. I'm unable to read anything beyond that, the anger is so blinding.

"What am I looking at?" I am tense all over at the sight of his full name.

"Someone I know works at the DMV. I asked him to run Peter's name through the database after I tried to find him on one of those online background-check sites." She pauses to gauge my response. I have no words. "There was no trace of him," she finishes.

My face is burning and all the saliva in my mouth has evaporated. I stand to get some water and reach for a glass of freshly poured pinot noir instead and drink it down in two giant swigs.

"Whoa, Char, slow down." Rachel stands and moves to put her hand on my arm, but I shrug her off and move to the other side of the kitchen.

"Rachel. What. The. Hell?" My head is pounding and I can taste a migraine coming on. "Why the hell were you doing a background check on Peter?" In all our years of friendship, this is the first time I've raised my voice to her. It feels awful. "Is this why you've been acting so secretive lately?"

"I—I—I was concerned, Charlotte," she stammers. "It seems like the more you told me about him, the less it made sense. People typically get *more* information the longer they date someone. Maybe you haven't been telling me everything you know, but based on what little you've shared—and, come on, we tell each other everything—things were not adding up."

"How dare you?" I'm so furious I can't see straight. "I didn't ask you to do any of this. This is such an invasion of privacy, Rachel." She looks like I've smacked her.

"Char, I know you are angry. And I understand why you feel that way. But can you be logical right now?" she reasons, her defensiveness less than a few moments ago.

I am speechless. I start pacing around the kitchen.

"Let's look at this objectively. What do you really know about this guy? He's got a government job, *allegedly*? Have you seen any proof? He's completely offline. He's a phantom. No trace of him anywhere. He uses *burner cell phones*?! He doesn't *believe in credit cards*?"

"I'm not going to go point by point with you on this, Rachel. This actually isn't any of your business."

She's determined. "You've never seen where he lives. What about any friends or family? He claims he's originally from Chicago, but there is no one with his name from the state of Illinois or nearby, remotely in his age range. If he actually lives in Quantico now, there is no trace of him whatsoever. I had a bad feeling about what I might find out, and that terrible sense only doubled when I put him into the background-check system and there was no sign of him *at all*. Doesn't that worry you?"

"How about you be logical? He works for the *US government*." I'm spitting, I'm so enraged. "Why would you be able to find anything about him online? Why would *anyone*? Those online services are bogus and don't have all the information; he's said so himself." She guffaws at this, but I am just as driven to have the last word. "Why would they make it easy to just look him up on some low-budget search site? Use your head." I hear my mother's voice coming out of my mouth and cringe.

"Right. But the Department of Motor Vehicles should. Which is why I asked my friend to do me a favor after my search came up empty. I thought you would want to know if this guy you have been obsessing about for a year isn't who he says he is. I did this to protect you."

I've never heard Rachel yell, and it's jarring. I'm shaking because she's hit an already raw nerve with a hammer. I won't admit it to her, but she's not confirming anything that I haven't already thought about.

"You need to leave." My voice is cold as I turn the fury at myself on to her. I turn away so that I don't have to look in her eyes. The wind has picked up and the chimes hanging outside of the kitchen door are twisting and clattering at full volume in the absence of her response.

"Charlotte. You are my best friend in the entire world. I care about you. I'm worried. I have a really bad feeling about this man."

I remain silent.

"Char. Please. It's like he doesn't even exist. Don't you want to know who he really is?"

I close my eyes tightly before the first wave of tears starts to pour down my face. "I cannot do this with you." I turn my back to her. "Good night, Rachel."

I don't open my eyes until I hear the sound of the door click behind her. Blood rushes in my ears so loudly, it sounds like I'm in a wind turbine. A moment of panicked regret seizes me and I move through the house and throw open the door as she's backing her car out of the driveway. She sees me and stops.

I walk up to the driver's side and she lowers the window, her eyes hopeful.

I hold my hand up to stop her moving any closer back in my direction. "I'm still pissed at you."

She nods and meets my eyes. "Okay. I understand." She looks devastated. "I'm sorry, Charlotte. I thought I was doing something good. I'm trying to protect you."

"I can take care of myself, Rach." As I say it, I wonder.

"I know you can. But I am worried. You could get really hurt by this person."

"I need to process this more before I say anything that I'll regret," I say truthfully.

"I completely get that. Do what you need to do." She's deflated that I'm not inviting her back in, but if anyone should appreciate me having strong boundaries, it should be her.

"I didn't come out here to talk about this more." I kick a rock near my foot from the driveway into the grass.

"Okay." She sighs. "Why did you come out here, then?"

"I wanted to make sure you . . ." I soften. "Just text me when you get home, okay?"

❖ ❖ ❖

After she's gone, I sit in the cold evening air on the steps, shivering without my jacket, unable to motivate myself to go back inside. I'm still flaming from our interaction. The bamboo wind chimes directly above me are twirling fast. I have so many fearful thoughts. I deeply believe in the power of reaping the energy that we put out into the world, and I feel betrayed by the major imbalance of new doubt, tragedy, and rejection that is swirling around me. I've only tried to be loving, positive, and supportive and have been met with resistance, rejection, and death. I feel adrift and lonely. I feel desperate for Peter to respond and tell me that everything is going to be okay. I close my eyes hard and wish for him. I feel my phone move in my hand. Hope blooms.

Home safe.

I'm sorry.

I start to respond and my disappointed anger halts me. I put my phone facedown on the step next to me and listen to the hollow wood pipes knocking against one another. For the first time in our friendship, I don't reply.

TWENTY-ONE

SILVESTRI

"CAN YOU GIVE the clicking a rest, partner?"

Wolcott's voice tugs me out of my head. "Huh?"

"You've been fiddling with that thing incessantly," he says, nodding toward the Bic pen in my hand. "It's fraying my nerves."

We're in the parking lot of the shopping center in Smithtown, sitting in the unmarked car in front of China Panda, clocking the office next door. "Still trying to figure out how a dead woman manages to place an order for a flower delivery."

"You and me both," he says. "Someone's leading us in circles here."

"Circle's gotta lead somewhere." I can feel the tension in the hinge of my jaw.

"I requested the call records for that morning from the phone company. That should help clear this up."

"Yeah," I grunt.

"What's got your beak in a vise?" He laughs. "You seem to be taking things awfully personally."

"This case is just throwing me off. Don't mind the mood."

He cocks a brow in my direction. "You sure you're not getting a little too close to this thing?" he asks. "The mirror's not getting a little fogged?"

"Ah, jokes."

"Maybe you've got a thing for dangerous broads." He chuckles.

I shake my head and stifle a laugh. "Man, I couldn't even tell you my type anymore."

"Oh." He brightens up. "The missus has been on me to have you over to the house for dinner."

"What, she wants to set me up?"

He waves off the thought. "Nothing like that. She just wants to get to know you. I think she has this picture in her head of you living in a cave and drinking bat's blood or something."

"And what in the world would have given her that idea?"

"I may have used the term 'brooding' to describe you," he says.

"Me?!" I shake my head. "I'm an absolute fucking delight, Wolcott."

His laugh is cut short by a flash of action from the door we're scoping out. Charlotte Knopfler exits the office and walks toward the green Prius parked a few spots away from us. We wait for her to drive off before we exit the car.

∲ ∲ ∲

"Ms. Sherman, is it?"

She barely pays Wolcott's inquiry any mind as she takes my hands in hers and studies me intently. "You must be Silvestri?"

"Your reputation precedes you," he cracks. "And I'm his partner, Detective Wolcott." He extends a hand to Rachel Sherman, who takes it with her right while keeping hold of mine with her left. I wonder if we're about to be pulled into a meditation circle.

"Detectives, I'm afraid you've just missed Charlotte. She ran out for lunch."

"That's a shame," I say.

"She'll be sorry to have missed you." She offers a warm smile. "Oh, any news on that poor woman you found? Char's been filling me in."

"We've got some solid leads," says Wolcott, nodding.

"It seems like such a wild case. I don't mean to be morbid, but I'm so intrigued."

"Join the club," he says, half a grin on his face. I watch his eyes sweep over to the floral arrangement. "Say, my partner and I were in yesterday admiring the flowers you surprised Ms. Knopfler with."

She inhales deeply and smiles. "It's so important to be surrounded by vibrancy and life in one's work environment, don't you think?" She catches herself. "I'm sorry. That was an insensitive thing to say to you both."

"Well, it's not all murder and mayhem," he responds. "In fact, my partner here is something of a green thumb. You've got that in common, I guess."

She shakes off the thought. "I'm no expert. I just enjoy the energy that flowers bring to a room."

"Don't be modest," I say. "You must know a good deal. I mean, you don't just stumble into ghost orchids without knowing what you're looking for. They're quite rare."

"Oh." She hesitates. "Yeah, right. Actually, Char knows a lot more than I do. I just try to pay attention to the names that she mentions. And those are her favorite."

"I see," says Wolcott. He holds her gaze for a long moment.

Her eyes finally shy away from his and find mine. She smiles again, but it's lost a bit of its luster. "Well, I'm sorry again that you missed Char." She's well versed in deflection, a tendency I recognize. "Is there anything I can pass along to her?"

Wolcott looks to me, then back to her. "Just mention that we were here and that we'll be in touch soon."

"Of course. And thank you for stopping by." She crosses to us and places a hand on each of our shoulders. She smiles as she gently nudges us toward the door.

"Thank you for your time, Ms. Sherman," I say.

"Of course." She beams as we exit the office. "And, please, call me Rachel. May you both have a blessed day."

✣ ✣ ✣

"Last chance for some lo mein," he says, nodding in the direction of the China Panda as we climb back into the unmarked.

"I'm going to hold off." I key the ignition and throw the transmission into reverse.

"Nice work in there, partner." He grins. "I gotta ask, are ghost orchids a real thing?"

"Oh, they're stunning," I say, backing out of the space. "But there were none in *that* arrangement."

"I see." He looks off. "And why, do we think, is Rachel Sherman lying for Charlotte Knopfler?"

"That woman's got some secrets," I say. "And a past. I'd bet big on that." I don't explain to Wolcott how my time in a twelve-step program has made it easy to suss out people of a similar bent.

"Well, let's pull her sheet and dig around a little. See what we can find."

TWENTY-TWO

CHARLOTTE

"CHAR, THANK YOU SO MUCH for fitting me in. I hate calling you so last minute, but I could barely move." Annelise winces as she pulls herself up on the table and I help her roll onto her stomach. She nestles her face into the open headrest and lets out a groan as her pelvis gives in to gravity.

Her pulse and tongue indicate far more than an inflamed lower back, one of the most common manifestations of major stress in people's bodies. And hands down one of the most common complaints among new patients. But Annelise is not a new patient. She was a high school friend with whom I was so grateful to reconnect when I first moved back in with Mom, and she's been coming to me since I started the practice. I'm more than a little hurt about her bailing on last night. But as her acupuncturist, I need to leave my hurt feelings outside the door.

"Of course. I can get you feeling better." I move her hips gently so that she's aligned on the table, and start with some calming needles along her periformis point.

"I can't believe how quickly the pain came on. I sneezed this morning and, bam, I was crippled. I guess this is what forty looks like."

"Trust me, it isn't just you. Everyone walking in here is feeling it. The fall-into-winter season in particular brings on back pain and tightness." I'm aware of how stilted my speech is. I'm having trouble finding my usual warm and cheerful bedside manner.

"I'm sorry I missed last night. Aidan had a terrible cough and the twins were both colicky beyond belief. I couldn't leave Lucas alone with

all three, and we've been fighting a lot about equal-effort co-parenting."
Her voice quivers. "Forgive me. I'm very sleep deprived and cranky."

"Of course. I totally get it." I don't like hearing that her kids are sick
or that she's having a hard time with her husband, but I am relieved that
her excuse for last night is a reasonable one. But there are three other
women who bailed, and I'm sure they don't *all* have sick kids or partners
they are fighting with.

"How was it? Did you guys howl at the moon by the end of the night?"
She winces when she half laughs. The meeting when we were dubbed
"the coven," there was a full moon and many bottles of pinot noir. We
ended up howling at the sky. It was an amazing night with wonderful
women.

"No howling." I put another needle in to release her psoas tension
and am happy to feel the channel open up more easily than I expected.
"Actually, everyone canceled, except for Rachel." I don't hide my disappointment. "But I made it an early night. I was exhausted."

"Oh no. I didn't realize that everyone bailed—I'm sorry." She sounds
genuine, but I find it hard to believe she wasn't aware that everyone else
flaked. I know they still have the unending mommy text chain, updat-
ing one another on every pediatrician trip and poopy diaper.

"It's okay. I know it's hard for people to get away. Between babysitters
and work."

I place a gentle hand on her hip as I insert a series of needles throughout her lower-back channels.

I twist the needle in the *dai mai* meridian line and it releases, and she
sighs with relief.

Annelise, like all of the women in my group, knows very little about
the period of time after I left our town and went to medical school. My
mom bragged about it to anyone who would listen, so everyone from
my high school friends who stayed in town to the UPS guy knows all
about my going to become a doctor. But she ran out of positive things
she could say. I've told my women's group bits and pieces, but nothing

about what happened during my residency or my hospitalization. Rachel knows the most out of my real-life friends, and even then, I've left things out.

I continue placing needles in silence. I feel tension between us but consider that it's probably my own. By the time I place the last needles in her, I hear her snoring softly. I shut the lights and the door quietly behind me.

◈◈◈

Trauma Survivors Private Chat Room: 10/5/19
5:00 p.m.

Woundedhealer: Good evening, ladies!

MaxineKD: Woundedhealer! We were just talking about you.

Makeupyourmindcontrol: Happy happy hour (uncorks box o' wine).

Miserylovescompany: And what does the uncorking of a corkless box actually sound like?

Makeupyourmindcontrol: Like heaven.

Harmnoone82: Cheers.

Woundedhealer: Have any of you ever had a situation where your friends don't like your significant other?

Miserylovescompany: Does it count if *I* don't like my significant other?

MaxineKD: For sure. None of my friends ever liked my men.

Harmnoone82: A long time ago. My sister didn't like my college boyfriend. It sucked.

Woundedhealer: How did/do you handle it?

Makeupyourmindcontrol: How close is the friendship?

Woundedhealer: Very close. She's my best friend.

MaxineKD: I thought we were your best friends?

Woundedhealer: I meant aside from y'all, of course.

Miserylovescompany: Hmm. Maybe not your *best* if she's down on your guy.

MaxineKD: If she can't support your choices, how much of a friend is she actually?

Miserylovescompany: I recommend Marie Kondo'ing the fuck out of toxic people in your life!

Harmnoone82: I think you have to figure out who is more important to you. Although, personally, if someone doesn't support my relationship, I'm not sure I want to know them.

Biggirlsdontcry54: I would handle it the same way I do most things. Disengage, retreat, avoid. No drama.

Makeupyourmindcontrol: What exactly is her problem?

Miserylovescompany: It is a really tough position to be in. What doesn't your friend like about him?

Woundedhealer: She doesn't think he is who he says he is.

Makeupyourmindcontrol: All fair points. But I guess the real question is: Do you trust him?

Woundedhealer: Yes, I think so.

Harmnoone82: No offense, but that doesn't sound very convincing.

Woundedhealer: I mean, I guess I have some fears and doubts, but I think that is natural given our situation.

Harmnoone82: So, no.

Woundedhealer: Well, not lately. No.

Harmnoone82: Is the distrust because of something he's actually done, or is the doubt influenced by your so-called friend?

Woundedhealer: Mostly about his being unavailable, especially when I need him. I'm going through hard things and he isn't around.

Miserylovescompany: Maybe your friend is jealous? Is she single?

Woundedhealer: Yes, she's single.

Miserylovescompany: She might be jealous of your happiness? Or maybe she wants to be with you?

Woundedhealer: No. I don't think that is it at all.

Miserylovescompany: Sorry! I just assume everyone is in love with me all the time.

Woundedhealer: We are. :) Rachel (my friend) is very overprotective of me. She knows as much about me as all of you. She's had her fair share of trauma too.

Makeupyourmindcontrol: Invite her to join the group! We'll set her straight.

MaxineKD: Well, maybe not if you feel like she's judging you or your relationship.

Woundedhealer: I'd like this group to just be mine.

Harmnoone82: Yeah. A safe space.

Biggirlsdontcry54: Of course. I feel the same way.

Woundedhealer: And we work together, so we are already entangled enough.

Makeupyourmindcontrol: Well, that'll keep things good and complicated.

MaxineKD: Yeah, what *don't* you do together?

Miserylovescompany: Not much, apparently.

MaxineKD: She sounds like a stage-three clinger if you ask me.

Woundedhealer: She doesn't even know about the group. No one in my life does. I like having this as my own secret escape hatch.

MaxineKD: I know what you mean. I like that it is a place just for us. No judgment.

Harmnoone82: We can just be.

Miserylovescompany: (And just be in our fat pants.)

MaxineKD: Ahem, eating pants. No fat shaming.

Miserylovescompany: Sorry!

Makeupyourmindcontrol: Hey, Woundedhealer, your friend, she hasn't met your guy, has she?

Woundedhealer: No, that's part of the issue. She can only go on what I tell her about him (or don't tell her). And she's been trying to get information outside of me about him.

Harmnoone82: Why don't you tell her more about him? Or us? You can be pretty secretive.

Woundedhealer: Because he's asked me not to. And I don't want to betray his trust.

Miserylovescompany: Maybe you should introduce them. See what he thinks about her.

Makeupyourmindcontrol: There's an idea.

Woundedhealer: I don't think so. I like the idea of keeping him just mine too.

Miserylovescompany: Well, if you ever decide you want to talk about this mystery man with us . . . we are all ears (and double chins).

Biggirlsdontcry54: Yeah. Promise we won't hate on him.

Woundedhealer: Thanks.

Harmnoone82: I say tell her how you feel. A real friend will support whatever life decisions you make.

MaxineKD: I say kick her to the curb. You don't need friends like that.

Makeupyourmindcontrol: Definitely not when you have friends like us!

Woundedhealer: Thank you. What would I do without you ladies?

The alarm on my phone chimes and I make my way back into my treatment room, where Annelise is still snoring quietly. Once I've woken her and removed the needles, I help her roll over and sit upright. "How does that feel?" I can tell by her expression that she's already experiencing relief. I'm glad.

"Oh my God. Charlotte. It is *so* much better. You are a godsend. I swear, girl, you have magic in your hands. Thank you so much."

"I'm so glad. Don't go dancing quite yet. Be gentle." She hugs me hard and I stiffen slightly. The hurt from yesterday resurfaces and I realize it's because I miss her. I miss my friends. I hadn't realized how cut off from everyone I've been feeling.

"Char, what's the matter?" She puts her hand on my shoulder.

"What do you mean? Nothing is wrong," I lie.

"I can see it in your face. Plus, you can't lie to me. I have toddlers, I can spot that shit a mile away now." She squeezes my arm.

Before I can do anything to stop it, tears are falling freely. I'm surprised at how much emotion is coming out of me, and a little embarrassed. I'm not usually the one crying in my office. And I've been crying more this week than I have in a long time.

"Oh, sweetheart. Let's get you some Kleenex." She moves from the table to the nearby box and takes me by the hand to my waiting room, where we can both sit. The door to Rachel's massage room is shut, which means she came in when my door was closed. She's likely avoiding me. Muffled voices float into the waiting room. She's in with a client and I feel self-conscious sitting so close to her office and talking with Annelise.

"Would you have time for a coffee? I don't have any other patients and would love to get out of here." I expect that she'll turn me down. I don't doubt that she has to get home to relieve her neighbor, who came over on short notice to sit for the kids.

"This requires something stronger than coffee." She types something into her phone and waits for a minute for a response. "Good. Lucas just got home. Let's go get something strong and alcoholic."

◆ ◆ ◆

Annelise came by Uber to my office, so I drive us to the nearest restaurant—La Vid. It is a big date-night place, but luckily we are sliding in before the dinner rush and get two seats at the corner of the bar. Annelise has already turned more than a few of the waitstaff's heads walking in, and I'm used to it. Her former-ballerina, six-foot-one, gazelle-esque body, coupled with her flawless caramel skin, huge brown eyes, and close-cropped hair, makes her stand out in any room. She is always graciously dismissive of how otherworldly her beauty is and the effect it has on mortal men.

The bartender brings our martinis and lingers at our end of the bar polishing a glass a little longer than necessary. Annelise turns toward me and away from him, and he gets the hint and moves to the other end of the bar. We laugh quietly as she pushes her glass over to mine in a grounded "cheers" since our drinks are so full. I follow her lead and lean down to the rim to skim some of the vodka and olive juice from my glass until we can safely lift our drinks without spilling the precious alcohol.

"Okay, that's better. Now, tell me." She holds her drink expertly and pulls her shoulders back to correct her posture on the barstool. "What is bringing you down, honey?"

I take another thirsty sip of the cool, briny liquid and let it hang in my mouth for a moment before swallowing. I love the way the cold quickly becomes warm throughout my body. I hardly ever drink anything stronger than wine these days, but a very cold and dirty vodka martini used to be my go-to.

I consider what I can tell Annelise without betraying Peter. I don't want to open up the can of worms that is Silvestri and the dead woman. I start with what is bothering me as it pertains to her. "Well, my feelings are hurt." As soon as I say this out loud, the tears begin to well in my eyes. "I feel like everyone bailing last night was too coincidental not to be taken personally." I take another sip of my drink. "Did I do something wrong?" A swell of emotion rises in me. I realize how quickly the vodka is kicking in and preemptively decide that I won't be driving home.

Annelise sighs and places her drink on the bar. She is frowning and I can see she's being deliberate about how to gently deliver whatever is causing her pained expression.

"Charlotte, you didn't do anything wrong." She sighs again, pauses, and locks her eyes with mine. I see her amazing maternal side shining through. I search her face for what is coming next.

"Then what is it, Lise? It isn't just last night. I feel like everyone in our circle has gotten really busy and unresponsive all of a sudden." I reach for the sweating glass of water sitting untouched next to my martini. "And not to be immature, but it feels like everyone just flaked on my birthday. It was my fortieth and, I don't know, I guess I thought you guys would all do something for it." I feel embarrassed for bringing it up, but in real time, I'm realizing how much the absence of anything really hurt me. "Rachel was the only one who acted like she cared."

"I don't know what to say." A few people have begun to filter in and claim seats nearby and she turns toward them.

I put my hand on hers to retrieve her attention. "Tell me. I can take it."

"It's complicated. I don't think people know how to talk to you about this." I can tell that she would rather be having any other conversation than this one. Annelise has never been one for big emotional talks; she prides herself on her unemotional, type A, practical problem-solving personality. It makes her an amazing CEO and mother of small children.

The bartender glances over and barely registers my outpouring before turning to a recently arrived group of men in suits. I'm finding that with each inhale meant to contain my feelings, more emotion escapes.

"It isn't you, okay?" She's still grasping for whatever she needs to say, and shifting uncomfortably.

"Then what?" I'm impatient.

"It isn't *what*, Charlotte. It's *who*," she says.

I don't need her to say; I already know. "Rachel."

She nods seriously. "Rachel."

In the Uber on the way home, I'm glad I had the foresight to leave my car in the restaurant parking lot. I'll get it tomorrow, when the world isn't spinning so quickly. Annelise has revealed so much that I didn't know, and I'm searching myself for an explanation of how I could have missed all of it. The thoughts and feelings are so dizzying, I worry I might have to ask the driver to pull over. I have nothing in my stomach to expel, but my heart rate and increased saliva tell me that it doesn't matter. My body wants to purge something. I shouldn't have drunk as much as I did, but the bartender brought us another round of martinis without prompting, and I drank mine down fast while Annelise told me multiple gripes that the group has with Rachel, many of those things having to do with me.

Luckily, the traffic lights are in our favor and there is little traffic. It is going on eight o'clock and the autumn night is crisp. The moon is nearly full when I step out of the car and take in a refreshing gulp of fresh air.

I see her sitting on my front stoop with a medium-size box wrapped in brown paper and tied with twine sitting on her lap. I can see that she's been crying. The impulse to comfort my friend is now replaced by coldness.

Annelise said so many troubling things once I'd stopped being defensive on Rachel's behalf and just let her talk. She described months' worth of weird behavior on Rachel's part that, when assembled, added up so perfectly, I couldn't believe I'd been so clueless. Things she'd said and done, seemingly "on my behalf," but had never told me about were many. Small gestures and correspondences with the group of friends I'd invited her into that had slowly begun to erode their trust and inclusion of me, because of her. And most worrying, her erratic behavior sounded like she could be using again.

"She's weirdly possessive of you, Char," Annelise had said. "She acts like she knows you better than all of us, and in reality she's known you the shortest amount of time. And more than that, she acts like she knows what is 'best' for you. Like she's your mother and your wife, and you are a child bride in the nineteenth century or something."

I steel myself for what I know will be another uncomfortable interaction. Rachel is the last person I want to see right now. I try to walk up the driveway as gracefully as possible but I feel unsteady on my feet.

She puts the box to the side and stands when she sees me.

"What are you doing here?" I ask her, wishing I was more sober.

"I tried calling and texting, but you didn't respond. I wasn't sure if you would be up for talking, but I had to try." She pauses and gathers herself. "Char, I'm really sorry. It was out of line for me to look into Peter's life." She moves closer to me and to the side, as though she is waiting for me to invite her in. I don't move.

"Rachel, I'm not ready to talk to you." I can see the coldness crushing her.

"I hate this. I need to know that we are okay."

"*We* are not okay, Rach. We are definitely not okay," I snap.

"I understand you are upset that I overstepped about Peter—"

"You more than overstepped! And not just about Peter!" She looks as confused as she is stunned. "How could you tell my friends not to throw me a surprise party? What right do you have? You told them that I didn't want a birthday celebration but I didn't want to 'seem ungrateful'? What were you even talking about? I didn't even know there was a plan to do something for my birthday! I thought everyone had just blown it off."

Something dark passes over her face, but she composes herself. An unsettling calmness sets in and I recognize it as her default when dealing with difficult clients.

"I told them not to throw you a surprise party because I knew you were supposed to be going away with Peter that weekend."

My heart drops as I remember that part of the disastrous birthday. I'd excitedly packed and had driven halfway to the campsite where Peter said he'd meet me before I received his text that he wouldn't be able to make it. I'd spent the weekend alone in my house before I fessed up to Rachel about the canceled plans. Peter had apologized profusely and sent me a gorgeous arrangement of apology/birthday flowers, but it took me a few weeks before I recovered from the disappointment completely. And it took the arrival of the copper necklace currently around my neck for me to completely forgive him. A twinge of residual anger eats away at me.

"Instead of putting you in the uncomfortable position of having to lie about where you were going, I thought it would be easier to say you and I had already made plans to celebrate out of town." Rachel is adamant.

Part of me feels foolish, like I'm overreacting, when I hear her reasoning. It is a feasible coming-from-a-place-of-love explanation. But it isn't just the squashed birthday plans. My anger flares again.

"What about telling the group that I wasn't interested in being set up with Annelise's work friend on a blind date? Why are you getting involved with my love life?"

Rachel shifts uncomfortably. "Well, I guess for the same reason. I know how much your relationship with Peter being a secret has been hard on you, and I didn't think you'd want to have to either come up with an excuse for not wanting to be fixed up or go out with someone even though you were committed to someone else."

"But isn't that my choice? Aren't both of these examples of things I should have a say over?"

She seems genuinely hurt by my anger. She's not holding back her tears as successfully as I am. "Absolutely. You are right. I thought that I was helping you. I honestly believed that I was keeping an already stressful situation less than."

"You treat me like I'm this fragile little girl sometimes, Rach. And I hate it. I don't need you to protect me or make decisions for me."

"I don't know what to say to you other than I'm sorry."

"I don't want you to say anything," I say icily. "I don't want anything from you."

She looks devastated. "I'm really sorry to hear that." Her face and shoulders drop in unison. "I'm just trying to be your friend. Your *best* friend. The one who keeps your secrets. I'm sorry."

"You are not the center of my life, Rachel. I have other people and I need space to have those relationships too."

She grabs her bike and pulls it upright. She retrieves her helmet from the front basket and sighs. "Right. I'm gonna go."

I feel like I should stop her, but I don't. Annelise has told me too many troubling things about her behavior, and I need to take some time to sort out what is really going on with her.

Before she's out of my driveway completely, I see that her box is still on the stoop.

"Wait, Rachel."

She puts her foot down to keep her bike steady and turns back to me, her expression optimistic.

"Your box?" I say coldly while holding up the wrapped package. Her face crumples.

"It was already here when I arrived."

She turns away and rides into the night.

I stand in place, shaking hard for a long time. Eventually, I feel the pull of gravity along with the tremors of anger releasing into my muscles and joints and sit. I snap up my phone and scroll through the last three weeks of one-sided texts from me to Peter. All unanswered. I know I should put my phone down and take a walk. I'm bordering on hysteria, and nothing good ever comes from being this keyed up. But I'm this upset because Rachel's right.

I'm not being logical. Who is this person? This is no way to have a relationship. The impulse travels from my brain to my hands faster than I can find a long, calming inhale. I type my message in fast and furiously and press SEND before I can stop myself.

> Peter. I don't think I can do this for much longer. I'm starting to doubt everything you've ever told me. I want to believe you when you say you love me. But how do I know that you are who you say you are? We need to talk face-to-face or I'm done.

I put my hand on the box. Mechanically, I undo the twine and unwrap the stiff brown paper. The box inside is a shoebox and light on my lap. When I lift the lid and hold the object inside close to my face to see it better in the dark, I'm walloped by the force of recognition and immediate shame when it registers what I am looking at. The box slides off my lap, the packing contents spilling out onto the ground and the glass shattering on the walkway as I throw up into the bushes.

TWENTY-THREE

WOLCOTT

I FLICK THE SHEET of paper onto Silvestri's desk like a card dealer. "You were right."

"Great," he says, pleased. "About what?" He leans forward, picks up Rachel Sherman's rap sheet, and begins to study it. "Oh shit." He blanches.

"Uh-huh," I respond. "Quite a past indeed."

"Damn. Possession, shoplifting, trespassing . . . ," he rattles off, then continues to read silently.

"And she saved the best for last."

When he reaches the end, his eyes pop, then dart to mine. "Jesus, man."

"Yeah. Seems she copped heroin for her and a boyfriend, then shot them both up. She survived; he didn't. They hit her with involuntary manslaughter; she got herself a good lawyer and managed to get out of it with only probation."

"This is nearly a decade ago," he points out.

"Right. She goes quiet after that, more or less. Couple of speeding tickets over the last few years, but that's the extent of it."

"Hmm," he considers.

"I don't know, man. Aside from leaning into the gas pedal a little too enthusiastically, she's a model citizen of late. Could be this is a fruitless tree we're barking up."

"Could be," he says. His stare gets stuck, and he appears to be doing some sort of arithmetic in his head. He blinks, then looks to me. "Could not."

TWENTY-FOUR

CHARLOTTE

THE KNOCK ON the back door jolts me upright. I still feel tipsy and disoriented. I steal a look at my phone while I walk to the door. It is only twenty minutes after my text to him. He looks concerned but smiles warmly when I open the door.

"Evening." He nods hello and I smile in spite of the awfulness of the evening.

"Thank you for coming." I clumsily step aside to let him enter.

"I tried the front door, but when you didn't answer, I came around back. Are you feeling ill?"

It takes me a minute to realize why he's asking, and I blanch at the realization that he's undoubtedly observed my vomit in the bushes next to the front door.

"Yes. I got sick earlier, but I'm okay now." I nearly excuse myself to brush my teeth for the third time, but I hold off.

"I'm sorry to hear that. Should we sit down?"

He is dressed more casually than I've seen him. He looks good in crisp jeans and a deep blue wool sweater, topped off with a subtle dark-colored houndstooth sports coat.

"Sorry. I fell asleep. It has been a taxing evening." I can hear the light slur in my voice. *Pull it together.*

"I assumed so if you needed to reach out to me after hours." I can see him assessing me before looking around the kitchen. I begin to regret asking him over, but it's way too late now.

"Tea?" I force my voice up an octave and move toward the kettle sitting on the stovetop and spark the burner. Having my back to him feels easier than trying to evade eye contact.

"No, thanks."

"I hope I didn't pull you away from something important." I retrieve one mug from the cabinet and then change my mind. I shut the burner off but linger over the stove instead of facing him.

"This isn't really a social call, Charlotte." His voice is stern. "Your text said something had happened?"

Before he can finish, my entire body falls into a quaking mess. I cover my face with both hands, then wrap my arms around myself and sob for a minute. The weight of everything breaks me apart. Silvestri is silent, but I feel him behind me, waiting.

"Charlotte. I'm sorry. I didn't mean to upset you."

"*I'm* sorry. I had a few drinks tonight. Alcohol makes me emotional."

"It happens to the best of us."

"I didn't drive, though. I took an Uber home from the bar." I feel foolish seeking his approval, but I do.

"Why don't we sit down?" he offers. I nod weakly and he follows me into the living room and onto the couch.

"I'm sorry if I sounded curt just now. I was worried about you after getting your text." He has the familiar, terrified face of a man who has unexpectedly made a woman cry.

"Please don't apologize. I probably ruined your night."

"You didn't ruin anything."

"Now I'm acting like a basket case. I just didn't know who else to reach out to."

"I'm glad you did. Why don't you tell me what happened this evening?"

"Rachel and I had a bad fight. She told . . . All of my friends are mad at me. There is so much happening right now." I stop myself from rambling any further and try to catch my breath before I start crying again.

"And I haven't been able to stop thinking about Brooke Harmon." Silvestri stiffens when I say her name. No turning back now. He looks like he wants to say something but holds back. I feel the alcohol turn my thoughts maudlin. "Detective, do you believe that people can change?" I grasp for a little more time before I come clean.

"How do you mean?" He's watching my face.

"If they've done terrible things. Do you think they can become better?" He appears to retreat into his brain while he considers this.

"It depends on the person and what the terrible things are. But, yes, in my experience, some people can change. They have to actually do the hard work, not just say they want to."

I consider the breadth of his experiences and the types of people he's encountered before I realize that he's clearly referring to himself. A fleeting moment of comfort in connection encircles us and I nearly grab his hands and ask him what he's had to change about himself. As if he senses my urge, he clasps his hands together on his lap. "Charlotte, what's this about? Have you done something bad?"

I shift uncomfortably on the shared cushion beneath us. When I collect myself and lower my hands, I see he's pulled a handkerchief seemingly from out of nowhere and is offering it to me. It is pristinely crisp and white. I accept it gratefully and dab my eyes, relieved that I didn't bother with makeup this morning.

"Thank you. You're very nice to me. You aren't like most men."

He lets out a short laugh. "I guess I'm not like most anyone."

The need for levity is palpable. "I don't even know your first name. I think you told me the first day we met, but, honestly, I have blocked out most of that day." I half laugh, and it feels good to have a break from crying.

He smiles. "Dennis."

"Dennis. That's a nice name." He straightens a little when I say this and I sense I've gone a shade too far. I see his eyes home in on my chest. I look down and see that my medallion necklace has peeked out of my shirt. I grab the chain and pour it back inside my shirt, where I can feel the metal against my skin.

"What is the name for that snake-around-a-stick symbol on your necklace? It is one of those images that we see a thousand times but don't really look closely at. Does anyone really know what it is actually called? Do doctors even know?" he muses.

I touch the metal through the fabric of my shirt. "The Rod of Ascle-pius," I tell him, sadness flaring in me. But I'm not thinking about the symbol or what it means; I'm only wallowing in how absent Peter is from everything that is happening in my life right now.

"Charlotte. I'd really love to help," he says gently, likely sensing my wistfulness. "Can you talk about what prompted you to reach out to me tonight? I'm assuming it's about Brooke."

"There's a shoebox on the kitchen table. Somebody left it for me to-night. You need to see what's in it."

He seems grateful for the excuse to leave the room. "Back in a flash." In the minute I have alone, I blow my nose, stand and stretch my arms up to get my blood flowing for energy, and overall compose myself.

He returns holding the edges of the box with a paper towel in each hand. He places it gingerly on the coffee table and retrieves the framed photo, again with the barrier of paper. It takes me a minute to process why he does this. It's not the broken glass. It's because it's evidence, of course. I'm silent as he regards the image before him, and I can practi-cally hear the gears in his brain turning. He looks up at me. Any previ-ous tenderness is gone. He's all business.

"This is Brooke Harmon. She's younger and her hair is different. But it is definitely her. Same freckle pattern and mole above her right eyebrow."

"Yes. It is definitely her."

He examines all sides of the box, presumably for any sign of its sender. I already know it is label-less and think about the broken glass, brown paper, and twine still in the bushes, and wonder if he spotted them when he rang the bell.

"Charlotte, where did this come from? *Who* did this come from?" His tone is steady but energized.

"I have no idea. It was here when I got home tonight."

"Has anyone else been in contact with the box other than you?"

"Rachel. She was waiting for me and had it with her."

His eyes narrow. "She was here this evening? Is that where your fight took place? Are you sure she didn't bring it?"

"She said it was already here when she arrived." He pulls a notepad from inside his sports jacket, flips it open, and starts to make notes with the pen clipped to the pad. "Charlotte, I'm going to need you to tell me everything, starting with how you suddenly recognize this woman."

"It took seeing the picture for me to connect who she was."

His brow twitches. "I'm going to need you to walk me through how you knew Brooke Harmon, and who would have sent you this photograph of her."

I take a deep breath. "I never actually met her." He looks at me skeptically and cocks his head.

"Charlotte." I can sense his frustration. "You need to be as specific and honest as possible."

"I am." My voice cracks. "I swear that I am being honest."

"What is your connection to Brooke Harmon?"

I can't look him in the eyes. "I killed her sister."

PART TWO

PART TWO

Date: 10/5/19
From: CharlotteKnopfler@gmail.com
To: Braindoc67@gmail.com

Dear Henry,

Brooke Harmon is dead. The police are asking questions. We need
to talk.

Charlotte

TWENTY-FIVE

RACHEL

I HAVE NOTHING left to lose.

The fight with Charlotte has flipped a switch in me and I need to release this rage. I replayed the argument with Charlotte a hundred times between her house and mine, each time reliving her anger toward me. I need to do something.

By the time I reach my driveway, I'm so furious that I throw my bike across the lawn and slam the front door behind me, hard. One of the glass wind chimes falls and shatters on the floor of the enclosed porch, and the artworks on the walls inside shake and threaten to come off their nails. The cats scatter in opposite directions as I walk to the kitchen cursing loudly and open the Yelp app on my phone. I type away on my phone furiously and let all the words pour out of me, no filter, no polishing. I rip my heart out and put it online for everyone to see. I want them to know the truth about her. Once I'm satisfied with my words, I post it and immediately feel better.

My relapse fantasies have kicked up with more frequency in the last month than they have in a decade. If that thought persists, I know what I need to do. I walk to the kitchen to retrieve the broom and dustpan to clean up the glass on the porch.

I reach for a sleeve of Thin Mints from the freezer. Standing over the sink, I inhale the entire sleeve in less than two minutes. As I move to fetch the broom, I think about how in my young days of using, I could never walk barefoot in my home because there was always broken glass. Broken bottles, stepped-on syringes, dropped wineglasses, and thrown dishes. If I forgot to put on shoes, which I did often, I'd cut my feet walking across the pitiful apartment I called home. Early in my sobriety, the realization that I could walk shoeless through my house unscathed brought me to grateful tears. Instead of the broom and dustpan, I reach for my phone.

Charlotte's phone goes straight to voicemail. I try two more times, think about leaving a voicemail both times, and then hang up because I have no idea what I want to say.

The cats slink out from their respective hiding spots and inspect me now that I'm noticeably calmer and, more important, in the kitchen. Their aggressive purring concern is because my outburst has greatly delayed their being fed. They make their dissatisfaction known by alternately ramming my shins. They nip at my hands before I've got the spoon and can completely out of their bowl.

I pour myself a large glass of cloudy homemade kombucha from the pitcher on my counter. The pulpy mother floats to the mouth of the pitcher and then back down to the bottom like a jellyfish. The sober, health-conscious person's tequila worm. I take three sips and pour the rest down the sink. I don't actually like it, never have. I consider how much of the "healthy" lifestyle I've adopted actually brings me joy and reach for the other Thin Mints sleeve while I ponder that thought.

I sit on my couch and watch the cats feast. When they finish, they clean themselves before silently consulting each other and making their way over to me. In perfect sync, they leap from floor to lap, and I appreciate the two purring bodies on me, a warm reminder I am not alone. I got the Siamese pair because the woman who sold them to me called them "the fiercest bitches of the cat world," a description that I think I misinterpreted, and I've been trying to win their love and approval every day since. Mercifully, they know when I really need some love. I shut my eyes, run my hands through their fur, and rerun the fight another ten times. I try Charlotte's phone again and it goes straight to voicemail. This time I leave a message.

"I'm so sorry, Charlotte. Please call me."

I was trying to protect her. I hope that in the light of tomorrow she'll be able to see that. Since she's not answering, I draft a text to her that I decide I won't send tonight at the risk of seeming too obsessive. Once I finish, I read through it a few times, tweaking it until I'm satisfied, and save it.

I set the meditation timer on my phone for twenty minutes and connect my earbuds to my phone and then put them in my ears. I situate myself as the app's chiming reverberates and blends into the trippy tones of the binaural beats, alternating in my eardrums and left and right hemispheres. I sit in my chair, back straight and bare feet placed on the parquet floor. With each deep breath in time with the metallic echo, I feel another wave of worry and regret swim through me, but I don't open my eyes or fight through the deep discomfort I'm feeling.

I think that I hear the sound of a car pulling into my driveway over the meditation soundtrack. I take one earbud out, and the sound of a door opening and closing brings me to my feet for a look through the window. I'm shocked and ecstatic to see Charlotte's green Prius is parked in front, and I nearly cheer.

I open the door and start to step into the enclosed porch barefoot but remember the broken sea-glass chime. "Go around to the back door!" I yell, seeing that she hasn't reached the outer door of the porch yet. I catch sight of her shadow retreating and moving around the side of the house, stopping briefly and then continuing around. There is a tentative knock at the back door.

"Coming!" I practically sing as I sail across the open space to the back door. She has her hoodie pulled up in the chilly night air and she is turned away from the window. She is still as a statue and is focused on something in the darkness of the yard. I hesitate as a nudge of dread knocks at my rib cage from the inside out, but I ignore it and fling the door open, ready to hug her hard. I'm crying happy and relieved tears. I conjured her and she came.

Everything is going to be okay.

TWENTY-SIX

SILVESTRI

COME ON, WOLCOTT. *Pick up, pick up, pick up.*

"Hey, partner." He yawns as he speaks. "What are you bothering me for?"

"I'm on my way over to your place."

"What?"

"Look, I'm sorry to pull you away from the missus. Can you meet me down in the driveway in five?"

"Silvestri, everything okay with—"

"Just meet me outside."

I hang up, drop the phone on the seat beside me, and roll through a stop sign.

◆◆◆

He swings the front door of the house open as I pull into the driveway. In his haste, he's tossed on a raggedy overcoat and a hat with ear flaps, to combat the cold. On any other night, I'd kick things off with a *Grumpy Old Men* joke.

"This better be good," he says, shaking his head as he nears my parked car.

"Well, we just figured out Charlotte Knopfler's connection to Brooke Harmon," I say.

His tired eyelids pop wide like a pair of window blinds being sprung open. "I must be asleep and dreaming," he says. "Did you just—"

"You're plenty awake."

"You've got my attention," he says, leaning against the hood of my car. He flinches from the residual heat and slides his hand toward the fender.

"I just got back from Charlotte's place," I say. "We had a very enlightening discussion."

"Partner, what sort of off-the-clock shit are you getting yourself—"

"Don't start that again, Wolcott. Look, I got a distressed text from her and thought I'd check it out."

He runs his tongue over his lower lip, then bores his stare into me. "She's a person of interest in a murder investigation, for Christ's sake!"

"Yeah, well, we may be a step closer to figuring that one out."

There's not a trace of patience in his expression. "Walk me through this."

"So, I get over to her place, and she's obviously been drinking. Not blotto, but a few in. She lets me into the house and sits me down. Shows me a package that she says had been left on her front porch." I reach through the window and pull out an evidence bag with the photo inside. "Look at this."

He takes in the image, then returns his eyes to me. "No shit?"

"Right? She starts to fill me in on the significance of the photo. She's rambling a bit, courtesy of the sauce, but I'm more or less able to follow. Turns out that before Charlotte Knopfler graduated to acupuncture, she was on track to become a brain surgeon. But she was discharged from her residency after a patient died on her table."

Wolcott's shaken off his fatigue. "Brooke Harmon's sister," he realizes.

"Correctamundo." I nod. "She claims to have not made the connection because they never actually met. It was this that tipped her off."

"Got it." Now he's grinding. "Okay, but why in the hell would the sister of a victim of a botched surgery have the perpetrator as her emergency contact?" He kicks this around for a moment before a thought hits him. "Wait, what if Charlotte hasn't been telling us everything? What if they'd been in contact? What if Brooke was afraid of Charlotte? Had her info written down to implicate her in case something like this happened?"

"Could be," I say, even though the theory doesn't sit well. "*Or* we've been looking at this thing backward."

"How so?" he asks.

"We've been assuming that this was murder all along. But what if it was a suicide? What if Brooke Harmon blamed Charlotte Knopfler for her sister's death?"

I watch the tumblers click into place. "And instead of going after Charlotte," he says, "she turned the pain in on herself."

"Put the person she held responsible down as her emergency contact . . ."

"Knowing that it would get back to Charlotte."

"One final twist of the knife," I add. "And it would make sense that Brooke mailed the photo, no?"

"That's gotta be . . . Wait, though." He shakes his head. "We've still got the business with the postmortem flower arrangement."

"And our guy from the phone company confirmed the time, right?"

"He did."

"That's . . . I don't know."

"I hear you," he says. "And I put in a call to her cellular provider, to try to get a bead on the phone. No dice."

"Fuck."

"Listen, let's get ahold of any medical and psychiatric records for Brooke Harmon. See if the suicide angle checks out."

"Right," I say. "And I'll put a call in to Fisk. See if she can shed any further light on our theory. And let's not forget about the surgery; we've now got an operating room full of people that we're gonna want to talk to."

"Yeah." I eye my partner, who wears the unfortunate expression of a man who's simultaneously exhausted and wired with energy. I've seen this look before, often while brushing my teeth. "Also, let's drop by Brooke Harmon's place tomorrow. See if we can't turn up some answers there."

"Right. Now, go inside and get some sleep, gorgeous."

"Uh-huh." He manages a weak chuckle. "Coffee's on you in the morning."

TWENTY-SEVEN

CHARLOTTE

Peter Stanton
+6466900469

I was very sorry to receive your text. I've just returned
home from a very traumatic and nearly fatal mission.

The belief of being with you kept me going.

I thought your childish insecurities were a thing of the past,
but evidently not. How utterly disappointing.

I wish you could see yourself the way I do, but you can't
seem to get out of your own way.

I don't want to believe that this is how we end, but perhaps
this is for the best.

Goodbye. P

TWENTY-EIGHT

WOLCOTT

"You two aren't going to believe this!"

Fisk is barreling toward us as we enter the ME's office. There's a pointed fascination in her expression. It might be the most animated I've ever seen her.

"Easy, Fiskers." Silvestri shifts to his back foot to let her forge between us. As she does, she grabs each of us by a wrist, dragging us in the direction of the autopsy space.

"No, you guys really have to see this!" She flings the door open, and we approach a metal table with a brain sitting atop it. Skipping the preamble, she jumps right in. "I *just* finished my reexamination. You guys were dead wrong."

"How so?" I ask.

She eyes us, then the spread on the table. Realizing her haste, she rewinds. "Okay, after your call, I went back in to check over your body." I realize that she's referring to Brooke Harmon. Fisk nods in the direction of the brain to indicate the correlation of the organ to its former owner. "No chance this was a suicide," she says with a satisfied grin.

"How'd you come around to that?" asks Silvestri.

"Look," she says, picking up a set of forceps. She uses them to retrieve a tiny object from a petri dish and hold it up for our consideration. Upon inspection, the object resembles a small coffee bean.

"Yeah?" I ask.

"This," she says. "I found it in her ear canal, tucked in there against the drum. Nice and deep. Missed it the first time."

"What the hell is it?" My partner shrugs.

She drops it back into the petri dish, and the object makes a pinging sound as it lands. "Foreign object."

"How would something like that become lodged—"

"It went in the same way it came out," she says, snapping the forceps together twice in quick succession.

"Manually?" gapes Silvestri. "Fuck."

I look back at the object in the petri dish. "What is that thing, anyway?" I ask.

My partner, leaning in closely to the dish, beats our ME to the punch. "Looks like the seed of a plant."

ᛀ ᛀ ᛀ

"If it's not here, then where is it?"

We're standing in Brooke Harmon's empty driveway. "Good question," I say. "I'll hit up the DMV for the make and plates and put out an APB." We cross the lawn and approach the front porch. "Now, let's see what we can see, partner."

I close the door behind me and survey the scene. Silvestri joins me in snapping on a pair of nitrile gloves as we begin to take in the space around us. A modest-size kitchen sits to our right. There's a cherry dining table just to our left, with four matching chairs.

The makeshift dining area flows directly into a living room space, delineated by an enormous woven rug. The midmorning light spills through the east-facing windows and washes over the hardwood floors peeking out from beneath the rug. The place is spotless, everything organized and stacked neatly. It would feel like an open house, if not for the morbid context.

We enter the living room. A sofa sits along the right side of the rug, creating a walkway between its back and the foundation wall. Flanking the sofa are two side tables, each with a lamp atop it. A hutch stands against the wall in front of the sofa, between the two windows. Dozens of framed photographs sit on the shelves of the hutch.

We move closer to examine the photos. The frames in the center feature Brooke Harmon with her grandparents and her sister, Michelle. The images span decades, starting from infancy up until just before the tragedy. There are a handful of the sisters alone, all of them suggesting a happy, loving sibling bond. Mom and Dad are conspicuously absent from the pictures.

"Wolcott, check it out," he says, pointing. There's a noticeably empty space amid the array of photographs. A thin strip of dust-free shelf suggests that a frame was recently removed from the spot. "I can take a guess where the photo that showed up at Charlotte's place came from."

Other photos sit on the periphery of the family shots. Brooke smiles a radiant smile in the company of friends in graduation gowns, Halloween costumes, and impromptu moments. A mix of men and women in her age range, some connections appearing more intimate than others. Each of the photos is thoughtfully, tastefully framed.

"A woman after my own heart," says Silvestri. I look over to the corner of the room and see him admiring the record collection on the shelf below a turntable and amplifier setup.

"You a vinyl hound?"

"No better way to hear the music, Wolcott."

"I'm with you on that," I say. "What's the reading list looking like?" I ask, nodding in the direction of the bookshelf next to the stereo.

He sidesteps to the shelf and begins to browse the titles. "Hmm. We've got a number of gardening books. Lots of literature: Didion, Zadie Smith, Lydia Davis, Henry Miller, Erica Jong, Twain, McCarthy, Alice Munro. Bunch of thrillers, some relationship how-tos. Couple of cookbooks."

"Pretty well-read."

"That's right."

We cross along the wall and through the doorway into the bedroom. We approach the queen bed, situated at the far end of the room. The comforter is pulled down on the right side, the only thing visibly amiss in the entire house. I approach on that side, Silvestri on the left. Light streams into the room through the skylight in the ceiling. There's an indentation in the pillow on the side I'm standing on. I lean closer and find a few stray hairs atop the pillow. The other side of the bed appears undisturbed. "Looks like she'd been sleeping alone," I say.

"Hmm. Real creature of habit, on the one side and all."

"Well, most people are."

"Yeah? I usually fall asleep on one side and wake up on the other."

"Well, you're you."

"What?" he says. "That's weird?"

"I don't know, partner. Abby has her side of the bed. I mean, *her* side. The left, always. People are particular with their rituals."

He nods, cocking an eyebrow. "You guys never switch it up?"

"When she visits her sister, I sleep on her side."

"Aww," he coos. "That's adorable, Terrence."

"Uh-huh."

"Also, you shouldn't have told me that. I'm never going to let you live that one down. You know that, right?"

"Oh, what?" I retort. "You don't think I've got dirt on you?"

He sucks his teeth and looks off. "Fair enough."

We cross to the desk in the corner of the room. An ergonomic office chair sits in front of it, and a corkboard is attached to the wall behind it. I peruse the board, which has a few notes and photos tacked to it. I read a printed schedule for shifts at the community garden where Brooke Harmon volunteered.

A laptop computer sits open atop the desk, the power cord plugged into the wall. I hit the RETURN key, and the screen lights up. The page opens to her Amazon Prime account, on a freeze-frame of Stana Katic in an episode of *Absentia*. There's a second open tab for a Yelp account. I close the laptop, unplug it, and slip it into the large evidence bag that my partner holds open. "Let's get this down to Clarence. Maybe he can help get us some answers here."

TWENTY-NINE

CHARLOTTE

THIS IS NOT the normal behavior of a grown-up.

My subsequent calls in response to Peter's text have gone unanswered, and I've been utterly paralyzed obsessing about his response. Each hour that passes that I don't hear from him, the more frantic and regretful I get about the angry, alcohol-charged text I foolishly sent him.

I feel so shamed by his words that I've completely lost the thread on what I was so upset about to begin with. I'm beyond relieved that he's alive, and now I feel a terrible sense of having ruined everything just when he has returned. I've gone back and reread the words I sent to him before he responded so coldly, reminding myself that I had reason to be upset.

I know what he is doing, because he's done it before when I've thrown down boundaries that he doesn't like. He is punishing me by silent treatment because it is the most effective form of retribution when I've stepped out of line. He's well aware that when he comes back after a long-enough silence, I'll forgive everything and drop the line of questioning and suspicion out of fear that I'll push him away again. Even though I can see what he is doing, I can't seem to resist it. Though this time does feel different: I'm not sure if he's coming back—and it scares me deeply.

I'm speedy with stress hormone overload and quickly career across the line of emotional control. Sitting still is not possible, and the overwhelming need to yank a handful of my own hair out prompts me to pull it into a bun. I manically pace around my room.

I've lost half a day and I haven't moved from my bedroom or let go of my phone. It has become my only beacon of hope and my constant source of anguish.

I should return Rachel's missed calls. I should call my mother, who has called me more in the last twelve hours than she usually does in a month. But I don't want to talk to anyone but him.

I feel chastised and diminished by his text. The only other person who came close to making me feel this way was Henry, after Michelle's death. I squash those thoughts. I don't have enough room for that particular pain today.

I've limited myself to calling Peter once every two hours and have only left four voicemails in the time that has passed. I don't want to go overboard, but I need to let him know that I'm not giving up and I'll fight for this relationship. I've spent the last two hours frantically typing and deleting twenty different responses to Peter's text, in addition to the handful I've already sent.

I read his text for the seventeenth time and try to interpret each phrase for a hidden meaning. But it may be the most direct Peter's ever been with me. I'm furious with myself for my tipsiness and passing out on the couch so that I didn't hear my phone chime when the text came in.

Where I'd usually stress about my light patient roster, I am thankful for the empty schedule today. I never would have been able to make it through a session without being able to obsessively check my phone. I allow myself to call him again. The generic voicemail comes on right away. I disconnect.

I sit on the edge of my bed. All of my meditative centeredness has been replaced by grim despair. I hurl my phone across the room, where it lands in the soft nest of my clothes hamper. I hear the phone vibrating in the basket and run to get it and curse out loud when I see it is my mother calling. I'll just wait another couple of hours and try him again.

I won't give up. He'll pick up eventually.

THIRTY

SILVESTRI

"ALL RIGHT, Starsky and Hutch. Here's what I've got for you so far."

We're parked in the interrogation room at the station house. Clarence, the computer forensics analyst the department uses, is helping us navigate Brooke Harmon's laptop.

My partner laughs. "Isn't that reference a little before your time, young'un?"

"C'mon, Wolcott. Haven't you seen the Ben Stiller version?"

I like the kid. He's got a breezy demeanor, and I can safely say he's the most laid-back IT guy I've ever encountered. "Okay, Clarence. Run us through it."

"Easy stuff first. I ran her Find My Phone program. There's a reason why you guys couldn't locate it. The last time I caught a ping, it was in a spot right next to Smithtown Bay. I'll let you gumshoes do the rest of the math on that one."

"Swell," I say. "Any more good news?"

"I don't know if this is helpful, but I pulled up her Yelp reviews. There were a bunch of savage ones for this acupuncture practice." He points to a scathing review of Charlotte Knopfler's business. "I'm talking dozens of these," he says.

I nod to Wolcott. "Uh-huh."

"It'll take a couple of days for me to run everything, but I did get into her Gmail account. I can give you her log-in info, and you can jump into that on your own while I've got the laptop."

"Solid work, Clarence. Thanks a million."

"No thing," he answers. "I'll hit you guys back when I've got more."

"Holy shit, Wolcott. Take a look at this."

We're back at our desks, and I've just pulled up an email from Brooke Harmon's account on my computer. The message is bcc'd to a small group; CharlotteKnopfler, Braindoc67, aeforester, and sassystacy314— the members of the team assigned to Michelle Harmon's surgery, judging from the email. Wolcott rounds the corner to my desk and leans in to read off of the screen:

September 25, 2019
To: Brookeharmon1@gmail.com
From: Brookeharmon1@gmail.com

I know the truth. Not the story you all were complicit in telling my parents and me, but what really happened that day.

I've accepted that you will never go on record and admit your part in this cover-up, nor do I think that would make any difference in gaining the much-needed peace around all of this.

I believe that my family and Michelle's memory deserve something better than bureaucratic denial, sealed files, and nondisclosure agreements. Her life was worth so much more than your self-preservation.

It has been a long, painful road, but I'm ready for this to be done. I will stop my campaigns against you, if we can all mutually agree on closure, once and for all. I hope you can all make the decision and see beyond your own self-interest to make things right.

On the day Michelle died, you didn't just end her life, you ended mine. I'm ready to start living again. Please do your part in helping me make this happen.

Brooke Harmon

"Well, well," says my partner. "Now I *really* want to speak with these folks. Let's let our fingers do the walking."

⊪⊪⊪

"Any luck?" he asks.

"I tried the nurse. Got one of those creepy automated voicemail greetings. Left her a message. You?"

"Thornton's secretary said he was in a meeting. Took a message."

"Cool. I'll try the anesthesiologist now." I pull up the number for Annie Forester, dial, and let it ring a few times.

"*Hello?*" The woman on the other end of the line sounds out of breath.

"Good morning, I'm looking for Annie Forester."

"*This is she. Sorry, I heard the phone ringing from the driveway and just ran inside.*"

"No problem, Miss Forester. Take your time."

"*Thank you.*" I hear her take a couple of long breaths. "*Okay, then. That's better. And who am I speaking with?*"

"This is Detective Silvestri, from the Stony Brook Police Department."

"*Stony Brook, huh? How's it going down-island, Detective?*" She lets out a soft laugh at her own joke.

"I think we're getting the same weather as you," I volley back.

"*I see. And what can I help you with today?*"

"Miss Forester, I understand that you worked as an anesthesiologist at the Greater New York Medical Center several years back?"

"*Gosh,*" she says. "*Feels like another life.*"

"And I also understand that you were the recipient of an email from a Brooke Harmon recently. Is that correct?"

She lets out a sigh. "*That poor girl.*" She's quiet for a moment. "*Yes, yes, that's correct.*"

"I'm sorry, you referred to Miss Harmon as 'that poor girl'?"

"*I just always felt bad for the family. After what happened with the sister. Such a tragedy.*"

"I see. Well, I'm sorry to have to inform you that Brooke Harmon's body was discovered the other day."

"*Oh my God,*" she blurts out. "*Oh no. What happened?*"

"We're looking into that now."

"*Has the family been notified? Those poor parents. First Michelle, now this.*"

"Miss Forester, I'd love to speak with you in person if you have any time. We could come to you."

"*Oh, um, certainly. I'm at home today, if you'd like to stop by.*"

"That would be great."

"*Now, I'm up in Northport, Detective. Are you familiar with the area?*"

"We know our way around there, yes. My partner and I can swing by a little later this afternoon."

"*Okay, great!*"

I write down the address she gives me, thank her for her time, and hang up. I catch Wolcott's attention. "That's one down. You up for a ride in a bit?"

"Sure thing," he says. "But let's eat first. I just called in a lunch order. Should be here in a few."

"My man."

THIRTY-ONE

WOLCOTT

SILVESTRI AND I are finishing our sandwiches when my cell rattles against the desk. I consult the display. "Oh, hold up. It's a 212 number. Might be the surgeon." Mouth full, he offers a thumbs-up as I answer the call. "Detective Wolcott."

"Good day, Detective. This is Tate Whelan, of Whelan, Robinson and Associates."

"How can I help you, Mr. Whelan?"

"I operate in the capacity of chief legal counsel for Dr. Henry Thornton."

"Oh, I see. We're trying to get in touch with your—"

"Yes, I'm aware of that, Detective. I'm phoning you on Henry Thornton's behalf. Henceforth, I'll request that all communication directed to Dr. Thornton go through my office." His tone is overly relaxed. He wants me to know that he's not sweating this exchange one bit.

"Mr. Whelan, I'm looking to ask your client a few questions regarding a former colleague of his." I'm all nonchalance.

"And I'm informing you that I'll be acting as the liaison between your office and Henry Thornton going forward." Decidedly business casual. "Now, are there any questions that you'd like me to direct to Dr. Thornton at this time?"

"Not at the moment, no."

"Very well, then. Can I give you my office line?"

"I'm looking at the number right here on my phone."

"Great." His voice jumps an octave. Now we're old friends. "Call anytime you need, Detective. Take care, now."

"You too." I hang up the phone and snort. "This motherfucker."

Silvestri swings his head out from behind the computer screen. "What's up?"

"That was Thornton's lawyer," I say. "The cat's stonewalling us."

"Wait, he's got his lawyer running interference off of an inquiry call? That doesn't look good."

"No, it does not," I say. "Now I want to know what this guy's so nervous about." I stand from my desk and take a lap around the room.

THIRTY-TWO

SILVESTRI

MY PARTNER RETURNS to his desk, a sinister grin curling the corners of his mouth. He pulls his cell phone from his pocket.

"Wolcott?"

He nods my way, eyes dancing. "Watch this." He taps the screen, holds the phone up to his ear, and begins to speak. "Yes, good afternoon. This is Roger Papworth, of the Papworth Group . . . Well, ours is a philanthropic organization looking to invest in socially responsible interests, and I'll tell you what! Your chief of staff, Dr. Henry Thornton, has come to our attention . . . Yes, yes, we're quite impressed with Dr. Thornton's work and would be interested in sitting down with him to discuss a sizable donation to the hospital . . . He's got a full day? I see. Unfortunately, we're only in town for the afternoon, wrapping up meetings . . . Uh-huh . . . Right. Well, I'd really hate to miss him. We insist on sitting down for meetings face-to-face when discussing endowments on this scale . . . Mmm-hmm . . . But of course . . ." He covers the speaker with his palm. "She's putting me on hold." He winks and returns the phone to his ear. His head dances side to side, mimicking the ticking of a clock. "Yes, hello again . . . Uh-huh . . . He *can* fit us in today. Terrific. Just terrific . . . Four o'clock it is . . . Yes, that's P-A-P-W-O-R-T-H . . . Thank you so much. We'll see you in a bit." He hangs up. "Thornton's schedule just opened up."

"Nice. We'll drive in after we stop by and see the anesthesiologist."

"Two birds," he says.

"Hey, what's the dress code for this meeting, anyway?"

He chuckles. "Money."

╢╫╟

"Detectives, please come in."

We're standing on the porch of Annie Forester's ranch-style home in Northport. She greets us with a wide smile and whisks us inside. "Can I take your coats?" Before we can answer, she's tucked in behind Wolcott and is helping him out of his.

"Thank you," he says.

"Oh, it's nothing," she answers as she plucks mine and crosses to hang them on pegs next to the front door. "You're a pet lover, Detective?"

"Two dogs," I answer. "You?"

I turn and notice that she holds my coat with an outstretched arm. "I wish. I love animals, but I'm afraid I'm highly allergic. Please, have a seat." She shoos us toward a pair of chairs in the open living space. "Can I offer you coffee or tea?"

"We don't want to put you to any trouble," I say.

"Oh, not at all," she answers, crossing the room into the kitchen. "I've always got a pot of coffee going. Have a bit of a caffeine issue myself." There's a cut-out in the wall between the kitchen and living room area, and she ducks her head to speak with us through the opening.

"As long as it's no trouble," I say, "we'd love a coffee and a tea."

"Certainly," she says, flitting around the space. "And how was your drive?"

"Just fine," answers Wolcott. "Good time of day to get up here. Not much in the way of traffic."

"Of course," she says. "Do you gentlemen take anything in the tea or the coffee?"

"As is for both," I say. "And thank you."

I take the opportunity to size up the space. The floors are carpeted, and the art on the wall appears to have come from a big-box store. There's a long, narrow table that serves as a border between the sitting area we're in and a lounge chair and flat-screen TV on the far end of the room. A collection of jigsaw puzzle boxes sits atop the table. I notice an absence of photographs on the walls.

The sound of china clinking is heard before she emerges from the kitchen. She crosses to us, tray in hand, and pauses in front of me. She picks up the coffee cup, then hesitates and looks at me. I smile and point to Wolcott. "Shame on me," she says, shaking her head. "We should never assume, should we?"

"It's happened before," he says, smiling. "No offense taken."

She laughs warmly, sets the respective cups on the coffee table in front of us, then lays a plate of sliced fruit between us. "Sorry it's not more exciting," she apologizes. "It's too much temptation for me, having sweets in the house."

"This is wonderful," says Wolcott. "I'm trying to eat healthier myself."

"Oh good," she says, and sits in a chair across from us. As we sip from our cups, I take a moment to consider her. I'd peg her around midfifties, with a warm disposition and an open face. She's brimming with energy, to the point where it appears to take a concentrated effort for her to sit still. She seems very excited to have a couple of detectives in her home. I'm hit with a feeling of sadness as I wonder what this woman's family situation looks like.

"So," she says. "What did you want to speak with me about?"

"Well," I begin. "We wanted to follow up on our earlier conversation about Brooke Harmon."

She shakes her head. "Poor thing. What loss that family has suffered."

"Yes, it seems as if they've had more than their share," I lament. "Have you had any dealings with Brooke Harmon in the years since the accident?"

"I have, yes. In fact, I received an email from her recently. She seemed very out of sorts. Was saying something about having found out the truth behind her sister's surgery and wanting to put all of it behind her."

I mentally review the content of the email. She's more or less on point. "I see. And do you know what she was referring to? The truth about her sister's surgery?"

"I'm afraid not. You know how it is these days, with the Internet. So much in the way of wild theories and misinformation out there. It's enough to drive anyone crazy. Especially someone who was in such pain and was searching for answers."

"Of course," I say. "And do you happen to know if anyone else received that same email?'

"I can't say for sure. But I could guess that she may have sent it to the rest of our surgical team. Definitely Dr. Thornton, and Dr. Knopfler and Nurse Phillips, probably."

"And have you been in touch with any of those individuals recently?"

"Well, not exactly," she says.

"I'm sorry?"

She rises from her chair and crosses back to the kitchen. "After Brooke's email, I got a phone message from Dr. Thornton." I hear a click, and it takes me a moment to realize that she's accessing an answering machine. A man's voice, full of aggression, comes through the speaker:

"Miss Forester, this is Dr. Henry Thornton. I'm assuming that you received the same email correspondence that I did, and I'd like to remind you that we all signed NDAs after the, ahem, incident. I suggest you leave the matter alone and don't do anything stupid. Thank you."

The message is followed by the sound of a beep. "Wow," I say. "Must have been a real treat to work with."

She shrugs and offers a smile in spite of herself. "You know."

Wolcott leans forward, catching her attention. "And *could* you tell us a bit about your experience working with the team?"

"Hmm. Well, Dr. Thornton was the senior member. A little arrogant, if I'm being honest. Had a very high opinion of himself. And a real bully, as you can probably tell. Dr. Knopfler? Well, that young woman was quite impressive. She was being groomed as the next big thing. Had some really groundbreaking ideas in the field of neurosurgery. Those two were working very closely on this experimental surgery. Of course, Dr. Thornton liked to take all the credit." She rolls her eyes.

"I see," continues Wolcott. "And how about Nurse Phillips?" he asks, consulting his notebook.

"Oh goodness. Stacy was lovely. Bit of a wild child, though. There were a few incidents of pills being diverted, and the general consensus—"

"Pointed back to the nurse?" I ask.

"Yeah," she says, wrinkling her nose. "I hate to spread gossip, but it was probably the case. If we hadn't all been dismissed after the tragedy, I think they would have let Stacy go anyway."

"I wanted to ask you about the dismissal. I've read the report, and I understand that the death was ultimately attributed to an allergic reaction to the anesthesia. Is that correct?"

She casts her eyes down to the floor and purses her lips. "I'm afraid so, Detective. We did our homework, in terms of Miss Harmon's medical history. We were quite thorough. But she suffered an anaphylactic reaction to the anesthesia, and since she was under, we weren't able to detect the signs in time. It's a very rare occurrence, but it happens."

"I'm sorry to hear that," offers Wolcott. "It's got to be tough to lose a patient like that."

"Of course," she says.

"I did want to ask you about Dr. Thornton," I say. "He was the only member of the team the hospital kept on staff in the wake of the tragedy. That must have chafed, no?"

"Well." She sighs. "You have to remember that I got into medicine a long time ago. It was a much different field in those days. Female anesthesiologists were not nearly as common as they are today. It was a real boys' club. I guess I got pretty used to the men in my field being looked after, when it came to job security."

"But you were forced to walk away from a lucrative career."

She considers the question for a few ticks. "Don't get me wrong; I held on to some resentment about the handling of that incident for a time. But in all honesty, it had become a different game. Between the corporate structuring, the bureaucratic headaches, and having to wrangle with the insurance companies, I had become pretty disillusioned. I'd had a long and satisfying career, and it seemed like a good time to walk away. The hospital took care of us on the way out the door, and I've been able to live very comfortably."

"That's quite the positive attitude," says Wolcott. "Don't know that I'd be as forgiving."

"What do I have to complain about, really?" She looks around the room, a smile taking over her face. "I'm a lady of leisure, with all sorts of free time on my hands. I'm active, I'm happy, and I'm taking care of myself." She pats her stomach on the last part.

"That does sound nice," I say, setting the teacup on the table. "Now, just to cover our bases, could you tell us where you were this past Tuesday evening, October first?"

It takes a beat for her to realize that we're asking for an alibi. "Oh." She giggles excitedly, as if thrilled by the thought of us entertaining her as a suspect. "Um, let's see. Tuesday night . . . I made dinner . . . Oh, I remember! I ordered that movie, *A Quiet Place,* off of Amazon. Have you seen it?"

"It's on the list," I say.

"Oh, it's very good! Scary, but good."

"I see." I jot the title in my notes. "Would I be able to use your bathroom?"

"Of course. It's the last door on the left, just past the office."

I excuse myself and follow the hallway down to the john. I finish, wash my hands, and head back toward the living room, first ducking in through the open door to the office. In front of me is a large wooden desk, a computer monitor atop it. A rolling chair sits on the other side of the desk, in front of a shelf filled with volumes of medical books and a large collection of sci-fi novels: Asimov, Bradbury, Philip K. Dick, and the like. I take in the room quickly before dipping out and back to the living space.

As I approach, Wolcott glances at his watch and stands from his chair. "We should probably get on the road, to beat the traffic into the city."

"Good call," I say, then turn to our host. "Thank you for taking the time to speak with us. We really appreciate it."

"Of course." She stands, bustles across the room, and retrieves our coats. "And please be in touch if you have any more questions."

"We will," says Wolcott, handing her a business card. "And please do the same, if you think of anything."

⬧ ⬧ ⬧

"What's your take, Silvestri?"

We're pulling out of Annie Forester's driveway as she waves to us from the front porch. I return the gesture. "Seems like a nice, lonely woman. Felt a little bad for her."

"Did you buy her story about the postsurgery fallout?"

"I mean, that would be pretty forgiving. But retirement seems to be agreeing with her."

"I suppose. Hey, did you notice there were no photos in there?"

"Yeah, I checked out her office when I hit the bathroom. None in there, either."

"What does that tell you?"

"Maybe there's no family around. Or they're estranged? Like I said, she seemed a little lonely."

"Yeah." He laughs. "She was awfully excited for a visit from law enforcement."

"I was thinking the same thing," I say. We make the turn onto 25A and head west. "Now let's go see what we can pry out of *this* fuck-ing guy."

He side-eyes me. "You sound excited, Silvestri."

"You're the one who should be excited, pal. Wait until you get a load of my outfit."

THIRTY-THREE

CHARLOTTE

THE ONLY THING that gets me out of bed is a frantic call from Lucy, who I'm genuinely surprised to hear from after abandoning her. She's either a masochist or really suffering, and I'm the only acupuncturist in town who has an open slot on short notice. She's having neck and shoulder pain and says she hasn't been able to sleep, so I tell her I'll meet her at my office at four thirty P.M.

As I pull myself through the necessary motions of actually getting up and showering, I feel like I'm moving through waist-deep snow. The hangover/heartbreak twofer is dragging me down hard. I turn on the water and step into the shower so distractedly that I don't realize I'm still wearing my socks until they are soaked. Too despondent to bother to take them off, I pour conditioner in my hand and pull it through my unshampooed hair in what seems to be some sad autopilot self-cleaning routine. Since my brain has clearly become so preoccupied with the crisis state I've found myself in, and it's anyone's guess what I'll end up falling short of in basic self-care next, I skip shaving my armpits and legs.

I think about my first day in Bellevue as I'm getting dressed. That is the last time I recall feeling this dissociated. And that was with 10 ccs of Temazepam in my system. I've effectively relegated my inpatient stint at the country's most storied psych ward to the deepest recesses of my amygdala, but the triggering effect of this week's onslaught has jimmied that memory safe-deposit box right the fuck open.

It was Henry's brilliant idea to have me committed against my will, and my mother was unshockingly agreeable in cosigning that sheer act of self-interest and desperation of his. I was the holdout between the two of us, refusing to go along with the official incident statement in the hospital board's investigation into the death of Michelle Harmon. Henry said my "emotions were getting in the way" of my common sense, but really, my conscience was getting in the way of getting him off the hook for his part in the disastrous surgery.

I shuck my soaked socks before I step out of the shower and hang them on the curtain rod, loud drops of water plunking into the porcelain bathtub. I look at my drawn face in the mirror as I rub moisturizer into my skin and pull a comb through my limp, overconditioned hair. I had a thunderous moment of realization the day that Henry picked me up at my apartment the morning everything changed. It was under the auspices of going to a final meeting with the hospital's board of trustees, where we were supposed to be discussing the "optics" of the investigation, but in the minutes between him bypassing our hospital and pulling into the drive for the Bellevue emergency room, a distinct feeling of understanding settled in me. That clarity was reinforced when I saw my mother waiting for us at the admitting desk, holding my summer camp suitcase.

Even on the day she was committing her own daughter, she was beaming at the sight of me on the arm of a handsome doctor, no matter that he was guiding me toward a monthlong stay against my will to treat my apparent brink of breakdown.

I was in bad shape and too bereft at the time to fight either of them. The prospect of retreating and not having to say or do much of anything sounded like heaven, once I got over the initial feelings of betrayal and rage. I'd been having some very dark thoughts since Michelle's death and was growing a little worried for myself. So Henry's ulterior motives for removing me from the picture ended up being the best thing for my mental and emotional fitness in that moment. (Something I'll never admit to either of them.) What it *didn't* benefit were my relationships with him or my mother, or my career, which was DOA by the time I was released and acquiesced to being driven back to my childhood home.

Without my job, I had no purpose, necessity for my apartment, or remnants of my life in Manhattan. Henry was noticeably absent at my release. The investigation had been concluded, without my being of sound mind. Henry spoke on my behalf.

The last time I saw him in person, he was signing my psychiatric ward admittance papers, his back to me.

THIRTY-FOUR

WOLCOTT

"Thank you for seeing us."

"Of course, gentlemen! Thank you for your interest in our program." We're sitting in Henry Thornton's office. He's got a grin shellacked on his face.

On our way up-island, we stopped off at Silvestri's pad to grab the flannel suit jacket and tie he's decided on for this meeting. I assume he was aiming for an old-money vibe, but the outfit makes him look like a debauched Alistair Cooke. "Nice place," he says, slumped in his chair.

"Thank you," says Thornton proudly. "Now, which one of you gentlemen is Mr. Papworth?"

"Ahh." I produce my shield. "He couldn't make it today."

The expression on Thornton's face takes a sharp detour south. "You," he sneers.

Silvestri flips open his shield and waves with his other hand. "Me too."

Thornton places a hand on the telephone receiver on his desk. "Seems like a long drive just to have me call security on you two."

"Now, that would be the move of a guilty party," I say. "We're just here to ask you a few questions about your colleagues."

He considers this for a moment and removes his hand from the receiver. "Okay," he huffs. "Let's get this over with."

"Excellent," I say. "Now, we understand you were the recipient of a recent email from Brooke Harmon, sister of—"

"Now, there's the real criminal!" he spouts. "You should be talking to her."

Silvestri hops in. "I'm afraid Miss Harmon isn't doing any talking these days." I study Thornton's face as the information sinks in.

"Wait." He shakes his head. "You mean . . ."

"Brooke Harmon was found dead. We're investigating her murder."

He involuntarily mouths the first syllable of the last word out of my mouth, his eyes wide. "Okay, listen," he stammers. "I had nothing to do with that."

Silvestri sets his phone in front of the doctor and taps a finger against the screen. "We're curious about your response to her email: 'What's it going to take to shut you up once and for all?' That sounds, well, threatening."

"That was in reference to the prolonged harassment. The emails, the calls to the hospital. She wouldn't let up. I had to get a restraining order against her, for Christ's sake." My partner and I remain quiet. Thornton squirms in his seat. "Detectives, come on." He sweeps his hand to illustrate his well-appointed office. "You think I . . . really?" I dead-stare the guy, which incenses him. "She was trying to shake me down, and now you have the audacity to come in here and accuse me? I'm going to have your fucking badges."

"Pump the brakes, guy." Silvestri ices him, which seems to deflate Thornton. "No one's accusing anyone of anything. But I do find your interpretation of Miss Harmon's email interesting. At no point do I remember her explicitly asking you for money." He turns to me. "Did I miss something in there, partner?"

"No, no, I don't think you did."

"Oh, come on. Don't be naive, Detectives. It's always about money."

"We've read the official report," says Silvestri. "Seems like it was a pretty straightforward case of accidental death due to an allergic reaction. What grounds would Miss Harmon have had to come after you monetarily?"

"Listen, people are greedy. They always think they've got an angle, and they're never shy about exploiting tragedy when money is involved. I can't tell you how many times this sort of thing happens."

"And how do you normally handle it?" I ask. "When 'this sort of thing happens'?"

His eyes narrow. "You've got some set of balls on you, Detective."

"Just one more question," says Silvestri. "Can you account for your whereabouts in the early hours of October second?"

"Okay," he says, incredulously, "I'll play this game." He picks up his cell phone, taps the screen, and scrolls. "October second . . . I was . . ." His smug smile drops. "Um, I was with a young woman."

My notebook is at the ready. "And may I have the name of the lucky lady?"

"Let me clarify; I was with a young woman *other* than my wife."

"I see. I'm still going to need the name of the woman in question."

"Come on, Detective." There's panic in his eyes. "I'm trying to be discreet here."

"Dr. Thornton, we're in the middle of a murder investigation. Your convenience is not our concern."

"Jessica Hughes," he seethes, and reads off her contact information.

I jot it down and close the notebook. "That wasn't so hard, now, was it?"

His rage boils over, and he slams his fist on the desk. "You actually think I'd throw this all away on that greedy twit?!"

"I'm sorry?"

"You know what the real tragedy here is?" He's at full throttle. "The techniques that I was pioneering were on course to revolutionize the field of neurosurgery. That operation would have changed the face of medicine, if only the incompetents in that room could have managed to keep up with me!"

"Uh, *that's* the real tragedy here?" Silvestri is incensed.

"I had nothing to do with that girl's death." Thornton's eyes shift between us. "Okay, playtime's over." He lays his hand back on the receiver, threatening action. "You two get the fuck out of my office."

THIRTY-FIVE

CHARLOTTE

Lucy is waiting outside my office when I arrive. I've gotten here a few minutes before our appointment, but she looks like she's struggling to stand fully upright, and there's an expression of consternation when I get close to her.

"Charlotte! Thank you so much for seeing me on such short notice. You are an absolute lifesaver! I really did a number on my body last night."

"Of course." I place a comforting hand on her arm and move her in the direction of the door while she talks.

"I wrenched something in my shoulder and neck, and my lower back is killing me." She winces as she recounts her pain points.

"Lucy, I'm so glad the spot was open. It is great to see you again." I feel a tad guilty for making it sound like I had other clients scheduled for today when she called. I usher her inside, switch the lights on, and take her coat and hang it in the closet along with mine.

"Just give me a sec, and I'll get you right in." Rachel's treatment room is closed. She's not back in until Tuesday.

I open the door to my room and do a quick sweep. Happily, I left the room set up after my session with Annelise. The bed is newly papered, and all of my needle packets, swabs, Purell, and essential oils are laid out.

"Come on in." She limps slightly as she approaches and I notice her posture might tip to scoliosis. I make a mental note to ask her about her back history. She intimated that there'd been a surgery in our first

appointment, but I'm realizing now that I never got the full story because of my fast departure.

"Lucy, I just want to apologize again for abandoning you during our
first appointment. I'm still mortified." I take a seat and gesture for her to
do the same.

"Oh, it's fine." She waves her hand. "Really! I didn't even notice you'd
been gone so long until your very nice colleague, Rachel, woke me! It
was one of the best naps I've had in a long time." She laughs lightly.
"That reminds me, I have to make a massage appointment with Rachel.
She was so nice, and I'd love to spend some more time with her."

If Lucy is harboring resentment, she's good at hiding it.

"Sure. I can help you schedule that today." I don't give any emotion
away in this, but it is thick in my throat. I know I'm not going to feel
better until I clear the air with Rachel.

Lucy takes a slow and careful seat on the chair opposite me and I pull
out her file, where I've made notes from our initial appointment.

"So, there are still some basic health history questions you and I
should discuss for your overall treatment. But how about we address the
acute pain today and get you comfortable, and then we can talk more
about longer-term treatments next time?"

"Yes. That sounds perfect. Anything to get this pain gone! Times like
this, I wish I was a subscriber to the idea of pain meds, but I know how
insidious that stuff can be. You won't see me going any stronger than
Advil."

I notice how well-spoken she is and wonder if she's a writer or a
teacher. There will be time for me to pry into her professional profile,
but now I want to get her on the table and address the present pain. Both
to ease her misery and to divert my own with some distraction.

"Can you point to where on your neck, shoulder, and back are the
most painful?"

"Here." She points to the right side of her neck and down to her
shoulder on the same side, and then stands, turns around, and gestures

to her right side down around her sitting bone and right glute, indicating pain radiating down her hamstring as well. "And all around here." She chuckles. "Basically my entire body hurts."

"Got it. Were you doing anything strenuous yesterday? Exercising or lifting something heavy?"

She laughs again. "God no. The last time I exercised was ages ago." I make a note: *Sedentary.* "Yesterday I was visiting a friend and running errands, nothing too exciting."

"Okay, Lucy, I'm going to treat you facedown today if that—" I immediately see her tense up. I don't press her; I don't want to make her uncomfortable. "You know what, on second thought, let's do faceup. There are some incredible acupoints in your hands that, believe it or not, are the most effective back-pain relievers." She looks grateful. But I need to remember for future reference that she doesn't want to be facedown. It isn't uncommon for patients with certain traumas to want to be able to see their surroundings at all times. I still feel anxious facedown.

"Thank you." She moves toward the bed.

"Actually, if you don't mind removing your shirt, I can give you this towel to place over your chest. I'd love to have access to your stomach today as well."

I see the tension return. "Oh. I didn't think I'd have to take anything off. I didn't last time."

"If you are uncomfortable, I can skip it and focus on other areas."

She considers it. "If you don't mind, I'd rather not. I've got some scars that I'm self-conscious about."

"Of course. I understand." She looks grateful. "Do you need help getting on the table?"

She nods. I take her by the elbow and guide her up on the table. She moves slowly and somewhat fearfully, like a much older person than she actually is. Once she's comfortable, I roll up the sleeves of her sweater and leggings and swab the intended points with alcohol.

"You remind me of my daughter." She's closed her eyes before I've begun placing the needles. "That's probably why I just feel super-comfortable with you." She exhales as though she's been holding her breath for a while.

"I don't know if you are quite old enough to be my mother!" I laugh but also find myself getting choked up. "I know what you mean." I wonder what it would be like to have a mother like Lucy. Someone I felt comfortable with and could talk to and feel like they really cared about what I had to say. "Are you close with your daughter?" She opens her eyes and looks at me. "I'm sorry, is that too personal?"

"No. It's not that." She sighs. "I wasn't in touch with her for a few years, and we've recently reconnected. She did some really unforgivable things to me and it is hard to imagine ever being the same after that."

"I'm sorry. I hope you can work it out. I have a complicated relationship with my mom too." All of the edges on my personal and professional boundaries feel like they are getting runny. I have an urge to tell Lucy about the text from Peter. The person I really need and want to be telling about it is Rachel. I'm anxious to see her and clear the air. I decide that I'm going to drive over to her house and, if she's not home, wait for her as long as it takes so that we can make up.

"How are you feeling so far, Lucy?"

She murmurs and smiles. "Charlotte. You are incredible. Everything stopped hurting."

"I'll be just outside the door. I promise not to go anywhere this time." We both laugh.

"This time, I'll hold you to that," she replies.

THIRTY-SIX

October 6, 2019
From: cdharris94@gmail.com
To: dsilvestri@sbpd.gov twolcott@sbpd.gov

The Two Jakes,
Just giving you guys an update on the laptop. Not much in the way of social media. She looks to have gone dark on Twitter, FB, and Insta. Did turn up a chat room that she frequented. Thought you might want to check that out. Hit me up with questions.
Clarence

THIRTY-SEVEN

CHARLOTTE

WHEN I PULL into Rachel's driveway, her car is in its usual spot. Nearby, her bike is on its side in the middle of the front lawn. I am thrilled to see that she's home and exhale a loud sigh of relief as I shut off the engine. One of the strays that Rachel feeds is stalking a crow that has landed on a low branch of the tree near where I've parked. The crow takes flight when I shut my door, and the cat hisses at me as she skulks off.

I walk over to Rachel's bike, pick it up, and wheel it over to the fence where she usually keeps it. A couple of morning papers are undisturbed in their plastic bag on the welcome mat, where her two cats, Thelma and Louise, lounge sphinxlike, lazily guarding the front door to her enclosed porch. This is odd; they are strictly indoor cats, which Rachel never lets out of the house.

Rachel's bungalow is small, and perfect for one person. One floor, with a spacious open-air kitchen and living room, and a medium-size bedroom and bathroom, it has more of a California feel than Long Island. In the summer you can hear the bay a few blocks away and smell the salt in the air. In the fall and winter, it gets bitterly cold, and I can see that she's already installed the layer of insulating plastic when I try to look into the first window on the side of the house. The curtains are open, but the plastic layer gives an opaque view of the interior, and I can only make out blurry shapes and dark spots inside.

I open the door to the winterized enclosed porch and am met with a wave of heat. Both cats dart in front of me. She keeps the space hotter than her actual house, the hanging plants, various large, overgrown potted ferns, and banana and ficus trees creating a tropical feel. I close the door behind me, taking in the space. It is as eccentric and unique as she is.

Her cats barely register my presence beyond flicking their tails until I reach her doorbell, when Thelma stretches, saunters over to me, and starts working figure eights through my legs, purring and bumping my shins for immediate attention. I reach down and stroke her head in a halfhearted acknowledgment. I'm too distracted and nervous for Rachel to come to the door to muster much more. I feel a crunching under my shoes and see broken glass and the tangled skeleton of a mobile chime from one of Rachel's trips to the West Coast. The cats bat the string and glass pieces around the porch in a loud display. I do my best to push the glass pieces into a pile with the unwrapped newspaper and scoop up the sharp pieces on the fold so the cats don't get cut. I place the folded newspaper on the windowsill.

I try the bell again, and after a few moments, and no sign or sound of movement from inside, I knock hard in case she's sleeping, although this would be way out of character given her aversion to naps. *"I'll sleep plenty when I'm dead, Char. I spent so much of my twenties in a stupor, I don't want to sleep through anything now."* My knocks are met with the same silence as the doorbell.

I call her phone and sit on the porch swing listening to the unanswered rings. I calm myself, silently reasoning that she could have gotten a ride to an NA meeting or gone for a walk to the water. She could have had a date and spent the night somewhere else. I don't necessarily know *everything* about her life. Any number of reasonable explanations could be at play here, but a deep sense of unease has knotted my stomach into a throbbing ache of worry, signaling that this might actually be an emergency.

I decide to go around to the back of her house and see if she's left a door or window unlocked. Thelma has resumed her pose on the mat, and Louise hasn't moved an inch, so I pull the porch door shut behind me, closing them safely inside. They are absolutely indifferent to my leaving the porch.

When I reach the back door, I look through the glass panels before knocking or trying the knob. I'm startled to see Rachel inside, sitting in a chair in the living room, her back to the door. She is very still, with her feet on the floor and her hands out of sight, which I assume are in a mudra in her lap or at her heart. I see the telltale white wire connecting her phone on the floor nearby to her earbuds. Of course she was meditating. She must have lost track of time. I laugh out loud.

I hesitate to disturb her, but I've come this far. I want to hug my friend and apologize more than I want to respect her practice. I knock lightly, but she doesn't stir, so I try the knob. It turns easily and the door pushes inward with little effort.

"Rach?" I say, just above a whisper. She doesn't move or answer. I creep through the kitchen and into the living room. The late-afternoon gloom has settled, as does a deep rooted dread, which grabs me hard by the throat and winds its way up and down my spine. I gasp loudly as an acrid smell fills my nostrils. But more than the overpowering odor, the emptiness of the room, the absence of Rachel's essence in spite of the presence of her body, pummels me to the ground to find my breath before retching.

I have been around enough corpses to know the difference between the stillness of peaceful sleep and that of death. She's gone. But denial is a powerful coping mechanism, and the brain will allow you to live there for as long as it thinks you need to.

"Rachel? Wake up, honey." I know better, but I still pray that I'm wrong. My legs give out as my brain catches the rest of my body up with the reality of what's happening. "*No. Rachel? Rachel. Nooooo.*"

I crawl to her and grasp at the side of the chair to pull myself closer. The slight movement causes her hands to fall limply to either side. I sob openly and can't figure out who is saying "No, Rachel, no," repeating it at an increasing volume, since it can't possibly be me—I'm struggling too much to catch my breath to muster words or sounds. I fight to pull myself closer to her. I put my hand in hers, and it is ice-cold. Her open eyes are milky and empty and her slightly parted blue lips render me hysterical. There is white foam collected in the corners of her mouth and I fight the urge to wipe it away.

I lie faceup on the floor and try to regain focus. The room is spinning fast around me, my chest is heaving, and I battle the sensation of losing consciousness. I try to find something nearby to focus on. I see her phone, which I reach for and hold in my hand, knowing I need to call someone, but not remembering how to do that.

THIRTY-EIGHT

SILVESTRI

"That wasn't so bad."

We're returning to Stony Brook after a rush-hour slog on the way back from our meeting with Thornton. "LeFrak's *always* a jam," I say. "And you get that bottleneck by the Douglaston Parkway exit. I guess not too much of a drag, all in all."

"You hungry?" he asks.

"Actually, yeah. All that getting yelled at really worked up an appetite."

"What are you in the mood—"

We're interrupted by the hiss of the radio. "*Ten-twenty-three. Request detectives at seven-two-five Lawson Way.*"

Wolcott and I look at each other. "Hold that thought." I grab the microphone to respond as my partner guns it.

As we enter the residence, the hallmarks of death loom heavily in the air. There's a stale quality to the whole affair, and an eerie sense of stillness despite the cats that slither between our feet. The odor of the deceased hits my nose. I remove a vial of peppermint oil from my pocket, apply a dab under each nostril, and pass it to my partner. I recognize the officer as he approaches us. "Litman?"

"Detectives, how you been?" His time on the job has lent the kid a level of self-possession. He carries himself with a heightened sense of confidence.

Wolcott extends his hand. "Officer. Good to see you again. It's been since the Sasha Anders case, I think?"

"Sure has," answers Litman as he leads us into the living room. "That whole thing took a wild turn, eh?"

"That it did." I chuckle.

"Can't believe you guys ended up popping the Maxwell woman on a cold case after all that."

"Stranger things," I say. We approach Rachel Sherman's body, sitting lifelessly in an armchair. "So, what are we thinking here?"

"Looks like smack," he answers, pivoting toward the body.

"OD?" asks Wolcott, leaning in to examine the corpse.

"Thinking so. The deceased looks to be midthirties. Lips blue, pupils pinned," he says, pointing between her facial features to indicate the hallmarks of a heroin overdose. "Some traces of old track marks, but nothing fresh. No signs of paraphernalia. Might have snorted it? And her friend is basically catatonic, so no help there."

"Her friend?" I ask.

Litman nods past Rachel Sherman's body. I walk around to the back of the chair to find Charlotte Knopfler sitting on the floor, knees pulled in tight to her chest, staring off at something in the next zip code. I approach her steadily and ease into a squat position. "Charlotte? Are you there?"

She looks to me. "This is my fault. I did this." Her body trembles, then quickly stills again. I kneel down and place my hand reassuringly on her shoulder. Her eyes snap to mine as she clutches her chest and lets out a pained groan. "I think I'm dying."

THIRTY-NINE

WOLCOTT

"Good morning, fellas. How does it feel to be such a know-it-all, Wolcott?"

We're back in the ME's office. Charlotte Knopfler has been admitted to the hospital, and Fisk has completed the expedited autopsy my partner requested.

"Not great, Fisk. Not great at all. Both things checked out?"

"Yeah, hotshot. Cause of death was heroin overdose. And I just dug this out of her ear canal."

"Poppy seed?" I ask.

"That's right," she confirms. "Can you two do me a favor and crack this case? If these seeds get any smaller, I'm gonna need to see my optometrist and up my prescription."

FORTY

CHARLOTTE

EVERY HOSPITAL has the same noises. Squeaky wheels on linoleum. Metal instruments on trays. Orderlies walking quickly and with purpose. Whether you are in a bed or looking over one, the finite variations of sounds are ubiquitous. The audio orients me before my sight kicks in. The combination is paradoxical: comfort in familiarity and terror of the unknown.

The lead weight on my brain can only be chemical. I can barely lift my lids, and when I do, it is a struggle to keep them open. I'm back in Bellevue. My chest begins to constrict and my throat burns. I can't be.

The room I'm in is fairly large for a single, and looks different from the one I was in before. There are quiet voices outside the door. The cadences are familiar, but too distant from where I'm struggling to focus to positively identify. My optical haze lifts slightly and I can see my mother in the corner of the room, her mouth open and head lolling as she sleeps soundlessly. The sight of her in person makes me anxious and indicates how bad things have gotten. The image of Rachel in her chair reintroduces itself to my frontal cortex and I whimper into a sob. Mom's eyes flutter open and she is on her feet in a flash and at my side with both hands on my right arm. She's never been particularly affectionate, and my reflexive flinching causes her to pull her arms into herself.

"Oh, honey. I didn't mean to hurt you." For a brief disoriented moment, I think she's apologizing for my childhood.

"How could you?" Each word out of my mouth is thick and slow.

She looks confused. "How could I what, honey?"

"You put me back in here?! How could you?!" I yell. I feel like I'm strapped down and start to feel panicked. I realize I'm able to lift my arms and legs.

It dawns on her quickly. My distress must be unique to that period of time. The one time she visited me, my unhappiness at seeing her was profound.

"Charlotte. Honey. You are not in Bellevue. You were brought to Stony Brook Memorial Hospital after you found your friend. You told the detectives that you were in cardiac arrest and asked them to bring you here."

I shut my eyes tight and moan. The Holter monitor starts to chirp. I expect the rotational nurse will reveal herself in the next five minutes. I try to remember who works in cardiology from my days in the halls of this hospital, barely conscious but going through the motions like a ghost after I came home from New York.

"How do you feel?" she asks gently. I'm a ticking time bomb that needs to be handled with care. The feeling of déjà vu right now is overwhelming.

"Logy." My eyes roll to the IV drip hanging above.

"They gave you Ativan to calm you down. I didn't get here until after; otherwise, I would have told them not to. I know how much you hate being sedated. Me, on the other hand, I would kill for some of what they have you on." I can see that she is trying hard to be maternal in spite of herself. I know it is as uncomfortable for her to assume that role as it is for me to be daughterly.

"How much do you remember?" She's negotiating how bad I am this time around.

"Rachel." I choke out her name and start crying.

"Well, I don't know much. The detectives wouldn't give me any details. But your friend is dead. I'm so sorry." Compassion is an underdeveloped muscle for her, but she's flexing it hard.

"I know." I'm numb as I say this. Fat tears roll down my face, and my nose begins to run. I couldn't wipe my own face if I wanted to, though.

"Let me go find some tissues for you!" She jumps up and runs straight past a box of Kleenex on the windowsill and out of the room.

I have less than a minute alone before the familiar voices outside the door reveal themselves. Wolcott leads the way, determined. Silvestri trails him more tentatively and meets my eyes before I look away.

"Ms. Knopfler. How are you feeling?" I'm too tired for the niceties or to ask Wolcott to call me by my first name for what feels like the fiftieth time. I feel a rush of irritation toward both of them, as misdirected as it might be.

"I feel awful." The drugs have rendered me into complete emotional putty. "I'm devastated."

"Totally understandable. It's been a traumatic few hours," Silvestri says.

"Rachel," I moan.

The two men look at each other. I gather they haven't fully decided who is going to break more bad news to me. Silvestri moves closer and clears his throat.

"Do you feel up to talking, Charlotte? Can you walk us through the time leading up to when you called 911 about Rachel?"

"I remember going to Rachel's house. We were in a fight." My voice cracks. "She wasn't answering her door or her phone."

"Around what time would you say this was?" Wolcott has a pad and pen poised.

"I went after Lucy . . . my patient appointment. It would have been around six P.M."

"Okay, so it's early evening, yesterday, and you get to Rachel's house. Then what?" Wolcott puts the end of his pen in his mouth.

"I went around to the back door because she wasn't coming to the front door and I couldn't find my keys. I thought she was meditating—" I choke hard.

Silvestri pats my hand lightly. "Take your time." He pours some water from the plastic pitcher on my bedside table into a tall cup with a straw sticking out of it.

I accept the cup, and the plastic IV tether tugs at my hand. I immediately want to take it out. I push ahead. "I thought she was meditating in her chair. I let myself in and I could tell when I got inside that she was . . . dead." I hear the sentence out loud but I don't believe it. "She and I had a fight," I repeat and choke back a sob. "I let her leave. Oh my God. I shouldn't have let her leave." I put my face in my hands. "How did this happen?"

"We're waiting on the toxicology report," says Wolcott. "It looks like she may have overdosed."

I gasp. "No," I say weakly. "She wouldn't do that. She's been clean for a very long time."

They both look at me sympathetically. Wolcott speaks. "We won't know anything for sure for another day or two at least. But as soon as we do, we'll let you know. We'll need your help, if you don't mind, determining who we should contact. Family members, close friends, et cetera. We have her cell phone, so if you tell us any names, we should be able to take it from there.

I think about this for a minute and break down. I look at Detective Silvestri. "She doesn't have any family. I was her only family. *I* was her 'in case of emergency' person." This makes me cry hard. The detectives stand awkwardly, both searching the room. They overlap each other's uncomfortable voices—"We'll go find tissues" and "Nurse"—and make a quick escape. Leaving me alone to dissolve into a puddle of hopelessness. An unfamiliar and terrifying urge overtakes me. I want my mother.

◈ ◈ ◈

After everyone, including my mother, returned with Kleenex, the detectives confirmed that I would come into the station tomorrow morning to talk to them further. I am desperate for some alone time to process everything, so I send my mother on a field trip for a smoothie, something I know she won't be able to get inside the hospital. I haven't been able to convince the nurses to take my IV out, and they've added another line of vitamins since I'm not able to stomach any food right now. I'm beginning to feel like an insect pinned to a foam board for everyone to examine.

I'm ashamed at my relief last week when the body I was called to identify wasn't Peter, and I wonder if Rachel's death is a terrible twist of instant karma. I allow the unbelievably painful wave of grief to take me down deep, where I can't breathe or see straight for a few eternal-feeling minutes. I will never see my sweet friend again. I don't understand how things got so horrible that she relapsed. This can't be because of our fight. But even with that, I can't accept that this is something she would do to herself.

Agent Silvestri sweeps back into my room. "Sorry to barge in again. I forgot my—" We both eye the charcoal wool coat that he's left on the back of the chair. He puts his hand on the collar but doesn't immediately retrieve it. I'm not in the headspace to have a conversation with anyone right now. Even him.

"I bet you're looking forward to getting home. I hate hospitals."

"I don't hate them normally, and I know this hospital well. I used to work here, after I left Manhattan and moved back. But, yes, I'm desperate to go home. I'm trying to shake my mother, who appears to have developed late-onset maternal instincts. She is insisting on coming home with me." I roll my eyes to punctuate my exasperation.

"Nothing like being trapped with your mom with no place to run," he says. "At least this way you have the drug button to take the edge off." He taps lightly on the IV line.

"It's just saline for hydration. I had them stop the drugs."

"I'm so sorry about Rachel. I know how difficult this is."

I nod through my tears and shut my eyes.

"We'll need your help figuring out what happened to her," he says seriously.

"I'm sorry I don't know more," I reply.

"You know more about the way the brain operates under trauma than any of us." He continues to stand. "You may have something else in your memory that hasn't come to the surface yet. There is a lot of grief and shock to wade through right now." He looks at the chair. "Do you mind if I sit for a minute?"

"Okay." I'm too tired to tell him I'd rather he go.

"Did Rachel have a significant other?"

"She broke up with someone a few months ago. It was mutual, though."

He takes out a pad of paper and makes a note. "We may need to contact him. We'll discuss more tomorrow. And aside from the fight last night, was there anything Rachel was upset about? Any money troubles or a history of depression? You mentioned she was sober."

"Money problems, yes. Our business has been suffering. But not depression. She is one of the happiest people I know." I can't bring myself to switch to the past tense. Not yet.

I think about how all of Rachel's pain recently was directly caused by me. Our practice having problems getting and keeping clients. Our fighting over Peter. I'm just realizing now how much our friendship has revolved around my problems. I haven't been a good friend to her at all. I wrap my arms around myself to create a straitjacket against my emerging grief. I really want Silvestri to leave now so that I can wail into my pillow unobserved. But he doesn't show any signs of moving from his spot.

"Charlotte, I wanted to talk a little more about the work you were doing leading up to Michelle Harmon's death. Would that be okay?"

"I don't know. My brain is so preoccupied with Rachel right now . . ."

"We are still working as fast as we can to solve Brooke's murder, and now that we know your connection to each other, any info you can give us could be crucial."

I feel too tired to collect any more coherent thoughts, but I don't think I actually have a choice in the matter. "Okay," I say weakly.

"Great, thank you. Can you walk me through what exactly your area of study and surgical practice was leading up to Michelle's death?" I'm surprised he cares about the minutiae, but I humor him, if nothing else, than for the relief from thinking about Rachel's body in that chair, cold and empty.

I absently fiddle with the plastic tube coming out of my hand and mentally switch into a monologue I've delivered many times before. "My postdoctoral work was studying the effects of violent trauma on the brains of people before a certain age, and then again after. Looking at people who had been physically attacked before their frontal lobes had completely developed, and those who'd experienced similar traumas after development. My focus was postulating the possibility of surgically steering the brain in people who'd been injured early enough in development to repair the damage. Essentially, curing PTSD by manipulating the brain centers that trauma resides in before it fully takes root."

"What about nonsurgical trauma therapy? EMDR, neurofeedback, psychedelics, and the like?"

"This was for extreme cases. The nonsurgical routes don't always work. Some people are resistant to the other modes of treatment. I wanted to find another option and create hope for the hopeless."

"Sounds fascinating. And then you parlayed that into your clinical work?" He's been doing his homework on me, which makes me uncomfortable. "I understand you were quite a cowboy, or cowgirl rather, in the field? Largest grant to the youngest psychosurgical resident in the history of the Greater New York Medical Center. That's impressive."

His voice has taken on a hypnotic quality, which may be the influence of the remnant Ativan in my system. "I don't know about all that. But I was working on a very controversial but groundbreaking surgery with my mentor, Dr. Henry Thornton. He was the reason I got so much support and attention so early in my career." My voice catches at the mention of Henry.

"He sounds like a real mensch," he says drily. "Please, continue."

"We'd had some success in reversing the effects of trauma on some patients . . . until Michelle's death." My throat tightens and I feel the words getting strangled. "I'm sorry. I'm feeling pretty emotional right now. Do you think it's okay if we take a break from this topic?"

"Of course. I didn't mean to upset you. I'm fascinated by your work. I have some personal experience with trauma on the job as well."

I can't help but raise my eyebrows. "Really?" It is hard to picture us having much in common.

"Before I was with the NYPD, I was a rookie in Baltimore. We were raiding a drug den, and one of the perps had a knife to my partner's throat. We needed the perp alive for a number of reasons, but I misfired and hit him in the temple instead of the shoulder. He bled out before we could get him to talk. First dead guy I ever saw, and I was the one who killed him." His face is surprisingly composed for the flood of painful memories pouring out. My empathy for him is strong.

"I'm so sorry. That must have been awful."

"It was. Even though he was a bad guy by all accounts, he was still someone's son and brother. People loved him. And it was a careless accident; I was trained better than that. But for some reason, that day, I screwed up really badly."

"How long ago did it happen?"

"Oh, it was back when I was a young pup. Going on twenty years. But it's a rare day that I don't think about it first thing when I wake up. You have to be a real sociopath if the death of someone by your hand doesn't eat away at you." There is deep pain lining his eyes that I recognize. The spark of recognition reverberates in me.

"Traumatic memories can feel new, even after decades. And new traumas can trigger old ones." I could say so much more on the topic, from both personal and professional experience. This used to be my favorite topic of conversation. But I'm too sad and exhausted now and only thinking about how I'll never see my friend again. I wipe the fresh tears from my cheeks.

"I can't believe that Rachel would hurt herself. It doesn't make any sense." I'm reeling, realizing for the first time that I'm connected to two dead women.

"As a suspect in Brooke's and Rachel's cases, you are the most important person to help solve these."

The statement is a punch in the gut. *"Suspect?"*

He's unmoved by my incredulity, which makes me think his word choice was not accidental. "My apologies, I should have said 'witness.'" He watches me process.

"You think *I'm* a suspect?"

"That's what we're trying to figure out, Charlotte. And the more you can tell us about your relationship with both of these women, the better."

I am speechless, and he doesn't wait for my response.

"See you tomorrow, bright and early at the station house. Rest up, now."

I let the sting of the encounter burn for a few seconds and take in what is really happening here. They think I am capable of murder.

FORTY-ONE

SILVESTRI

"There he is."

I've just walked into the diner down the road from the station house to coordinate with Wolcott ahead of our interview with Charlotte Knopfler in the morning. My partner's seated at our usual booth near the front door. "Sorry I'm late."

"No sweat," he says. "Got your text. Went ahead and put in the order."

"Oh great. I could eat the wallpaper right now."

"Would you settle for a turkey club?" he asks.

"That'll do." I shrug.

"Then we're in business." He claps his hands together. "Oh, I got ahold of Thornton's girlfriend. She alibis him."

"Do you buy it?" I ask.

"She sounded nervous. But she was also copping to an affair with a married man. Either way, she emailed me a hotel receipt from a place in midtown, so he's covered."

"He's got her paying for the hotel?"

"It's so the wife doesn't find out. That's what the girlfriend told me. She sounded young, too."

"This guy's a real prince."

"You surprised?"

"Not one bit."

"Any word back from the nurse?" he asks.

"Not yet. I need to follow up with her."

"Okay, cool. I reached out to Clarence to set up a meeting. Sounds like he's going to have a full rundown on Brooke Harmon's laptop soon."

"Great. Thanks, brother."

"No thing," he says. "So, how'd the old 'forgot my jacket' trick go for you? Get anything fresh out of her?"

"We talked a bit."

"Whoa," he cracks. "Don't bombard me with everything at once."

"Right. Well, remember me telling you about that stash house we raided in Baltimore when I was first on the job down there?"

"Yeah," says Wolcott. "You plugged a perp in the shoulder."

"Bingo. So, I shared the story with Charlotte, but exaggerated a bit."

"Exaggerated how?"

"Less 'flesh wound,' more 'pine box,'" I explain.

"Sneaky." He snickers.

"It was important to ingratiate myself. Create a common experience in her mind, with her losing a patient on the table. Seemed to do the trick. Needed her guard down so I could gauge her reaction when I flipped things."

"How'd you do that?" he asks.

"I let the word 'suspect' drop, to see how she'd react."

"What'd you pick up on?"

"She seemed genuinely startled. Taken aback. You know how it goes, with a guilty party. The guilt betrays them. You pick up on that flash of relief when they know they've been caught. But I didn't get that with her."

Wolcott leans in. "What's your take on her being hazy with the details?"

"She seems convincing. I don't know. That level of trauma can certainly do it."

"Yeah," he says, nodding his head.

Phyllis approaches the table with both plates artfully balanced along her left arm. "The turkey club for you," she says in her pack-a-day rasp, and sets it down in front of me.

"Thank you," I say.

She lays a steak salad in front of Wolcott. "You boys all set here?"

"Yep. Thanks, Phyllis." We speak in stereo.

"Freshen your coffee, doll?"

"I'm good," answers Wolcott, passing a hand over his mug.

"Enjoy," she says, walking back toward the counter.

He tucks into his salad as I salt and pepper my sandwich. "So, the mom's a real piece of business, eh?"

"You got that right. Completely self-absorbed. And clueless. I explain to her that her daughter's just been in a room with the dead body of a friend, and she reacts like the kid chipped a nail. Makes me want to give my own mom a very big hug."

Wolcott swallows a bite of his salad. "Yeah, some icy personalities in the picture on this one. Thornton's about a stone's toss from a full-on psychopath."

"That's the truth," I say. "So, how do you want to go into our interview tomorrow?"

"Well, Cyrano, I'm inclined to let you take the lead. Soften her up a little."

"Really ridin' that bit into the fuckin' ground, aren't you?"

"Hey, keep tiptoeing around that particular elephant all you want," he says. "But I for one would love to get to the bottom of this case."

FORTY-TWO

CHARLOTTE

"I'm going to pull the car around while they get your discharge stuff together." My mother is freshly showered and coiffed and holding a coffee stirrer like a cigarette. She's been popping in and out of my hospital room like a mosquito at a barbecue, unable to land on any one place for more than a few minutes before setting off to find a new person to annoy. Every time she leaves the room I feel my heart rate settle along with my blood pressure.

"Okay, Mom. Can you shut the curtain so I can get dressed?" I say to further encourage her exit, and she pulls the fabric along the hanging circular metal track, enclosing me in a hoop of ages-old polyester cream and mint green swirls. I'm halfway into my jeans when a booming voice carrying my name rings out.

"Dr. K!" I recognize Nurse Murphy's voice before she's halfway behind the curtain. I pull my other leg through the free pants leg and lean into her enormous hug. I feel tears welling up and gulp them back and smile big when we part.

"Murphy," I say warmly.

"What are you doing here? I didn't know you were staying with us or I would have been here yesterday! The only reason I knew was because I saw your mother flitting around the halls like a regular queen bee." She pulls her glasses from the chain dangling around her neck to get a better look at me. "She hasn't changed at all," she says with the perfect balance of snark and sympathy.

In my short, miserable stint working here in Stony Brook Memorial Hospital after my Bellevue stay, Moira Murphy was one of the few people I interacted with beyond work matters. She saw that I was suffering right away and made a conscious effort to check in with me weekly. It took me a while to open up, but when I did we bonded over difficult parents; she was caring for her elderly mother at the time, who'd become increasingly prickly in her dementia.

"How's *your* mom?" I ask her.

"She passed away last year. It was the best thing that could have happened. She only got worse as time went on." Her smile betrays sadness through the stoicism.

"I'm so sorry. I should have been in touch. I didn't know." I squeeze her hands.

"Don't be silly. How would you have? And I know how much you wanted to leave this place. I didn't expect that you'd look back or end up spending the night here! What on earth?"

"Just a run-of-the-mill panic attack. I'm fine. I got a good night's sleep and the world-class cuisine of Stony Brook Memorial Hospital." I strive hard to keep things light and make it home before falling into despair and grief completely.

"Who is your doctor, hon?" She reaches an arm through the curtain and pulls my chart from the door before I can answer. She grunts when she sees the name. "Dr. Barron. Well, he's a rotten apple, and one that should have been retired out years ago. He's still telling dirty jokes to the nurses." She balls her fists. "Nothing much has changed around here."

"Luckily, I've had very little interaction with him. I think they just kept me overnight because the police brought me in—"

I'm interrupted by the sound of someone calling for a crash cart and a number of rubber-soled shoes moving quickly on linoleum.

"Lemme go see what this is about, sweetie. I'll stop back when I can." She ducks around the curtain and is out the door in a flash.

I realize my shirt is on inside out and I pull it over my head, turn it right side out, and have it three-quarters of the way on when I see the dark outline of a figure through my shirt's light material and the curtain.

"Knock, knock." I'm immediately disoriented by the sound of Jack Doyle's voice in my hospital room. I pull my shirt the rest of the way down and pull back the scrim between us.

"What are you doing here?"

"Well, hello to you too." He grins at me.

"Hi. Sorry. I wasn't expecting you." I look at my feet.

"I work here. The more pressing question is what are *you* doing here? And did you miss me?"

Not only is he a surgeon, but his place of employment is the setting of one of the lowest points of my life. Something about the two being conjoined bothers me deeply. I feel ashamed at the thought that we overlapped and he somehow was able to read my mind during that time.

"How long have you worked here?"

"Two years in January. I transferred from San Diego Memorial. My, uh, wife wanted to move back east to be closer to her family. That didn't exactly go as planned, but I ended up liking the Atlantic Ocean more than I expected."

"I see." I feel uncomfortable with his bright eyes boring into mine, so I turn to look at my phone, which is on my bed. I'm surprised that my mother hasn't called, impatiently wondering where I am. In the moment that I pivot away from Dr. Jack, he grabs my chart from the door.

"Hey!" I exclaim. I don't want this near stranger looking at my info, and pull it hard from his grip.

He looks startled and then embarrassed.

"Sorry. Force of habit." He lowers his hands to his sides.

I pull the chart to my chest and wrap my arms around it and myself protectively.

"Cardiology is never a good ward to be camped out in. What's going on with your heart?" he probes.

"Are you a heart surgeon?" I ask him.

"I've operated on some hearts, but it isn't my area of expertise," he says without a trace of flirtatiousness.

"I'm fine. It was an acute panic attack. I thought it might be myocardial infarction when it was happening." He raises his eyebrows and I realize I need to speak like a nondoctor or I'm going to have to explain myself. "They kept me overnight because the police brought me in and they know me here." I've said way more than I should have and have no intention or patience to unpack any of the things I've just revealed about myself. I need to stop talking.

His eyebrows remain raised. "Police?"

"My best friend died." The first time saying it out loud cuts my heart into pieces. "And I found her." I pull my arms tighter around me. "When the police got there, I thought I might be dying. I felt like I was."

His face takes on a quality of curious concern as he processes. He reaches his hands out and pulls the clipboard from my grip and places it gently on the bed, which I don't resist. Once he does that, he takes my hands in his and looks into my eyes and through me.

"I'm terribly sorry to hear that you went through that." My surprise melts into gratitude when he gathers me in his arms and holds me tightly. His breath and voice are low and warm through my hair and into my ear. "I'm so sorry, Charlotte."

I easily melt into the embrace, the enormity of my grief emerging again and becoming bigger and bigger. We stand quiet, holding each other for a long moment, until I feel something vibrating in his pants.

"Dammit. Sorry." He releases me and takes a step back. Frustration passes over his face when he unlocks the screen of his phone. "Shit. I gotta go. I'll be back to check in on you when I can." He's out the door without my responding.

I pull the curtain completely open and take inventory of the contents of my purse versus what I remember being brought in with, and everything is accounted for. My phone is still quiet, so I sit on the edge of the bed and look out the window. A flock of southbound geese move together in the cloudless sky. I close my eyes.

"Please show me a sign that you are here, Rach." I taste the salt running into the corners of my mouth from my eyes. I strain my ears to hear her in between the sounds of the hospital around me.

"All right, my love! I heard you were being set free on my way out of that defib scene, and I'm going to do your discharge."

Murphy pushes a wheelchair into the room and looks like an angel in her pristine white scrubs and halo of bleached hair, crested in hairsprayed peaks of pin curls around her face. Her full cheeks are pink with heavy blush and some ruddiness, probably from many years of afterwork drinks. Her immaculate white shoes and scrubs gleam against the beige walls of the room. She is one of the few nurses here who opted for the all-white look over the patterned or child-friendly scrubs, like teddy bears with balloons, most of the RNs wear.

I feel a swelling of gratitude that she's come back, and I'm so relieved she is doing my discharge. She sees the pain in my face and takes my hand. "Let's get you the F out of here." She laughs. "Hospitals are no place for healthy people."

She looks down at the packet of paperwork in her hand and back to me. "You don't need me to go through this, do you?" I shake my head. She nods and wraps a warm arm around my shoulder. "Come on, time for me to roll you out."

As she pushes me down the corridor and to the elevators, I crane my head toward her, a thought forming.

"Hey, Murphy? What floor does Dr. Doyle work on?" I turn back in the direction we are moving and avert my eyes from a few familiar faces I'd rather not interact with.

"Doyle?" She clicks her tongue. "No doctors here named Doyle, pumpkin."

"Dr. Jack Doyle? I just spoke to him. He's in surgery. Been here for two years," I tell her.

"Baby, you know that I know everyone from top to bottom in this place," she says proudly.

I press the down button when we reach the elevator bank and maneuver the chair to face her. "He definitely works here. He was in my room just minutes before you came for me. Dark reddish hair, around six feet. Very striking green eyes."

"Handsome?" she teases.

"I suppose so," I reply.

"Well, you could be describing John—Dr. Lyons. I love to tease him about how he's always tugging at his beard. I haven't seen him for a minute, though; we've been working opposite shifts lately." She chuckles as the doors open and she pushes me to the back of the empty car. "He's a sweetheart. Moved out here from the West Coast about two years ago. Just went through a divorce."

FORTY-THREE

WOLCOTT

"Charlotte, thank you for coming in to speak with us today." Silvestri deploys his most soothing, even tone. He sits across the table from me, our suspect seated at the head. A bottle of water sits in front of Charlotte. She looks rigid and squints slightly.

"Sorry about the lighting," he continues. "It's not the easiest on the eyes."

She laughs, seeming to relax as she does. "It's no worse than the hospital, honestly. I'm just relieved to be out of there."

"I'm sure," he says. "That's never an enjoyable stay. Have you had a chance to stop home and get settled?"

"A bit," she answers. "Although my mom is insisting on staying with me for a couple of nights. So that's always a production."

"Charlotte," I begin. "We were wondering if anything may have come back to you since we last spoke. Any memories, or even snippets of detail. Anything that may have clarified itself in your mind since you've been out of the hospital."

She concentrates on her hands. A look of frustration deepens as she takes a long, silent moment. Finally, she exhales slowly and deliberately. She looks me square in the eye. "Detective, I wish I could tell you more. Believe me. Ever since I got the phone call about Brooke's body, I feel like I've been underwater. Everything has seemed hazy and out of focus. I just . . ."

"Take your time," says Silvestri, cocking his head to the side as he looks at her.

"Thank you, Dennis," she says. "But time doesn't seem to be helping me any."

I lean in, propping my elbows on the table. "Charlotte, may I go back just a bit in our conversation?"

"Sure," she responds.

"When we were discussing Brooke Harmon a moment ago, you used only her first name."

She looks at me, unsure of the question. "Okay?"

"It just seems like a familiar way to refer to someone you never actually knew during her lifetime." I look at Charlotte for a long moment, assessing her response. Her shoulders tense up. "I'm correct in thinking that, Charlotte? You never actually *knew* Miss Harmon when she was alive?"

She squints hard and takes a deep breath. "I mean, no, not technically. But making the connection to her sister changed something in me. I feel so much closer to Brooke than I realized I could. I don't know. Does that make sense? This case has brought up a lot of things from my past that I had really tried to leave there, you know?"

I sit with clasped hands, stock-still, staring at her. "It's a funny thing about the past, though, Charlotte. What's that old quote? 'The past is never dead.'"

She leans back in her chair, crossing her arms. "How do you mean?"

"We spoke with your former mentor, Dr. Thornton."

Her body tenses at the mention. "Is that right?"

"Very passionate guy. Really takes his work seriously."

Her shoulders relax a touch. "Yes, well, the work that Henry and I were doing together was quite important. I guess he always maintained a certain intensity around that."

Okay, time to thread the needle. "The work you did *together*? That's an interesting way to word it. Makes it sound as if you were more or less equals in the OR."

The rigidity returns to her body. "And why wouldn't we be?"

I remove the notebook from my jacket pocket and flip open to the page I've dog-eared. "Well," I say, reading back from my notes. "He discussed the neurosurgical techniques that *he* was pioneering. Mentioned how frustrated he was with the other members of the surgical team— how did he put it—uh, not being able to 'keep up.'"

Charlotte stares straight ahead, cheeks flushing. "'Keep up,' eh?" The anger radiating off of her is palpable. "Wow. Only someone who's '*failed* up' so completely would have the nerve . . ." She trails off, the sentiment clear.

"Failed up?" I inquire. "How so?"

She lets out a breath. "You're aware that he's now chief of staff at that hospital?"

I consult my notes. "On the board of directors, as well." I want to see how far we can take this.

"Of course." She nods her head. "All I'm saying is, the anesthesiologist, the nurse, and I were all dismissed from our positions at the hospital. Only one person in that room managed to stay on staff."

"I see. So, Dr. Thornton's promotion was not merit-based?"

"The hospital needed to spin the situation as much as possible. The surgery that we were attempting was essentially experimental, and they had invested a lot of trust and resources in it, and in us. When things went the way they went, they were concerned about the optics, with the lawsuit and all. I was the junior physician on the team, Dr. Forester was aging out, and the nurse was a pill head, so they figured they could get rid of us and take Henry off the floor. That would appease everyone."

"Well, not everyone," I say. "What about you and Dr. Forester?"

"They made it worth our while," she says, rolling her eyes.

"Oh?" I say.

"Basically, they paid us off to go quietly. And they took very good care of us. I guess it was worth it for them, to avoid the lawsuit and the bad press."

"But isn't it true that the Harmon family attempted to initiate legal action against the hospital, and against the individual physicians involved? And that Brooke Harmon was outspoken about your culpability?"

"That is true, yes. But the case was ultimately settled out of court."

"I see. Now, that brings us to our next point. This woman, with whom you have a tragic connection, ends up living a few towns away, several years later, seemingly with an ax to grind. Then she turns up dead—poisoned, to be exact—and has you as her emergency contact."

She takes a stab at speaking but comes up short. All she can manage is a weak shake of the head.

"On top of that, a close friend and colleague of yours—a woman you had recently been in a heated argument with—turns up poisoned as well."

Her eyes go wide. She looks to me, desperation taking hold. "Oh God. Rachel was . . ." I study our suspect as she processes the information. Realization suddenly sinks in. "Wait, Detective. Do you think *I* killed these women? It's just not . . . I could never . . ."

I lean in and soften my tone. "I want to understand where you're coming from, but do you see how it looks, on the face of things? The similarities in these cases?" I take a beat. She's reeling. "You're sure that Brooke didn't reach out to you or approach you in some way? I mean, I could imagine that the prospect of someone in her position coming back into your life might seem threatening, or—"

"She was never in my life!" Charlotte blurts out. She takes a moment to compose herself. "I mean, not directly, at least."

"Okay," says Silvestri. "We're just trying to get to the bottom of this. With your help, of course."

Charlotte looks between us. She makes a visible effort to hold back the tears welling up in the corners of her eyes. She takes a deliberate breath and lands back on Silvestri. Her tone is as measured and even as can be expected. "Look," she begins. "I'm not a killer. I can assure you of that. I've been hesitant to dredge up the details of my past. Some of those events were deeply traumatizing, as I know you can understand." She looks at Silvestri with a pleading expression. I remember his admission of embellishment in their conversation and clock his look. He blinks for just a moment too long and returns a steady gaze to Charlotte, along with a nod of acknowledgment. "And in order to pick up the pieces and move on," she continues, "I've had to do a lot of work toward leaving the past in the past. I promise you that I will be as open as possible with you in this investigation, however uncomfortable that may be for me. But I am not a killer." She hits each word on the last sentence pointedly. She inhales sharply and blots the corners of her eyes with her sleeve. "I'm sorry, this is just taking a lot out of me."

"You're holding up great," Silvestri assures her.

She musters a halfhearted smile. "Thank you." She again looks between us. "Is there anything else you need to ask me right now?" There's an exhausted desperation in her face.

I look to my partner. We exchange an almost imperceptible nod. I turn back to Charlotte and lay my palms on the table. "Thank you, Ms. Knopfler," I say. "We'll be in touch with you soon, but right now you're free to go."

FORTY-FOUR

CHARLOTTE

As I near my house, I feel a hellacious headache coming on. My morning in the police station felt like a time warp, simultaneously short and eternally unending. My phone tells me it is nearly noon already and my interrogation lasted more than an hour, not long by comparison, I'm sure, but I feel like I've completed a triathlon.

I'm utterly exhausted by how the various corroded layers of my life have conspired to bring me down. I'm struggling to keep any of my thoughts straight, and it feels like the more I try to focus on the basics, the "good cops" playing three-card monte with every mistake I've ever made has pushed me to the brink. I can barely grasp at the basics of recall, like where I live, and drive past my house and cruise for a few miles in my fog before I realize I've overshot it.

I think about the ten grand in my bank account, the last of the hospital money paid to me if I would go quietly, after renting my house and paying for acupuncture school, and wonder how long it would float me in a new life somewhere else. But I know better. Wherever I go, I will be. I can't outrun any of this, because all of this is me. All the old shame and fear are still just as potent as always; they have just been lying dormant.

Now the second challenge after my morning police interrogation is facing my ultimate opponent. Conveniently, she's waiting for me in my own home. The only upside in all of this chaos is that all of my attention has been taken off Peter's falling off the face of the earth again.

"How was the police station?" my mother chirps upon my entrance. She is lounging on the couch with a book and a cocktail. Her tone suggests that I've just returned home from a party.

"It wasn't a social call, Mom." Every word is vinegar in my mouth.

"Well, excuse me for showing an interest in your life." She says this with the intonation of a sitcom catchphrase. She knows this is exactly the kind of shit that drives me especially crazy. I'm not taking the bait. My tank is on empty and I don't think I have any fight in me, even if I wanted to.

"Can I make you a spicy red snapper, dear?" She shakes her glass and the sound of ice tinkling in my direction fills the space between us.

"Mom, it's noon."

"And it is a breakfast cocktail!" She shrugs her shoulders at my lack of response, tips her glass back, and turns her attention to the TV, where MSNBC is on with subtitles. I'm thankful for small favors like the mute button.

I stare out the window to the backyard, where Rachel and I sat last week in the sun and talked. I look at my phone, empty of messages from Rachel or Peter.

"I was trying to reach you the last few days." Her tone is off.

"I know, Mom. I'm sorry. I was busy. I have a lot going on right now."

"This was before Rachel died."

"I had a lot going on before Rachel . . ." I cover my face with my hand.

"I was worried about you." She turns off the TV, which surprises me.

"Since when?" I scoff.

"I'm trying. You don't make it easy." She opens her arms.

"Are you really going to make this about you right now?"

She pulls back. I've inflicted damage, which is unusual. Maybe my uncontrolled emotional state is contagious. She can't be comfortable feeling her emotions. It stands in the face of everything she's about.

Maybe it will encourage her to leave sooner.

She has spread out the contents of her suitcase on every available surface of the living room, making my usually tidy surroundings a war zone of strewn clothing, books, and cosmetics. I place my purse on one of the few open spaces on the table and realize that my laptop is on and my Gmail account is open. My stomach somersaults.

"Mom? Were you on my computer?"

She glances up from her book with a faint look of irritation.

"I was catching up on emails." She looks at me like I've said something incredibly foolish and blinks a few times before resuming reading, the ice cubes in her glass clinking loudly as she takes a sip. I riffle through my purse for aspirin.

"Did you send your emails from my account?" I click into my sent folder and see that she has in fact sent a number of dispatches to her friends from my email address. This annoys me a lot more than it probably should, but given the high boil I walked in with, I'm ready to overflow.

"Oh, did I?" She chuckles and gets off the couch with her glass and heads toward the kitchen, presumably for a refill from the cache of bottles I expect she's brought with her. "You know I'm confounded by technology," she quips over her shoulder.

"*Mom*. You can't just get on my computer and into my email. We need to talk about some ground rules while you are here," I yell in her direction.

She pops her head back into the room. "Why are you so snippy today? Jesus, Charlotte. I just sent a couple of missives to my friends about your situation. This isn't exactly a walk in the park for me. I have a life that has been disrupted and need support from my friends. Is that okay with you?" I scoff and she disappears back into the kitchen. I hear the sound of an ice tray being brought down hard on the countertop.

She reenters the living room with a fresh drink and a smirk, and arranges herself on the couch, ready for her close-up. She plays with the elaborate gold-coin statement necklace she's got on today. It is reminiscent of Liz Taylor's *Cleopatra* look, and an extravagant one for day drinking indoors. "Let's chat." She is patting the seat next to her. "I need to talk to you about something."

Whatever it is, I'm not interested.

"Mom. I can't. I'm sorry." I grab my purse and move toward my room. The only thing I can think about doing right now is crawling into bed and pulling the covers over my head.

She shrugs again and sighs. "This is how you treat someone with cancer?"

I freeze in place. "Do you have cancer?" I hold my breath.

"Well, no. But if I did, you'd feel terrible." She pulls a vape pen from her purse.

"I'm going to bed, Mom."

"It's only noon." She smiles, pleased with herself.

I walk to my room, shut the door behind me, and hear the MSNBC volume increasing by the second.

FORTY-FIVE

SILVESTRI

"Whoa, tiger!"

Wolcott and I stand on the front porch of the house next door to Rachel Sherman's. A Boston terrier stands guard inside the front door, barking.

"Rufus, sit!" The muffled voice and sound of footsteps grow louder. "I'm coming." A man looking to be in his midthirties approaches the door, keeping an eye on us as he leans down to pet the dog. "May I help you?"

We flash our shields. "I'm Detective Wolcott, and this is my partner, Detective Silvestri. May we ask you a few questions about your neighbor?"

His expression shifts from wariness to comprehension. "Of course," he says. "Please come in." He corrals the still-excited dog as he opens the door and bids us inside. Wolcott thanks him, and we idle in a small kitchen area, the dog nuzzling my leg.

"What was your name, sir?"

"Oh, I'm sorry. I'm Pete. Pete Woods. I saw the ambulance out there the other night. What happened?"

"Mr. Woods, your neighbor, Rachel Sherman, was found dead inside her home."

"Oh man. Damn. How'd she die?"

"We're still waiting on the autopsy results," he answers. "Did you know Miss Sherman?"

"I mean, not well. Just to say hi. You know."

"I see," says Wolcott. "Had you noticed anything out of the ordinary going on next door as of late?"

"The other night, I heard some noise over there. I'd just gotten back home from visiting my brother in Chicago, and I was in here, getting Rufus fed. I heard a door slam, and then something like glass breaking. That sort of high-pitched sound."

"And which night was this?" asks Wolcott, opening his notebook.

"This would have been Saturday."

"Okay, go on."

"So, Rufus finishes his dinner, and we head out for our walk. I take a quick look at the house, because of the noise and all, but nothing seems to be going on. I guess she had a visitor, but it seemed calm."

"A visitor?" I ask.

"Yeah, there was another car in the driveway. A green Prius."

Wolcott looks up from his notes. He eyes me, then returns his attention to Pete. "And what time was this, Mr. Woods?"

"Right around nine o'clock," he says. My stomach plummets as the sound of their voices muffles in my head. "I remember checking my watch as we were leaving the house."

"You still wear a wristwatch, eh?" My partner flashes his own. "I thought we were the only ones left," he says, nodding between us.

"Yeah, I've been trying to do a tech detox. Every time I pull out my phone to look at the clock, I get distracted by ten other things."

"I hear you," says Wolcott. "Listen, thank you for your time." He returns the notebook to his pocket and pulls out a business card. "If you think of anything else," he says, handing the card to Pete.

"Will do. You guys have a good day, now."

◈◈◈

"What time were you over at her place?" he asks sheepishly as we pull out of Pete Woods's driveway.

"Got over around ten."

"Uh-huh." He doesn't want to acknowledge what's now painfully clear to both of us—that Charlotte Knopfler texted me that night in an attempt to alibi herself out. We're still waiting on Fisk for official time of death, but the pieces are all falling into place. "You going to be okay handling this?"

"You kidding?" I say. "I can't wait to put the cuffs on her myself."

FORTY-SIX

Trauma Survivors Private Chat Room: 10/9/19
4:00 p.m.

Woundedhealer: Hi.

Miserylovescompany: Hey, girl!

Harmnoone82: OMG! We've been wondering about you. You disappeared.

Biggirlsdontcry54: We missed you.

Makeupyourmindcontrol: Yeah. Way to leave us wanting more!

Woundedhealer: Something really bad happened.

Harmnoone82: Oh no. What is it?

Woundedhealer: My best friend died.

MaxineKD: Fuck.

Woundedhealer: Yeah.

Biggirlsdontcry54: Oh my God.

Harmnoone82: That's awful. I'm so sorry.

MaxineKD: WHAT HAPPENED?

Woundedhealer: We fought a few nights ago about my relationship. I lost my temper.

Harmnoone82: Wait . . . you didn't? I mean, did you do something?

Woundedhealer: No!!! Of course not.

Harmnoone82: Phew. I thought that you were saying you lost your temper and . . .

Woundedhealer: It could be my fault that she's dead.

Harmnoone82: DON'T do that to yourself.

Woundedhealer: I should have handled it better.

Harmnoone82: You poor thing.

Miserylovescompany: I've been there. It is the worst. You can't stop asking yourself what you could have done differently.

Makeupyourmindcontrol: I'm really sorry, Woundedhealer. You can't blame yourself, though.

Biggirlsdontcry54: There is nothing anyone can really say that is going to take the pain you are feeling away.

Makeupyourmindcontrol: So true.

Woundedhealer: I'm trying so hard to be a good person, but bad stuff keeps happening.

Makeupyourmindcontrol: I know this is going to sound harsh, but when a lot of bad things are happening around you, it might mean you have to take a hard look at your behavior.

Biggirlsdontcry54: Um, rude! These are things outside of her control.

Woundedhealer: I *am* the common denominator.

MaxineKD: Maybe you can't view everything in your life as "happening to you," maybe it is "happening around you," and the decisions you're making are leading up to the bad things, or how you are responding to it all, aren't the best?

Biggirlsdontcry54: Ladies. I don't think this is what she needs right now. This is a support group, not an unsolicited life advice group.

MaxineKD: Is there a difference?

Makeupyourmindcontrol: Sorry, Woundedhealer.

MaxineKD: What can we do to support you? I can tell you bad jokes.

Harmnoone82: We could all meet up. Talk in person. I know how much it helped me.

MaxineKD: That's a great idea.

Biggirlsdontcry54: OK. I will leave my house. For you, Woundedhealer. At least, I'll try. No promises.

Makeupyourmindcontrol: I'll bring supplies: Kleenex and chocolate. And wine obviously.

Harmnoone82: What do you say, Woundedhealer? Can we take care of you for a change?

Woundedhealer: Yes. That would be . . . amazing.

Harmnoone82: You need all the support you can get right now.

MaxineKD: We'll take good care of you.

Harmnoone82: Wonderful! Where should we meet? Same spot as last time?

Woundedhealer: Hold on just a minute, my mother is

MaxineKD: Hello?

Woundedhealer: *Is now offline.*

Harmnoone82: HELLO?

FORTY-SEVEN

CHARLOTTE

"Mom, I don't want to talk right now!" I sound like my teenage self as I wipe the grateful tears for my chat room friends away with the back of my hand. If my mother has seen this, she doesn't let on.

With two nearly full drinks in hand, she's barged into my room and I've snapped my computer shut on the chat, surprised and frustrated by the intrusion.

The idea of being surrounded by friends right now, and being away from my mother, sounds like the safest place I could be. But I don't dare try to respond with her in the room. I don't need her prying and judging the one place I have left in the world for comfort and support.

"Charlotte, I've been thinking." Nothing good will come from this. She flips the light switch, which hurts my eyes, and puts the two full glasses of what look to be mojitos down on my bedside table.

"What are you doing, Mom? I really want to be alone."

"Happy hour, darling. It's a time-honored tradition. Indulge me." She sits next to me on the bed, retrieves the drinks, and hands me one ceremoniously. I accept it, as much as I hate to. I'll take the escapism from this terrible sadness wherever I can get it.

"Here's to those who've seen us at our best and seen us at our worst and can't tell the difference." She taps her glass lightly against mine, even though I've made no move to indicate that I'm participating in any of this.

After a healthy swig, she takes a dramatic breath and scans the room as though she's looking for the camera she should be speaking into. "How are you *feeling* about everything?" I fear there may be a YouTube video of "How to Talk to Your Fucked-Up Adult Children During a Time of Grief" at play here.

"Well, I feel like shit, Mom. Maybe the worst I've ever felt. My life is coming apart at every possible seam."

"And what else?" She rubs her chin thoughtfully. This must be her attempt at active listening.

"And I'm more than a little disconcerted by how you are acting right now." I take a swig of the cocktail, which is triple the strength of any reasonably mixed drink, which shouldn't surprise me.

"Let's open a window in here! It is really stuffy." She moves to the black-out curtains and flings them open, practically spilling her drink in the process. The gray sky does very little as far as changing the feel inside the room, but the fresh air coming in when she cracks the window is needed.

She looks out the window and hoots. "Guests! And handsome ones! Good thing I bought extra mint and cachaça."

My head begins to throb. "What are you talking about?" I hold the cold glass to my forehead. "No guests." If she's invited people over at a time like this, I'll at least have a good reason to ask her to leave.

She looks at me and smiles sweetly. "Well, in that case, you are going to break that very inhospitable bit of news to the nice detectives yourself." She struts to my full-length mirror and examines herself as I absorb the news.

"You know I'll never turn good-looking men away, especially during cocktail hour."

The doorbell rings and, before I've moved, it is followed by an aggressive knocking.

"Get the door. It will do you some good to get up and move around," my mother tells me.

I take the remainder of my drink in two mouthfuls. I half walk, half slide down the carpeted stairs but pull myself together before I reach the doorway.

When I open the door, the detectives are standing shoulder to shoulder, blocking me from the rest of the world.

"Hi—"

"Charlotte Knopfler." Dennis's tone is unrecognizable. He is robotically militant. I feel his anger coming off of him in waves. His chest rises with his breath. "You are under arrest for the murder of Rachel Sherman." A flash of light goes off in my head. I'm blinded from the inside out.

Before I can process, Wolcott is firmly guiding me by the shoulder down the stairs of my front stoop. He is turning me around as the sound of handcuffs being placed around my wrists by Dennis culminates in a terrifying metallic click. The metal is colder than I would expect.

"You have the right to remain silent. Anything you say can and will be used against you in a court of law. You have the right to an attorney. If you cannot afford an attorney, one will be provided for you. Do you understand the rights I have just read to you? With these rights in mind, do you wish to speak to me?"

He's facing me now. I just stare at him. His eyes are empty and resigned as he looks through me. He actually believes that I could have done this. I'm crushed.

Before I can even begin to muster a response, I hear my mother coming down the stairs in the house behind me. I'm facing the street and I see a neighbor's car slowing down as they pass to get a better view of my new worst life moment. It is unreal how many of these are piling up this week.

"Who wants a caipiriiiiinha . . . wha?" They don't acknowledge her as they walk me to their car and put me in the back seat.

"Charlotte??" Her muffled voice is for once without a singsong quality or a hint of sarcasm. She sounds scared. Which in turn snaps me out of my shock and straight into the horror of what is unfolding. "What is happening?!"

I don't turn my head to look at her as they get in the driver's and passenger's seats and start the engine. I can't let her see me crying.

PART THREE

Harmnoone82: Is anyone awake?

Miserylovescompany: I'm here.

Biggirlsdontcry54: Greetings.

Makeupyourmindcontrol: Guilty. I'm Google stalking my exes.

Harmnoone82: Thank God. I didn't think anyone would be up.

MaxineKD: Just us vampires.

Biggirlsdontcry54: Seems like Woundedhealer might be the only one of us sleeping this evening.

Harmnoone82: I was hoping she'd be on tonight.

MaxineKD: Hey, what are we? Chopped liver?

Harmnoone82: Sorry! Of course not. I'm so relieved you are all awake.

Miserylovescompany: What's troubling you, Harmnoone82?

Makeupyourmindcontrol: The usual nightmare of being alive?

Biggirlsdontcry54: God, you are always so pessimistic.

Makeupyourmindcontrol: Well, I am a highly traumatized and sensitive person living in the world.

Biggirlsdontcry54: It isn't that bad out there.

MaxineKD: Says the woman who hasn't left her house for three years.

Makeupyourmindcontrol: What's wrong, H?

Harmnoone82: I think I made a big mistake.

MaxineKD: Big mistake how?

Harmnoone82: I stood up for myself.

Biggirlsdontcry54: GOOD!

Harmnoone82: HE took it really badly. Worse than I expected.

Makeupyourmindcontrol: Shit.

MaxineKD: Okay, well, you knew this was a risk. You put yourself out there, that is what matters.

Harmnoone82: I think I went too far. He wants to "shut me up, once and for all."

Makeupyourmindcontrol: Is he really capable of that?

Harmnoone82: I mean, he's done it before.

Biggirlsdontcry54: Based on what you've told us, he's clearly a sociopath.

MaxineKD: Are you safe to be alone?

Harmnoone82: I'm really freaked out.

Makeupyourmindcontrol: Well, this is officially feeling very creepy.

Biggirlsdontcry54: Remember when we talked about inappropriate times for humor?

Makeupyourmindcontrol: I'm sorry. I know. My shrink says humor is my defense mechanism. I thought I was just really funny. (Turns out I'm just really fucked-up.)

MaxineKD: Harmnoone82, do you want to talk in person?

Harmnoone82: Is that allowed? I thought we were supposed to keep this anonymous.

Makeupyourmindcontrol: We can do whatever we want! Our room, our rules.

Biggirlsdontcry54: Amen, sister. And also NO BOYS ALLOWED.

Miserylovescompany: I can meet up. Or come to you?

Harmnoone82: That would be great . . . to meet up.

Miserylovescompany: I can meet you right now if you want.

Harmnoone82: That would be amazing. I'm definitely not going to be able to sleep.

Miserylovescompany: There's a twenty-four-hour spot, the Beacon Diner, on Route 15.

Harmnoone82: Great.

Miserylovescompany: Any other takers?

Biggirlsdontcry54: I would almost leave my bubble for you guys. But . . . I can't. Maybe next time.

Makeupyourmindcontrol: I wish I could, ladies. Unfortunately, I'm half a bottle in. No operating heavy machinery for me. And I've been banned by Uber (another story for another time).

MaxineKD: I can be there too. An hour?

Harmnoone82: That works for me. How will we recognize each other?

Miserylovescompany: Hmm. I'll be the only woman holding a single flower.

MaxineKD: How very rom-com of you! I like it. I'll wear something pink.

Miserylovescompany: Better rom-com than horror.

Harmnoone82: I can't thank you enough. You are lifesavers.

Miserylovescompany: That's what friends are for, honey.

MaxineKD: Never fear. As long as you have us, nothing bad will happen to you.

FORTY-EIGHT

WOLCOTT

"*You guys in?*"

Clarence's voice is piping through the speaker on my desk phone. He's given us the log-in information for a chat room Brooke Harmon belonged to. Silvestri and I have been scrolling through the backlog and have just discovered a chat from the night before she was killed. "We sure are. And we just stumbled onto a big clue."

"*Cool, cool.*"

"Hey, Clarence. Could you dig up whatever info you can find on the other members?"

"*On it, fellas. Working on those addresses as we speak. I'll let you know when I've turned anything up.*"

"Beautiful," says Silvestri. "Thanks a million." We hang up and stare at each other. "Well, this case is getting wackier by the fucking second, eh?"

"Seems to be," I say. "Let's hit the diner and see what we can turn up."

Before I finish the sentence, Silvestri's up from his desk and pulling his coat on.

FORTY-NINE

CHARLOTTE

HE SHUTS THE DOOR TIGHTLY once he shuttles me through the entryway and keeps a hand on my shoulder while sealing up any chance of escape. The lock catching makes the same doomed metallic click that every other door in this place makes. The sound that says, "You are trapped."

There is a medium-size table in the middle of the room with four chairs around it. One of the two facing the door is occupied by a young woman with blond hair and bold red lipstick. She looks more like a hostess at an upscale restaurant than a court-ordered shrink. She stands to greet me while my mute escort with the name tag ROBERTS unlocks my handcuffs and ankle restraints. The whole arrangement seems a bit like overkill, but here at the Suffolk County Jail, they are very serious about prisoner accessories.

"Hi, Charlotte. My name is Dr. Louisa Russell."

I'm too focused on watching Roberts transfer my handcuffs in the direction of the loop on the table to pick up my cue.

"That won't be necessary, Officer." She smiles big and he wordlessly shrugs his shoulders and turns to leave.

"I'll be right outside the door."

"Have a seat." She refers to the chair across from her and I slide into it. "Thank you for meeting with me." The situation feels vaguely like a job interview.

"I didn't really have a choice."

"I suppose that's right." She laughs lightly. "But I appreciate you being here. I'm going to be recording our conversation, if that is okay with you."

I shrug in response. Nothing is okay with me anymore. I'm so consumed with every negative emotion, I feel like I'm wearing a five-hundred-pound suit.

"I know that you are going through a very distressing time right now." Dr. Russell looks to be about twenty-two, if she's a day. For some reason, her youth infuriates me as much as her restating the obvious. Maybe because it suggests that I'm not important enough to have been sent someone with more experience.

"Have you been told why I am here?"

"You are here to figure out if I'm crazy or not, right?" I say this without attitude.

"I wouldn't put it so crudely. This may feel like a punishment, Charlotte, but this is to help you."

"It would be far more helpful if people didn't think I was a murderer." I put my hands on either side of my head.

"That isn't for me to decide." She looks shaken. "I've been asked by Detectives Silvestri and Wolcott to do a standard psychiatric evaluation today." I can see her trying not to waver from her training and to keep her cool.

"Sorry if I'm being rude. I haven't slept much and, well, you know, I'm in here," I say.

"I understand. The goal is to determine your state of mind currently, and your state of mind in the last couple of weeks when the deaths of Brooke Harmon and Rachel Sherman occurred. Specifically, this is an in-custody evaluation to determine if you are fit to stand before the judge for your bail hearing." She appears to be consulting the folder sitting in front of her for her lines. I nod. "Do you understand the goal of our conversation today?"

I nod again.

"I'm going to need you to verbally answer for the recording."

"Yes, I understand, Dr. Russell." The *ls* are bitter coming off my tongue.

"And for the record, you have declined having your public defender present for this evaluation."

"Yes. That's right." I don't feel the need to explain to her that I'd rather take my chances at saying the wrong thing than have another stranger present for an inevitable, invasive line of questioning. I know it is probably supremely stupid, but I am too exhausted to wait the extra two days for the lawyer who they've appointed to me to be available. I had a lawyer for the aftermath of Michelle Harmon's death, but I would sooner defend myself than call him ever again.

"Great. Let's begin." She straightens in her chair and takes a deep breath. She appears to be nervous, and I wonder how many of these evaluations she has done. It occurs to me that as far as she knows, she is sitting in a very small room with a murderer.

"Please state your name, age, date of birth, marital status, and gender, for the record."

"Charlotte Anne Knopfler, April 1, 1979, age forty, female, single."

She slides a piece of paper over to me, and a newly sharpened pencil. "Please check the following words you would use to describe yourself."

I look down at the page and the words swim around. It takes a few seconds before they stabilize on the white space and I can read them.

_____ Intelligent _____ Confident _____ Worthwhile _____ Ambitious _____ Sensitive _____ Loyal _____Trustworthy _____Evil _____Full of Regrets _____ Worthless _____ A Nobody _____ Useless _____Crazy _____ Deviant _____Unattractive _____Ugly _____Considerate _____ Unlovable _____Inadequate _____Naive _____ Confused _____Hardworking _____ Incompetent _____ Stupid _____ Attractive _____Persevering _____ In Conflict _____ Honest _____ Suicidal _____ Can't Make a Decision _____Memory Problems _____Good Sense of Humor

I put check marks by the words that apply and slide the paper back to her; she doesn't register any tells in her expression after reviewing my work. Satisfied, she continues.

"Great. Now, where were you born? And how long did you stay there?"

"I was born in Stony Brook, Long Island, and lived here until I was seventeen."

"What other places did you live, and for how long did you live there?"

"I lived in Cambridge for my undergraduate degree for four years, and then New York City for medical school and my residency for eight years. I've been back in Stony Brook for six years now."

"Do you have any siblings?"

"Not that I know of." I can't help thinking about how similar these questions are to a few first dates I've been on. If only this was one of those times. I'd be dressed better, for starters.

She raises her eyebrows. "None that you know of?"

"Sorry, bad joke. I'm an only child."

"Got it. Okay, now, how about your father? Is he alive, and what is his age and occupation, or if he's deceased, what age did he die, and cause of death?"

"No idea who my father is or if he's alive or not." There is not any discernible emotion in my answer, at least not any more than there is in my heart.

"Okay, how about your mother? Same questions."

"She's very much alive. She's sixty-nine going on sixteen. Retired."

"Retired from what?" She is clicking the pen gently.

"She has done a number of things. Worked in an office, done tele-marketing, apparently she did a stint in a floral shop. I learn about a new vocation of my mother's every time we speak. She was probably in the circus at some point."

Dr. Russell laughs politely. "What was your relationship like as a child?"

"Let's just say that if emotional abuse was an enforceable crime, Mom and I would be cellmates."

"So I'm inferring that the relationship was not good? It was abusive?"

"Abusive may be overstating it. Maybe just dysfunctional." I have to keep myself in check and not pull my mother down with me.

"And how about your relationship as an adult?"

"The playing field is even now that I'm an adult. But the game hasn't changed much."

"So you are not on good terms, I take it?" She leans on her clasped hands, which she has balanced on her elbows. She's incredibly thin.

"We are on fine terms. Normal for us."

She refers to the pages in her folder and skims a few paragraphs. I focus on the top of her head and start to hum softly.

"You were living with your mother for a length of time when you came back to Long Island six years ago, is that correct?"

"It must be if it is on your printout." Dr. Russell frowns. I relent. "Yes. That is correct."

"And, Charlotte, was that period of time particularly stressful?"

"Yes, you could say that."

"Would *you* say that?" Her voice jumps an octave.

"Yes, it was acutely stressful."

"And what prompted you to finally move out?"

"I got a job. I reconnected with old friends and made new friends and started seeing someone who helped encourage me to get out of her house. My mother was ready for me to leave a few days after I arrived. She amused herself greatly when she drew up an eviction note as a 'joke,' but the message was received loud and clear. At least she gave me a slight break on the rent."

In a surprising moment of humanity, Dr. Russell wrinkles her nose disapprovingly. "Your mother sounds charming." We both laugh. Dr.

Russell pulls a second page from her material and pushes it over to my side. "Here is another batch of words that I'd like you to review and check if any of the following apply to your childhood or adolescence."

____Unhappy Childhood ____Family Problems ____School Problems ____ Emotional/Behavioral Problems ____ Alcohol Abuse ____ Drug Abuse ____ Medical Problems ____ Legal Problems ____ Physical Abuse ____ Sexual Abuse ____ Emotional Abuse ____ Other

I run through the collection of phrases in front of me and sigh. "This is beginning to feel like a women's magazine quiz. What kind of lover are you?" I drily joke as I check all of the terms that apply.

"How did your mother discipline you? Did she ever hit you or use physical punishment?"

"She employed varying degrees of emotional warfare and gaslighting. My mother is a huge fan of Joan Crawford's work, on- and off-screen."

Dr. Russell blinks at me with her enormous green eyes, hardly eclipsed by her stylish Warby Parkers. They blink quickly and look doll-like, as though they are made out of glass and paint. I gather from her blank stare that she has no idea about or appreciation for my *Mommy Dearest* reference.

"Sorry. I'm just kidding. She never hit me with or without coat hangers," I tell her, slightly ashamed of myself.

"Okay, let's move on to an area that will hopefully be a bit easier, Charlotte. Let's discuss your education history."

"Bring it on."

"What degrees have you been awarded?"

"I have a bachelor's in biology; an MD, specializing in neurosurgery; and a master's of science in acupuncture."

"What type of grades did you receive?"

"I had a 4.0 in high school, college, and medical school. I graduated top of my class."

"For which levels of schooling?"

"All of them."

She looks at me with a little more respect than when I first joined her at the table. I feel a small but smoldering sense of superiority.

"Were you ever held back a grade or promoted an extra grade?"

"I skipped second and third grades." She's right. This line of questioning is much easier.

"Were you ever diagnosed with a learning disability or ADHD?"

"No." I say this with confidence, although keeping my attention on one thing currently is a challenge and part of me wonders.

"Please detail any suspensions, detentions, or expulsions you may have received."

"I never got in trouble."

"Okay. Well, then, let's delve into your counseling history."

"Okay."

"Have you ever been in counseling or psychotherapy?"

"Yes."

"How did you make the decision to seek counseling or therapy?"

"It was made for me."

"Are you currently on any medications for a mental disorder?"

"No."

"Have you taken medication for a psychological problem or mental disorder in the past?"

"Sure."

"What medications?"

"It might be easier if you have a one-sheet of medicine names that I can put check marks by."

She doesn't look amused and slides a blank page over, where I write down my greatest pharmacological hits and their dosages.

"When did you start taking medication, and how old were you?"

"Six years ago. Age thirty-four."

"And when did you stop taking them?"

"Age thirty-five."

She looks at her notes. "About the same time you ceased therapy and were living at home with your mom, is that correct?"

"That is correct."

"What was it prescribed for?"

"Depression. Anxiety."

"Have you ever been hospitalized for psychological problems?" She looks down as she asks this and I'm positive that she knows the answer. She seems unsteady with this new topic. She should be.

"Now we are getting into the fun stuff."

"Is that a yes to the question, Charlotte?"

"That is a resounding yes."

"When was your first hospitalization?"

"First and only. Six years ago."

"Where?"

"New York City. Bellevue Hospital. Inpatient for two months."

"Please explain what brought you to the hospital."

"Don't you have all of this in your file? I know Detectives Wolcott and Silvestri must." I let my irritability leech into my words. She looks up from her file.

"If you want to take a break, we can do that. How about some water?" she asks with just a little too much condescending perkiness in her tone.

I'm losing my grip on any remaining affability I have reserved. "No, I'm fine."

"Great, let's continue, then." She assumes an empathetic and eager pose.

"Six and a half years ago, I was a surgical resident at the Greater New York Medical Center, in their psychosurgical unit. I was chief resident. It was my first surgery as lead on a relatively new surgical approach that I'd assisted on a number of times before. The patient was a young woman named Michelle Harmon."

"Michelle Harmon, as in the victim Brooke Harmon's older sister?"

"She *was*." I'm as annoyed with her interruption as I am with her habit of asking questions she knows the answer to already.

"Right. Was. Okay, please go ahead."

"Michelle had been beaten badly and left for dead when she was in high school four years earlier. She survived the attack and had miraculously come out of a three-month coma but developed severe and rapid-onset symptoms of post-traumatic stress disorder. She became a threat to herself and everyone around her, with episodes of violence and delusional behavior that were escalating quickly." I pause and see that Dr. Russell is rapt with attention. "Her family was close to having her permanently institutionalized but then heard about the success we'd had with a number of patients using psychosurgical approaches, namely, a high-profile NFL player who'd sustained multiple head injuries in his career and was arrested for domestic abuse multiple times, and a jockey who'd been thrown into a concrete pylon at the speed of fifty-five miles per hour and begun to self-harm following his trauma."

I stop again and reach for the unopened bottle of water in front of me.

Dr. Russell sits patiently, her hands folded in front of her. She has a triumphant look, and I gather it is due to my first serious, more-than-five-word response. I need to give this woman a break and let her do her job. I have a flash of the patronizing treatment I received as a young and eager resident.

"Whenever you are ready, Charlotte. Please continue."

"The surgery was going along as planned and I successfully removed the section of Michelle's hippocampus where we believed the concentration of trauma was residing and causing her most extreme problems . . ." Dr. Russell looks expectant and taps her pen on the table lightly. She encourages me with a nod. I take a deep breath and have trouble finding the space in my lungs for any air.

"Michelle coded and never regained consciousness. She had an adverse reaction to the anesthesia."

I am whispering at this point, and looking down at the table. Tears are falling from my face and onto the surface in a small puddle.

"Sorry. This is hard." I put my face in my hands.

Through my fingers, I see Dr. Russell press the red circle on her smartphone and pause the recording. When I lift my head, she looks at me compassionately and reaches her hand across the table and gently pats the top of mine. "Let's take a break. This is a lot."

I put my head down on the table and cry into the absent space of my joined arms. We sit in silence for a few minutes. I pull myself together and sit up.

"So have you?" I ask her.

"Have I what?" She looks tense.

"Determined my 'state of mind.'"

"Yes, I believe I have," she responds evenly.

"Great. That makes one of us."

FIFTY

SILVESTRI

"Oh, there we are."

He points to the light blue Honda Civic parked on the far side of the lot. We cross to the car and peer inside. The interior is clean and bare, nothing visible in the way of personal possessions. I try the door, to no avail. "Hmm. No wonder the APB didn't turn it up. She's tucked way over in the corner here. Guess it was a busy night?"

"Or she wanted to keep a low profile," he offers. "Maybe she was nervous that someone had eyes on her? In any case, it looks like she got a ride out of here."

I consider the thought as I call in a tow truck to come down and impound the vehicle. We cross the lot and enter the diner, which is bustling with the lunch rush. A server whisks by us. "Two? You guys want a booth or counter?"

I pull out my shield. "Just a chat, thanks."

She skids to a stop and huffs. "Brenda," she calls over her shoulder. "Cover my tables, hon?" She looks between the two of us. "What can I do for you, Officers?"

"Any chance you were working the night of October first? Tuesday before last?"

"Yeah, I'm always here Tuesday nights. What's up?"

I pull out my phone and bring up a photo of Brooke Harmon. She studies the image and a vague look of recollection sinks in. "Yeah, I remember her. She came in right around the end of my shift. Sat in a booth over there," she says, pointing.

"Do you remember if she came in with anyone? Met anyone? How she seemed?"

"Seemed tense, maybe? Came in alone and sat alone. She was looking around the room, like maybe she was expecting someone. But I took off shortly after that, and I don't remember seeing anyone in the booth with her when I left."

"And what time was that?"

"Twelve-thirty a.m."

"Could you tell us who took over your tables that night?"

She rolls her eyes and snorts. "Uh, that would be Christina. She ran off with one of the line cooks a few nights ago, and no one's heard from either of them since." She pulls her phone from her pocket, scrolls through, and finds a number, which she writes on a cocktail napkin and hands to me. "Here you go. Maybe you'll have better luck turning her up."

"Thanks," I say. "Would we be able to get a look at your security footage from that night?" I nod toward the camera in the corner.

"Not that far back. The system archives the footage for a week; then it gets scrubbed." She looks around anxiously. "Sorry, guys. I'm kind of in the weeds here."

"Quite all right." Wolcott hands her a card. "If you remember anything else, during a quiet moment, would you please be in touch?"

"No problem, guys." She offers us a smile before gliding off to the coffee station.

◆◆◆

I'm driving us back to the station house. No sooner has my partner hung up with Christina's voicemail than his phone rings. "Wolcott . . . Oh, hey, Clarence . . . Okay . . . Right, right . . . Really?" The change in tone catches my attention. I see his eyes widen in my peripheral. "Damn, that's . . . Okay, appreciate the call." He hangs up and turns to me. I glance in his direction and catch a look of surprise on his face.

"What's up?"

"Clarence just ran down the IP addresses of the other members in Brooke Harmon's chat room."

"Yeah?" I ask.

"Silvestri, you're not going to believe *this* shit."

FIFTY-ONE

CHARLOTTE

RACHEL SITS ACROSS FROM ME, *her legs in lotus position, beaming as brightly as the sunlight cascading down around her.*

"There's something I want to ask you," I say, as I have many times before.

"Ask me anything," she replies brightly.

Even though we've had this conversation before, this time feels different.

"If you could change one thing about your past, what would it be?" She appears to take this in very thoughtfully, even though I always ask the same question.

She pulls her hands together and puts them up to her heart while she closes her eyes. "Hmm."

I know what she'll say; she always answers the same way.

And I always say, "Really, nothing?"

"I wouldn't change a thing," she'll repeat.

"Really? Even his death?" I always press.

"Even the worst things I've ever done. I wouldn't change a thing. Because it all led me here," she will answer. And every time this comforts me.

But now she doesn't say anything; she just watches me waiting for her to answer. I begin to fidget while we sit in silence, the air around us growing thick with the smell of something burning.

She smiles oddly, like she has something sharp in her mouth. There's a darkening mischief in her gaze. I suddenly feel afraid.

"I know what I would change," she says, her voice deepening as she reaches her hand up to her neck and tugs at her throat like she's removing a necklace. I

try to reach out to her and pull her fingers from her throat, but she's suddenly
very far away from me. She rolls the skin upward and pulls her face up and
away and there is only dark nothingness underneath.

"I would have killed you sooner," says a voice.

But the voice is not Rachel's. It is Peter's.

◆ ◆ ◆

"Rise and shine, Ms. Knopfler. You've got a visitor."

I'm grateful for the sound of Officer Roberts's voice and keys rescuing me.

Although the multiple horrors of my new reality upon waking aren't any less horrifying than my vivid dreams. There is no safe consciousness left. My bed is not my own; it is state issued and what I imagine sleeping on a pommel horse would feel like. Rachel is dead anew each time I wake up, and the brief sublime moment before the remembering is savagely ripped away again and again. I'm locked in a cage, both inside and outside my head.

I sit up too quickly and floaters dance in my peripheral vision. I've been dizzy and nauseous since I got here. The food not only tastes awful but is comprised of only two ingredients: sugar and salt in multiple variations. I'm lethargic and sinking into total slothdom. I can't fathom what I'm going to feel like after a week or a month.

"Up and at 'em. You don't want to keep your mother waiting, do you?"

"My mother?" Heart palpitations and dry mouth join the list of jail-flu symptoms.

"Yep. She was first in line for visiting hours. She's quite a character, isn't she? I met her on the way in."

"Do I have to?" I've put my head in my hands.

Officer Roberts shrugs. "Technically, you don't have to see anyone you don't want to unless it's the cops. But why not? You've got something better to do?"

"I don't feel like seeing anybody right now." I smooth my hair down and gather it into a bun.

"Some people don't have any visitors *or* mothers. You should consider yourself lucky," he preaches.

"Easy for you to say. You weren't raised by her." He frowns.

Officer Roberts is the tall, dark, and judgmental type. He keeps telling me that I should consider myself lucky. I am lucky for having a cell to myself and I'm lucky I'm not getting hassled by the other inmates. I'm lucky that I'm healthy and I'm lucky I'm not in a different county jail where the guards aren't as friendly as he is. I know he's right, but it's hard for me to see my many blessings from my six-by-eight vantage point.

"I can tell them you don't want visitation today." His disapproval is apparent. I have to wonder how the quality of his life is, working in a place like this.

"No, I'll see her. I might as well talk to someone other than myself. I'm starting to feel a little crazy in here with the lack of conversation."

He shoots me a surprisingly wounded look that I'm immediately shamed by.

"No offense."

"Honey, you look terrible." Her "What's that bad smell?" expression is comical despite the grimness of our surroundings. "I barely recognize you."

"Coming in strong, Mom. Thanks." I sigh.

"What are they doing to you in here?" She looks from side to side.

I'm focusing on the chartreuse jumpsuit she's wearing. Other inmates and their visitors keep looking over at us.

"Mom, I've only been here for two days. I can't look that different. And it's jail, not summer camp. They are keeping me contained and feeding me. That's about the extent of it."

Her lip trembles a little bit, which makes me deeply uncomfortable. "You don't look like yourself."

"Well, I don't feel like myself either." I hop to the next subject. "Interesting outfit choice, Mother." I try to keep my delivery as light as possible to evade any real emotional exchange here.

"Isn't it wonderful?" She looks down at herself proudly, ignoring my sarcastic tone. "Vintage Halston. Older than you are! I had to dig it up, but I thought for solidarity, it was worth going deep into my vault for."

I sweep a hand up and down my government-issued tan ensemble. "I'm sorry to disappoint you, but they don't actually have us in jumpsuits."

"I see." She gives my outfit a once-over. "More like scrubs, aren't they? Well, at least it's something you are familiar with wearing."

I groan.

"How are they treating you?" she asks in a stage whisper.

"Fine."

"Why aren't you accepting the public defender?"

"How did you know that I didn't?" I reply.

She leans in conspiratorially. "The guard I was chatting with earlier told me."

"Because I didn't do it, Mom," I answer in a normal volume. "And because the last lawyer I had screwed me. I'm not interested in a plea bargain. I talked to the well-meaning but extremely inexperienced person they sent for five minutes and realized I would be better off not having anyone at all. I don't need to become the subject of a millennial-hosted true-crime podcast."

"Are you sure that is wise?" She picks at a cuticle.

"Yes. Actually, I am. Going with someone who is only focusing on pleading me down to a lesser sentence for something I *didn't* do is not the right path." My voice cracks. "I refuse to even go through the motions of that."

"You seem angry," she says.

"Wouldn't you be, if you were in my position?" I shrug and look away from her.

"You seem angry at *me*, in particular."

"I'm furious at the whole situation, Mom. And I'm not really sure why you are here." I sigh.

"Charlotte, I'm sorry I couldn't post bail for you." Her defensive discomfort is undeniable.

"I didn't realize that you hadn't. But good to know." The aching disappointment of her admission surprises me. I guess I'm not as immune to my feelings in here as I thought.

"It's a lot of money, sweetie. And I've been trying to talk to you about this for a few weeks now. I'm actually having some money problems at the moment—"

"*Mom.* I am not going to talk about your money problems while I'm in *jail.*"

I see something cross her face that I haven't seen in a very long time. Real emotion. Rage. She leans in and grits her teeth.

"Charlotte. I don't know exactly what has you so pissed off at me, but you need to snap out of it, and quick. You've made it no secret that you think I'm a bad mother, but you seem to selectively omit that I'm the one who is there for you when things get *real.*"

"I didn't say I was angry, Mom—"

"Aside from *keeping you alive* until you left for college, I am the one who picked you up from the mental hospital and took care of you until you could rejoin the living. And presumably, I'm going to be doing the same thing when I pick you up from *prison.* Do you really think you are in a position to be judgmental of me?"

I'm speechless. She sits back and smooths the front of her jumpsuit and the sides of her hair with her hands. I see they are shaking.

"I don't know what to say. I didn't realize you thought I was such a terrible person," I say, petulantly.

"Grow up. You don't know how I view you because you have taken it upon yourself to do the thinking for me."

"Oh Jesus, Mom. I've already seen a shrink this week. Do you really think this is the best time to tear me down? I'm already on the ground." I give her a withering look.

"Yes, I do, actually. You are a captive audience, for once."

"Fine. Give me your best shot," I say snidely.

"How on earth can you heal someone if you have such negative energy running through you? How can you bolster people when you clearly have such low self-worth? I didn't teach you that."

"Mom, I tell you what I want you to know and show you very little about who I actually am," I reply icily.

She scoffs. "Darling. I made you, raised you, and know exactly *who* you are."

"And what? You brought me into this world, and you can take me out of it?" I counter.

"No, but you can. And it certainly seems like you are trying hard to do that." We stare at each other.

"Becoming a surgeon was your dream, not mine," I say quietly.

"If that were true, why would you be angry about that? Until the tragedy with Michelle Harmon, you were on track to be a superstar," she says evenly.

"If you hadn't pushed me into becoming a doctor, I wouldn't be living with the death of another human being on my conscience now. I wouldn't have been betrayed and abandoned by my industry and people closest to me. I wouldn't have had a breakdown."

Her expression softens.

"Alex Myer," she states.

"Who?"

"He was the reason you wanted to become a brain surgeon?" She watches my face closely.

I draw on the name but don't have a face or memory attached. "No idea. Who is he?"

"He was a little boy in your kindergarten class. The two of you were playing with a kickball at recess one day and he kicked the ball into the creek across the street from school."

Images are coming back to me. There was a car.

"He chased after the ball and got hit. You witnessed the whole thing and stayed with him there in the middle of the street while the ambulance came."

"Oh my God. I completely forgot." I search my memories for that day. I remember there being a lot of blood and his eyes being shut. But I can't recall anything else.

"He lived. Got something like two hundred stitches in his head and body, but he survived, miraculously. You were at his side at the hospital every day after school until he got out."

"I was? I completely blocked that out."

She nods. "But he wasn't the same. He became erratic and really badly behaved. He tried to hurt you and some of the other kids in your class a few times. You didn't understand. I had to explain to you that the accident had damaged his brain so badly, he wasn't himself any longer."

"What happened to him?" I ask, riveted by this past life I'd completely lost track of.

"His family moved away. I lost touch with his mother. I'm not sure what happened to him. But I know what happened to you." She looks at me tenderly.

"What?" I ask her, anticipating her response.

"You became fascinated by the brain and with healing people. It was, and still is, an amazing quality in you." She beams.

"Thanks, Mom," I say to her. It is all I can muster.

"Charlotte. Forgive yourself. For all of it. Let it go." She presses her hands on the table.

A terrible thought blooms. "Mom. Do you think I'm guilty?"

I brace myself by digging my hands into the fabric on my thighs, the metal of the handcuffs digging into the delicate skin on the insides of my wrists.

She doesn't answer right away, and her hesitation is the most painful thing so far today.

She blows air out of her mouth so hard her lips make a fluttering sound. "Char. Of course I know that you did not murder your friend." She moves closer to me. "But I know that as long as you carry around what happened to Michelle Harmon, you might as well be guilty of every death you are in proximity to, with the way you blame yourself."

"This is completely different. What happened to Michelle Harmon *was* my fault!" The guard shoots me a warning look and I check my volume. "And Rachel's death may have been my fault, too." I say this much more softly to my lap.

"I'm sorry that you believe that and that you are putting yourself through this." She holds my eyes for a moment and I actually feel her empathy, which levels me. "The situation is tragic enough without your self-torture, but I need you to listen to me right now." I can see her jaw muscles are clenched as she winds up.

"Underneath all the bad feelings, you are strong and resilient and resourceful. That is what you need to be taking hold of. Not the sadness. The despair is just going to pull you under, and I can't do anything to help you if you are in here and giving up." She leans back

I blink a few times and tilt my head closer in her direction to try to enable understanding, but my confusion remains. I hear her voice, but the words themselves are perplexing. It almost sounds like she is on my side.

"You think that I'm strong?" I ask her, praying that she'll fall on the side of sincerity.

She nods. "I do. And I believe that you can and will pull yourself out of this self-pity hole you are in right now and defend yourself. You've done it before."

"I'm grieving, Mom," I counter.

"No, you are wallowing. Grief comes when you have the space for it. You are in jail right now for a crime you didn't commit, and you are fighting me harder than you are resisting what is happening to you. If you think that your innocence is going to conquer all and that this will just sort itself in some natural order of the universe, you are being extremely naive."

"That's not what I'm doing." The defense sounds flimsy as I say it.

"Well then, the other alternative is that you are surrendering to this wrongful imprisonment as some self-inflicted punishment for Michelle Harmon." My body tenses into one giant fist.

"If that is the case," she continues, "I shouldn't have to tell you, no matter whether you are in here punishing yourself for something that can't be undone, or doing it out there, what's done is done. And in both scenarios you are in a jail cell. You need to start forgiving yourself or you might as well give up completely, plead guilty, and let New York State own your life."

"Or maybe you are just projecting a lot of shit on me that has no truth. You don't know everything, Mom," I retort weakly.

"You have always been brilliant, with a particular genius for brattiness. You must have gotten that from your father's side of the family."

I start laughing. And she does too. My laughter turns into loud tears, and I'm crying hard. Shockingly, so is she.

"I need you to fight," she says. "Figure this out, defend yourself, and then you can start grieving *everything*." When the guard's back is turned, she reaches across the space between us and wipes away my tears with the heels of her hands. The gesture is small, but also enormous.

"And I can be there for you, if you want me to." She pauses. "Or I can go away. But we'll fight about that later, if we are lucky."

FIFTY-TWO

WOLCOTT

"We just want to speak with the detectives in charge," a voice bellows from the direction of the front desk. I pick up my pace and round the corner to find Greene seated at his station, extending his hands palms in an effort to placate a fellow who slams a meaty paw repeatedly against the lacquered surface. A petite woman stands beside the irate man, one hand on his broad shoulder, the other balled tightly at her waist.

I slip in beside her and extend mine for a shake. "Hello, folks," I say, smiling. "Detective Terrence Wolcott."

He looks me up and down, then frowns at her. He returns his eyes to me and thrusts a mitt in my direction. "Bob Harmon," he says sourly. "This is my wife, Kathy."

Oh boy. "Mr. and Mrs. Harmon. Of course. We spoke on the phone. Please, follow me. We'll find a place to sit and talk." I resist the inclination to place a comforting hand on Kathy's shoulder, as I suspect it might incite Bob to tear the attached arm out of the socket and beat me with the limb.

We pass the desks on the way to the interrogation room. Silvestri leans back in his chair, legs kicked up on his desk, flipping through a stack of papers. I shoot him a look, and he immediately swings his legs to the floor, stands, and smooths his shirt with an open palm.

"Mr. and Mrs. Harmon," I say. "This is my partner, Detective Silvestri."

Silvestri clears his throat and displays a solemn look. "I'm terribly sorry for your loss," he says, extending a hand to the couple.

"Thank you," says Bob distractedly. He looks around the cluster of desks and shakes his head. "Is there anywhere we can go and talk with a little more . . . privacy?"

"Of course," I answer. "Follow us."

◆◆◆

"Can we get you anything? Coffee? Water?"

We're sitting in the interrogation room. Kathy folds her hands in her lap, while Bob leans forward, elbows perched on the edge of the table. "We're fine," he says, answering for both of them.

"Our apologies for the setting," Silvestri pipes up. "I'm afraid it's the only room in the building that affords us the chance to have a quiet conversation."

"It'll be fine," says Kathy, forcing a polite smile. "So, you've arrested Charlotte Knopfler?"

I'm grateful for the prompting. "That is correct, Mrs. Harmon. We have Ms. Knopfler in custody, awaiting a court hearing." I need to handle this situation very gingerly. Bob's just lost his second child—at the hands of the same suspect, no less—and is quite understandably on the edge of sanity. "Over the course of our investigation," I begin, "we learned of the devastating loss of your daughter, Michelle. I can't imagine what this experience must be like for you both. Our team is working around the clock to put together the strongest case possible, to make sure that the person responsible is brought to justice."

"So, I guess three's the charm, then?" Bob's hand quakes as he speaks. His face is a shade of crimson, and his voice cracks with a mixture of rage and grief. "Let this bitch get good and warmed up before you finally bring her in?"

"Bob." Kathy speaks with a bit more force and volume this time. "Please."

I shift in my seat in an attempt to ground myself. I open my mouth to begin a sentence but think better of it. The words "your daughter" nearly tumble out, but I catch myself. "Brooke was the first victim." I make deliberate eye contact with both of the Harmons as I continue. "We began an aggressive investigation immediately, but evidence was scant, and we unfortunately found ourselves at the mercy of some forensic findings that took longer to sift through. We assure you that we—"

"Bullshit!" he spits. "First Michelle. Now Brooke. Should my wife and I be fearing for our lives too? Jesus! Can't any of you ever be bothered to do your fucking jobs?!"

"Enough." Kathy Harmon's hands shoot out of her lap and up in front of her. The volume of her voice doesn't climb, but the tone is steady and forceful. She slowly lowers her hands to the top of the table. It has the effect of a conductor leading an orchestra. The room around her falls silent. She gently places a hand on her husband's forearm, which seems to have a tranquilizing effect on him. She looks at him, raises a hand to his cheek and strokes it gently. The rage and anger in his face give way to something softer, more gentle and vulnerable. His eyes well up, and he takes a deep breath.

She returns her hand to his forearm and her attention to me. "Charlotte Knopfler. She's a sick woman, Detective Wolcott?"

I maintain steady eye contact. "We're waiting on the results of a psychiatric evaluation. But, yes, we believe that Ms. Knopfler is unwell."

She breathes in the information, sits with it for a moment, and exhales. "And you've got strong evidence against her?"

My partner slips in. "We're building a very strong case against Ms. Knopfler, thanks in no small part to our findings in Brooke's email exchanges."

"Detective," says Kathy, "I'd like to have access to her email account."

"We can certainly arrange that," I assure her.

"Okay." She looks to Silvestri, then back to her husband. She squeezes his arm gently as she stares off toward the far wall of the interrogation room. Then, in an eerily calm tone, she speaks, more statement than question, with utter resolve. "So Charlotte Knopfler's not going anywhere."

FIFTY-THREE

CHARLOTTE

WHEN SILVESTRI WALKS into the room I can barely look him in the eye. But I force myself. I asked him here, and thankfully he agreed.

"Charlotte." He seems to be struggling with maintaining eye contact as much as I am.

"Dennis. Thank you for meeting with me alone."

"Charlotte, for the sake of clear boundaries, I'd prefer it if you called me Detective Silvestri from here on out."

"Of course." I barely have the energy to conceal the sting of his request.

"Great." He clasps his hands in front of him. "I need to let you know that anything we say in this room will be recorded, and potentially used in a court of law, should your case go to trial."

"I understand." There is no room for our friendly connection here any longer.

"Well, then." He sits back and appears to relax. "Now that the house-keeping is out of the way, let's talk."

I try to emulate his relaxed pose, but it is a challenge given my height-ened sense of anxiety.

"I was sorry to hear that your mother wasn't able to post bail for you." A noble, if not inflammatory, attempt at small talk.

"She was able to; she just chose not to." I consider that maybe I'm wrong about this but move on. "But she came to visit. So that is something."

"Does she believe that you're guilty?" Seems like Silvestri can read my mind. I don't know if that is a good or terrible thing at this point.

"I wouldn't put it past her." I reconsider. "No, actually, she doesn't. She supports and believes in me." I need to work on losing the "I hate my mother" routine, I realize. I'll add it to my growing list of self-improvement to-dos.

He raises an eyebrow. "Charlotte, what's on your mind? I don't imagine you asked me here to talk about your mother."

"Certainly not." I laugh drily. "I wanted to talk to you alone because I feel like you understand me, and possibly, hopefully, don't really believe that I had anything to do with Brooke and Rachel's deaths. I'm not sure that I ever had Detective Wolcott's faith, but I definitely don't now." This likely sounds rehearsed because I've rolled it over in my head so many times in the last hour.

He leans forward and places his elbows on the table and his right palm on his cheek. I realize it is probably strategic body language to disarm me.

"I want to believe you, Charlotte. I really do. But my job is predicated on finding common denominators, determining motive and opportunity, and piecing together compelling evidence. And, as much as I hate to say it, I'm afraid that you are the apex of everything." His eyes travel to my chest, where I realize I've been absently tapping at my heart acupoint. He averts his gaze quickly.

"Sorry. It helps to calm me. I'm feeling a little anxious." I migrate my active hand into a medium grip around my wrist and use my thumb to tap into the point between the tendons to calm myself.

"Charlotte, I appreciate the seriousness of your situation and the obvious stress that it brings. I also know you have lost someone incredibly important to you. What I'm struggling most to understand is what your motive in killing Rachel would be. Can you help me comprehend this?"

"I didn't kill *anyone*. I didn't have any reason to!" My voice is shrill.

"Okay. Let's back up. You have a background in science. You under-stand and appreciate rational thinking better than anyone. Put yourself in Wolcott's and my positions." He pauses. "Let me break it down for you from our perspective, and maybe you can help explain where we might have it wrong?"

I nod obediently.

"It seems like this was a deadly chain reaction. Once you committed the first murder, the second was put in motion. With planning and pre-meditation, you killed Brooke because of the guilt you felt about Mi-chelle's death, felt threatened and provoked by her relentless bullying from afar, and were ultimately losing a grip on your job, your financial security—"

"But I would never—I didn't know it was Brooke who was bullying—"

"My bet is that you killed Rachel out of necessity because she real-ized your part in Brooke's death and was unwilling to protect your se-cret. After the blowup at your house, where we imagine she may have threatened to turn you in, you killed her in her home, attempting to make it look like a suicide, to keep her from exposing you. Her murder had more of a compassionate air to it, suggesting you were conflicted. You killed her with something you knew would make her feel good on the way out. And then you couldn't leave her alone after you did it." He stops for a minute, and I notice veins in his forehead and neck pulsating. His eyes have darkened, and I can see that he is struggling to compose himself as well.

"And you used me for an alibi. I'm not going to begin to tell you all of the ways in which this was a terrible decision. But that is the kind of thing that doesn't just make Wolcott and me consider that you are ca-pable of murder, but also whether your role in Michelle's death was ac-tually accidental."

I feel like he's punched me in the face. My knuckles are white as I try to keep hold of myself. I'm not sure if the pause is a cue for me to re-spond, but I remain quiet.

"Charlotte, can you see how you are the most likely suspect? Everyone else with any possible motive has an alibi. And all I've recounted are just the basic facts. I haven't scratched the surface on the MO of the murders, which overwhelmingly implicate you, given your areas of expertise."

He leaves this utterly perplexing comment dangling, I assume, to see if I'll give something away in my subconscious movements. I can only offer absolute bafflement.

"Have I missed anything?" His face is neutral.

"Everything you've said is completely wrong," I spew desperately.

"Okay, then, please tell me. Where are we wrong in all of this? You are a brilliant woman with a deep understanding of the human brain. This all seems pretty logical, doesn't it? I would love for you to give us another plausible scenario that exonerates you."

My racing thoughts are jumbled and I am grasping at the most salient one to talk myself out of this. He's right—it absolutely looks like I could have done these terrible things. And restating that I'm not capable of killing anyone clearly doesn't mean anything, even if the only life I've actually taken was taken accidentally. I cannot become openly enraged unless I want that to be used against me down the line.

"Detective Silvestri, I can see how the puzzle pieces all come together, and why it appears that I'm your person. But the motives don't add up, because I had no reason to kill Brooke, and didn't kill her, so the incentive to kill Rachel would be nonexistent."

"How can you explain the happenstance of Brooke moving to Port Jefferson? A couple of towns over from the one that the woman who accidentally killed her sister resides in."

"I had no idea she was here. I haven't been in contact with her! I've never even been in the same room as her." I see impatience in Silvestri's face. This isn't good enough; my word means nothing to him.

He pauses for a sip of water and pulls his phone out of his back pocket and places it facedown on the table between us before continuing. "Based on what we know about your connection to her, and your interactions with her, it seems like you are not only the sole person who would have a possible motive, but there is ample evidence that you also engaged in a lengthy process of manipulation before taking her life." Silvestri stops and reclasps his hands together in front of him, waiting.

"I don't understand. Manipulation?" My heart is racing.

"It is interesting that you used the phrase 'in the same room,' Charlotte."

"What do you mean?"

"Well, you have been in the same room with Brooke more than twice, haven't you?"

I shake my head vigorously. Silvestri looks unmoved.

"What are you talking about?"

Calmly, he puts his palms on the table and locks eyes with me. "Okay, Charlotte. Let's say, for argument's sake, you've never physically been in the same room as her." He passes the bottle of water back and forth between his hands. I'm trying to keep focus on him and not this distracting action. He's toying with me. Wearing me down and trying to make me admit something I didn't do. I'm starting to feel crazy.

"But you were in a virtual room with her, weren't you?"

"I don't even know what that means."

"You are an active member in an online trauma survivors chat room, correct?" he asks.

I'm stunned. "Yes, I am."

"And you created the group to lure Brooke Harmon into joining, and groomed her under the guise of being a support system for her?" Every last hair on my body stands on end.

"*No.* I didn't start the group. I joined it. And there were already active members in it when I did."

"Members that eventually included Brooke Harmon. That seems like a remarkable coincidence."

I feel all of the color drain from my face as my blood pressure drops. "I had no idea Brooke was one of the members. We were anonymous." Silvestri is watching me closely as I'm turning over the news that I've been chatting with Brooke unaware. "Detective Silvestri, you have to believe me. I did not start this group. I had no idea that Brooke was one of the members. I swear to you."

"You expect me to believe that you wouldn't connect Brooke to her story in a confessional online support group, or she to yours? I have to assume that the trauma of her sister dying during surgery came up once or twice. From one or both of you? It is a pretty significant and unique event to have in common."

"I never talked about Michelle's death in detail in the room. I mostly talked in general terms, and more about my childhood than my residency. And none of the other members ever mentioned their sister dying during a brain surgery. I would have remembered that!" I mentally scan the members of the group. Harmnoone. Her sister was murdered. I feel feverish.

"I didn't do this! You have to believe me," I beg.

He's unaffected. "What happened? Did Brooke discover who you really were, and you had to kill her?"

"None of this is true." I throw my shackled hands up as far as I can move them. The knots of this story are getting more tangled and I'm losing the resolve in my innocence the more he says.

"Well, we haven't been able to recover all of the chat room archives yet, Charlotte. But I'm confident that when we do, we'll be able to fill in the blanks."

"Have you questioned the other members of the group? They'll be able to confirm that I joined before Brooke, but after they did."

"Well, that's the tricky part, isn't it, Charlotte?"

"I don't understand."

"I'm questioning all of the members of the chat room, minus Brooke, right now, aren't I?" An indecipherable smile crosses his face.

"I'm sorry, I'm not trying to be difficult. I'm really not following," I say.

"Charlotte, the IP addresses for the other members of the group trace back to a single server. They originated from the same computer. All of the supposed traumatized members of the group were actually you, alone. Isn't that correct?"

"What?" I feel sick. My blood pressure plummets and I start to feel a cold clamminess creeping up the back of my neck and around the sides of my face. "That is insane! I didn't create the group. I wouldn't know how, even if I wanted to. The members are not all me. How would that even be possible?" I feel a small sense of relief amid my befuddlement and fear. This is all so far-fetched, unbelievable, and untrue, they'll have to believe me.

Silvestri's phone chirps and he flips it over and quickly glances at the screen. "I'm going to need to take this. But I'll be back shortly. Why don't you take the time to dig back into your memory and see if you can suddenly recall how this all started. I imagine there is an amazing story waiting to be told."

I barely look at him as he exits the room.

FIFTY-FOUR

WOLCOTT

When I arrive at the Suffolk County Jail, Silvestri's waiting for me. After I show my credentials and sign in, a guard escorts us down the main hallway in the direction of the holding cells. My partner is raring to go.

"So, let's run through everything," he says. "We've got the direct connection to the dead women. There's her easy access to the poisons in both cases."

"The motive with Brooke Harmon, with Charlotte's business taking a hit with the bad Yelp reviews, and the continued harassment," I add. "Not so clear with Rachel Sherman, but we don't know what that fight was about."

"Right. Then the neighbor places Charlotte at Rachel's house around the time of the murder. She lies about having been there during our conversation later that night."

"And don't forget about her use of the chat room to lure Brooke Harmon."

"Seems like we've got enough to bring this thing home," he says. "Let's get back in there."

"*Back* in there?" I ask. "You already went a round with her?"

"Just warming the room up for you."

FIFTY-FIVE

CHARLOTTE

ALONE AGAIN, I find a focal point on the wall across from me in a cluster of chipped paint. I focus on the point to calm my hysterical nervous system and let my gaze become blurry. I try to clear my mind, but I keep thinking about Rachel.

"I wish you were here. I don't know what to do," I say out loud to the empty chair across from me. Of course, my plea is met with silence. But the hair on the back of my neck rises when I feel a distinct crackle of energy around me. "Please help me."

I close my eyes and imagine we are sitting in the backyard, but the once peaceful and comforting vision is now tainted by my nightmare. I open my eyes and shiver. I feel a sharp pain in my left big toe like I've been stung, and the jolt brings with it a conversation that she and I had early on in our friendship. It was when she was practicing reflexology on me in school.

"What's that point you are working on?" She'd been pressing hard on the upper part of my big toe, and I could feel the current of energy traveling up through my foot along my spine and into my cranial field.

She laughed. "Of course that is the one you'd ask about. This is the brain acupoint."

I'd recently confided in her about my past life as a surgeon. I didn't want anyone else in the program to find out and google my name. She'd been appropriately surprised and, I sensed, a little judgmental.

When she moved to my other foot and began working on the same point, she'd asked, "So, what made you interested in cutting into human brains?"

I'd given her my usual canned response, which always felt like a lie. "I always found surgery really fascinating, I guess. And brains were the organ with the most mystery about them, in my opinion."

"I always felt that way about the heart," she'd replied.

"But you didn't end up cutting into them," I'd countered.

"What trauma inspired you to spend half of your life in medical school studying other people's?" she'd asked knowingly

I'd had to think about it. I couldn't really remember a time when my becoming a doctor wasn't just part of my personal narrative. My mother had been reinforcing it for as long as I could remember. But that day, lying on my back with my new friend pushing into my foot and feeling a very clear sense of healing energy moving through my body, I tried to recall what I remembered, not what I'd been told.

"Honestly, I can't recall." I'd tried to imagine that early thought process, or an experience that made me want to devote my life to helping people with PTSD, but there was just a blank space.

She'd stopped pressing on my toe and come around to the top of the table.

"Have you ever been hypnotized?" Her eyes were lit up.

"No. But I read a lot about it in med school. There was some good controlled-study research for quitting smoking."

"And also for recovering memories. I'm surprised you didn't come across that in brain school." She'd been playful, but I remember feeling vaguely offended.

"Sure I did. There is a lot about repressed memory recovery. But also a lot of skepticism around hypnosis."

"Well, then. Let me teach you how to self-hypnotize. Maybe we can solve the mystery of why you wanted to become a brain doc."

It hadn't worked ultimately, but it was a big day for our friendship, when our bonding really began. "You are probably just one of those people who aren't highly suggestible," she'd said. "Probably a good thing." Now I wonder.

Back in the room, I will a wave of calm over me as I close my eyes and picture the number ten. It takes many repeated attempts, but sometimes extreme cortisol floods can help in self-hypnosis, if you know how to harness them. I'm able to visualize the number ten clearly after a few times. While it disappears from my mind's eye, I open and close my eyes quickly and picture the number nine, while I reach for another wave of calm. I open and close my eyes quickly once the nine fades. I repeat this until I get to number one, praying that I can successfully get my disjointed neural pathways to make contact and jog something in my brain that can help me. The familiar feeling of tingling and detachment courses through me. Entranced, I imagine myself in a movie theater, sitting in the front row and following a scene of myself on-screen.

I am walking the hallways of Stony Brook Memorial Hospital, newly hired as a rotational GP six months after moving back to Stony Brook and again living with my mother following my breakdown. I see my hopeless, beaten-down self going through the motions of someone half-asleep. I watch myself standing in front of the locked pharmaceutical room, silently deliberating over which fast-acting chemical exit I would use. It is the lowest point in my life.

I follow myself going from the hospital with a purse full of ill-gotten Dilaudid, opening my laptop to compose an email of apology to my few remaining loved ones, and being sidetracked by the rare nonspam email at the top of my inbox. It was from a friend of a psych nurse at Bellevue whom I hadn't remembered giving my info to, but I had been on a lot of Thorazine and didn't question it. Her message was saying she'd started an online support group for trauma survivors a few months earlier and our mutual "friend" had thought I might be interested in joining.

I clicked on the link in the email and was transported to the first safe and supportive place I'd been in since Michelle's death. There were people like me waiting to support and relate with, living with their guilt and shame, talking anonymously and openly about their worst moments and thoughts. In the safety of their virtual room, from the semi-safety of my actual room, I was able to share and be heard nonjudgmentally. I'd started tentatively, but quickly came to need the room to get through the day, and to sleep at night. I was able to laugh and cry with people who understood. They saved my life.

I engaged with them daily over the year and a half it took to get my head together. I confessed to them about not wanting to be a doctor any longer but still wanting to heal people. They cheered for me when I made a friend my first day studying acupuncture at the Center for Healing and moved into my new home, all in the same month.

In my hypnotic trance, I watch myself getting stronger and happier as I settle into my new life, opening my practice and changing my entire lifestyle. I start to feel the possibility of being in love again, and the group encouraging me to date. I become excited about a new member of the group, with whom I find myself sharing the same middle-of-the-night hours and chatting one-on-one when everyone else is asleep. We completely click. She and I couldn't be more alike.

Eventually she confides that *he* is actually a man posing as a woman in our support group, because he was unable to find a men's group online that he felt he could really open up in.

I am surprised about how undisturbed I am by this revelation. Part of me is even excited. He and I have already connected over our crazy mothers and keep finding the most random parallel things in common. I see myself crushingly disappointed when he doesn't come back to the group and no longer reaches out to me. I miss him deeply. I watch myself send a private message confiding as much, and to my delight, him responding, admitting he missed me too and how relieved he is that I don't hate him for lying, and how grateful that I kept his secret. He tells me that this is very important to him, "someone who he can trust to keep his secrets."

And then I relive our regular connecting on text and then by phone.

First a couple of times a week and then every day. My life becomes completely centered on when I'll hear from him next. I let the images and revelations trickle through me calmly. I observe myself rapidly falling in love with this person I never meet. Someone I feel so thoroughly understands me and doesn't judge me for the pain I've caused and the terrible mistakes I've made. Someone who went from being a screen name I was so excited to see appear—Openhearted2—to a person with an actual name—Peter—whose words and voice became something I came to depend on more than anything else in the world. And when I felt myself completely dependent and desperate to meet him in real life, he started to disappear and pull away.

It was him all along. Everything. He was using me, playing with me, getting off on my suffering. I was stupid and gullible enough to fall for it. How I could not see the most obvious piece of this puzzle levels me. I begin to shake.

Silvestri enters the room, pulling me back into complete consciousness. He's followed by Wolcott, who nods solemnly in my direction. He pulls the open chair noisily next to Silvestri. Silvestri leans against the wall, his gaze locked on his colleague before moving to me.

"Charlotte, we have a lot of ground to cover, and it is best if we do that with Wolcott here." Wolcott watches me but doesn't say anything right away.

I nod weakly. I'm reeling from the connections I've just made. I can't even begin to think how I can articulate it all to these men.

"I hate to be a third wheel, but you don't mind if I join, do you?" Wolcott finally chimes in.

I can barely move to acknowledge that he's spoken. My mind is overflowing with one horrible realization after another. All the things I believed to be one way were something completely different. I've been in one protracted, deadly hallucination for the past year. Longer, even. When did this all really start?

Peter. But why? My heart breaks all over again. I clutch at my chest, the metal of the restraints clanging noisily.

"Do you need a bathroom or stretch break?" Wolcott asks, concerned.

I shake my head.

Silvestri speaks. "Okay, then. Let's start at the beginning and talk about when you started the group and at what point you lured Brooke Harmon into it."

Brooke Harmon. Harmnoone82. My lungs are struggling to get a full breath in. She'd joined a few months after Peter had left the group. She and I had bonded quickly. It felt as though my circle of genuine, loving, chosen family was only getting bigger with each passing day.

"Detective Silvestri."

"Yes?"

"Remember you asked me if I was single?" I don't look at him when I ask this, and Wolcott's face takes on a vaguely strained affect.

"I don't believe that I phrased it that way, but you implied that you were unattached the first day that we met, if I remember correctly." He frowns. "Was that not the case?"

I hold on to my response for a split second as I attempt to fully accept the dawning truth about Peter. There is no reason to keep any of his secrets any longer. Every absurd, implausible, outlandish detail that I believed in good faith. I am stunned by my stupidity.

"Yes. I lied."

I have their attention now as I scan both of their faces. Wolcott looks intrigued, Silvestri brooding.

"Okay, Charlotte. So you have a significant other that you lied about. I'm assuming this person factors into proving your innocence in the deaths of Brooke and Rachel?"

"Yes."

Before I can continue, Silvestri shifts away from the wall and scratches his head. I think he's going to speak, but he remains quiet and pensive.

"I believe that the person I've been having a relationship with for the last year is somehow responsible for their deaths."

Silvestri shifts on his feet. They are stonelike, waiting for me to continue.

"And I believe he's framed me for both murders." My statement hangs heavily in the air between us. I search their faces for any indication of belief. I only see silent gears turning and shades of doubt.

"And why do you believe this person would want to frame you?"

"I honestly have no idea," I say.

"And what is this person's name, Charlotte?"

"Peter Stanton." I feel lighter saying it out loud.

"And where can we find Mr. Stanton?"

The momentary lifting reverses and my chest tightens. "I don't know."

"Why is that?" Wolcott asks gently.

"He's missing."

Dennis narrows his eyes.

"Then we'll need you to give us a physical description, and we'll put out an APB on him right away. If this man has anything to do with these deaths, we need to find him immediately."

"I can't do that," I say softly.

"Why is that?" Dennis presses.

"Because." My voice quivers. "I've never met him."

The room becomes airless and the detectives silent. Their indecipherable expressions stay fixed on me for a full, agonizing moment before they look at each other and appear to have an entire conversation with each other silently.

I sit in the chair and make myself as small as I can. Outside of the deep shame I feel, I am also experiencing a growing sense of relief now that I've said the unspeakable.

Wolcott breaks their mind meld first, turning to me slowly. "Charlotte, just so we are one hundred percent clear on this, you had a lengthy relationship with this man, but you never met each other in person?"

I nod. "That is correct." I look down at my lap, humiliated.

Silvestri speaks up. "And how exactly did you cross paths with this mysterious man?"

"In the chat room," I respond.

"The *women's* support group?" he asks.

"He was posing as a female member," I whisper.

Silvestri takes a sharp inhale. "Charlotte, are you telling us that this person you've been in a relationship with for a year is not only someone you've never met but who was lying from the jump?"

He rubs his temple with one hand and extends his other out in a gesture of disbelief.

"Yes."

"I'm not going to lecture you on how dangerous this all is," he says to the wall.

This is sickeningly funny, because "Peter" has already lectured me about the dangers of people posing as someone they're not online. I wouldn't suspect the online fraud expert of online fraud, naturally.

"I imagine you have texts and exchanged pictures you can share with us?" Silvestri probes.

My stomach drops. "They don't exist."

"Of course they don't," he quips.

Wolcott interjects. "That's problematic, Charlotte. Why is that?"

"We used an app that automatically deletes texts after twelve hours. It is untraceable. Peter insisted that it was the safest way to communicate."

"And have you been in touch with Peter in the last twelve hours?" Silvestri questions.

"No. I haven't heard from him in almost a week. Before that, it was a month."

Silvestri and Wolcott trade glances.

"And did you ever speak on the phone?" Wolcott jumps in.

"Yes, but he always called me."

"Of course he did," Silvestri mutters.

"Was Peter Stanton perhaps married?"

"No." As I say it, I realize I have no idea if that is the truth. Nothing else he told me was true, evidently, so why would something inconsequential like being married or having, say, a family be something he'd be forthcoming about? I am dying a thousand deaths in this chair.

"And why did he say it was 'safer' to use a disappearing text app?" Silvestri resumes control.

"Because of his job."

"And what line of work is Mr. Stanton in?" They both seem mildly amused now. They clearly think I'm making this up as I go along.

"I don't know exactly." I blow the hair that has fallen into my eyes out of my face. "He told me that he was in a department of the US government that was highly classified and couldn't breach protocol by telling me any details."

Silvestri and Wolcott exchange a look of complete disbelief without even attempting to hide it from me.

"He did tell me that he was a specialist in online crimes, and that the reason he was in the chat room in the first place, posing as a woman, was because he was investigating online chat room scams."

I can't tell if the expression of incredulity on their faces is directed at the absurdity of an obviously fabricated story or my stupidity for believing any of it.

"Look, I realize this all sounds crazy and fictitious. I'm processing it all in real time too. I didn't realize that Peter was involved in any way until you told me about the chat room and Brooke. I don't understand how he did it, but it has to be him."

Wolcott speaks. "Okay, Charlotte, you've got our attention. We'll follow you down this rabbit hole for a bit and see where we end up. We are going to need any information that you have. Phone numbers used, any emails or texts, anything that could help us locate him and obtain proof of his whereabouts—"

"And his existence," says Silvestri acidly.

FIFTY-SIX

SILVESTRI

"I'M ALMOST INCLINED to give her an A for creativity." I chuckle. I make a point of speaking softly, as our voices echo through the empty hallway.

My partner snorts. "Let's go ahead and save that A for arrogance. She really tried to pull that Secret Agent Man bullshit with us? What, does she think we walked in here out of a cornfield?"

"Uh, Wolcott. There are cornfields up and down Long Island—"

"Okay, wise guy. You know what I'm getting at."

"I do. What do you expect, though? She's desperate. It's gotta feel like those walls are squeezing in on her by the second."

"Yeah," he says. "Well, I can't wait to see how slick she tries to get when the parents of the deceased are staring her down in that room."

"There you go, pal. Pulling the ace. Feel better?" I ask.

"Oh, I'm not even mad. More amused than anything."

"Good," I say. "Let's go drop the hammer on her."

Wolcott rubs his hands together. "Let's."

We turn and walk down the hallway. *There's a man who leads a life of danger / To everyone he meets he stays a stranger.*

My partner turns to me, wincing. "Save it for the shower, Silvestri."

FIFTY-SEVEN

CHARLOTTE

I'M ABSOLUTELY NUMB from the conversation with the detectives and the realization about Peter and am lying nearly comatose when Silvestri tells me that the Harmons have requested to meet with me. I hesitate only momentarily before agreeing. I know I may never get another opportunity to make amends in person, and in my heart I know it is the right thing to do. Anger probably isn't a strong enough word for how they feel toward me, and I'm imagining they will be waiting for me in a windowless room with bats and bricks. Even so, being the object of their rage will maybe feel better than my current state.

There was a moment after Michelle died when the only thing I wanted in the world was to apologize to her family. By the time I came to my senses enough to express this desire, I was in and out of Bellevue, and the hospital considered anything having to do with Michelle a closed matter. My former employer's malpractice lawyers forbade me from speaking directly to the Harmons and concocted a sanitized statement of condolence only to be released after the case was finalized. So the only form of apology the Harmons ever received from me was written by a crisis management consultant, signed in my name.

The day of the surgery, Henry was the one who ended up telling the Harmons—Brooke included—that Michelle had died. It should have been me, but I was barely coherent, so I stayed behind while he went to do the hardest part of a surgeon's job. He didn't give me a choice, though, just told me that I needed to pull myself together and get back to work.

I return to the moment again and again and wish I'd been able to compose myself enough and fought Henry for the opportunity that should have been unquestionably mine. It was my surgery and my responsibility. In the moment I was relieved that Henry did the difficult thing that I wasn't able to. It took some years of distance to see how he manipulated the whole narrative of that day from the moment Michelle took her last breath.

There was something about the way Henry acted about the surgery after the fact. Bedside manner was never his strong suit, but he was so brilliant and confident in the procedures, his brusqueness was generally accepted.

"Sometimes things just don't work out" were the words of wisdom my mentor and romantic partner shared with me after Michelle died. He said it with the same level of concern he might have about getting ketchup on a favorite shirt. His detachment stuck with me for months after and made me question if he was at all the person I thought he was. A detached bedside manner was one thing, but a complete lack of empathy for everyone was another.

My recollections are interrupted by an officer I don't know unlocking the cell and ordering me to stand and follow him. My heart beats as heavily as his footsteps as we near the visitors' room and I'm led to a table where the Harmons are waiting for me. My palms are damp and I rub them on the synthetic material of my prison scrubs—unnecessarily, since there are no handshakes extended.

As soon as I take my seat, Mr. Harmon slides his chair back, stands, and leans in close to my face. "I should kill you right now for what you've done," he growls.

"Hey! No contact. Keep your distance, sir." The beefy visitors' room guard advances on us at the same time that Mrs. Harmon snaps her husband back a few feet by the arm. He turns sharply on his heels and faces the window with his back to me. His shoulders are up around his ears and I can see that he is breathing fast.

She rises to join her husband and leans into him and says something in his ear.

"Kathy. I can't do this. I'm sorry." He bolts for the door and the guard holds up his hand.

"Sir, if you leave now, there is no reentry."

"Out of my way!" he bellows in response, and the guard steps aside while he storms off.

The other family in the visiting room seems undisturbed by Mr. Harmon's dramatic exit and barely look up from their engrossed conversation.

"Mrs. Harmon, I'm very sorry for everything that has happened. I know there isn't anything I can say, but I have never been able to tell you how sorry I am about Michelle."

I have to use every bit of might to make eye contact with her. She locks my gaze and I am looking directly into hatred.

"Don't you even say her name," she spits. "I am not here about Michelle."

I'm cowed. I don't say a word and look at my hands on the table.

"I would let my husband choke the life out of you if I didn't think it would be too much of an easy way out. I would like to see you suffer for a very long time in prison," she hisses.

Ashamed, I attempt to modulate my voice so I don't sound like the scared little girl who is sitting across from her. I take a breath before speaking.

"Mrs. Harmon, I swear to you, I did not hurt Brooke. I've never even met her in person." I want to tell her that now that I know that Brooke and I were friends, I feel the huge loss as well. But I know making any of Brooke's death about my grief might be the worst thing I could do.

"As far as I'm concerned, anything you say is pure and absolute lies. You are clearly mentally ill and living in your own imaginary world without rules or any regard for other people. You are about to have quite a painful reality check, though."

She reaches into her purse. My heart stops for a minute and I look to the guard, expecting to feel the business end of a knife plunged into my jugular before he makes it across the room. Instead she withdraws a folded piece of paper, lays it on the table, and slides it across to me.

I look at the guard again to see if my accepting this offering is against the rules, but he's focusing on one of the visitors struggling with the vending machine and not even looking in our direction. I don't make a move.

"To be honest, Charlotte, I didn't want to see your face until it was sitting in the defendant's box of a courtroom awaiting your sentencing. You are an evil person."

"Mrs. Harmon, I understand why you hate me."

"I wish you could give your life to bring my daughter's back. But Brooke was a far more loving and forgiving person than I am, and that is why I'm here." She gestures at the piece of paper and covers her face with her hand and shakes slightly.

I unfold the page and see that it is an email addressed to me. I jump to the bottom of the text and see Brooke's name.

"What is this?" I ask, afraid to read any of the words on the page.

"It's a letter addressed to you that Brooke had saved in the drafts folder of her email. She wrote it recently. So your claim that you didn't even know she was in town seems pretty flimsy to me, since you were clearly still in the forefront of her mind. I don't know what kind of head games you were playing on her, but after I read it, I realized that there would be nothing I could say to you that would be worse than your seeing how much better a person Brooke was than you."

I'm speechless as my vision blurs when I attempt to get a grip on the words on the page. I wipe the tears from my eyes and swallow. There is a knot in my throat the size of an apple. Crying in front of Mrs. Harmon feels wrong for a lot of reasons. She doesn't look at me and I start to read.

Dear Charlotte,

I'm writing this letter after six and a half unbearable years without my older sister and best friend, Michelle. In that time I have fantasized about what I would say to you if I had the chance. You have been the focus of so much of my rage for so long, I started to get used to it as its own emotion that I carried around with me as regularly as sadness. It got heavier with each year that passed and I'm ready to let go of that weight and move on.

After Michelle died, my mom and dad moved out of the country for a fresh start. I was so angry at them for moving so far from where Michelle was buried, our relationship disintegrated. I had no direction or joy in my life, and no family. I couldn't work. My marriage fell apart. I stopped seeing my friends. I felt like you had not only taken my sister from me, but my entire life.

For every holiday, birthday, and life event that passed without Michelle, I harbored this deep anger that was consuming me from the inside out. I became sick and hopeless. I lost track of the fact that I was the sister who was still alive. I thought if I could hurt you, it might take away some of the incredible pain you've caused my family.

A few things happened in the last year that changed this darkness in me. I found support in people who knew what it was like to survive incredible loss. I started fresh in a new place and found that I was still very much alive.

I am ready to let go of the anger. I want to forgive you. I accept that you made a terrible mistake, and one that I think you'd probably give anything to undo if you could. I hope you have forgiven yourself by now, but if you haven't, I hope that this letter helps you get closer to that.

Brooke Harmon

I wipe my face with the back of my hand and look at Mrs. Harmon, who is staring at me coldly. I know I can't say what I want to, as I imagine my thanking her in this moment might send her into a fit of rage. I'm at a complete loss for words.

"I don't know what to say. This is incredible." I am overwhelmed.

"My husband thought I was crazy giving this to you. He doesn't think you deserve anything from us, and certainly not from Brooke. But I wanted you to know the character of Brooke, so that one day when you fully realize what you've done, you can live with the shame that she was ready to forgive you."

"I'm so sorry she's gone. I'm so sorry." I'm rocking in the chair a little bit and wincing at the pounding behind my eyes.

"Two minutes left, folks. Wrap it up." The guard shouts too loudly for the barely populated room.

"Please believe me, Mrs. Harmon. I'll do anything to help find the person who did this to Brooke. I had no reason to do this. I would never hurt anyone—" She's on her feet as fast as she can stand up and begins yelling over my pleas.

"I hope you suffer every day for what you've done to us," she spits. "My daughter may, but *I* will never forgive you for as long as I live."

FIFTY-EIGHT

WOLCOTT

"Silvestri," I shout excitedly into the phone.

"Was just calling you," he responds. "Been a busy day over here. Christina, the server from the diner? She came down to the station to follow up on the messages we left her, after the romp with the line cook."

"Silvestri—"

"I show her a photo of Brooke Harmon. No recollection whatsoever. Claims to have been stoned to the gills through her whole shift. And considering how glassy her eyes were in the station, I have little problem believing it." He chuckles. "So, dead end there, I'm afraid."

"Silvestri, shut up for a second."

There's a pause in the sound of papers being shuffled on the other end of the line. "What's up?" he asks.

"Charlotte didn't do it," I say.

"What?" asks Silvestri, tentatively.

"The timeline. Fisk just confirmed that Rachel Sherman was killed at ten P.M. on the fifth. *You* alibi Charlotte out."

There's a long hesitation on my partner's end. When he finally speaks, there's a discernable brightening of his tone. "Holy shit. That's . . . Wait, though. What about her car?"

"That was my first thought, too. Went back and did the math from that night, with you showing up at our place from Charlotte's house. Even had Abby confirm the time. Once I cemented that, I called Rachel Sherman's neighbor, to double-check his recollection of the time frame. Remember he mentioned having just gotten back from a trip to Chicago?"

"Yeah."

"When I pressed him, he realized that he hadn't set his watch back to eastern standard. He was off by an hour. I don't know why the car—"

"Oh shit! Wait."

"What's up?"

"I was so thrown by the timeline when we first spoke with the neighbor that I completely missed it; when I went to Charlotte's that night, her car wasn't in the driveway. She mentioned having taken an Uber back to her house."

"From Rachel Sherman's?"

"It didn't sound like it, but I guess it must have been."

"Well," I say, "we can sort it out when we go bust her out of jail."

"On my way."

FIFTY-NINE

CHARLOTTE

I BARELY REMEMBER the ride home as we pull into my driveway, only that it has been quietly tense. Neither Detective Silvestri nor I have said much, beyond him clearing his throat a number of times and my saying "thank you" or "no, thank you."

It feels strange to be wearing my own clothes and holding my phone and purse again. I'd started getting used to having nothing. My phone is dead, so I haven't been able to check it for messages yet, but the police are now tapping it in case Peter reaches out. I don't expect that I'll hear from him, but it may just be that I've gotten so used to him abandoning me, especially when things get difficult.

Even so, if Peter wanted to be in touch, I have to imagine he expects that I'm being watched and protected by the law. Whether he assumes I'm being watched from inside jail or out is what I can't envision at this point. This has been such an elaborate game that I didn't know I was playing in, I can't even guess what his next move will be.

Silvestri insisted on giving me a ride home and I was too sleep deprived to resist. Even though I'm no longer a murder suspect, I requested to sit in the back seat just the same. I couldn't face sitting beside him. Less than twenty-four hours ago, he believed that I was a murderer.

When we reach my home, he clears his throat again when he turns off the engine and offers his hand as he opens the back door for me. I don't acknowledge the gesture and move past him from the car to the driveway. With my back to him, I hear his footfall on the gravel and I move a step away.

"I bet you're going to be happy to sleep in your own bed tonight." He is handling me like I'm an injured bird, and I should welcome the tenderness, but my earlier warmth toward him has been replaced with a dull detachment. There have been too many emotional dials turned up to the max in the last few days, and I am spent.

"I'm very happy to be home," I say wearily. My back is completely out, which is greatly contributing to my crankiness.

There was a slight air of sheepishness and apology from the detectives when they explained that I was getting out. Something about the time of death for Rachel not adding up, among other things. The noise in my head from my sit-down with Kathy Harmon was still on full blast, and I missed a lot of their explanation beyond "You are free to go." I suppose I should feel more joy and relief about being exculpated, but my head is a flurry of emotions, and none of them are positive or comforting in the least. And even though I'm out of the suspect position, Peter is still out there, and probably watching me.

The squad car that trailed us from the station is idling at the foot of my driveway. I turn my attention in its direction and see the driver, who looks no older than thirteen. His partner is an even younger-looking woman who has her black hair pulled into a severe bun. They are chatting and watching us. Silvestri gives a wave and the baby-faced cop cuts the engine. I avoid catching eyes with Silvestri as I turn my attention back toward the house.

"Officers Smith and Tedesco are good cops. They'll be posted outside your house around the clock. If anything or anyone looks suspicious, they'll alert us and will secure the premises. We've already done a sweep of your house, and everything is as it should be. Your mother was very helpful. You'll be completely safe at all times."

"I don't know about that." I glance at my mother's car, parked squarely in the middle of the driveway. I had hoped dearly that she would be long gone by now. As usual, she has succeeded in dashing my dreams.

"How's that?" He seems genuinely concerned.

"The call is coming from inside the house," I deadpan.

He lets a chuckle escape. "Are you going to be all right?"

"Probably not. But anything is better than where I've spent the last two days."

He nods sympathetically. "Indeed." I think I see a tinge of guilt in his face, but I could be looking for that. "Would you like me to walk you in?" he offers.

I shake my head sulkily.

"Maybe I can illuminate the situation a bit for her, so that you don't have to?" He's trying, and I'm giving him nothing.

Anger rises in me. "Maybe you can illuminate it all for me as well while you're at it?"

He looks surprised by my flare-up but doesn't push the issue. "Okay, then. If you leave, don't go too far," he says lightly.

"And where the hell would I go?" I look him square in the face and am startled at my own growing fury in his direction. I'm strung out from my sleeplessness. Beat up. Everyone who was supposed to be on my side feels like an enemy right now.

"Sorry. Get some sleep. We'll need to talk with you again soon."

"Fine. When?" I seem to be unintentionally channeling my mother's attitude the closer in proximity I get to her.

"We'd like you to come back in as soon as possible. Once you're feeling a little better, of course. Would that be okay?" He seems flustered, and I suddenly feel guilty for being so angry in his direction. I center myself and reframe.

"Whatever I can do to help," I say.

"We've got our resident computer forensics guy recovering the chat archives and tracing Peter. We'd love your input, in case there are any clues that you might catch that we wouldn't."

"Okay. But I really don't think I'm a good judge of anything Peter says or does."

"You know the guy better than any of us. He may have given something away that you didn't realize at the time," he says.

This brings up a much stronger emotional response than I expect, and I put my hand over my face.

"Sorry, Charlotte. I know this is a lot of loss for you at once."

"I thought I knew him. I'm so ashamed that I let things go as far as I did. I was a fucking brain surgeon, for God's sake! Rachel knew something was very wrong and tried to help me. I should have listened to her." I drag the tip of my clog across the gravel.

Silvestri puts a firm hand on my shoulder. "Don't torture yourself on top of the grief you are processing now. You wouldn't believe how many smart, caring, honest people get taken in by these animals. It really isn't about intelligence; it's about trust and vulnerability."

"I appreciate that. But the fact remains, I trusted and *loved* someone that I had never even *met*. I'm having a hard time reconciling that."

"This guy is the worst kind of sociopath. He's the combo platter: a con artist *and* potentially a cold-blooded killer who fancies himself smarter than everyone else. He thrives on the long game and on tricking people who threaten his intelligence." He puts his other hand on my opposite shoulder and squeezes me.

"I just wish I had the first idea why he wanted to ruin my life. It doesn't make any sense. And to do it so elaborately."

"We'll figure it all out."

"I want him caught so that he doesn't hurt someone else."

"Or you." He looks me straight in the eye.

"I doubt he's going to contact me, especially if he finds out that you no longer think I'm responsible for Brooke and Rachel. Not that I'd recognize him if he walked up to my front door and rang the bell." I cringe.

"That's what worries me the most." His expression darkens.

"There isn't really anything left he can do to me," I say, defeated.

Silvestri gives me a concerned once-over. "Not from where I'm standing."

◈ ◈ ◈

Its early, and I'm tucked into my bed, grateful beyond belief that I am where I am right now. I hear my mother running a bath and singing a show tune that I don't know the name of but that brings me back to childhood. Surprisingly, she's left me alone since I arrived home.

I'm scrolling through photos of Rachel on my phone from a yoga retreat we went on together a couple of years ago, a trip to Sedona two winters ago, and, most recently, a silent meditation retreat in Woodstock last spring. One by one, the images provoke immediate despair into aching into love into deep appreciation for the many wonderful experiences she and I had together. And anger at having to be without my friend. I open a close-up of her beaming face, looking incredibly happy and light. She reminded me often about how lucky she felt to have come back to life and been given a second chance.

"Give me a sign that you are still around, Rach. Please."

I sit with my eyes closed for a few minutes before I hear a tinny ringing sound coming from the spare bedroom/office, where my mother is camped out, and it takes me a minute to register that it is the house landline. The previous owners left the throwback handset telephone still plugged in. The service came with Internet, so I held on to it for no reason other than it seemed easier to keep it than cancel.

"Also good to have in case of a zombie appocalypse or if the grid goes dark," Rachel had joked when I first moved in, and I called her cell from the line to figure out what the phone number was. She'd call me on it every once and a while for the nostalgic thrill it provided.

As I walk toward the sound, I feel exhilarated by the possibility that it is Rachel communicating with me from another dimension. It isn't until I have my hand on the phone that I have the passing thought that I should get my cell phone and call or text Silvestri right away. It feels as plausible that Peter would be calling on the line as it does that it could be my dead best friend from beyond the grave.

I have the receiver in my hand mid-ring.

"Hello?"

The line is quiet.

"Rachel?" I feel immediately foolish and catch sight of myself in the mirror holding the phone, and flash back to my youth.

"Charlotte?" the man's voice on the other end asks, and my stomach starts to churn violently. I sit on the edge of the bed.

"Peter?" I gulp.

"No, this is Jack," he replies gently. "I wanted to check on you and see how you are doing. You were discharged by the time I made my way back to your room."

I gather he hasn't spoken to Nurse Murphy yet if he's still identifying himself by a fake name. I am tempted to call him Dr. Lyons to see how he reacts, but I decide against it. I'm also trying to imagine how he could have gotten this number. I'm definitely not associated with it anywhere that I can think of.

I decide against interrogating him. I have decidedly bigger fish to fry as far as men not saying who they really are. I just need to get rid of this one.

"That's nice of you, and totally unnecessary. I'm doing just fine." I stumble over "fine."

"Good. I'm glad you are feeling better." He hesitates. "Listen, I just want to tell you how sorry I am about Rachel. I've lost people close to me in my life, and it is incredibly difficult. Especially close friends. I'm sure she was very grateful to have you."

I'm annoyed this man has insinuated himself where I haven't asked him to be. "Thanks. Yes, it is very hard right now . . ." I trail off.

"When are you planning on going back to work? I'd love to come in and finish what we started last time," he says. "My shoulder is killing me and I've really been feeling my pre-op anxiety. I promise not to make any more bad jokes about being a human pincushion." He pauses for laughter. I am silent. "Well, no more bad jokes after that one, anyway."

"I'm not sure when I'll be back. Maybe early next week. I haven't gotten that far yet. But you can look online and book through our site. I'll make sure the dates I'm returning are available."

"Okay, then. I'll keep trying." He sounds frustrated or something. Maybe even a little pissed. I am not taking that on right now. The call has already lasted longer than I wanted it to.

"Jack, I really need to go now."

"I'll be thinking about you, Charlotte. I may even drop by to check in next week, just to make sure you are doing okay," he says sweetly.

"Bye," I say quickly.

The receiver is barely back on the cradle when it dawns on me that I never identified my "dead friend" as Rachel to Jack.

⸾ ⸾ ⸾

I'm not sure what to make of Jack Doyle, or whoever he is, but I decide to call Silvestri to tell him about the strange call. As soon as I unlock my phone, my heart swells at the snapshot of Rachel filling my screen and I fall back into the rabbit hole of my friend's images. I return to combing through photographs that I will cull for Rachel's memorial service, which I can't even fathom organizing. Numbly, I create a new photo folder named "Rachel" and slot it between two existing folders, "P" and "Receipts," and my heart stops cold. I click on the "P" folder, one that I'd completely forgotten I'd created. Inside: two photos of Peter. From way back in the very beginning of our courtship, if I can even call it that. I saved the first two photos he sent me before he convinced me to switch over to the Specter app, where everything is automatically deleted. I'd downloaded the pics to my phone to show them to Rachel before they disappeared. And because I'd wanted to look at his face when I couldn't talk to him.

With shaking hands, I text Silvestri and attach the photos. I feel excited that I have proof of him and crushingly sad looking at the two shots. It was a year of my life I spent talking to, texting, planning with, fantasizing about, and missing this person. A year of my life, and the longest, most intense relationship I've ever had. Which is probably why I fell for it all in the first place. All of those years when everyone else was tripping through adolescence and falling headfirst into love and betrayal and all of the highs and lows of sex and dating and marriage and divorce, I was studying.

I lie down and feel the heavenly softness of my own bed and close my eyes.

SIXTY

SILVESTRI

"THIS GUY HAS to have been right in front of us all along."

We're back in the interrogation room at the station house, looking through exchanges from the chat room that Charlotte and Brooke Harmon belonged to. Clarence is sitting in front of an open laptop, helping us navigate. Wolcott and I are looking over his shoulder as Charlotte sits at the table next to him. She's agreed to come down and run us through the chats, in the hope of helping find any bread crumbs that might lead back to our perp.

"Here's the thing with that," says Clarence. "Whoever it was who ran game on you guys spoofed the server. As far as we can tell from *this*," he says, nodding at the screen, "these messages originated from somewhere in Cambodia."

"How'd they do that?" asks Wolcott.

"Basically, they falsified the IP address, so it looks like these are coming in from a different geographical location entirely. But that's not even the craziest part," says Clarence, sucking in his breath.

"Oh no?" asks Wolcott.

"Remember I told you that all of the usernames originated from the same address, except for this one?" he says, pointing to "Woundedhealer" on the screen—the handle we now know to belong to Charlotte.

"Right." I nod.

"So," he continues. "I went back further. Turns out that up until

October first, all of the chats from 'Harmnoone82' also came from a different address. After that, though? Same IP address as the others."

"*After* her murder . . ." Charlotte trails off, dazed, the tone in her voice mirroring the ghoulish reality of the situation.

"Jesus," says Wolcott.

"So it was just me in there with Peter," says Charlotte, shuddering.

"Whoever this 'Peter' really is," I say. I look to Charlotte, and I'm struck with a pang of sympathy. I'd become as convinced as Wolcott that she had to have been involved in this mess, and I can't imagine what it must have felt like to be so utterly alone and scared over the course of these last several days, proclaiming her innocence to deaf ears. She appears to be as pulled together as can be expected of someone in her position, but her nerves show some fray.

"About that," says Clarence. "These photos you had me run?" He points to the two on the screen—the same ones that Charlotte Knopfler texted us. "Turns out they're model stock photos. Whoever this actually was just ripped them and sent them to you. Happens all the time with catfishers."

The audible gasp pulls my attention to Charlotte. She shudders as the color drains from her face. She appears to be deflating, right there in the chair.

"Okay," says Wolcott, in an effort to assuage her obvious discomfort. "Let's go back to the jump here. Likely suspects. Time to take a fresh look at who we're eyeing."

"There's Henry Thornton," I say. He does have the hotel alibi, though his girlfriend sounded nervous when we spoke. I make a mental note to follow up with her, and turn to Charlotte. "You worked with the guy. Do you think he'd be capable of something like this?"

She mulls it over for a long moment. "I don't know, but I've learned that his lack of empathy makes him capable of a lot of things that I might not have suspected at first."

"Something to consider. Okay, Annie Forester. I checked her Amazon Streaming history. She did in fact order a movie the night of the murder, like she told us."

"Not an airtight alibi, but we can circle back to that. How about Stacy Phillips? Still haven't been able to track her down."

"I'm sorry," Charlotte interjects. "Did you just say 'her'?"

"Yeah," says Wolcott. "The nurse."

"Um, Stacy Phillips is a man."

Clarence looks wide-eyed from Charlotte to my partner. "Yo, you guys assumed . . ." He shakes his head, suppressing a laugh. "That's priceless."

"Well, looks like we've got omelet on our faces," says Wolcott, cheeks reddening. "Probably why we had such a tough time finding anything on him." He looks to Charlotte. "Any chance you've got a line on *Mr.* Phillips?"

She shakes her head. "I haven't been in touch with Stacy since the surgery. But I wouldn't worry about him."

"How's that?" my partner asks.

"Stacy's as gentle as they come. The worst thing you could accuse him of is making bad jokes . . ." She trails off before her eyes widen. "Wait a minute!"

"What's up?" I ask.

"Jack Doyle," she says. "I mean, um, John Lyons."

"Who?" I ask.

She takes a moment to get her thoughts together. "Okay, so a new patient shows up at my office for an appointment. He introduces himself as Jack Doyle. Pays in cash. I can't really get a good read on him. Confusing energy. Pretty arrogant, honestly. He turns out to be a doctor." She lets out an uncomfortable laugh. "Should have known. He reminded me a lot of Henry, actually." The mention of Thornton stirs my gut. I feel a fresh urge to get a bead on him. "Later," she continues, "when I'm checked into the hospital, I find out from a former colleague of mine that this doctor's real name is John Lyons. Then, the other night, I get a sympathy call from him on my landline, with his condolences about Rachel. Only I have no clue how he got that number, and I never told him that Rachel was the friend who had died."

I feel a tingle up my forearms. Wolcott, pitched forward in his seat, turns from her to me. "What do you say we go corral ourselves a doctor?"

"Actually," I say, "I've got a couple in mind."

SIXTY-ONE

CHARLOTTE

I'M BACK FROM the police station for fifteen minutes and settling in for an emergency meditation session. As soon as I get comfortable, there is a knock at my bedroom door. I think about not answering in the hope that she'll think I'm sleeping and retreat. But before I have a chance to lie down and feign sleep, I see the doorknob turning.

"Char? Honey?" She pushes the door open cautiously and I glance at her for a quick second, long enough to see that she's going full Norma Desmond, with a silk turban and a velvet cape draped around her shoulders.

"What is it?" I can barely look at her without wanting to laugh.

"I'm glad you are home." Her sincerity is unsettling.

"Turns out you didn't have to pick me up from my latest fiasco after all, Mother." We haven't spoken directly since I was released. She was passed out cold in front of the TV when I came home, and I've been hiding in my room for the last two days, mostly in a state of delirious sleep. I'm rocked by dreams about Rachel and the Harmon sisters.

"How are you feeling?" she asks carefully. "I left some supplies outside your door yesterday. I didn't want to disturb you." She's referring to her idea of comfort food: a bottle of gin, a half-eaten bag of Milano cookies, potato chips, and a couple of pills, which looked to be Valium, all arranged on a silver platter.

"I'm alive." I'm feeling worlds better than I did forty-eight hours ago, but I'm still not feeling strong enough to go a few rounds with her. She lingers in my doorway.

"I'm really sorry that I couldn't bail you out, Charlotte."

"It's fine." I look back down at my phone and send a text to Lucy, confirming our appointment in an hour. I agreed to see her earlier than I'd planned to go back to the office because she was clearly suffering by the sound of her voice when she called earlier today.

The two officers who've been watching the house are waiting to escort me to my office and stand guard for Peter, on the insistence of the detectives. I'm happy to have the protection.

"Do you want to . . . talk about things?" It appears this "talking about things" is threatening to become a regular practice with us.

"I've got to get to work. I have a patient coming in." I catch the flicker of surprise in her face and look away.

"Really? Isn't it a little quick to go back to work, dear?"

I really wasn't planning on getting back into things so quickly, but the combination of not wanting to be trapped in an uncomfortable conversation like this one and my patient being in distress motivated me to return to it.

"It has only been a couple of days since you've been home. Is that healthy? After everything you've been through?"

"I'm fine, Mom."

She sits on my bed and changes her approach. "It is just wonderful news that you've been released. I knew you didn't do anything wrong."

Anger bubbles. "Did you, Mom? Is that why you left me in jail? Did you think it would be a good character-building exercise?"

"Oh, Charlotte. It wasn't about you."

"It never is, Mom."

I'm shocked to see her burst into tears.

"Mom, what is it?" I ask.

"I'm broke. That is why I didn't bail you out. It wasn't a personal statement. You know I would have if I could have."

"What are you talking about? What about your retirement money?"

"Gone."

"What about the money you 'borrowed' from my settlement money? And all the rent I paid you?"

"*Long* gone."

"How have you been supporting your gimlet habit, then? And your clothes?" I gesture to her elaborate getup. "Capes aren't cheap."

"I've been Airbnbing the house to a bunch of pornographers so that I can make my monthly debt-consolidation payments." She lets me absorb this. I'm speechless. She forges on. "I'm destitute and am going to lose the house at the rate I'm going."

"Wait. What? What do you mean *pornographers*?" I'm dearly hoping I've misheard her.

"I got an offer from a young independent filmmaker to rent the house, and it was twice what I thought I could get. I went by the house this week to check on things, and they were filming a rather racy scene in the living room. They didn't know I was there, but I caught the tail end of . . . oh, never mind, it was the tail end of something. Or someone."

I can only imagine how depraved what she saw had to be if she was scandalized by it. "Oh Mom. I don't even know how to process this information right now."

Suddenly her excitement and insistence to stay at my place is making sense. As is the inordinate amount of stuff in the trunk of her car. I sigh.

I feel a rush of empathy for her. "Mom. Don't worry. We'll figure this out. Okay?"

She's shocked. "Really?"

I say it because I know it's true. It has to be. I will help her, in spite of my better judgment. She was there for me at my worst.

She looks surprised and grateful, two emotions that are also new for her.

I take a look at my phone and see the time. "I need to get going, Mom. We'll talk about this later, okay?" She nods and steps aside to let me through, and shockingly pulls me in for a tight hug. I stiffen and then go limp.

Path of least resistance.

SIXTY-TWO

WOLCOTT

"How may I help you, sir?"

I'm standing at the reception desk at Stony Brook Memorial Hospital. Silvestri and I have split up, and he's out attempting to track down Henry Thornton. The young woman I'm speaking with offers up gleaming-white rows of teeth.

"Yes, I'm looking for Dr. John Lyons."

The smile remains intact as she goes rapid-fire on the keyboard. She consults the screen in front of her, then picks up the telephone handset. "Is Dr. Lyons still on the floor?" she asks, and waits patiently on the line. "Okay, thank you." She hangs up and returns her attention to me. "It appears that Dr. Lyons wrapped up surgery and has left for the day. May I . . ."

I flash her a quick eyeful of shield, which promptly switches her smile to the off position. A look of concern takes its place. "Would you be so kind as to provide me with a home address and phone number for Dr. Lyons?" I ask.

She returns to her keyboard, and in a few ticks she's turned the info up. She pivots the monitor toward me. I jot it down, return the notebook to my pocket, thank her, and wish her a lovely day.

SIXTY-THREE

CHARLOTTE

I'M SHAKY and the simple act of driving feels harder than it did this morning when I drove to the police station. Officers Tedesco and Smith follow at a safe distance, but never too far that I can't see them in the rearview. They feel like a human life raft right now.

When we pull into the parking lot, it looks darker along the strip than usual, and I see that the China Panda's lights are off and the lobster tank in the window is empty. A large sign on the door informs that it has been shut down by the health department indefinitely.

There is the same spot available near the entrance from last week, which I opt not to take and instead park farther away. I power down the Prius and gather my stuff. The crisp fresh air hits me as I exit the car.

As I put the key into the lock and push the door open, I vow that I'll look into finding a good therapist on Monday. It feels crazy to make that promise after swearing off shrinks completely post-Bellevue, but I need to live as though I'm my own best friend now, and give myself the advice that Rachel would have: ask for help. I can't get through this alone. And as much as I hate to admit it, I need to find peace and common ground with Mom. Without Rachel, Peter, and my entire online support group, she is my only "in case of emergency," whether I like it or not. And most likely, my roommate for the foreseeable future. I shudder at the image, just a forty-year-old head case living with her insane, aging mother. How long will it be until we start dressing alike, sleeping in the same room? We are about two raccoons short of Grey Gardens.

I am in the door and have the lights on and my coat off when Lucy enters. I realize I haven't locked the door behind me. I need to keep not only myself safe, but also my patient.

"Lucy." I gesture her farther inside and shut and lock the door behind me. She notices.

"Locking it?"

"Just in case. I never know if someone is going to come in when I'm in the treatment room, and there are some valuables out here."

"Smart thinking. Thank you for seeing me again on short notice. I'm never this needy, I swear!" She chuckles. "Well, maybe I am."

"Of course. I'm happy to see you. Not happy you are in pain, but we'll work on that."

"Wonderful." She looks around the room, and at the door to Rachel's treatment room. I feel a pang of longing.

"Why don't you take a seat. I just need a few minutes to get the room ready. Then we'll have you feeling good."

"I don't know what I would do without you, Charlotte."

SIXTY-FOUR

SILVESTRI

"Thornton's alibi is blown."

"*Oh yeah?*" Wolcott says into the phone.

"Tried to get him at the hospital first. They told me he took a personal day. Tried him on his cell. No dice. Circled back with the girlfriend, who finally admitted that he asked her to lie for him. Said they left the hotel at ten o'clock."

"*Giving him plenty of time to get out to Stony Brook that night, if he was the doer.*"

"Exactly," I say. "Where are you?"

"*Just left the hospital. Lyons wrapped up surgery and skipped out of there. I'm heading over to his place to try and doorstep him. Where are you?*"

"On my way to Northport. Thornton being in the wind is making me antsy. We've got the detail on Charlotte, but I feel compelled to look in on Annie Forester. You know, just in case."

"*Our anesthesiologist. Good man,*" he responds. "*I'll hit you back when I turn up Dr. Lyons.*"

"Sounds good, brother. And be safe out there."

SIXTY-FIVE

CHARLOTTE

"Okay, Lucy. I'm ready for you. Why don't you come inside? So, you said on the phone that your back and neck are feeling bad?"

"Well, this pain has flared up again like something fierce. And my hands have been getting numb." She adjusts her glasses.

"Do you sit in front of a computer a lot? Look at your phone multiple times a day? Watch a lot of TV?"

"No to the computer—I barely know how to turn it on. A reasonable amount of time on my phone; I don't have that active of a social life these days. It's the TV time that is excessive."

I nod nonjudgmentally. "How much screen time are you clocking in general?"

"A lot. Too much." She scrunches her face.

I nod as I make notes. "Don't worry. We all do. I can show you some tricks to make all of these things less harmful to your body."

"You are a lifesaver. I already feel better."

"Oh, and I've been meaning to ask you: What kind of work do you do, Lucy?"

"I'm between jobs right now, but I do a lot of freelance and volunteer work. I've done a little of everything, though. I never really found my true calling, I guess. Some people are just luckier than others when it come to that kind of thing," she says.

"Volunteer work is wonderful. I need to do more of that myself," I say, wanting to bolster her. She smiles gratefully.

"Okay, well, let's get you up on the table." I pause. "What would you feel comfortable doing today in terms of undressing? As far as giving me access to your skin? I'd love to do some needles in your shoulder . . . We can put towels over any parts of you that you are feeling self-conscious about."

"I think I'm comfortable enough with you now that I can let you see my body. Fair warning, though: It isn't pretty."

"This is a judgment-free zone, I've seen all kinds of bodies, and everyone is beautiful. I'll step out so you can get situated. I'll be back in a few minutes." I shut the door behind me.

Once back in the waiting area, I look for my phone and can't find it. I check my coat pockets and my purse, but it is nowhere. I conclude that it must have fallen out of my coat pocket in the car, and I'm frustrated with myself for not keeping track of it. I don't have time to worry about it now with Lucy waiting for me. From the treatment room, I hear the sound of paper crinkling and know she has pulled herself onto the table. I triple-check the lock on the front door and put on the chain bolt, which we never use, just to feel doubly safe, especially now, without a phone.

As I pass the closed door to Rachel's room, I pause and place my hand on the knob. I start to turn it but stop myself. I rest my forehead on the wood and can smell the lavender essential oil in her treatment room. I feel like I will never be ready to walk through this doorway again without feeling destroyed. I say my new mantra silently: *Show me a sign that you are still with me.* I hover for a moment and accept that she's gone. I know there will be a million more moments I'll have to continue that acceptance.

I move to my door, knock lightly, and hear Lucy reply, "Ready."

When I enter, Lucy's laid out on the table. She has draped the towel over her chest like a bandeau, and her stomach is exposed. She has the other towel draped over her crotch area, leaving her thighs and legs exposed. Her head is turned away from me and facing the wall. I see what she was self-conscious about, but I would never draw attention to it even if she hadn't warned me. Everyone's body tells a story of the things they've endured, and unsurprisingly, Lucy's story tells a lot.

"Did I do the towels the way you wanted them?" She's facing toward me now, clearly expectant for a reaction to her body.

"You are perfect." I sanitize my hands and start unwrapping my first packet of needles.

"I'm going to start putting needles in. If any of them hurt or feel weird, just let me know."

"I'm ready." She seems relieved that I haven't run screaming out of the room and smiles at the ceiling as I move around her body swabbing the intended meridian points with alcohol.

I feel comfort in the familiar movements and a small sense of lift from the doldrums of the last couple of weeks. With each needle inserted, I feel the energy releasing in Lucy's body as she relaxes into the experience, a little bit deeper with each pass.

When I get to Lucy's legs, I see a series of abrasions around her ankles and up and down her calves. They look to me like animal scratches.

"What happened here? Do you have a cat?" I ask.

She pauses and casts her eyes down to her ankles and feet. "Oh, those. I scratch in my sleep. It is an old habit from childhood. I don't have any cats; never liked them. I'm definitely a dog person."

I glance at her fingernails, which are cut extremely short and in their current state wouldn't be able to do any damage, let alone the scene on her legs, but I don't push. It would make sense if she trimmed her nails after doing this, but these don't look like human scratches.

"So, do you also have a patient in the other room?"

"No, actually. Not today. Usually the massage therapist is in that room." My voice starts to catch.

"Rachel, right? She was very nice. And really funny. She is a character, isn't she?" Lucy smiles. "She was so generous and offered me a free massage, which I'll definitely take her up on!"

The flood of emotions and the desire to tell Lucy about Rachel's death is swift. My eyes well up and I'm glad Lucy's eyes are shut.

"She is . . . she isn't here . . . she isn't working today. She won't be back . . . for a while," I stammer as I regain composure before I put the last needle in.

"Oh? I just assumed there was a patient getting needles in that room. When you were setting up earlier, someone was moving around in there."

A sharp ringing starts in my left ear and a cold sweat breaks out all over my body. "Lucy. What do you mean someone was moving around in there?" Her eyes flutter open and meet mine.

She looks chastised and visibly embarrassed. "I'm so sorry. I was totally being a snoop!"

I hold my breath, the information permeating and my pulse quickening. "Sorry." I realize I've been too abrupt. "It's okay. I'm not mad. Can you just tell me what exactly you heard?" I'm using every effort to remain calm.

"Well. I thought I heard someone moving around, so I put my ear to the door and heard the sound of someone breathing, pretty heavily too."

SIXTY-SIX

WOLCOTT

"John Lyons, I presume?"

"Yes?" He stands with the front door cracked open, one arm holding the handle while he crosses his stomach with the other. His eyes are narrow as he sizes me up. "Can I help you?"

I flip open my credentials and they go wide, showcasing a set of bloodshot whites. "Detective Wolcott." He's visibly alarmed. "Dr. Lyons, do you mind if I come in for a moment?"

"Um," he hems. "Not really the best time."

"It'll just take a few minutes, I assure you."

He scratches his side absently. "What is this about, anyway?"

I break eye contact, both to put him at ease and to steal a look into the house. "Just wanted to ask a few questions about an acquaintance of yours."

"And who would that be?"

"Mind if we sit down? I've been on my feet all day."

"Again, not really the—"

"Dr. Lyons, is there something in there you don't want me to see?"

He stiffens, which causes me to move my hand inside my jacket. I maintain a neutral expression as the adrenaline rises. "I just . . . Okay, here's the deal," he says. "I wrapped up surgery earlier, and I smoked a little bud when I got home. There's some in plain sight on the table in the other room."

I feel my stomach calm as I slide my hand out of my jacket. "Listen, I couldn't care less about that. It's practically legal at this point."

"Okay," he says, relaxing. "Maybe I'm a little paranoid." He opens the door and steps aside to let me in. As he leads me down a hallway, the musky scent tickles my nostrils. We reach the living room, where he motions for me to take a seat on a sofa as he flops into an armchair opposite me. The coffee table in between us is laden with large, pungent buds and a vaporizer. He sees me eyeing the stash. "I'd offer, but . . ."

"Appreciate the hospitality. All set."

"Right." He nods. "Who was it you wanted to ask me about, anyway?"

"You're familiar with a Charlotte Knopfler?" I say.

A grin takes over his face. "Oh, Charlotte. Of course."

"You recently contacted Ms. Knopfler at her home. May I ask how you came across that information?"

"The hospital I'm at is the same one where Charlotte used to work. I dug up her number from an old directory. I was calling with condolences for a friend that passed away."

"This friend being Rachel Sherman?" I ask.

"Right." His eyes drop to the floor.

"And how did you come to be aware of Miss Sherman's passing?"

"We were, uh . . . Well, I guess it doesn't really matter now."

"What's that?" I ask.

"Her anonymity." He seems to weigh the word as it leaves his mouth. "Rachel and I knew each other from Narcotics Anonymous. Another reason why I get nervous about that," he says, nodding toward the coffee table. "Technically a no-no, but the harder stuff is what gave me problems. Anyway, that's how I came into Charlotte's orbit in the first place. I stopped in one day and chatted her up. Caught myself a little crush."

"Hmm," I say, and lean forward. "And the name Jack Doyle?" I ask, catching his glance.

His face goes a shade of pink, and he titters self-consciously. "Yeah," he says. "Look, I was a little embarrassed about going to an acupuncturist. You know, being an oncologist and all. The whole East-West thing. I was just trying to cover my tracks on that one. Honestly, I'm still not sure if I really subscribe to all of it. But Charlotte . . . Well, I'll be real with you. Half the reason I made the appointment was to get closer to her. That woman really gets my pulse going."

SIXTY-SEVEN

CHARLOTTE

My heart is pounding so hard I'm sure she can hear it. I put my hands by my sides as I try to calculate what I need to do first. Multiple scenarios blossom in my head. I feel stupid for not checking Rachel's room.

Do I take Lucy's needles out and whisk her out of here without explanation? Or tell her there's a gas leak? Or do I get to my phone to send a text to Dennis? Of course, my fucking phone is in the car. And if Peter is in here, who knows if I will even make it to the door? I can't leave Lucy alone in here with him. I feel my panicked breathing starting up. I don't want to freak her out, especially if it is a false alarm. But I can't put her in danger either.

I take stock. As far as she knows, everything is fine, although her gaze on me is looking more concerned with each passing moment that I don't say anything.

"Charlotte? Is everything okay?"

I think quickly. "Oh! I completely spaced. That must be the cleaning lady. You startled me for a second, but I was just mixing days up."

She nods, smiles, and shuts her eyes, unperturbed by my explanation.

"How are you feeling right now?" I keep my voice steady.

"Dreamy." She looks exactly that. I am vacillating between overreacting and vigilance.

"Are you comfortable? Warm enough?"

"Yes and yes."

"Terrific. I'm just going to let you sit with these for about twenty minutes. Okay? I'll be right outside if you need anything at all."

"Wonderful." Her breathing is deepening. "I'll probably fall asleep." She sighs happily.

I lower the lights as I normally would and slide out the door as calmly and quietly as possible.

My pulse is racing so fast now, I worry I won't make it to the main door. I am frozen in place, considering what might happen if I open the door and try to get the officers' attention. If Peter is already inside, will he try to lock me out and hurt Lucy? Going into Rachel's treatment room to inspect if he's in there by myself seems tragically dumb. I think about my laptop, and opening it to send an email, until I realize I've stupidly left that in the car as well.

Don't panic. I'm hypersensitive right now. Logically, the sounds that Lucy heard could be any number of things. Maybe people at China Panda moving things out the back entrance, which butts up against the windows of Rachel's treatment room. Maybe there's a draft from a cracked window creating movement inside.

I start for the front door, deciding that the only smart option is to get Officers Tedesco's and Smith's attention. My hand is on the chain lock when I hear the sound of paper crinkling and a hard thump on the floor, followed by a groan.

"Lucy?" I call, with my hand still on the lock. There is no response. I move back in the direction of the room. "Lucy? I'm coming in, okay?"

I hear her moan, and the sound is coming from much lower in the space than it should be. Like she is on the floor. I try the knob, but the door is locked.

"Lucy, I need you to let me in, okay?" I certainly didn't flip the lock when I left her. I try the knob again. There is no question.

"Charlotte?" Her voice is strangled. My blood runs cold.

"Yes! Honey, open the door. It's locked from inside."

"Charlotte, please help. I'm hurt."

"I'm trying. What happened? Did you fall off the table?"

She is silent for a full minute and I feel like I'm going to burst from the tension.

"Lucy?"

"I'm not alone in here." I see a shadow of movement through the bottom of the door and gasp. I back up quickly, lose my balance, and seem to fall end over end as I move to get to the front door backward. To my surprise, I am still vertical as I put my hand back on the chain lock and undo it. I unlock the knob and get a grip around it. I hear the door behind me open and I turn, prepared to come face-to-face with Peter. Finally. I will see him in the flesh after all this time. As I move my body in two directions, one arm moving to pull open the door and the other pivoting to see who is emerging from the room, I feel a sharp sting in the side of my neck.

Everything around me gets fuzzy and dark fast. I can't see, but I can hear the sound of someone stepping over me and relocking the door and putting the chain in place before I'm grabbed by the ankles and dragged far away from my possible escape.

I jerk violently back to consciousness, and a hundred bees sting my face and neck simultaneously. There is a throbbing pain in my neck where it feels like I've been poked with something sharp. I cry out and attempt to move my eyes without further disrupting my head, to avoid another cluster of shooting pain. As my eyes adjust, I see many small shadows in my near periphery on all sides. It takes me a moment before I realize what I'm looking at. There must be at least thirty needles stuck into my cheeks and forehead, creating a garden of slim metal stems over the landscape of my face.

It takes a few seconds to get my bearings. My surroundings are familiar, but the vantage point is off-kilter. The room is barely lit, and it is hard to see anything beyond a few feet in front of me. What I can see is tinged with a yellow-green hue. The heavy curtains have been pulled closed and there is candlelight licking the walls.

I'm unsure of how long I've been out. I can't crane my neck to see the clock behind me without inviting great pain. As my eyes adjust to the gloom, I realize that I'm faceup on the treatment bed. My arms and legs feel like they are bound, but I don't seem to have anything around my wrists or ankles. Once I have the thought, I feel the phantom pressure of the handcuffs and shackles from earlier this week.

My chest feels constricted, like I'm under a leaden blanket. There is an upward stabbing sensation with each inhale. I've been drugged, as my motor skills are offline and my respiratory system is close behind. Given my increasingly dry mouth and the urge to throw up, I'm guessing it is something highly toxic and fast acting.

"Hello?" I whisper. I know even without a response that I am not alone in the darkness.

"Charlotte." A familiar husky voice croons from behind me. "Finally."

"Peter?" I can barely find the air to get his name out. It feels like something is cinched tightly around my neck.

"Hello, darling." His voice is low and hushed. He sounds different than he did on the phone, but it is undoubtedly him.

I dig deep for the strength and calm to get me through this. Waves of supreme nausea are rising and falling rapidly. There is a slight tremble in my voice that is impossible to hide. "This isn't really how I pictured meeting you for the first time."

He laughs drily. "Oh, Charlotte. You are adorable. But you and I have met plenty of times."

"What are you talking about?" Each exertion is getting harder.

"You are just so completely self-absorbed. You've been in the same room with me more times than you probably realize."

My mind is reeling. Even though I'm terrified to see his face, his dis-embodied voice is scarier.

"What are you talking about?"

He laughs. "Not only have we already met, we worked together, closely."

I'm at a complete loss. I try to think about all the men I've worked with and try to place him.

"You were just too self-involved to see how much I've changed."

I can see slight movement in the shadow on the wall to my right. He is still standing behind me but has moved closer. I feel breath on top of my head as he leans closer. My heart palpitates.

"You all did quite a number on me, kiddo. But don't worry. I'm very resilient."

"I'm so sorry. I don't know what I did. But I never would have inten-tionally hurt you." I feel like I've been hurled into a whirlpool of dark water and I'm losing the strength to swim against the current.

"Did I ever tell you about my brother?" he asks.

"No," I murmur.

"Hmm. I guess that's right. I led you to believe I was an only child like you, didn't I? I was trying to ramp up the bonding.

"Although, in a way, it wasn't a lie. I really was an only child after a certain pont. Then an orphan and a ward of the state. My childhood ré-sumé was quite a bit more dire than I divulged in our endless back-and-forths. We talked so much about yours though." It sounds like he is walking back and forth behind me. Like a caged animal.

I cough weakly.

"Feeling unwell, sweetheart?"

"I'm really sick, Peter. What did you give me?"

"It goes by many names and grows from the ground." He laughs. "Does that narrow it down for you?"

My stomach painfully contracts and I realize I may very well loose my bowels on the table. I'm so far beyond caring about vanity at this point, though. Any relief from the terrible contractions and nausea would be welcome.

"Peter, where's Lucy?" I'm straining to widen my view of the room, but the needles are digging into my neck with even a microinch of movement.

He snorts. "Look at you worrying about someone other than yourself. How very off brand for you."

"Please." I can barely get a breath out. "She has nothing to do with this." My voice breaks and the deluge begins.

"She's fine. Better than fine. This is *actually* a moment when you should be worrying about yourself."

"I'm worried about *you*, Peter." I remember hearing somewhere that when someone is freaking out, saying their name repeatedly can help ground them. "I want to help. You are upset with me. Tell me how I can make it better."

He snorts. "Are you seriously trying to convince me that you care about me right now?" I hear a bag being unzipped.

I'm cycling through each of my medical school peers or other residents. Maybe he was a patient? Or someone at Stony Brook Hospital after I moved back and had my miserable year there? I'm stumped.

"Peter. This is crazy. Please. I don't understand. I thought you loved me. I loved you."

"Yawn. I fucking despise you. Whatever you thought our relationship was, it was pure imagination," he snarls.

I'm trying to keep my crying as contained as possible but everything hurts so much, I'm unsuccessful. "I'm so sorry for whatever I've done to hurt you."

"Oh dear. We are light-years beyond an apology."

My vision is tinted in shades of and yellow and green. I am having a vague recollection of a course about toxic plants used in treatment from my early Chinese medicine days, where we covered one poisonous plant in particular that had this specific psychedelic symptom, but there were so many toxic flowers among us, I'm finding I can't pin any one thought long enough to conjure the name of it.

"What have you dosed me with? I'm having a lot of trouble breathing." As I utter the words, my chest constricts further.

"A beautiful flower that is deadly as hell at its roots. Absolutely perfect for you."

Oleander, hemlock, white snakeroot, wolfsbane. Fuck. My heart starts pounding even faster and harder, exactly the opposite of what I want my vascular system to be doing right now.

"Wolfsbane?" I squeak.

"I prefer the scientific name *Aconite*. Sounds so much less pretentious," he says.

My hope plummets, along with my blood pressure. "How much?"

"My brother introduced me to the wide world of killer plants. He poisoned my dog by feeding him water hemlock as an experiment. I was devastated. He blamed it on me, and I was the one who got in trouble. He was always doing terrible things and making it look like I had done them. No matter how much I tried to convince them, my parents always believed him over me," he says, acidly.

"How *much Aconite* did you give me, Peter?" I gasp.

"Oh, a good amount," he says offhandedly. I moan in pain. "As sad as I was about my dog and upset that I got in trouble," he continues, "the whole event did teach me many formative life lessons." His voice goes up an octave.

"Peter," I say in a pained whisper. "I'm going to die if you don't help me."

"That's the aim, honey. I'd say you have about fifteen minutes." His voice cracks with excitement.

I need to keep my nervous system as calm as possible to slow my metabolic rate. "Peter. There is still time."

"Just enough time for a quick surgery," he quips. "Much quicker than the ones you are used to. Except for maybe Michelle's—that one went south quickly, didn't it?"

My stomach seizes violently and I cry out in pain.

"Let's shed some more light on the situation."

In my now very blurred vision, I see his shape walk through the gloom toward the light switch and flip it. I shut my eyes quickly. I feel him standing beside me. I am barely breathing. He leans in closely and I force my eyes open, my vision adjusting slowly and painfully. His face comes into shocking focus before a rocket of pain plunders through me and my sight becomes blurry again. I can barely get the words out. "Oh my God. You?"

SIXTY-EIGHT

SILVESTRI

"Have you turned up Lyons yet?"

Wolcott's on the other end of the horn. I've arrived at Annie Forester's place, with no sign of Annie. The house is quiet, and her car's not in the driveway. I've just walked around to the back of the house to get a look, and he's in my ear. *"Lyons ain't our guy."*

"Shit. You don't say."

"Yeah, found him at home, just kicking back. He's clean. Alibi and all. But I did finally get a call back from Stacy Phillips."

"Really? Where's he been hiding?" I approach the back door and peek through the glass inset. The house appears empty.

"He didn't get back to us right away because he thought he was in trouble."

"Huh?"

"I guess Brooke Harmon reached out to him, looking for closure. He felt guilty, let it spill that her sister's case was in fact malpractice, due to Thornton's arrogance. The hospital was afraid they'd lose their funding, so they pinned it on the anesthesia. That email we read? After Brooke sent that to the rest of the surgical staff, Stacy got a threatening voicemail from Thornton. So when we called, he thought he was in hot water for violating the NDA."

"Well, that account puts a different spin on things."

"Sure does," he says. *"Oh, and this is curious; at one point in the conversation, he asks about Annie. I guess he was fond of her. I make mention of her having enough energy to run a marathon. He can't get on board with this being the same person he remembers. Thinks I'm confused about who she is, to the*

point where he texts me an old photo of the surgical team. Remember how Annie made that comment about watching her weight? Seems to have really paid off."

"Oh yeah?" I approach an open trash can, jammed to the brim, and see a box of wine sticking out.

"She must have lost . . . I don't know. It's like I'm looking at a different person, Silvestri. Guess the diet's working."

"Looks like she's been cheating a bit," I say, discovering a flattened pint of Chubby Hubby wedged in next to the wine box.

"I'll text you a photo," he says.

As I look at this woman's trash, an eerily familiar feeling washes over me. "Wolcott, you remember that chat room exchange?" I say, as much to myself as to him.

"Huh?" he says distractedly.

I stare at the box. *"I'll see your box of wine and raise you frozen calories . . ."* My eyes move to the ice cream container. *"Tonight I'm having a ménage à trois with Ben & Jerry . . ."* My mind flashes to the bookshelves in Annie's office. The Ray Bradbury novels. *"I keep thinking about that Disney movie from the eighties,* Something Wicked This Way Comes . . . *"* The phone dings. I pull it away from my ear and open the text that Wolcott's sent. I'm looking at Annie, standing among the surgical team. She has to be seventy pounds heavier, with straight brown hair. I'd never recognize her. Suddenly, the rest of the photo goes blurry as I lock onto the necklace she's wearing—the copper Rod of Asclepius coin I've seen recently, hanging around a different neck. My eyes burn, my mind races, and my heart's in my throat. "Holy shit!" I manage. "Wolcott, it's her!"

SIXTY-NINE

CHARLOTTE

"It's me!"

"Lucy?" I squeak.

"Well, I'm not Peter, but I'm thinking you figured that one out." She is really enjoying herself, as I sink deeper into shock both from the aconite and from the realization that she is even less the image of Peter than I ever imagined. I've become very cold even though I am profusely sweating.

"Does it really matter? Lucy, Peter, MaxineKD and the gang, none of them are me, but then again, I guess they all are, aren't they? I gave you so many clues and you still didn't figure it out. My actual name"—she pauses for dramatic effect—"is Annie Forester. Remember me? Surprise."

She watches me put the pieces together.

"Been a while since you thought about me, hasn't it?"

I'm struggling to keep my vision focused on anything, but I force myself to look hard. Annie Forester, of course I know her name. The anesthesiologist for Michelle Harmon's surgery. But this woman doesn't look anything like her.

"Maybe if I take my glasses off?" She does and laughs hard. "I don't really need them anyway."

I can start to see some resemblance, if I imagine her with different hair and about eighty more pounds on her. The weight made her look younger, and the drastic haircut and color have transformed her. Now I understand the vast amounts of loose extra skin she was concealing. Even if I had seen that earlier, though, I never would have made the connection.

She spins around. "Hard to believe, isn't it? A lot has changed about me since we were in the OR together."

I'm gobsmacked and utterly confused about what is happening. The poison in my system is severely impeding my cognitive function.

"Why, Annie?" I say weakly.

She reaches behind me and grabs something. She is now standing over me with a McKenzie leucotome in one hand. The sight of it brings me back to the first time I held one by its narrow metal shaft with wonder, before inserting it into the back of a cadaver skull and cutting my first piece of brain tissue. It was simultaneously the most exhilarating and scary moment of my career, until I did the same thing for the first time on a live patient. She sees me eyeing the instrument.

"It is astonishing what you can find online. You know what else you can find? Geovernment IDs and passports of dead people. Easily doctored." She winks at me. "I will give you credit for taking a hard line with Peter over giving you proof about his job. The whole secret agent thing was pretty outrageous, but fun as hell to go along with."

I am swallowing regularly to keep my salivary glands active and blinking rapidly to keep my eyes alert.

"The secret flower code was probably my favorite Peter flourish; you were such a sport to go along with that. When I sent the bouquet with Brooke's credit card after I killed her, I was a little sad because I knew it would be the last one I would get to send. I wanted to make it extra special," she chirps.

I am trying not to look directly at the sinister tool she is brandishing closer to my face.

"Don't worry, it's clean," she assures me.

I've begun to pant, and cardiac arrhythmia is getting more pronounced, which is a sign that my respiratory system is worsening and I'm getting into an advanced stage of poisoning.

"What are you going to do?"

"I thought I would do a little reenactment of Michelle's surgery to-day. A do-over, for closure, you know? But instead of boring old anesthesia, I thought I'd make things interesting with a little Eastern flavor. The ultimate integrative practice. East meets West." She hums as she rubs the leucotome down with a polishing cloth. She's fucking insane. I'll get her to talk about herself to keep her distracted, since she doesn't seem to be able resist that.

"Annie, why did you kill Brooke? I don't understand. She lost her sister, for God's sake." I struggle to string the words together.

"I was trying to help her. I felt awful about what happened to her and her parents. I thought if I couldn't bring her sister back, I could try and become another sister to her. Before my brother got me sent away, I was a very good sister to him. Because I have compassion, Charlotte, something most people say they have, but don't actually."

She's talking and scanning the room manically. I don't interrupt her. As long as she rambles and I keep myself conscious, there's still a chance that one of the cops outside will realize how long I've been out of communication and check in.

Annie continues. "I reached out to Brooke after Michelle died in spite of that goddamn settlement saying we couldn't have any contact. I found out which dog park she walked her cocker spaniel, Butter, at and brought my pug, Thor, along. I led her to believe that my brother had died much more recently than he actually had, and confided in her about how much I was struggling, and we became a major support for each other. At first she didn't know who I was—she never saw me in person the day of the surgery—and we became friendly." Annie pauses pensively.

"But once she found out who I was because someone from the hospital recognized me when we were together, she turned on me fast. Because of that lie you all agreed to, she held me entirely responsible. I tried to tell her the truth, but she wouldn't listen. I would have given all of the money back just to clear ny name. She turned all of her rage and vengeance onto me," she says dejectedly.

"You agreed to that settlement too," I whisper, realizing that Annie is far more concerned with not being seen as making a mistake than with Michelle Harmon's death.

"I was bullied into it! Henry Thornton made my life a living hell until I had no choice. When I first pushed back on the settlement, he sent men to my apatment to intimidate me. He only cared about saving himself and getting someone 'lesser' to take the blame. No one would have believed that Stacy, a lowly nurse in his eyes, would have any real impact on the patient, so that left me. And of course *you* enabled him in the lie! You and I both know what happened that day, Charlotte. Michelle Harmon's blood is on your hands. Not mine."

"But so much blood is on your hands now. Brooke's. Rachel's," I cry weakly. *Probably mine soon*, I think.

"Brooke brought it on herself. Once Brooke made the connection about who I was, she came at me worse than Henry had. She hated me with a vengeance. She was out of control and looking for someone to feel the pain that she was. Every job I tried to get after that ordeal, she found out about and called my potential employers and told them I was a murderer. I wasn't even trying to work in medicine any longer, but no one was going to employ me with Brooke Harmon making it her misson to take me out. She got me evicted from my apartment, she spread rumors about me with my friends at the dog park, and then, Thor"— Annie's voice cracks—"my baby, Thor, died from antifreeze poisoning! I know it was Brooke who did it! And if it wasn't her, it was that asshole Henry Thornton trying to scare me for contacting Brooke.

"After that, I had nothing left to lose. Brooke Harmon ceased being that poor woman who lost her sister and became only my contstant abuser in my eyes. I had to put a stop to it. It was self-defense!" Annie is wild-eyed. Her ranting is clearly crazy, but the longer she is talking, the longer it is that she not is cutting into my body.

"Why did you kill Rachel?" I whimper. "She had nothing to do with this."

"She was collateral damage. Rachel was snooping. God, was that woman nosy as hell. I wasn't planning on it, but she kept digging into Peter and filling your head with doubt and suspicion. She was getting in the way. But she did add some value," she says, amused. "I mean, the fight at your house alone provided me with so many fun twists. Rachel getting there right after I left the box for you was priceless. And I never could have planned on you leaving your car at the restaurant for me to use!"

"I don't understand." I'm moaning and crying now.

"I wasn't planning on going into your house that night, but after I left the box, I had to hide when I saw Rachel riding up on her bike."

Every word is sapping me of energy. I'm in agony. "You were in my house that night?"

"I was there for the whole fight with Rachel."

"How? Where were you?" I ask.

"During the fight I was lying on your bed, actually." She laughs maniacally. "I was laid out like I was at the beach and I had a front-row seat for your and Rachel's tiff through the window, which I opened just a few inches, to hear what was going on. And then I hung out under your bed when you came inside. My fear that you would somehow look under the bed and discover me was gone when I realized how tipsy you were. And with the bedroom door open, I had the perfect view of the living room. I let myself out before you fell asleep on the couch."

"Oh my God."

"And then when the detective came over and you told him that you'd left your car in the parking lot of La Vid, I was struck by a stroke of brilliance. I waited until you'd passed out cold, took your keys and bike, and helped myself to your car. I paid Rachel a visit and then returned your car to La Vid's parking lot and your bike back where I found it. No one was the wiser! It was like the universe was just laying things in my path left and right to even the score. It was all meant to be."

SILVESTRI

"I think she's in the office!" I yell into the phone to Smith, who's parked in the lot keeping watch over Charlotte.

"Who?" he asks.

"Our perp is a *she!*"

"Ten-four," he spits back. "We're on it."

CHARLOTTE

I am stricken with a violent wave of chills and my teeth begin to chatter loudly. Annie is undeterred. "It wasn't the first time I'd been in your house. It was usually when you weren't home, but sometimes when you were sleeping I just let myself in. I got curious about you, and it was useful to know things about your life that you weren't volunteering when I was playing the role of your 'soulmate,' Peter." She makes a gagging sound. "I had to cool it, though, as much of a habit as it had become to invade your space. Obviously, when things heated up with the cops and your mother came on the scene, I had to stay away." She takes a step closer to me, the end of the metal catching the light.

"Annie, please don't hurt me!" I'm trying not to stare at the sharp end of the leucotome.

She looks at it and frowns. "You know, you're right. This is all wrong." She lowers her hand. I feel a glimmer of hope. She moves to the area behind me and I hear metal on metal. "I think I'd prefer to go with something a little more modern, in honor of your extensive appreciation for the art of surgery." She brandishes a stainless steel Walter Freeman orbitoclast, which to most people looks like an artistically rendered ice-pick, but I only see the beautiful streamlined update of the leuco-tome. Along with it, she holds its companion, a steel mallet, and hovers the pair over my face. "Beautiful couple, aren't they?"

"Annie, why do all of this? I don't understand."

"I'm so glad you asked," she purrs. "Because I had a lot of time on my hands, thanks to all of you. After Brooke dismantled my life, I wanted to make some big changes. I'd always needed a makeover but had never had the motivation or the means. Like you, I was all about my career. All of a sudden I had endless hours in my day, money in the bank, and a handful of people whom I needed to teach a lesson. My job was my life, Charlotte. When that all got stolen, I had to reinvent myself. I had to become someone completely new.

"I'd always been unhappy with all of my extra weight but never had the time or a good enough reason to do something about it. I got gastric bypass from a doctor out here on the island that I knew from my resi-dency days. I bought myself a little house, got the surgery, and spent the next six months recovering and deciding how I could take my power back."

I'm happy she is monologing instead of cutting into me. I silently scan through my body as she rambles. Each detail is more disturbing than the one before. She pauses and looks at me for a second, and my heart halts. She continues.

"Since I had so many more hours in the day without my career, I de-cided to learn a new skill. Remember when I told you that I could barely turn a computer on?" she crows loudly. "Oh, I can definitely turn one on, and much more. It turns out that I'm a natural coder. I didn't under-stand why I was moved to learn it at the time; I just thought it was a smart thing to know how to do in this day and age, and it was fun. And then it hit me that it was the perfect entré into connecting you and Brooke, something I thought would be a fascinating social experiment. But I didn't want to feel excluded again. Friends are vital to sanity, Char-lotte," she asides creepily, and I get a wave of chills. "I wanted to be close to other people in the way that I had in the dog park days with Brooke, before she found out who I was. I hadn't realized how much I needed the support of other women about the traumas I've experienced in my life." She stops to walk behind me and I hold my breath, thinking she's getting her surgical itch again, but I hear her open a bottle and take a sip of something. The sound of it makes me realize how unbelievably parched I am.

"Annie? I'll do anything. Please call 911," I beg. My body has taken on a numb sensation, which is better than the unbearably ill feeling but decidedly not a good sign of the course of the poisoning.

"Are you out of your mind? I've done way too much to get us here. Why would I undo all of it now by doing something stupid like that?" There is anger emerging in her voice again.

I decide indulging her is far safer than inciting her any further. I begin to pray silently for someone to help me, steadily losing hope the longer I lie here. "Annie, why did you get me into the chat room? Why even pretend to be Peter and frame me?"

"I wanted to get back at you in a way that could give me something to do. I needed a sense of purpose after everything in my life was burned to the ground by all of you. Once I started it all, it became a game. And it was too much fun not to stop."

"Wouldn't it have been easier to just kill me?" I hear the defeat in my words as much as I feel it in my will to keep fighting.

"It didn't feel like just killing you would be satisfying enough." She has begun to pace and I can see she's becoming angry. I need to try to calm her.

Paresthesia has set in, and rounds of burning and prickling are alternately moving from my torso through my extremities. "I'm sorry you got fired, Annie. I didn't know that you were going to lose your job. And I would have done anything not to have let that happen—"

"But you didn't do *anything,* did you! You just cosigned that bullshit statement with Thornton, letting me take the hit. I lost my reputation and my career of thirty years, Charlotte!" she spits furiously. "Do you know how much that job meant to me? It was all that I had next to Thor. And you all treated me like I was invisible. You people were the closest I had to a fucking family!" It dawns on me that her estranged daughter must have been a fiction, and this saddens me deeply, and oddly, given the current events of the moment. Making up a daughter who doesn't speak to you feels even worse than actually having one who isn't speaking to you.

She rails on. "And you threw me under the fucking bus to save yourselves. And you were going to get away with it." She is tapping the hammer against her palm furiously.

"Annie. I completely understand. You should not have taken the fall. It was my fault what happened. I wanted to tell everyone that. But Henry . . . he had me hospitalized when the investigation was going on to keep me out of the process."

She stops pacing and looks at me. "So you let him take the credit and the blame for everything, huh? At least you are consistent."

"I lost my career too, Annie."

"It's not the same, Charlotte. You were a fucking child, not a fiftysomething-year-old woman trying to get back into the workforce with a high-profile malpractice smear on her résumé. Especially once Brooke Harmon got involved."

"We got the settlement money. What about that?"

"You are missing the point, you self-important little bitch. This is not about money. I have plenty of money. This is about the fact that while Henry Thornton failed up, you helped him, and you both let me suffer for your mistakes. Where is the fucking solidarity? I was kind to you. I would have been a mentor to you and helped you navigate all the sexist politics that I had to deal with coming up as a woman in medicine. But you barely registered anyone else's existence in favor of him. You sided with him. I showed up one day to do my job well, as I always have, and in a flash, lost everything. And none of you thought twice about me."

I'm fading. "I am so sorry, Annie. Henry screwed me over as much as he did you. I would have stopped him if I could have. Michelle's death ruined my life too."

"Oh, I know it." Her face twists into an expression of bitterness. "I know everything about you, Char. You shared so much in the chat room and on the phone. For the last year, I have listened to you talk about yourself. I probably know more about you than Rachel did. Or your own mother." She twists the virtual knife and enjoys it.

I wither but take a different approach. "I thought you cared about me. I thought you all did. Was that all pretend?"

"It is a funny thing, Charlotte. When I found out that you'd been committed to Bellevue and then moved home with your mother, I almost felt satisfied that you'd adequately suffered. But when I heard from one of my old friends at Stony Brook Memorial Hospital that you'd re-emerged and were practicing medicine again, I got pissed. But it seemed like total kismet that you, Brooke, and I had all ended up out here, and I took it as sign that there was an opportunity to balance the scales.

"Like I said, I was craving the camaraderie and the support I'd had with Brooke and the dog park crew, but I didn't want the rejection from either of you again. I've never had an easy time making and keeping friends, on account of my being very straightforward."

And on account of you being a psycho, I say to myself.

"I also wanted to know how you were feeling about everything that happened, and that gave me the idea to connect all the dots. I knew Brooke had been harassing Henry, which made me endlessly happy, but I felt like you'd unfairly gotten off the hook—"

"But Brooke did attack me. She went after my business," I counter.

"Not in a significant way, in my opinion. She'd lost her steam with you after Henry put a restraining order on her, it seemed. It enraged me how you always seemed to land on your feet no matter what you did. You know, I was nice to you when we worked together, and you barely acknowledged my existence. You are unbelievably entitled, Charlotte, and now, thanks to our candid relationship, I know all the reasons why," she says meanly.

"Were any of them actually you?" I ask feebly.

"All of the members of the chat room are aspects of me. Peter, not so much; he was very real once. I had fun becoming him. I kept pushing it further and you ate it all up."

"I'm trusting, Annie. I trusted you." My breathing is strangled.

"We had fun, though, didn't we? All of our thousands of texts. Checking in all the time. It felt good to know Peter would be on the other end of the phone when you picked it up every single time."

"Except when he wasn't," I say unexpectedly. "Except when he disappeared." I feel myself dissociating from the reality of Annie being Peter, and my feeling of being angry and heartbroken by the man I fell in love with without ever meeting.

"It was essential to the story to have Peter be elusive. It kept you hooked," she says.

"I was hooked because I was lonely. Peter was just a stand-in," I drop, curious if my self-awareness does anything to her.

I can see the whites of her knuckles around the orbitoclast. I feel myself flinching ever so slightly and am surprised that there is some faint movement in my right hand if I focus on it.

"Oh bullshit, Charlotte. I know you loved Peter. I was there, remember? All of his flattery and endless attention. The nauseating soul-bearing confessions. The fantasies."

I feel tears running down the sides of my face. This pleases her.

"But it really is all fake, even when both people meet in person and *know* who they are with. The initial spell of obsessive love will burn off and there will inevitably be disapointment. It just isn't sustainable, which is why I never bothered with it. At least you got to think you had someone who loved you and cared about what you were doing every day, for the time that you did." Her pupils have dilated so significantly, it looks like she has empty, black, sharklike eyes.

"I think of something Rachel once said to me: *'Most people are afraid of dying, but they shouldn't be. It is much worse for the people left behind. When you die, you go somewhere better. I truly believe that.'"* I cry harder at the possibility of seeing my friend again. My body surges with pain and a tremor shoots me into a convulsion.

"This is a lot to take in, I know." She puts the steel pick down on the table and moves behind me. As long as I keep her talking, I am keeping myself conscious and her distracted from sticking anything into my brain. When she returns to my sight line she is snapping surgical gloves on.

"Now shhh. Too much talking. I want to make sure you are conscious for the main event, and from the looks of it, you are not long for this world."

SILVESTRI

"We can't get in!" Smith yells into the phone. *"There's something blocking the front door!"*

Fuck. "Hold tight," I say. "Almost there." I hang up, then call for backup and a bus.

CHARLOTTE

The next time she moves out of the frame, I focus every last bit of energy into my right hand and am surprised to find that I am able to open and close it. Now I just need to somehow conjure enough momentum to move my arm from my side up to my face and pull any number of the needles out without her noticing.

"Did you know that as far as Western medicine has come, scientists don't actually *know* how anesthesia works? I always loved that fact. Like I was the most important person in the OR because I kept people from feeling fear and pain, but no one could actually identify what it was about anesthesia that made it work. I was a magician." She whistles as she futzes around nearby, but the twilight state I'm flipping in and out of is making it hard to focus on any one thing for long.

The tiny needles are hardly a formidable opponent to her heavy steel weapons, but it is the only defensive strike that I can think of, and I can't let her into my brain more than I already have, without at least putting up a fight.

"Annie?" I croak.

"Yes?" She's impatient. I can see stabby eagerness pouring out of her.

"There are police officers in the parking lot. If I don't walk out of this office in the next five minutes, they are going to know something is wrong and come looking for me. And Detective Silvestri is outside too." I say it with all the hope in the world that somehow this is true.

She cocks her head and gives me a once-over before spreading a sickeningly toothy grin across her plain face. "You are so sweet to be worrying about me." Just as quickly as it spread, the smile is gone, and her voice drops into a deepness that chills me. Peter's voice. "I've got it covered."

My heart drops into my gut in between its sporadic bursts of arrhythmia.

"You very helpfully double-locked the front door, and then I pushed that surprisingly heavy desk in front of it, so it is going to be a bitch for your dick in shining armor to get through it in a hurry without a battering ram. I have plenty of time to spend with you uninterrupted."

"And how are you going to get out of here once you've killed me? You are trapped." I am finding a new, deeper reserve of energy in me. The poison is destroying my body's enzymes one organ system at a time, but I am grateful for the faculties that are still hanging on. I still have my brain, barely. But keeping it intact is highly motivating.

"Oh, don't you worry about me, honey. And you forget. Your good guys are looking for your bad *guy*. Not me. When they are finally able to get in, I will be barely coherent enough to describe the horrible man who was waiting for us both before he knocked me out, locked me in Rachel's office, and had his way with your brain. I will tell them that I became worried about you because of the threatening calls I've been getting from Henry. They know he is unhinged and has been trying to shut us all up. And when they see the brain surgery he's done on you, they'll see he's finally lost his damn mind over not being allowed to operate any longer. I was very happy to learn that while they didn't fire him, they took his toys away. That's for the best anyway; you were always the competent one in that partnership. The only thing he was truly good at was stealing the spotlight."

"Why me? Why not Henry?" I ask weakly. "He was the one who orchestrated the settlement. It was Henry who bullied you and maybe killed Thor."

"He's going to get his, don't you worry." She savors my terror in her pausing. "But I guess I got more creative with your punishment because his behavior was typical. Predictable white-man-privilege bullshit. But you were totally mystified by him, and completely took for granted the fact that I would have supported you, would have been on your side in solidarity. I could have been a mother to you."

"We barely knew each other," I say.

I see a flicker of something in her eyes beyond the sharklike blackness I've been staring into. Pain. "I guess I looked at our relationship differently than you did. I thought we were kindred spirits. Especially after that time you confided in me." Her eyes return to their darkened state and her expression is stone. "Of course you don't remember." She shakes her head. "You were crying in the bathroom. I thought it was because all the residents were talking shit about you."

I'm conjuring a vague memory of Annie catching me after a particularly stressful thirty-hours-straight shift and a frustrating conversation with my mother, who showed up at the hospital tipsy and disruptive to say "hello." I'd burst into tears and lamented to her that I wished I had a normal mother. But it had been so offhand and I'd completely forgotten about it until this moment. Her experience had clearly been something entirely different. The loneliness of this woman is becoming painfully evident.

I change my approach. "How are you going to explain you being here and Henry not?"

"He will be long gone by the time they get in, but I have plenty of his DNA, thanks to his penchant for afternoon delight sessions with his girlfriend at the same time and place every week. It is unbelievable how easy it is to pose as housekeeping, just by dressing the part and hanging around a hotel hallway. I got plenty of the good doctor's spunk to spackle this soon-to-be crime scene. Then he can take the credit for something else he didn't do. I will have to play the part of 'nearly victim number two' but be the one who miraculously lives to tell about it. I bet you I'll get a book deal and a TV option. I'll dose myself with some aconite, but not nearly as much as I gave you," she confidently asides, "and I'll be fixed up right as rain with a charcoal smoothie. I mean, is there anything that stuff can't do?" She is very pleased with herself.

My semi-conciousness has rendered me in a dreamlike state. I am not ready to leave this world today. I think about my very limited resources and wish that the *dim mak* Kiss of the Dragon fatal-pressure-point move really worked outside of kung fu movies. But it gives me an idea.

SILVESTRI

I whip into the lot, throw the car into park, and hop out. I sprint past the uniforms toward the entrance to the China Panda, pulling off my jacket as I go.

CHARLOTTE

Her back is turned while she sets up something on the shelf behind her.

"Annie?" I sputter. "Peter was your brother's name, right? You've talked about him in the chat room?"

She doesn't turn around, but I see her shoulders droop. I hadn't put it all together until she said, "He was very real once." Now I'm hoping that I can stall her even for a few minutes longer to will the energy I need into my right arm.

"Yes," she replies quietly. "Peter was my older brother. He was supposed to watch over me, but instead he did terrible things and blamed me. First it was poisoning my dog, then it was a shed fire that almost took the main house out, then he tried to poison one of the kids in the neighborhood. My mother thought he could do no wrong and never believed me when I told her what he was doing. He convinced her and my father that I was the bad seed. And they chose him." She hasn't turned around yet, but I can hear the bitterness in her voice. "They sent me away to boarding school. I barely saw any of them after that. I pretended I was an orphan and never looked back. Unfortunately, I would lose everything I cared about more than once because of people putting the blame on me. I guess we each have our own shitty patterns to overcome." She snorts.

While she's further spiraling into her crazy, I send every possible drop of energy into my right hand and am able to lift it to my face and extract two needles before my arm gives out and falls limply to the side. Miraculously, my finger grip is strong enough that the slim objects stay firmly between my thumb and pointer finger.

"Enough about the past. Let's be in the present! You are all about that, aren't you, Charlotte?" She picks up the orbitoclast and hammer and moves closer. "Now, I know I don't need to talk you through what I'm going to be doing. I have to say how pleased I am that you are as coherent as you are for this. You have quite a fight in you, Charlotte. After injecting you with seven grams of pure aconite, I would have thought you'd be pretty comatose by now. Some people's constitutions are just better served for toxins than others. Rachel didn't stand a chance."

I don't speak and barely nod in acknowledgment. I use the rage surging through my body and channel it. It is rocket fuel to my waning energy. I keep still and reserve any life force that I have left.

"Oh, I almost forgot!" She reaches into the pocket of her button-down and withdraws a contact lens case.

SILVESTRI

I wrap my jacket around my left arm and use it to club through the front door of the darkened restaurant. As shards of glass cascade around my feet, a bolt of sharp pain shoots up my arm, and I feel my eyes tear up. I slip through the door frame and sprint toward the hidden entrance to the bathroom in Charlotte's office.

CHARLOTTE

She places the pick and hammer on the table beside her and unscrews one of the reservoirs of the case. After placing the screw top next to the surgical tools, she uses bipolar forceps and extracts a small brown object, which looks like a small olive pit. She holds it over my face and brings it close to my right eye so it becomes blurry. "Le seed de résistance!"

I blink back a wave of tears. This is happening. This moment, right now, and I'm so present and mindful of it, I can't stand it.

I take a beat as she swaps the forceps for the orbitoclast and hammer. "I'm just gonna get in there and dig around and do some damage to your upper frontal lobe before I get to seed planting. I placed the other seeds in the ear canal, but I think to really make a splash with this and make it signature Henry, I'll go big. I may ask your advice as I do the procedure, at least as long as you still have use of your verbal skills." She is cracking herself up, and I am a handful of breaths away from real cardiac arrest.

"You may or may not be fully dead when I get to that point, but your brain will be! It's not every day that I get to mess around with a brain surgeon's gray matter. I've watched quite a few YouTube videos on brain surgery to brush up. It's been a long time since I had the privilege of watching you and Dr. Thornton work."

I'm trying to recall if I ever sensed that Annie was crazy when I knew her. I just remember her being unassuming. Friendly, kind of quiet. A little shy and reserved. She blended into the rest of the hospital. I was so caught up in the glamour of possibility that I didn't see so much of what was happening around me. I didn't see the people. "Annie, I'm really sorry. Please don't do this. You are my friend. Do you really want to hurt me?" I plead. "Lucy and I bonded, didn't we?"

She hesitates. "That was a part I was playing. Like the women in the chat room. Like Peter. It was all make-believe."

"But there was a bond there. *Is* a bond there. I know you feel it. All of the conversation we had in the room, all of the texts as Peter you sent me, and when I treated you as Lucy. That may have been imaginary in parts, but you were there in all of those connections."

Her face contorts slightly. I'm not sure if she's holding back pain, anger, or love. Whatever it is, she's holding strong.

"Are you kidding? I've been planning this for over a year now. And it has all come together better than I could have imagined."

"Wait. But you saved my life," I push.

"What are you talking about?"

"You sent the email about the trauma survivors group, right? To lure me in?"

"Yeah," she says proudly. "You made it easy and totally took the bait on that right away. I thought I'd have to spam you a few dozen times before you'd take it."

"How did you know that I was suicidal? Your email came the same night I was going to end my life. That is how despondent I was after Michelle's death."

She considers this. "I didn't know. I guess it was just a happy coincidence. Huh. That's funny." I can tell from her tone that she is not remotely amused.

"So you did save my life. Unintentionally, but that group was what kept me from committing suicide that night, and every night after. *You* being the members of the group helped me heal. Why do all of that work, just to kill me now?"

She's quiet and I can't tell if this is helping me or enraging her further, but any additional time that I can keep her from digging into my brain is more chance that the cops will realize something is wrong.

"Hmm. Well, I didn't have all of the information at the time. It certainly wasn't my intention to make your life *better*. I was gathering information and having a fun time catfishing you as Peter. I thought breaking your heart, while framing you for murder, before ultimately killing you and framing Henry for it, had a nice story arc. Funny how much of what we plan doesn't quite end up like we thought it would."

"Annie. You've ruined my life. You killed my best friends, Rachel and Brooke. You broke my heart. I will never be the same again. Isn't that enough?" The clarity of everything now is profound. My heart rate is too slow to sustain me much longer.

"You make a good point, but this is too exciting to not see through." She's resolved. "You don't mind if I film this, do you?" She nods in the direction of her phone, positioned on my bookshelf, camera side facing out. She shimmies her shoulders a little bit and squeals, and I shiver at the complete absence of soul in her eyes as she leans toward me.

"I'll need something back from you now." She points to the necklace and reaches to unclasp it. In a flash, I swing my arm, and the two needles make contact with her right iris. I use all of my hand coordination and remaining strength to gouge the points as deep as possible into her eye socket. She screams animalistically.

"You fucking bitch." She's wailing and dazed. There is blood streaming down her face as she wails in pain.

She removes her hand from her eye and I see the ends of the needles barely sticking out, and I'm surprised by how deep I was able to plunge them.

"Don't think that this is going to make me kill you any faster!" she bellows before grabbing the orbitoclast from the table and pouncing on me, pinning down my arm and shoulder with the weight of her body, her breath hot on my neck. As I see the sharp end getting closer and closer to my eye, I close them and pray that it won't be too painful or long. And like an alarm at the worst point of a nightmare ripping me from sleep, I hear the peal of wood splintering and Dennis's voice.

"Drop it!" he shouts. Her weight lifts and, startled and wild, she lunges for him.

The chime of metal hitting the floor and the sound of his voice cradle me. I hear sirens approaching in the distance. Before I can say a word, I feel my heart arrest, my breath becomes inert, and all of it deliciously falls away into a wonderful stillness of warmth, light, and silence. And I see Rachel's face.

SEVENTY

SILVESTRI

"HERE YOU GO," says Wolcott, tossing the folder onto the passenger seat through the open window. As he leans in, he spots the cage in the back. "And who do we have here?"

"Just had to swing by the SPCA and grab them. I'll see you in the morning, pal."

"I worry about you, Silvestri. You building an ark in the backyard?"

"Ah, jokes," I say. He leans away from the car and waves as I pull out of the parking lot and slip into traffic.

◆◆◆

"Oh, hello, Detective Silvestri. And who are *these* beauties?"

I'm standing on Charlotte's porch, holding the cage as I speak to her mother through the half-open door.

"Ms. Knopfler." I nod. "Nice to see you."

"Oh you rascal! Call me Margaret."

"Mom, who is it?" I hear Charlotte's voice approaching from inside the house. She reaches the door, and her smile brightens as she sees the Siamese cats I'm holding. "Thelma! Louise!"

"Charlotte, aren't you going to—"

"Give us a moment, Mom." She waves off Margaret, who disappears inside. "What a wonderful surprise," she says, turning her attention back to the cats. "Thank you, Dennis." I open the cage, and the cats hop down onto the porch and weave between her legs. She crouches down to pet them, then looks up at me. "Trying to give me a jump on the whole spinster-cat-lady thing?" She laughs.

"I thought they could use a loving home," I say.

"You thought right," she says, and watches the cats slither inside before letting the door close. "It's nice today. Shall we sit out front?"

"Sure." We cross to the corner of the porch and take seats facing each other. "So," I ask. "How you feeling?"

"I'm not entirely sure," she says, shaking her head. "It's all a little surreal. Glad to be home, even with the world's most persistent houseguest."

I laugh. "You gonna make it?"

"You know what? I'm not going to put any more energy into that situation than I absolutely have to. And who knows? My mother craves an audience. If I ignore her, maybe she'll find one elsewhere."

"Sounds like a remarkably healthy attitude."

"Yeah, well, near-death experiences have a way of reminding you of the important things, I guess." She holds my gaze for a long moment. "I really need to thank you, Dennis."

"No, you don't. It's what I—"

"I do. I've been thinking a lot over the last few days about everything that happened, and I keep landing back on the positive stuff. Yes, I experienced a chain reaction of insane events, all for the gratification of this incredibly sick woman. But in the end, she actually gave Brooke and me something very valuable."

"How so?"

"Brooke and I were brought back into each other's orbits through the chat room. We were able to comfort each other through our shared trauma, even without realizing how connected we were all along. And we were both able to find some peace. The support we experienced, even if it was staged, allowed Brooke to forgive us and let go of that anger and negative energy that were weighing her down, and her forgiveness absolved me of a lot of the guilt that had been eating away at me.

Not to diminish the tragedy of the situation, but I refuse to let it all be ugly and dark. Rachel wouldn't have let me wallow that way."

I nod silently and pull out my phone. "I wanted to show you this," I say, pulling up the unsent text from Rachel and handing it to her. "I can give you a moment alone." I begin to stand, but she holds out a palm.

"Sit with me," she says, and begins reading.

"You are absolutely right. I went too far, and crossed lines that I never should have. I accept responsibility, and I hope you can accept my apology. I hope you'll also accept that you are the person I love and value most in this world. I know I'm not a perfect person by any stretch, and will never be able to master moderation in anything I do, especially in my friendships, but I will keep trying to be better. Because you are the most important person to me, I will never stop watching out for you. I will never stop being protective. I will never stop making sure you get home safely.

"Thank you for being my friend, and the sister I always wanted, and for showing up for me when so many people in my life haven't been able to. Friendships like ours are rare, and I cherish it so much. Charlotte, you are my family and as long as you are safe and happy, I will be too. I love you so much."

She blots the corners of her eyes and smiles. She looks up, her face heavy with emotion. "Thank you so much for showing that to me."

"Of course." I return her smile. "Also, I wanted to let you know about Dr. Lyons."

"Okay," she says with a look of curiosity.

"It was through Rachel that he ended up in your office. They knew each other from NA."

"But why would he . . ." She trails off.

"I don't know. It sounds like he took a shine to you, and felt conflicted about coming to see you. That's all I know."

"Thank you," she says distractedly.

"Charlotte, there's something else I need to tell you."

"Okay," she says, re-engaged by my change in expression. Her brow creases. "What is it?"

A hollow feeling seeps into my gut. "I wasn't completely honest with you."

She regards me skeptically. "How so?"

"That story I told you, about the shooting in Baltimore? That wasn't entirely on the level."

"I don't understand," she says.

"I did shoot a perp during a raid, but I didn't kill him." I feel like this is spilling out of me all wrong. "I . . . I needed you to open up to me, and I embellished in order to get you to do that."

She turns her head in the direction of the street and exhales slowly. "I, um . . ." Her eyes shift to the side, but she can't bring herself to look at me. "I see."

"Charlotte, I'm very sorry. I was doing my job, but I hate that I treated you like a perp."

She brings her eyes to mine tentatively. "You really have a way with words, Detective Silvestri."

"Yeah, that's my reputation around town." I muster a chuckle.

"Well," she says, "I guess I wasn't exactly honest with you either, about Peter and all that."

"It was kind of a weird foot to get off on," I say.

"It sure was." She shakes her head. "I don't know. Fresh start?" She holds out her hand hopefully.

"Fair." I shake it, smirking at the formality.

She looks at my left arm with a concerned expression. "How are you healing up, anyway?"

"Fine. Some soreness and bruising. But I'm getting there."

"Well," she says. "When you're feeling a little less delicate, I'd be happy to get you on my table. I think it could really help with your recovery."

"I'd like that," I say, letting my eyes sit with hers.

She smiles. "Me too."

EPILOGUE

THE HEAT AND MUSIC are blasting from the vent above our booth. With the temperature drop and a report of an incoming storm, the diner has leaned hard into keeping its patrons warm and entertained. People are removing sweaters and coats left and right. I am debating losing my cardigan, which will leave me in a tank top, which seems a little too revealing for our first date. If this is a date, which I'm not entirely sure about. I can't see his face behind the giant menu, so I resume trying to focus on the laminated atlas in my hand.

He puts his menu aside and I do the same. I started salivating before even walking in, knowing that I'd one hundred percent be getting a cheeseburger and onion rings. My appetite has started to return to normal, along with many other things in my life, even though I still think about Rachel many times throughout the day every day and ask myself, *What would Rachel do?*

"Know what you want?" he asks.

"Yep. Salt and fat and more salt," I say proudly.

He winks. "I appreciate a decisive woman."

I groan. "Don't wink. And the innuendos, John . . . seriously." I shake my head from side to side vigorously. "Not a good look, and *completely* tone-deaf."

He turns an impressive shade of red. "I'm so sorry." He coughs into his hand. "I swear I'm trying to be better. I realized way late in life how my nervous habit of trying to act smooth in the presence of women has just been coming off as smarmy."

"*Now* you are realizing this? Better late than never, I guess," I say critically.

"Brilliant women make me very insecure," he says.

I raise my eyebrows and frown.

"That isn't a line! I'm being honest!" he says, seemingly genuine.

I am kind of flattered in spite of myself, but I won't let him know right now. I am still on the fence about John Lyons, formerly Jack Doyle. There are a lot of red flags to clear before I can know for sure if he's someone to whom I want to give any of my time. But when he reached out and said he wanted to share some things about Rachel, I couldn't say no.

"Honesty is good. Let's stick with that," I say.

"Do you happen to know any neurological experts who could help me understand neural pathway reprogramming to break bad habits?" He touches his beard, which has grown in pretty impressively since I last saw him six weeks ago at Rachel's memorial service.

"Have you been googling me?" I ask wearily.

He hesitates. "Yes."

I glance down at the table. There has been so much written about me in the last several weeks. I shudder at the thought of what he's read.

"Sorry. It was just that with all the coverage, I couldn't avoid it. And I got curious about your surgical work. So much of what people have written about you has been about your current work."

"Yeah, because I won't give them anything new," I mutter.

"You are really impressive, Charlotte," he says.

I try to let go of the now-daily feeling of being exposed all over again. "Luckily the news cycle is losing steam and people are hopefully on to the next thing." I dodge his compliment.

"Isn't the trial starting soon?"

"With any luck, it won't go to trial. There is overwhelming evidence, the detectives did their jobs right, and Annie is expected to plead guilty on all counts. But who knows. She could pull something at the last minute."

"Will you have to take the stand if it goes to trial?" he asks.

"They are working on a plea bargain that might keep me from having to testify, which I'm hopeful about. But I will, if it comes to that." I sigh. It's the last thing I want to do.

"They should lock that psycho up for a very long time," he says spiritedly.

I shrug.

"Don't you want her to suffer for what she's done? Aren't you furious? I am." He hits the table dramatically to punctuate.

"Yes, I think she should be held responsible. But I don't like the idea of anyone suffering. And Annie was obviously a person in a tremendous amount of pain." I think about my short time in jail. "Being locked up for the rest of your life sounds horrific."

"Well, I definitely don't share your equanimity. This woman murdered your friend—our friend—and almost you." He flares his nostrils. I don't entirely love his quickness to anger, but I appreciate where it's coming from.

"And Brooke Harmon," I say wistfully.

He nods. "You are just furthering my case. I hope she never sees the light of day again," he responds acidly.

"Annie wants me to do a sit-down special with Gayle King," I tell him. "Her press rep reached out to me."

"For real? Gayle seems cool . . ," he jokes.

"My life is so surreal right now." I shake my head slowly from side to side.

"Are you going to do it?" he asks.

"Not a chance," I say resolutely.

"I think it is amazing that you haven't done any media or taken any of the offers," he says. "I'm impressed. I don't know if I would have the same self-control. I'd love a few minutes to get on my soapbox and take that crazy bitch down." He clocks my reaction. I frown. "Sorry. Not cool," he says. "What is it okay to call a cruel female woman who impersonated a chat room full of people, tricked, stalked, and harassed and murdered two, almost three people?"

"Well, I guess she is a crazy bitch, technically speaking." We both laugh. "And it looks like Annie may have killed more than two people. They are investigating the deaths of her brother, who died under mysterious circumstances, and possibly her parents, years ago," I tell him.

"Jesus," he says.

"Rachel wouldn't have wanted any of the attention on her life. And I definitely don't want it on mine," I say.

"No, she wouldn't have," he agrees. "And I totally understand."

"I'm glad that the truth is out about Brooke's death and her parents now know the full story about everything. I just wish the phone calls and emails would stop."

He nods, listening intently. It feels good to talk about this with someone other than my therapist.

"If you need any help with the press, I have a patient who does crisis management who owes me a few hundred favors for saving her life," he offers.

"Thank you. I actually have a self-appointed, live-in press agent. She has mastered the art of saying 'fuck off' in a hundred ways and lives to do it. And she actually has the members of the media trying to get off the phone with her by the end," I marvel.

"This wouldn't happen to be the woman at Rachel's memorial service who looked like she was either on her way to or arriving from a Jackie O look-alike contest?"

"That would be the very one," I confirm. "She was also successful in finally getting Yelp to take down all the terrible reviews about me. So my practice is starting to pick up again."

"Is that why you were too busy to see me for an appointment?" He starts to wink and then realizes midway through, which leaves him in a comical frozen blink expression.

"Well, no. I want to be careful about boundaries. I don't treat people that I'm—" I catch myself before I vocalize the embarrassing presumption of what I was about to say.

He's highly amused and closed-mouth grinning like a cat with a mouse tail hanging from between his lips.

"People that you are . . . ?"

I blush and look away. "Having friendly coffee and conversation with," I respond. I pivot from the awkwardness. "I really have been overloaded, though. I'm actually not taking any new patients right now, and have another acupuncturist moving into Rachel's room next week to help with the workload."

It was a hard decision to make, allowing a stranger to come in and occupy her space, but a healthy one according to my shrink. "I am happy the new recruit seems really excited and open. She's already painting and decorating the treatment room to make it her own." Which I'm deeply grateful for. I still have a hard time going in that room as is.

"Oh, and that love letter of a review that is up is probably helping things too. I read it and felt a little threatened, to be totally honest," he shares.

"Love letter review?" I ask. I've kept my promise and not looked at the site, even now that Rachel is no longer here to watch for me. My mother versus Yelp was her idea, and while I appreciated it, I've let go of caring about that stuff. It isn't important in the grand scheme. I see that now.

John pulls out his phone, touches the screen a number of times, and hands it to me.

The Yelp app is open and I read the top review.

Dr. Charlotte Knopfler is the best kind of healer, the kind who empathizes deeply, believes in the power of love and connectedness, and makes everyone who comes into her presence feel safe, valued, and special. Every time I have encountered her, I've been made whole. She takes away pain, replaces it with love, and holds your hand through even the most difficult things. There are not enough stars in the universe to rate her with.

I look at the screen name and the posting date: OmRach. The night she died. I hand the phone back to him, speechless.

"Are you okay?" he asks.

"Yeah. I hadn't seen that before."

"There are a ton of other glowing reviews. Not so much about your practice, but about what an inspiration you are. How amazing it is that you defended yourself. A lot of female empowerment happening on your page."

I'm a little dumbfounded. "I assumed the influx of new patients was because of the news coverage and people's morbid curiosity about me. That is pretty incredible." I know I could tell him that it was her, and probably one of the last things she did before she died. But I want to keep it to myself.

He scans the restaurant. "Our waitress appears to have gone on break. Are you starving? Maybe I should track her down?" he offers gently.

"I'm fine. I'm not in a rush and not starving. It's just nice to be out," I say, appreciating his efforts to tend to my potential hunger. I'm a little surprised that a surgeon picked a diner for our rendezvous and wonder if he is sending a decidedly "undate" message with the understated venue choice.

"You know, Rachel and I used to come here after our NA meetings," he says, intuiting my speculation. "We definitely had some laughs about our own wild days. I miss the hell out of her." He looks out the window, the glass reflecting our images back at us with the dark outside.

"Me too. So much it hurts. I know I can't do anything about it now, but I am having trouble letting go of the fact that she and I were in a fight when she died," I reply sadly.

"I feel the same way, actually. She was furious at me when she died," he says gravely. "I keep trying to let go of it, but it is difficult. I've even been dreaming about it and apologizing to her in my dreams. Isn't that silly?"

"Not at all. I've been doing the same. And she always forgives me," I say. "So I feel better temporarily."

"Me too."

"What was she furious about?" I don't want to be unkind and tell him what I'm thinking, that she'd never mentioned his name or existence to me even once. It is ironic that Rachel was hiding details about a man in her life as I was, but given the anonymity of their connection, I understand.

He balls his hands up and looks uncomfortable. "That is why I asked you to meet me." He stops short and we sit in silence for a minute. "I'm going to need to just get this out and let you have whatever reaction you are going to."

"Okay." Given the buildup, I'm considering running for the exit.

"A month before Rachel died, she passed out in a yoga class and someone called the paramedics. She'd come to before they arrived and refused their attention, but they insisted she go to the ER because her blood pressure was so low. They brought her into Stony Brook, and by coincidence she saw me on my way out of a surgery and begged me to intervene. If we hadn't had the connection we had, I wouldn't have stepped on my colleagues' toes, but she was adamant."

"Okay." I'm hanging on every word. I had no idea that any of this happened and am feeling hurt beyond measure. "She didn't call me. Didn't tell me any of this."

He nods. "Yes, by design. She explicitly asked me not to call anyone on her behalf and pleaded with me to be her contact person so that she could be discharged. Which I agreed to do once she let the intake doctor run some basic diagnostics."

I am nodding and taking repeated sips of the water in front of me, out of the need to do something with my hands and my growing anxiety. The waitress finally appears with a pitcher and refills my glass. She is about to speak and I say, "Not now," firmly, and I wave her away, which she abides obediently, but with a look of disdain.

John continues. "The irony is, the chance encounter in the ER prompted Rachel to lasso me into being her proxy, but once the test results came in, I would have been called in for the consult anyway. I was the only resident oncologist on duty that day who was not in surgery." He gauges my face to see if he should continue.

The emerging truth is pulling at every nerve ending in my body. John sees the pain in my face and moves his hand slowly across the table toward mine. I let him squeeze it before I pull it away. I'm not anywhere near letting this man comfort me.

"Please." I attempt to clear my coated throat. "Continue."

"The results of her tests were undeniably indicative of something pervasive in her body. Her white blood cell count was dangerously low." I see him remember that he's speaking to a doctor and he adjusts. "There was a significant elevation in her carcinoembryonic antigen and CA 19-9."

"Pancreatic."

"Yes. And it was very advanced based on the CT scan I finally convinced her to let me do," he says solemnly. "I gave her three months, tops."

"So, you said this was four weeks before she died. But that can't be. She would have told me. I would have walked her through the process. Taken her to Sloan Kettering. Done all of the things." I'm leaking tears without even realizing I've begun crying. John slides a napkin over to me.

"It was a really long shot that chemo would have done anything other than make her feel terrible. And she was unrelenting about not having any surgery." I can hear the emotion coming through. "I tried, Charlotte. I swear to God. I tried hard to get her to do something. I was so desperate." He wrings his hands. "That's why I came to your office and used a fake name. I didn't want her to know I was reaching out to you. She found out and tore me a new one. I figured if anyone could talk sense into her, it would be you. She'd shared about you so lovingly, many times. I felt like I knew you without ever having met you."

"I know the feeling," I reply softly. I move my head to acknowledge that I'm still participating in the conversation, but I'm quickly transported miles away, processing all of the truth that has been heaped on me. The sounds of the diner take on a muted humming quality all around me.

"Charlotte, are you okay?" He looks concerned.

"I am." I close my eyes. "I understand."

"You do?"

"Rachel believed that we heal ourselves. She didn't believe in surgery," I say steadily.

He meets my eyes when I open them, and I can see the skepticism in his face.

"Her dad died during a routine surgery when she was a kid, and I think it really scarred her. And then all of her beliefs developed against Western medicine. And in Eastern modalities, practitioners believe that cancer is a result of energy blockages, and some hard-core people don't believe in surgical or chemical practices."

He looks unsatisfied with this explanation, which I can understand. He's doing what I was mere minutes ago. Making this about *his* beliefs. But this is Rachel we are talking about. *Give me a sign that you are still with me,* I say to myself. *Please.*

"And she didn't want to tell me, I'm sure, because this was one subject we agreed to not talk about," I reassure myself.

"About medicine?" He looks incredulous. "But you were a doctor!" He bites his bottom lip and composes himself. "Sorry. You still believe in medicine, don't you?"

"I do. Of course I do. But after everything happened with Michelle Harmon, I didn't want to talk about my time as a surgeon ever again; at least that is how I felt when Rachel and I first became friends. And she honored that. And I knew she didn't want to talk about her feelings about Western medicine, or talk about what I was trying to do in my surgeries, which I think she had a real problem with. So we had an unspoken agreement."

"And it just happened that the one thing you both didn't want to talk about was the thing you should have," he says frustratedly. "That makes no rational sense."

I am heartened by his emotion, and I see how much he cared about Rachel, which makes me like and trust him more than I have yet. But I won't try to explain to him why nothing I would have said to Rachel would have made a difference. That rationale was not the place she lived, and no one, not he or I, was going to ever change that about her. Which is the thing we both loved about her. Her resolve in herself.

"I know from your point of view, none of this makes sense. But it does to me." I focus on his beautiful clear eyes. "I feel so grateful that you are telling me that she was sick, *terminally* sick. I hate that Annie took her life, but given the choice to go out the way she did or dying slowly and painfully, I think Rachel would have chosen fast oblivion. That gives me some peace of mind."

His face twists into an indecipherable expression.

"What?" I ask.

"You can't say that someone who had the amount of sobriety time that she did would have wanted to die high. You just can't." I'm surprised to see a tear roll down his cheek, which he swats away aggressively and bows his head.

"You are right," I say softly. "I didn't think about that."

"But then again, given the choice, I know what I would choose." He sighs.

"This is a way that you knew her better than I did." I extend my hand across the table. "I'm so glad to know that she had you as a friend, and that you can tell me more about her. I'm grateful you told me everything."

He leans forward. "Don't take this the wrong way, but you are processing this news a lot better than I expected. My therapist prepared me for the worst," he says.

I bow my head when I hear the lyrics clearly and let the light fill me.

"Everything is okay." I tell him, then pull my hand from his and place both of my hands over my heart.

"It is?" he asks, mildly confused.

I silently point to the ceiling, where the song hits its chorus again. Rachel loved this song. *We* loved this song. The last time I heard it she was singing and dancing along to it.

John tilts his head to hear the words being sung along with the chords of an acoustic guitar.

"Listen," I tell him.

> *Woke from a dream, was soaked in sweat;*
> *I'd never known you, we'd never met.*
> *I'd never known how sweet life gets;*
> *When you find the piece that fits.*
> *The one who sees you, knows your soul;*
> *Knows each part and loves you whole.*
> *I'd never said, to my regret;*
> *How much I love you, my best friend.*

And I listen for my friend between the words.

ACKNOWLEDGMENTS

WE ARE SO grateful to our incredibly talented agent, Christopher Schelling.

We have the publishing dream team at Dutton. For the unparalleled editorial talent of John Parsley, who is patient, wise, and an all-around mensch; Maya Ziv's sage editorial notes; and Cassidy Sachs's sharp eye and amazing support, we are so very grateful. So many thanks go to our powerhouse publicity and marketing crew, made up of Amanda Walker, Jamie Knapp, Kathleen Carter, and Stephanie Cooper. Special thanks to Christine Ball for championing us early on, and to Madeline McIntosh, Allison Dobson, Lauren Monaco, and the PRH sales team for their enthusiasm for our books. And to David Litman for the stunning jacket design, art director Christopher Lin, and everyone else who typeset, copyedited, designed, etc.

A huge thanks to our film agent, Pouya Shabazian, and to our foreign rights and translation team: Chris Lotts, Nicola Barr, Lara Allen, Jacob Roach, thank you for all your work on our behalf to bring this book all over the world.

To our incredibly supportive families: Anne, John, Eva, Rich, Taylor, Connor, Will, Veronica, Carole, Firth, Hedy, Madeline, John, Charlie, Thomas, Jesy, and Bernadette. To Lori and Lis, and especially Tom and Nina for wise writing and life advice. And thanks to all our many aunts and uncles and cousins who always show up for us. Thank you to the Pedone family.

To all our beloved creative compatriots, thank you for the inspiration, conversation, pep talks, and emotional support, with special thanks to Augusten Burroughs, Scott Leeds, Lisa Weinert, Ruiyan Xui, Brian Selfon, Mikael Awake, Jason Boog, Joelle Renstrom, Holley Bishop, Rennie Dyball, "Utah," Liz Scheier, Liz Stein, Maris Kreizman, Sacha Wynne, Sarah Stodola, Erum Naqvi, Tyler Gore, Douglas Belford, Matthew Gilbert, Matt Laird, Dave Hill, Sebastian Beacon, Jesse St. Louis, Michael Dowling, Eugene Cordero, Ron Petronicolos, Chris Swinko, Ayana Brooks, Jeff Sheehan, Dante Clark, Barbara Lynn Cantone, Colin Poellot, Liza Colby, and Geoff Poppler.

A special shout-out to writers Samantha Downing, Wendy Walker, Chandler Baker, Cristina Alger, Liz Fenton and Lisa Steinke, Teresa Sorkin and Tullan Holmqvist for your wonderful books and for your support.

Heartfelt thanks to Pablo Rodriguez, Robert Clauser, and Alison Benson for their incredible support and encouragement.

Deep gratitude to the amazing booksellers we've met in our travels who support authors and readers; you are the heart of the book world.

There are so many wonderful bookstagrammers who helped to spread the word about our first book, especially Garrett Billings for your early and enthusiastic championing, for driving across state lines to support us, and the best virtual casting to date. Thank you.

A deep thanks to Amy Fitzpatrick and Casey Leigh Carty. You have been incredible resources of inspiration and healing on and off the table.

To Fiona Davis for her ebullience, love, and soul-soothing.

To Brian Pedone for love, laughter, encouragement, and daily acts of life-saving, on and off the mountain.

To everyone from Screaming Muse Productions, and for lifetime friendships onstage and off, Maurice Smith, Jason Weiner, Daniela Tedesco, Mike Bromberger, and Natasha Tsoutsouris.

A special thanks to J L Stermer, whose unconditional friendship, sense of humor, and impeccable sense of style has been critical for the writing and living process.

And to the people who are no longer with us, but who've been so important in our lives, we thank and miss you: Richard Wands, Tom and Nora Keenan, Patricia and Gordon Sabine, Paul Williams, Bill Rosen, Elizabeth Danser, Elizabeth Calhoun, and Carey Longmire.